The Trainee

A. F. Knott

The Trainee

Original Copyright © 2006

Second Edition 2016

ISBN: 978-1-912017-68-3

Hekate Publishing Ltd

2 Lydiard Green

Lydiard Millicent

Wiltshire SN5 3LP United Kingdom

admin@hekatepublishing.com

https://www.hekatepublishing.com

Thanks to Rowan Leigh and Hekate Publishing
Cover Design by A.F. Knott

DEDICATION

To Brendan and Ian

1
THE LOOK-ALIKE

The face of the man who boarded the bus in Baltimore resembled mine precisely. In addition, he carried a duffle bag just like mine. He regarded each passenger one by one, walked down the aisle and sat across from me. In revealing no hint of recognition, I could only conclude he sought that particular seat in the manner of someone drawn to review their reflection in a mirror.

I removed both notebook and pen from breast pocket, made note of his arrival then studied my look-alike as he gazed out the window. Our sense of fashion was dissimilar. His hair, brown like mine, was unwashed and extended to the middle of his back. He wore a gold hoop earring in each ear and held a pack of Chesterfields in his left hand. The man did not appear concerned or anxious in the least. His intellectual deportment differed in that he did not jot down observations, and did not seem to carry a notebook nor any form of writing instrument. No accessible reading materials or projects to occupy his time were visible. He simply looked out his window and protected the duffle bag between his legs. Twisting in my seat to assure privacy, I wrote:

Look-alike's duffle appears not unlike the scarecrow of Priapus warding off thieves and the evil eye, protecting the orchards while ensuring abundant crops.

I underlined the association, added two exclamation points then snapped the notebook closed. I brushed off my own duffle bag and propped it up.

I had no direct interaction with my look-alike until Fayetteville, North Carolina, where several soldiers boarded. After they had settled in their seats, he caught my eye, leaned into the aisle and pointed toward the front of the bus with his chin.

Following his gaze, I regarded the backs of the soldiers' shaved heads, searching the surfaces for meaning and metaphor. Cropped hair and bony protuberances did not easily accommodate analysis; I noted, however, that every soldier carried at least one pack of cigarettes. On taking a seat, each removed this pack from their shirt pocket and tapped outward a single unit. I noticed many different brands: Marlboro, Kent, Winston, L&M, and Pall Mall.

The snit snit snit of lighters sounded as if it were raining. Only one soldier used matches and cupped his hands together as I had seen the Marlboro Man do on television as a child. The soldiers jutted their lower lips forward and blew smoke upward while engaged in conversation. Cigarettes dangled from their mouths; these looked to be on the verge of falling.

My look-alike placed an unlit Chesterfield into his mouth, leaned across the aisle and asked me for a match. His voice sustained such an unusual hoarseness that I was compelled to study his face. Under the dark canopies of both his eyes hung an admirable hollow fatigue. I patted my pockets and shook my head.

He asked, "Where going, bucko?"

"New Orleans."

My look-alike tapped his head. "You could pretend you're in the military with that haircut."

I had maintained my hair closely trimmed for several years due to a persistent fungal condition acquired through long hours spent in the sub-basement level of the University library, a biosphere for all major genera of dermatophytes.

"You definitely could," he added, shrugged his shoulders and resumed staring out the window. We spoke no further.

This suggestion was helpful. Pretending to be a military man was appealing although I could not yet be certain of the utility in doing so. The desirability for hoarseness and a modicum of facial hollowness was self-evident. Right then and there, I decided to buy cigarettes and begin smoking them as soon as possible. I wished to ask my look-alike some questions concerning the smoking of cigarettes yet was not comfortable speaking aloud within the prying earshot of the soldiers. If unexpectedly pressed into a conversation, I remained mute as a matter of course; At times when I did converse, discerning whether dialogue was taking place internally or externally remained problematic.

I recalled the expression of my University physics adviser when I mentioned this predisposition. He became overly concerned. I explained that in utilizing all the resources within the sub-basement of the University library, my interests had broadened to include not only physics, my area of study, but 18th century romantic poetry, Theatre of the Absurd, psychoanalytic literary theory, the biological implications of non-equilibrium thermodynamics, and the investigation of classic anatomy texts. I had also come to champion the French existentialists, in particular, those who had scribbled thoughts in posthumously published personal notebooks. I shared my intention to become a notebook keeper. My adviser, a tenured member of the physics department faculty with numerous publications on low temperature phenomena to his credit, had removed his glasses and implored me to seek a psychiatric evaluation. He related numerous examples of how other students and faculty had followed this advice and were back on track.

By way of emphasizing my resolve, I insisted, "If necessary, I will drink my own transforming potion." My adviser became distraught and left the room; he returned a few minutes later having splashed water on his face. I attempted to qualify further my desire to understand the ways of man and to experience the spontaneity of life; I explained that my dreary world had been derived solely from observations related to books quietly read or movies viewed while seated in darkened theaters with no participation in the data acquisition process itself.

"I am choosing the way of the notebook," I had reassured him, and even went so far as to raise one finger above my head to accentuate the seriousness and irrevocable nature of the contract.

After examining me carefully, my adviser threw up his hands and exclaimed, "Fine."

The very next day, atop my usual study carrel in the sub-basement level of the University Library, I discovered a one way Trailways bus ticket to New Orleans tucked just inside the jacket of Jean-Paul Sartre's essay on Jean

Genet. Directly under Sartre's book had been placed an exquisite photographic essay of Gothic wrought iron balconies derived from architecture within the famous French Quarter of that same city. As it happened, an hour before, I had attended a lecture on astronomical relationships, learning that the diameter of the Moon was precisely four hundred times smaller than the diameter of the Sun and four hundred times closer to the Earth; the coincident ratios gave rise to precise conditions which allowed for a total eclipse to be observed from Earth. Knowledge of this juxtaposition of celestial bodies in conjunction with the sudden appearance of the two attractive books with accompanying bus ticket constituted a paranormal mandate: Only New Orleans could become my destination if not destiny.

I withdrew from classes and returned home to say goodbye to my parents and assemble a library requisite for the journey. My father did not approve of my intended career as a notebook keeper. Ironically, my parents had both been professionals in the theater, one a writer, one an actress, and in that way, I had grown up in a milieu which rarely distinguished between the domain of drama with the domain of reality. In a practical sense, they had known of this schism and remained adamant throughout my upbringing that I should avoid the creative arts at all costs. On this occasion, my father paced back and forth across the living room, emphasizing that a career in notebook keeping represented an implausible choice despite him having invested in what I saw to be a similar one. My father had even picked up my beloved copy of Dostoyevsky's *Crime and Punishment*, waved it through the air and insisted,

"This is of no interest to anyone. People who write this kind of thing are freaks."

"No, they're not, Dad. They're not," my mother had argued quietly.

I made up my mind I would come to my own conclusions.

After informing them I had found a bus ticket on my desk at the library, and thus selected my destination and destiny to be New Orleans, my parents began behaving bizarrely. They regarded one another without speaking, made several urgent phone calls after which they argued behind closed doors. I paid little attention to their comings and goings, too preoccupied with the planning of my upcoming adventure.

Back on the bus, the process of cigarette brand selection required my undivided attention. I could allot little time for staring out the window. Within my pocket notebook, I made a list of as many cigarette brands as I could recall and studied them. I turned to the final page of my notebook on which I had previously transcribed an arrival agenda and amended this to include the purchase of cigarettes.

While the bus refueled at the Tallahassee station, my look-alike disembarked. I observed him make a phone call. He pointed and gestured with great animation during this call, at one point extending his arms outward while tilting his head to the side and closing his eyes. I stood up and regarded the other passengers. Not one had pursed their lips, raised even a single eyebrow or sucked on an eyeglass strut.

I had been the first to recognize it.

I cleared my voice and announced, "It's a Christ-like posturing."

There was no acknowledgment. I spoke louder: "He's a Christ on the cross." I waited a few moments then sat back down.

Upon reboarding, my look-alike slowly and with odd intention walked up the aisle studying each passenger one by one. He stopped, caught my eye, and asked one soldier for a match. Rather than replying yes or no, this soldier made an offhand remark to a companion seated across the aisle. Without hesitation or hint of emotion, unlit cigarette still in mouth, my look-alike gripped the soldier's ear, yanked his head into the center of the aisle and crashed an elbow down upon his temple. Several other soldiers arose, pushed my look-alike onto the floor, and kicked and punched him. As they dragged him from the bus, my look-alike maintained a firm hold on his duffle bag.

I stood up to watch the assault. With heavy boots, one of the soldiers stamped my look-alike's forearm while others tried to pry his hand off the strap of the duffle.

The bus began to precess and tilt around me, ever so slowly, like a gyroscope. I was forced to sit and place my head upon the armrest. After a few moments, the spinning stopped, and I could raise my head. The instant I peered out the window, my look-alike's forearm snapped in two like a bread stick. Another soldier yanked the duffle bag from his grasp, opened it and shook the contents onto the bus station sidewalk. Rather than clothing or books, out spilled coils of rope, rolls of tape and what appeared to be an assortment of weapons. I noticed his package of Chesterfields had fallen onto the asphalt.

Though the man's arm was fractured he continued to issue forceful reprisals; kicking one soldier in the knee, another in the groin, yet another in the chest. He lunged toward the duffle bag and fell, his head instantly breaking open against the corner of a concrete curb. The other soldiers closed in and kicked him. I shut my eyes as violent spinning recommenced.

Police and ambulance crews arrived while the bus was pulling away from the station. I craned my neck to glimpse the arrest of three soldiers and observe paramedics bending over my look-alike, his body shaking and bouncing without reason upon the concrete.

Battered by wave after wave of unremitting vertigo, I made an urgent notation of all I had witnessed and felt little inclined to sleep after that. At University, I had read much of death and had found it confounding yet understood that I was duty bound to dwell upon it. Given the empiric data available, an individual's life formally ends with the termination of brain function; that puzzling transition to an inconceivable state. As a child, I had viewed the small dot on the screen at the start and finish of *The Outer Limits* television program with unease. The recollection of my look-alike's final tonic-clonic movements forced itself into a similarly small dot within my mind's eye.

As dawn approached, I decided Chesterfields would become my personal brand of cigarette and amended my written agenda to reflect this change:

1) Arrive at Trailways depot.

2) Purchase Chesterfield Cigarettes and smoke them. Swagger before or after purchase.

3) Commence Process of Self-Actualization

4) Locate Hotel

5) *Gain employment*

As the bus crossed Lake Pontchartrain, I dragged my duffle down the aisle and waited just behind the white line, holding pocket notebook at the ready. Once the bus entered the city, I observed with great vigor, leaning this way and that to view streetscapes as faithfully as possible. I noted whitewashed shotgun houses to my left, iron balconies to my right, a uniformly gray sky above and the heavily pot-holed road below. The driver grunted every few seconds while gazing into his mirror at me. Subject to his stare while simultaneously viewing the swirling vapors parting around the wide front window, I questioned whether I had fallen asleep in my seat and was floating within a disturbing reverie. Cigarette smoke and bus seat ethers clung to my nasal mucosa, confirming that what I experienced could only be a bland waking reality. These odors triggered a similar nausea with which I had been afflicted earlier during the observance of the horrendous killing of my Christ-like facial identical, whose eyes had met mine just before his final stand.

I counseled myself: This is no dream, Rodney Pepper. The terrible event you just witnessed constituted precisely that grim reality you've been seeking.

In continuing to stand just behind the white line near the door as we moved toward the downtown area, the driver's mirrored gaze remained intermittently fixed upon mine with a look suggesting significant vexation. The bus finally entered the Tulane Avenue station and stopped, air expelling loudly from a valve just before the door opened. I descended to the bottom step and paused to concentrate on placing my running shoe down upon the asphalt surface. I felt it appropriate to offer remarks of mythological import: "As Neil Armstrong applied his spaceman's boot down onto the Sea of Tranquility, I now take my own first tentative step." Before continuing, I inhaled the ambient exhaust fumes as a wine master would the olfactory bouquet of his cork and remarked,

"I will proceed directly to the kiosk and purchase Chesterfields, my chosen brand of cigarette."

The driver interrupted me: "Please get off my bus, asshole."

2
THE ARRIVAL

I flipped my notebook open and slashed *Displaced Anger* onto a blank page, snapped the book closed and yelled, "His teeth need a good kicking in!"

Composing myself, I chuckled in recalling that my father would always say so and so needs his teeth kicked in or, so and so's teeth need a good kicking-in. I entered the empty Trailways depot ahead of the other passengers and in doing so envisioned the cresting of a Swiss mountain top. My arms rose and spread outward. I twirled, swinging my duffle bag around and around and around.

The twirling motion proved unstable and one of my knees buckled. Julie Andrews had been far luckier to have executed her twirling without a duffle bag, as a result experiencing a far greater sense of exuberance. I considered what her trajectory might have resembled had a weighty literary opus been placed in each of hand just before the cry of roll 'em. *Under the Volcano* in the right and *Crime and Punishment* in the left would have sufficed to test her mettle.

In the midst of my ecstatic revolve, I noticed a man in a dirty pea coat and black knit cap recessed beside a stack of lockers, regarding me. Toppling sideways, aware of being observed, I emitted a flatulent which resounded throughout the depot like a cymbal crash. Given its tonality and color, anyone listening could have only surmised that I had shat my pants.

This discharge, however, in lieu of a violin string snapping, comprised the most succinct expression of my self-actualizing soul.

While toppling, I further glimpsed a woman on the street cupping both hands over her forehead and peering through the bus station window just underneath the Trailways lettering. Her breasts flattened against the outside of the glass like two enormous squashed bullfrogs. I drew in a breath and shifted my gaze to survey the waiting room, placing one hand on the floor for stabilization and assuming, for an instant, the persona of a French fencing master, appropriately coiffed in a powdered white wig. Although mightily inspired, even this posture could not provide sufficient buffering to make bearable the surrounding all-too-real bus terminal aswim in voyeurs.

Thoroughly disequilibrated I found it difficult to swagger toward the news stand as I had intended at the precise moment of cigarette purchase. I salvaged the agenda to an extent by commissioning my pack of Chesterfields with an audible voice. Catching sight of myself in a small mirror behind the counter, I was appalled to observe one eyebrow descending toward the bridge of my nose with the severity of a cliff face precipice; the pallor of my sleepless face rendered it not only macabre but nearly unrecognizable.

I wedged the Chesterfield pack into my shirt pocket, lifted the duffle onto one shoulder and pushed through the doors onto Tulane Avenue, instantly colliding with the woman I had seen peering through the glass moments before. She stopped and stood, hands on hips; I felt myself being drawn inward, towards the contour of her chest wall, as a meteor might have been perturbed into the gravitational field of one of the larger outer planets of our solar system.

The woman in front of the Trailways depot had dropped her newspaper as a result of our collision. I bent down, picked it up and offered it to her. Her hands remained on her hips. She asked,

"Have a cigarette?"

Placing the papers under one arm while still supporting the duffle over one shoulder, I attempted to pull the pack of Chesterfields from my shirt pocket with the opposite hand. I could only work the pack from side to side, moving it upward slowly. When it refused to budge further, I released my duffle bag, placed the papers between my knees, took hold of the pack with both hands and while utilizing double pincer grips, pulled. The knuckles of both hands flew upward, cracking against my chin. My head snapped backward, and I bit my tongue. Moaning, I held the freed pack up with one hand like an adroit shortstop holding up the ball after snagging a screaming line drive.

I had difficulty undoing the little red drawstring embedded in the wrapper.

"Here." The woman grabbed the pack, tore it open with her teeth and spat out the cellophane. She tapped out a cigarette, placed it in her mouth and withdrew a gold plated lighter.

Snit, snit, snit.

The rhythm of this woman's snitting suggested a greater casualness than the snitting of the soldiers on the bus. She inhaled, blew smoke through her nostrils and handed me the cigarette while waving the pack in front of my face. She asked,

"May I keep it?"

"Yes, of course." Thankful that I could again formulate coherent speech, I added, "I smoke Pall Malls for the most part."

She held the pack in front of my face and guffawed, raising her eyebrows as if I had made a joke. She tucked the pack just inside her blouse and a mammoth right breast. She removed her sunglasses and stared, without a hint of shyness, directly at my crotch.

"Your tidy whities must have shrunk in the wash, sweetie," she chuckled as puffs of smoke staccatoed from her mouth and nose. I did not understand the sense of her quip.

Without warning, she gripped my chin, turned my head from right to left, placed both hands on my ears and pulled them outward simultaneously. Using the tips of her fingers, she palpated the top of my cranium with the same degree of intention Dr. Leakey might have exerted in examining a newly unearthed Australopithecus in Olduvai Gorge. The nature of her examination remained obscure. I had much to learn regarding the everyday commerce of Homo sapiens.

"That haircut makes you look twelve." She stated.

By the age of twelve, I had not yet reached puberty.

I considered lying to the woman. My look-alike had suggested that I pretend to be a soldier; this would place me at eighteen, the minimum age for enlistment. And yet, I was twenty-two, a full ten years older than twelve and four years beyond eighteen. Internally speculating while the woman stood before me, I sensed an increasing rigidity within my vocal cords. Dark cloud-like spots appeared on both the right and left sided visual fields. Disconcerted by both the sudden ambiguity of my perceived age and the woman's physical modulations, in order to maintain my ability to speak, I defined aloud the principle of inertia, hoping that its irrefutable relevance within the physical sciences and without would quench at least a portion of autonomic craniosacral outflow generated by unconscious mediating centers within my central nervous system.

"Inertia," I began. "A property of matter by which it continues in its existing state of rest or uniform motion in a straight line, unless that state is changed by an external force."

The woman's expression changed to annoyance. "Enough." She replaced her glasses, glanced down the street and lowered her voice. "The piece is in the room. When his head is against the door, the peephole can be pulled out. You stick the piece into the peephole. Done."

What this woman said made no sense. I considered that she might be a madwoman; wandering the downtown streets of New Orleans in early morning hours, as Foucault had suggested, deceiving deception itself and speaking of love to lovers. I lightly caressed the notebook embedded within my breast pocket, longing to make an entry, and not only an entry: an entry in her presence.

I reconsidered my relationship with this woman: Her tone, imbued with ease and familiarity, suggested she had mistaken me for someone else. This person with whom I had been confused seemed fascinating with his curious stick-the-piece-in-the-peephole directive. Content to say nothing and promote this misimpression, I nodded and smiled ever so slyly.

The woman had not seemed displeased by my Chesterfield selection. The person she believed me to be was certainly a smoker. I attempted to inhale the lighted cigarette while assuming a cigarette smoking countenance. The smoke stung my eyes, and I shut them reflexively. Coughing once, the Chesterfield shot from my mouth as my hands jerked outward, groping to retrieve it mid-flight. Only after the ocular irritation subsided was I able to raise my lids. The woman had disappeared.

I recalled how the initial sensations in the presence of the woman heralded a familiar onset of symptoms which I had experienced intermittently during my years since puberty. The associated pathophysiology arose from amplified activation of my Vagus nerve along with associated parasympathetic nervous system excitations.

This visitation had caused me significant issue regarding a certain University Freshman English Composition Instructor; she, a graduate student at the time, quite innocently had been possessed of enormous breasts. After attending her initial class followed by a one-on-one tutorial, I recognized the speech center of my brain to have become partially disabled as the result of exposure to this stimulus; the resultant aphasia accompanied an abrupt onset of dizziness and ringing within the ears. Dependent on the instructor's choice of attire on any given day, the tinnitus could become so amplified and persistent as to force me to arise and stagger from the classroom lest I lose consciousness. I found I could hold the syndrome at bay to some extent; in order to retain the ability to speak, the speech offered had to entail accurate recitation of scientific definition previously committed to rote memory.

The frame of the woman I had bumped into was similarly broad and widely contoured. Her orange blouse adorned with white tiger stripes, featured frills which hung from the top of her breasts. Her abdomen protruded slightly over a broad black belt worn casually askew at the waist. Her skirt was composed of a brown leather fray, revealing portions of her thigh.

In form, she bore a striking resemblance to a depiction of the Queen Goddess of the World featured in a University library sub-basement level psycho-mythology text to which I frequently deferred and deliberated upon. Her lipstick and tiger stripes, however, suggested the complementary image referenced in that same volume, namely that of the Devouring Mother archetype. As I stood and considered further, the woman could conceivably symbolize the embodiment of what was referred to as the bad breast within the lexicon of Object Relations theory. I had understood there were two sides to every breast, a good side and a bad side; the breast that feeds the hungry infant was the good breast whereas the hungry infant who found no breast at all to feed upon turned to some notion of a bad breast for sustenance. I further imagined Bad Breasts to be large and imposing and always rendered in capitals, although I could not substantiate this. Through research at the University's Medical School Library, I came to appreciate presyncopal physiology and had convinced myself that nothing out of the ordinary transpired during these episodes; the sensations had been manageable except for the aforementioned encounters with that very specific University Composition Instructor.

In the meantime, all my symptoms had abated.

The filter of the burning cigarette lay on the sidewalk smeared with her red lipstick. I touched my lips, regarded the tip of my finger and sniffed ever so fleetingly. Grinding the cigarette against the sole of my sneaker, I discovered extinguishing it was far more challenging than anticipated. After grinding for some time with smoke continuing to issue from underneath, I regarded the bottom of my shoe. The Chesterfield had wedged itself into one of my heel treads and remained lit. In viewing the tenacious Chesterfield, I realized the woman had almost certainly mistaken me for the cigarette smoking look-alike whose convulsions I had witnessed on the Tallahassee bus station curbside only hours ago. And whereas I had filled my duffle bag with books, his had been chock full of weapons.

I removed the newspapers from between my knees. Sandwiched between the front and the back page of the Times-Picayune was a single sheet bearing the heading, rooms. Red lipstick conspicuously encircled an announcement:

Lafayette Hotel, St. Charles Avenue, $17.50. Daily. Weekly Rates. Transients.

I traced my finger about the lipsticked perimeter and raised that same finger to hover under my nostrils. While a gross misunderstanding had taken place, I felt a sense of belonging in having been welcomed at the bus depot by this mysterious large breasted woman who handed me my first Chesterfield. New Orleans was proving to be everything I had hoped. A room for the day was just what I needed now to recover from my sleepless night and start my life anew. I began to walk, forcing a fatigued eyebrow to arch upward, providing any onlooker with the suggestion of savvy.

After a time I noticed other pedestrians regarding me oddly. Some moved out of my path entirely to stop in the middle of the sidewalk and stare. I touched my face then examined my shirt and fly in sequence; both were intact and fastened. Catching sight of my reflection in a store window, I appeared to be leaning forward as if confronted by an extreme headwind. I stopped walking and removed my pocket notebook. At the top of a blank page, I created the new heading *Whimsical Observation.* Underneath this, I wrote:

People ambled in New Orleans. I had been walking very fast, far faster than anyone else.

Before my trip, I vowed to blend in at all cost, to live and function as the unobserved observer. Struck by the irony of my disparate gait, I shook my head from side to side like a bemused Herman Munster, nipped into the nearby alcove of a storefront and counseled myself aloud:

"I won't be able to simply close my eyes and skip along, singing 'if ever oh ever a wiz there was, the Wizard of Oz is one because, because because because because because…' and so forth."

I had to appear as if I knew where I was going and as if I were going somewhere, especially if I resembled a twelve-year-old. Having studied numerous books on charlatans and con artists to prepare for my relocation, I knew that if I did not give the impression of being savvy, there could be trouble. Exactly what this trouble entailed, I had no clue; most volumes exploring specific forms of trouble had consistently been checked out or gone missing from the University library shelves.

In assuming a slow gait, no one paid me any mind. Content with this resolution, I nonetheless longed for my pack of Chesterfields, the first I had ever owned and felt disappointment, even a tinge of bitterness, in having relinquished it so easily.

Life was proving far harder than expected.

Finding myself at the corner of North Rampart and Canal, I approached a pay phone and reached into my left-hand pants pocket. I had placed a predetermined measure of quarters, dimes and nickels there at the start of my trip, knowing full well that even a split second of fumbling while on the streets of this port city, would compromise my ostensible appearance as a sagacious notebook keeping bird of passage and possibly invite the attentions of a Big Easy Bill Sikes and the Big Easy equivalent of his prostitute girlfriend Nancy.

"Lafayette." The voice conveyed a considerable dullness. This person knew something of life.

Attempting to sound dull myself, I said "Yeaahhh," but after that remained at a loss and spoke at a rapid rate: "My name is Pepper, Rodney Pepper. I am calling., well, I have no reservation but would like to know if it is at all possible to get a room without one, without a reservation, that is."

I held my breath having inadvertently spoken with the cadence of a squirrel.

"Single, seventeen fifty," the voice stated with no inflection whatsoever.

Words lurched from my mouth at an even high register as if I were now Alvin, the head chipmunk: "Can I make a reservation?"

"Don't need one," the voice stated. I listened for any qualification. None followed.

"Thank you. Thank you so very much." I listened to scraping followed by silence.

An elderly black man stood on the corner facing away from me. He appeared to be doing nothing. His hair was strikingly gray, and one of his trouser legs had a tear in the knee. This man knew something of life's ultimate meaning, the very commodity I sought. I wondered, however, why he was standing.

Why wasn't this man going somewhere or doing something?

I knelt beside my duffle bag and tried to open it. Before departing, I had placed a New Orleans street map at its mouth. Something was wrong. My hands pried and twisted the clasp joining the eyelets at the top. I had practiced undoing this very clasp before the bus ride knowing full well there might be cause at any moment to remove an item from the bag without calling attention to myself. I twisted the clasp with all my might. I had not anticipated this type of delay just as I had not anticipated having difficulty removing the pack of Chesterfields from my shirt pocket earlier and certainly not anticipated having further issues in grasping the little red tag embedded within its cellophane wrapper. Recollection of these events precipitated a brief stir of vertigo. I focused my attention upon my hands and twisted the clasp while utilizing a mental image of myself possessed by superhuman strength. Twisting the clasp first in one direction then in another, my arms quivered at the furthest extent of each twist and counter twist. I breathed heavily and began to sweat. If I could access this map, there would be no need to ask directions. "I would be taken for someone who not only knows where he's going but who knows what's what," I murmured, attempting to mollify myself; I well knew this clasp twisting fiasco made me vulnerable to potential attack from any number of unknown agents. Near exhaustion, I lost patience, savagely kicked the bag and cried out as powerfully as a priest might in the final throes of exorcism:

"Fuck it all to goddamn hell!"

I bent my knees; filled with punishing rage, my plan was to jump on top of my non-compliant duffle and throttle it with both feet simultaneously. I did not do so as the elderly man had now turned and was staring at me. I straightened, pretended to stretch and meandered toward him.

"Do you know the way to St. Charles Avenue?"

The man continued to stare without answering. He glanced at my duffle then at me. I tried to control my breathing.

"What are you looking for?" he asked.

As described in numerous accounts of the epic human quest, this standing man was purposefully refraining from directing me to St. Charles Avenue. He wished for me to find my own path. With his deceivingly innocent question he had established himself as a haggard Zen Roshi asking for me to succinctly communicate the full import of my life until that point in time. And he undoubtedly expected a koanistic reply. This put me on the spot. I attempted to clear my mind after the fashion described by Suzuki in his *Essays in Zen Buddhism*, lowering my voice and speaking from well below the diaphragm. Trying my best to sound like the Mongolian throat singer, imbued with natural wisdom, I intoned,

"I am Lord Jimesque, you might say."

I winced visibly and uncontrollably as if a bullet had struck my forehead; I winced a second time as if being electrocuted, responding to the initial act of wincing.

My reply had been flabbergastingly anti-Zen.

My face assumed a grimace: I had blurted this literary allusion as a quadriceps muscle might contract following the impact of a reflex hammer upon the ipsilateral patella tendon. To have torn a page from my pocket notebook, folded it into the form of a paper airplane and propelled it into his face would have demonstrated a far greater insight. In Japan, I would have received the instructional sting of the master's bamboo sword across the crown of my head accompanied by the ominous beating of a tsuzumi.

I had jumped the gun and blurted out the wrong answer in the great class of life.

Previously, I had found it impossible to prevent the wincing which inevitably followed this form of inadvertent faux pas or the recollection of an embarrassing life event. Besides the wince itself, I typically lost conscious control of my skeletal musculature facilitating recovery of the awkward event; my arms would fling themselves outward of their own accord while my hands would grope, fingers opening and closing in a desperate attempt at reclaiming and nullifying whatever virtual insult had presented. This tic caused me considerable embarrassment and usually generated a series of secondary winces and flinches, similar to earthquake aftershocks.

The man, squinted, spat, and turned away without speaking.

I surmised there would be many more tests to come although had no idea if any would prove as difficult as this first one.

I proceeded along Canal, walking ever so slowly, holding the old man's haggard countenance in the center of my mind. Glancing at my reflection in a storefront window once again, I arranged upon my face a similar haggard expression. Haggardness, with a capital H, was surely prerequisite to Wisdom, with a capital W. For the time being I decided to feign Haggardness, and through practice, would eventually become truly

Haggard, and thereby Wise, spelled with upper case W. Using appropriate punctuation, I would record all these thoughts into the seminal ideas section of my pocket notebook at earliest convenience. For now, I dare not pause in my purposeful striding.

Knott

3
UNCLE GAMBI

The distant moan and echo of a ship's horn bade me stop and cup a hand to one ear. I could not have predicted this sound, so often described in books, would have proved as spectacularly despondent as the one I now heard. With no recourse but to follow its reverberations, my itinerary would have to wait.

I proceeded down Canal toward the river until encountering a series of parking lots. Turning left on Clinton, I came upon Jackson Square, recognizable by my preparatory study of maps and photographic surveys within the sub-basement of the University library. To my right, over a single set of railroad tracks, had been placed benches facing the river. I crossed these tracks and strode down to the little boardwalk. A small sign read Moon Walk.

I sat on a bench at the conclusion of the wooden walkway close to the grassy levy and observed the attitudes of my seated comrades. All leaned back with arm resting atop the bench; heads cocked to one side. Only a few seemed to be tourists observing dawn breaking over the Mississippi, which, according to the guidebooks, constituted a popular romantic past time. Mostly, the benches were populated by men in ill pressed clothing all appearing as if lead weights had been affixed to both eyelids and cheeks, countenances revealing no traces of enthusiasm let alone romance. I gripped my face with both hands and pulled downward. As the men shifted ever so slightly in their seats, I too shifted. I stared first at my hands then at the river and made the appropriate postural corrections.

With eyes fixed straight ahead, I opened my pocket notebook and recorded clandestine observations, the gravity of my anonymity being equivalent to that of a double agent standing at the Tränenpalast border crossing; microfilm canister embedded deep within his rectal vault.

Water churning, sweeping, overlapping, backtracking, pulling, pushing, tugboat diesel evoking impossible memory over powerful neurotic, psychopathologic eddy currents, the Mississippi and its bend, not a disappointment.

My abdominal muscles tightened. A man passed behind my bench. He moved over to a spot on the grassy levy, squatted on his haunches and gazed at the river as I had been. I snapped my notebook closed, replaced it in my breast pocket and glanced around, making certain that I continued to be unobserved; therefore, not subjecting to perturbation the system which was under my observation through the very act of observation itself.

The clouds hung low and gray; I felt sleepy, yet amidst my haggard brethren on the Moon Walk benches I also felt at peace.

The squatting man wore an old pea coat with a black watch cap similar to the fellow at the bus station who had observed me from the shadow of the lockers. The chance these men would be the same was unlikely although as coincidence was commonplace in novels I speculated it might well be the case in life. The man was watching the river intently. I felt compelled to sit and watch as this man sat and watched. I opened my notebook and wrote:

He examined every ship that passed, animated in his stillness, maintaining his weight forward, poised as if confronted with the impasse of the river, searching for a way across or, debating his suicide: a logical suicide devoid of emotion, a suicide by drowning in the Mississippi's collective unconscious.

I had to utilize extreme caution. In observing this man, the act of observation naturally elicited, for me, a pursing of the lips. And in pursing the lips, I would reveal to anyone observing me I was not only an observer but an astute observer. Before closing my notebook, I added hurriedly,

The man's brows looked knit to such an extent that it appeared his head might explode at any moment.

The morning had grown chilly. One by one the bench sitters took up their bundles and left. Only the most destitute remained, and myself. I observed a man arise and casually traverse the entire length of the moon walk. With no introduction, he sat at the opposite end of my bench. The two adjacent benches were unoccupied, yet he chose mine, the very last.

The man paid me no mind and sat with one leg hanging over his opposite knee, hands crossed. Remarkably, a Chesterfield balanced between two yellowed fingers. I was thrilled to recognize the Chesterfield name and hungrily awaited an opportunity to tell the man that not only did I smoke that brand of cigarette but that it represented my life brand.

The man turned his attention toward the remaining individuals seated several benches down then regarded the river for a moment. He turned and stared past me. I turned my head to follow his gaze toward the pea-coated man squatting nearby.

Minutes passed in silence and I relaxed, assuming I had chosen one of the most desirable benches and this man had simply been assertive in his sharing. His posture and body habitus suggested an aggressive nature. He wore a tight-fitting shirt which I thought unnecessarily accentuated his chest muscles and biceps.

As soon as I resumed my concentration upon the river, the man spoke. "Nice morning but it's going to get colder. I can tell you that right now."

I turned to examine the man's face. Its severity and lack of plumpness resembled no University lecturer I could recall yet he fell within the age range of an associate faculty member. In further contrast, no Professor, either junior or senior, in Sciences or Humanities, would be inclined to maintain their biceps or pectorals menacingly accentuated.

"What?" he asked. "I can't hear what you're saying." He slid over towards my end of the bench. I had not spoken a word. Without prompting, the man shared with me he had been working on a land-based wildcat drilling operation as a cook and that he had moved around Illinois while living in a tractor trailer cab. "I was the cook, you know. I cooked out of the truck, you know, lived in the truck, cooked out of the truck."

The man glanced at me as he spoke; I could not understand why he alternately glanced and spoke, with more glancing than speaking. I subtly communicated through knitting of the brow that I understood his subliminal communication. In having become savvy to subtexts through an intense regimen of preparatory readings spanning sociologic, anthropologic and literary disciplines, it occurred to me this man might be a member of the well documented French Quarter homosexual underground as described in tourist guidebooks and that he was relating in that context. But this man had lived in and cooked out of wildcat drilling operation trucks, which placed him squarely in the center of the heterosexual bell curve, if not at its most virulent apex.

The conversation seemed comfortable along the waterfront. I speculated this camaraderie was all too common while seated on Moon Walk benches at dawn. I again wished that I had not given away my pack of cigarettes as readily. This opportunity would have provided the ideal moment to light a Chesterfield and casually laugh as I shook the match out; even if the likelihood of inadvertently coughing, sneezing or having to suddenly squeeze my eyes tightly shut from the sting of smoke was not insignificant.

"My brand is Chesterfield," I offered.

The man pointed at his ear and said, "I can't hear you," and again moved closer. I was disappointed that he had not acknowledged my affiliation with the Chesterfield brand name. His new degree of closeness was disquieting. I remained comforted by an awareness that my books, remaining secure within my duffle bag resting against my left leg, were unaware of the stark reality which unfolded on this gong-tormented Moon Walk bench.

The man suddenly pointed toward the levy and exclaimed, "Right there! Right over there." I was startled; I straightened. He leaned forward, stretching his arm out to point, directing my attention toward the vicinity of the old man wearing the pea coat.

When I returned my scrutiny to the taut shirted man, he had again moved closer by another foot. His hands were crossed once again, although this time, one of them, I was aware, dangled close to mine.

"I saw him cut across that time. Goddamn thing was about the size of a football. Goddamn wharf rat," he hissed, and I now felt something cold pressing against my hand. To my horror, he cradled the barrel of a revolver and pressed its handle into the palm of my hand. The man observed me observing yet did not indicate that anything out of the ordinary was transpiring.

He was robbing me at gunpoint.

In films I had watched depicting just such a scenario, the gun barrel usually pointed toward the victim. In this instance, the gun barrel pointed toward the robber. I remained motionless, not wishing to create any disturbance which might alert the man to his error and cause him to flip the gun over.

The forever-moving-closer-reverse-gun-robber remained calm as we sat side by side gazing at the river. He continued to slide the butt of the revolver farther underneath my fingers. After a time, he spoke with annoyance.

"As far as I'm concerned, me bucko, this hotel plan of hers is amounting to one big pain in the ass. I'd soon not have to catch this fucker on my day off." The man was lamenting what sounded to be a work-related issue. He asked, "You said you want one of my Chesterfields?"

I was unsure what the appropriate response should be. On one hand, I was very pleased to have been offered a Chesterfield, my personal life brand, but did not entirely trust this man nor understand in the least where his actions were leading. I was aware the accentuated fellow had addressed me as me bucko. Hours earlier, while on the Trailways bus bound for New Orleans, I had been addressed similarly by my now deceased look-alike. No one, in my entire life, academic or otherwise, had called me either bucko or me bucko. I suspected that I had again been mistaken for my long-haired look-alike and suspected this look-alike had been immersed in a world of violent intrigue differing considerably from my University milieu. Nausea swept over me. I recalled the froth emerging from my traveling companion's mouth as the bus had pulled away from the Tallahassee station.

I wished more than ever I had proceeded directly to my hotel from the bus station instead of following the despondent ship's call to the banks of the Mississippi. To extricate myself from this mess I decided to inform my aggressive bench mate there had been a profound misunderstanding; that I was only twelve years of age and had become separated from my parents during breakfast that morning.

Before I could do so, he flinched, withdrew the revolver from my palm, and arose from the bench as the watch capped man staggered towards us supporting a cinder block over his head. As the two men faced each other, one with a brick, one with a gun, I pressed myself against the back of the bench and twisted sideways, toppling my duffle bag and nearly falling on top of it.

The taut shirted bench mate shifted his weight and hopped to one side, holding up one arm for protection. He slid the weapon into his pocket then strode up the boardwalk without a word.

"Your teeth need a good kicking!" the watch capped man called out.

My previous bench mate glanced once over his shoulder with an odd smirk, then spat and proceeded on.

The watch capped man continued to support the weight of the block with trembling arms until the reverse gunned robber disappeared into Jackson Square. He tossed the block over the bench onto the grass and sat down next to me, breathing heavily.

Disconcerted that yet another stranger had encroached upon my bench, I was grateful to this man for resolving my standoff as well as being intrigued by his spontaneous turn of phrase, identical to a familiar expression of my father. The events of the morning confirmed my previous suspicion that unbridled romance infused every waking hour of each and every day outside of University. The watch capped man and I sat side by side observing a tugboat push a barge upriver. In listening to the echo and reverb of its engine, I turned and asked, "Do you know how to get a job on one of those boats?"

The man continued to stare at the river. I waited several minutes for a response, grew uneasy by his silence, arose and hoisted my duffle bag onto one shoulder. As I proceeded along the Moon Walk, the man called out, "You want to work, is that it?"

I stopped, turned and assured him, "Yes, I want to work."

"You want to work on one of those ships? Is that the kind of work you want to do?"

As I had read several books on job interviewing strategy before my journey, I replied assertively, index finger trained upwards: "That is precisely the kind of work I wish to do."

He nodded; I returned to the bench. The man leaned forward, clasping his hands between his knees. I did likewise. We watched a large Lykes Brothers container ship move diagonally into the bend in the river which I knew to be the Algiers turn from my preparatory study of New Orleans maps. The stern of the ship swung around toward the East Bank. A reverberating growl filled the air. The water behind the ship churned as its stern shifted to line up parallel with the bank. The growling stopped and echoed.

"You know they are eating steak on that ship this very minute." Now closer, the man's pea coat appeared far more tattered; the breeze also brought with it the odor of acrid sweat.

"Steak?" I would not have thought they would eat steak at that very moment so early in the morning.

"As many steaks as a man wants. Pies, cakes…" The man became silent and stared at the ship. He made a violent motion as if discarding refuse with one hand. "*Bi-lacho*! On the ship, you work, you eat, get paid and get off. This is no good. You work with the men, drink with the same men. *Lovina*. You drink all they pay you. And if you don't drink with your mates; well, you have no choice. You have to drink with your mates. In one week, all your money is gone. All love is gone."

I would record this observation in my pocket notebook once at the hotel: that one must drink with one's mates and that in the real world there is no choice. I did not understand, however, why love would be gone as a result.

The man went on. "I have already spoken with the Dutchman, and he has found me a ship. I will be eating steak shortly," he said, "And not return here."

I assumed this Dutchman was a ship's broker of some sort. We continued to sit in silence and watch the Lykes Brothers ship disappear beyond the Algiers bend. The man had alluded to steak more than once; most likely he was hungry.

"My treat. I'm buying you breakfast," I announced.

"McDonald's," he responded without hesitation, rubbing his hands together. He slapped both thighs and arose. As we walked back toward Canal Street, he lowered his voice. "They have recognized me as a Gambi but don't yet realize that the chest is buried within the city."

I knew of no chest and stammered, "I think he was trying to rob me." Intending to describe how the robber had pushed the wrong end of the revolver into my hand, the tattered pea-coated man gripped my arm and interrupted.

"I am not sure if she understands precisely who you are, but she knew of your arrival. So, it begins. Her stated reason for wishing us dead is our bloodline. This is a lie. Her bloodline is a sham. This is about money. She will keep you alive as long as she does not have the gold. You will become her friend, her lover, her son, her daughter, whatever she needs you to be to gain control. She swallows everything in her path."

Not only did I not know this man but I was unaware of anyone who would wish him dead. And why anyone would want to kill me; I had been nothing more than a University student until recently; I did not understand precisely who I was, that is, who this mysterious madman presumed me to be, or why I would share his nature. He gripped my arm even tighter and asked, "How much has your father told you?"

My father had told me nothing and was quite sure had nothing to tell.

My mother and father both derived their work out of the theater industry in New York City and, the one thing made clear while growing up, was that neither had any interests outside of that.

"You know nothing then. Am I right? Nothing. And what's more, you have yet to get into any real trouble, so you know less than nothing. How we handle trouble is the only thing which defines us." The man seemed amused by this and spoke with a jovial tone as we walked. I frankly found it difficult to pay attention and resented his presumptions that I was ignorant. I had been to University. He went on, "I can see, you are a solitary, like me." He examined my sleeve as if gleaning information from the material itself. "They will say, you are not good to yourself, you are not healthy, do it this way or do it that way. Join us; they will tell you. But you cannot join them. Gambis have never acknowledged this form of logic. These people do not comprehend the state in which we need to reside. At first, I thought, oh how marvelous that the world and its promise turned out to be, as in a fairy tale. And how wonderful that it was all so self-contained, as within a book. As years passed, I came to understand that there was far more to consider and hardship in forms that I could not have anticipated. No, you are just like me." He clapped his hands together gleefully. ". . . But at the beginning."

This man assumed that I knew nothing, was just like him and that others might assume I was not good to myself. I did not like this man creating postulates concerning my nature or that he continued to rave on and on with such annoying assurance.

"Our family married into gypsy blood over a hundred years previously to protect themselves. The Lafitte brothers assumed we had their gold, you see. They didn't realize Vincent's whore had taken it all. The Lafitte's began cutting our throats one by one."

His tattered clothing and the prominent smell of sweat suggested the consideration that his intriguing history, interactions with me and presumptions were all delusional, and this man either belonged in a hospital or had escaped from one. He and his tales were more than what I could comfortably receive in the course of my first morning in New Orleans. Once at my hotel, I would record our interesting conversation within my notebook, perhaps creating a mental illness category to situate his monologue within an appropriate context; I would not consider allotting more than three to five pages for the entire analysis. Already within the duffle was an assemblage of books awaiting my thorough review.

The man stopped and commanded, "Look at me. I was born into Kalderash Natsia within a small kumpania in Bulgaria. I'm your Uncle Gambi!"

I bit my lip. I had no Bulgarian uncles. Out of pity, I did not correct the madman but regretted having offered to buy him breakfast.

"I had grown up under Rom protection while your father chose to come to America." My father had moved to New York City as a young man, but his parents had been missionaries. They had died before my birth.

"When I came to this country I had nothing," he went on. "I understood only Romani words. Your father and I had grown up hearing their stories, you see. I began looking for her as soon as I arrived. Ten years it took."

Uncle Gambi spoke with unusual urgency as we made our way onto Canal Street. His delusions were deeply rooted and the more he elaborated, the more disturbing it became to hear. The poor fellow truly believed us both to be descendants of this Vincent Gambi, an Italian pirate of whom he spoke with whimsical affection. He related how our ancestor had justifiably appropriated a large portion of Jean and Pierre Lafitte's pirate cache hidden in and around Southern Louisiana and this fortune been robbed by his prostitute, unbeknownst to the rest of the world. He insisted that after that, pirate ancestors, criminals, even governments had relentlessly pursued the Gambi bloodline until the present day and were still doing so.

Oddly, I had heard and read of the Lafitte brothers, real people in their time, whose exploits had been told and retold to the point their lives could be construed as fictional creations to those not historically aware. Any madman could be inspired to compose a fantastical narrative by reviewing any number of references describing their well know exploits.

He related having stolen the original fortune back from the last of the Gambi whores thirty years previously. Uncle Gambi further explained that within the treasure chest thirty million dollars were accounted for not only in the original doubloons, but that Swiss bank account vouchers, safety deposit box keys, passwords, stocks, bonds and assortments of world currency had also been contributed over the years. He reported having spent little of the fortune since acquiring it, only on the occasional rare wine or brandy. He implored me to trust no one and breathe not a word of this treasure, or you will end up their prey. These wolves will claim Lafitte blood.

After making this declaration, the man stopped to knead the top of my head and jaw exactly as the woman had done in front of the Trailways depot. Afterward, he seemed satisfied and resumed walking.

"You see, we share the same physiognomy."

Pushing through the door of the McDonalds, Uncle Gambi once again gripped my arm and pulled me closer to him. With disconcerting intensity, he pronounced an unfamiliar word directly into my ear: "Matelotage." I jerked my head away. As we waited in line to order, he continued to rave on with breath so fetid it forced me to step back and cough.

At one point, Uncle Gambi announced to the entire restaurant: "I offer Matelotage as Vincent Gambi had offered it to his own matelot two hundred years ago, just before being murdered. I am the eldest, and it is within my power to do so." The woman behind the cash register remained still as Uncle Gambi gripped my head with both hands and pushed me down to the floor with a grunt. "I bestow upon you the responsibility, burden, and legacy of a Lafitte Lieutenant." Flushed with embarrassment, I arose and ordered two Egg McMuffins, potato patties, orange juice and coffee. We made our way to the last vacant table in the center of the restaurant. I had resolved to eat as fast as I could then leave.

"I have spent twenty-five years cultivating our family treasure through sacrifice and significant losses of freedom," he said, unwrapping his Egg McMuffin. Before taking a bite, he added, "So knowing that someone like you will be taking over management of our legacy makes me very happy indeed. I have felt great anxiety about this for a very long time that it would all amount to nothing or that the treasure would be lost." Several patrons turned to stare pointedly in our direction.

From my readings at the University Medical Library, anxiety was defined as an affective disorder, a psychiatric diagnosis amenable to various modern treatment modalities, pharmacological or otherwise. I had been possessed by fits of anxious thought from time to time which had given rise to recalcitrant eczematous eruptions. At University, I had done quite a bit of research regarding dermatologic conditions in addition to issues of madness and delusional thinking. The notion of bearing the burden of a Lafitte Lieutenant was oppressive in that my vocation as a notebook keeper would beholden me not only to embrace its associated responsibilities and be light in travel but to be free from encumbrance.

The man had not, by the looks of it, purchased a new coat in many years yet purported to be the keeper of an immense fortune. The intricacies of his mad tale were intriguing but rife with inconsistency. His audacity in enrolling me within its delusional framework was equally astounding. As I sipped my coffee, I considered briefly that my self-actualization might involve coming to terms with a previously hidden pirate lineage. I dismissed the notion as highly improbable if not absurd.

Violently masticating his Egg McMuffin, Uncle Gambi banged his fists on the table. He announced, "I have not been with a woman in months!" With this he chewed even more violently, took up his carton of orange juice and rather than tilting it, crushed the container in his hand; the liquid inside propelled outward, drenching his face and throat. He finished his fried potato patty by pushing it into his mouth en masse, then slapped me hard on the arm and bellowed, "You must marry a South American woman! They are loyal and work like horses!"

He leaned back in his chair and chewed loudly. He told me with increasing volume that, "American women are the worst women in the world. American women aren't women. They are men. In South America, man is king. He is the king."

A similar pronouncement made within the University cafeteria would have invited heated debate or even violence. I slid downward in my chair. A large woman stared at us, chewing slowly. I averted my eyes and crinkled my potato patty wrapper.

"When I saw the woman waiting outside the bus station, and I knew I had gotten there too late." The man who stared at me across the table like a rabid animal was the same man observing me earlier behind the bus station lockers. "When you made visual contact, she had already placed herself in your head; she knows this. She will now attempt to dig herself in deeper. You must realize, if you associate with her, your reality will distort. You need to be able to visualize her inside and understand what sort of person she is and what is happening. That is if you wish to refer to her as a person at all. I don't. Once visualized, however, you will have to pull her out. Have you pulled your own teeth out with pliers?"

"No," I said. Uncle Gambi had a significant issue with the woman who lit my Chesterfield. Of course, I had never pulled my teeth out with pliers and would never think to do so; we lived in an age of modern dentistry. Uncle Gambi held unusually severe expectations regarding women in general and this woman in particular.

"She does not care whether you survive or not, only that she does. If keeping you alive will assure her own survival then she will keep you alive. She will eat you from the inside out while enjoying a glass of Merlot. You do not yet realize what danger you are in or the magnitude of the mistakes that can now be made without the necessary awareness of what you are doing. . ."

Uncle Gambi was proving himself increasingly unstable. I had encountered opinionated individuals at University, individuals who had made me feel similarly uncomfortable; I could challenge these University individuals with that question frequently posed by my physics mentors: Is the data sufficiently robust to support your statement?

In Uncle Gambi's instance, I was reluctant to provoke him further with additional questions. The more Uncle Gambi ate, the louder became his public celebration. At one point Uncle Gambi stopped speaking, looked about the room, leaned over the table and rasped, "It is no secret that the Lafitte fortune and the entire American economy is founded on chests of money laying at the bottom of a blood-filled ocean."

I glanced about the dining area as he pontificated of a slave trade carried out by the Lafitte brothers and their lieutenant, Vincent Gambi. Most patrons within the McDonald's were African American, yet he spoke without inhibition, sweeping his arm about the dining area and over his head like a rodeo cowboy riding a bucking bronco. "The presence of the blacks here is solely due to the legacy of slavery which you and I started! And now," he paused and clapped his hands together. "We are all Americans! What you see here are descendants from our African slave trade. The Lafitte's bought a slave from Cuba for one dollar a pound and sold this same slave here for four dollars a pound!" He banged his fist on the table concurrent to uttering the word pound.

The patrons had stopped eating and were listening to him, turning in their seats to stare at our table. I did not like his implication that I was complicit in the slave trade. I had taken no part in any Diaspora during this century or any other, although curiously, at that moment, felt an immense sense of guilt and personal responsibility. My skin became clammy. I was appalled this man had revealed these painful historical facts aloud within the McDonalds dining area. I knew from University that topics concerning issues of race were also of a sensitive nature. In every instance, one had to be very precise in one's language chosen to discuss these issues, not flippant and jocular. Uncle Gambi was asking for a misunderstanding if not a physical confrontation.

Thankfully he brushed his mouth with a napkin and changed the subject. "I only ask you to do me two favors, two quick errands. Two mathematics books sit on my bedside table. I borrowed them from the Public Library and both I'm certain, are overdue." I was relieved as the other patrons now returned their attentions to their breakfasts. "One of them will be significance for you while the other may prove misleading. I simply can't recall which is which. When you bring them, we can discuss this. I must explain what I've done." He added, "I would also ask you to fetch a small package addressed to me, and delivered to a house on Napoleon Avenue at which I had once stayed. I didn't like it there. The doorways were too low, and I would hit my head." He snapped his fingers. "Please, your newspaper." He reached across the table and snatched the paper from my hands. "And I need your pen." I reluctantly removed my pen from my breast pocket and handed it to him.

He made several notations and handed back both paper and pen. "I would not go near the hotel circled in your paper. The devil woman will subject you to psychological manipulations as soon as you step foot in the door." He looked about the dining area, removed an object from his coat pocket and pressed it into my hand. I closed my fingers around a key.

"As your uncle, I have to ask for your help. I cannot return to the first address on Prytania Avenue where my two books remain. The landlady had found a bottle of my wine on her roof. I had apparently wedged my library card through the spout in a moment of irony. I could not deny the bottle belonged to me, but she became unreasonable. I told her that I could not remember throwing the bottle onto this roof. She accused me of lying which had not been the case. I simply could not remember. How could I?" His prolonged laughter was disproportionate to the humor in the actual joke. I saw no joke.

Again I reviewed my encounter with the alluring woman at the bus station and wished I had without hesitation responded to her something to the effect of, "What are you talking about? You have mistaken me for someone else." But I had not responded in that way. I had lied in my omission, and the upshot was my current predicament, now enrolled to bear the unwanted burden of a Lafitte Lieutenant! I became even more strongly motivated to break away from Uncle Gambi, find my hotel and lay down in a comfortable bed, there to fall fast asleep. The notion that someone would inflict psychological manipulation on me was too far-fetched to be believed. Why would a hotel not simply be a hotel?

I arose without explanation and hurried out onto Canal Street, quickening my pace to a trot as much as my duffle would allow. The pathetic man hobbled after me, begging me to stop. When I continued, leaving him farther behind, he cried out, "We will meet then tomorrow night at nine o clock behind the YMCA, under the expressway. Please bring my books to me! Both of them."

I stopped and looked back. He leaned over, hands on knees and gasped for air, attempting to wave. Reaching into my pocket, I walked back and handed him a ten-dollar bill.

"So you may eat," I explained. He regarded the money with visible distress and backed away, horrified.

"No. You forget I have two whole days before shipping out. *Tachiben*, I cannot…" He pushed the bill back into my hand. "This has to be the last I eat or drink for two days."

I thrust the bill back into his hands and walked away, unable to bear further protestations from this starved lunatic.

"You are certainly a Pepper," he called out. "I can see that. If you choose to recover what lies underneath the filth, you will be rewarded. The problem to solve is usually quite simple involving only trigonometry. You only need the equation and usually a unit of measure. *O lungo drom*." He looked about himself nervously, pocketed the money, turned and trotted down Common Street.

Uncle Gambi had addressed me by my surname. I continued up St. Charles, light headed in considering that I had not once introduced myself formally as a Pepper.

4
REGISTRATION

Having fed Uncle Gambi's ravenous delusions with nods of encouragement and fueled him physiologically with Egg McMuffin, coffee, and potato patty, the man's psychopathologic gear train had increased its torque. I had been dragged into the cogs and nearly crushed by his machinations of lunacy. The only consolation was the unlikelihood of meeting him or any of these other specters again. Once safely within my hotel room, at leisure to transcribe the morning's hallucinations into my pocket notebook, my true unencumbered life as an experimentalist could begin on its own terms.

Uncle Gambi had suggested that I was, as he had been, naive at the beginning of life's journey, perceiving all that unfolded around me to be marvelous, as if taking place within a far-fetched literary tale. He implied that I would soon learn that life wasn't so amazing and that I had not considered many of its associated aspects. I disagreed. Life was unfolding exactly in keeping with my expectations. Why would it not unfold and continue to unfold otherwise?

Hoisting my duffle onto one shoulder, I caught sight of faded lettering along its side. Pepper had been written in magic marker some years previously. This observation proved a great relief, suggesting that Uncle Gambi had spied my name and used it as bait, as any carnival fortune teller might glean information by rifling through a rube's wallet. The breakfast adventure had at least provided a much-needed distraction from my long and disturbing bus ride.

Uncle Gambi's outward trappings implied he was internally discordant. He had likely created a philosophy for himself which applied to he alone, justifying his aberrant behaviors and actions of the past. This philosophy led him ultimately to squat destitute upon the Governor Nichols grassy levy staring toward the powerful undercurrents of the Mississippi. My appearance had somehow offered his imagination a last-minute solace. The term rationalization had been cited as the very point of reference which both my University adviser and father had invoked regarding my stated aspiration to become a notebook keeper and an experimentalist. They could not be more wrong. Uncle Gambi's conjectures were desperately fictional while my experimental notebook keeping resided in a realm of objectivity and devotion, protected by a prodigious sword of truth, gallantly *wooshing* and *swooshing* through the opaque wall of the world's psychic vapors.

Speeding up my pace along St. Charles Avenue, I soon noticed a large sign one block ahead: Lafayette Hotel. To my left was a small park, its plaque reading Lafayette Square. At the time of my arrival, men had arisen from blankets and newspapers were spread on its grass.

I studied one fellow attempting to stand by pushing his back against a tree. He arose from a squatting position and with successive jerks pushed himself upward, little by little, until upright. He spent an inordinate amount of time adjusting the angle of his orange beret and flicked several blades of grass from his coat sleeve; he took one step forward and fell, his beret tumbling off. He crawled on his hands and knees to retrieve the hat then returned to the same tree, sat with his back against it, and recommenced the entire process. Simultaneously, in the middle of the lawn, two men gripped the opposite arms of a woman, pulling her first in one direction then another while exchanging angry shouts and curses. The woman appeared groggy and endured the tug of war until all three toppled over and lay still on the grass.

I became enveloped by a group of men moving around me like a school of fish. The impression created was that a movie had just let out and that the patrons had just left a theater en masse. I surveyed the street, yet saw no evidence of a marquee. One of the men caught my eye and brought two fingers up to his mouth. He nodded expectantly. I shrugged and shook my head. The next man as well brought two fingers up to his mouth and nodded. I shook my head again and continued to turn from one to the next, shaking and shrugging. All the men possessed scrapes and scabs on their faces and foreheads with faded tattoos on their arms.

Once clear of this destitute congress, I removed my pocket notebook, dropped to one knee and wrote in block capitals:

I WILL ENGULF MYSELF IN SORROW, CATER TO MISFORTUNE

AND THEREBY EMBRACE LIFE'S TRUE MEANING.

Sorely regretting not having purchased two packs of cigarettes at the bus station that morning, I could have, at this very moment, been liberally distributing Chesterfields among these deserving men; and what despondent cheer this would have spread. Arising, I let my shoulders drop to lend the appearance of a soul beaten to a pulp and pocketed my notebook.

Lafayette Restaurant was printed across a dirty plate glass window facing St. Charles Avenue. Along the Lafayette Park side, several glass panes had been replaced by plywood. An Open sign hung inside although dusty chairs had been stacked some time ago, perhaps even years.

While examining the defunct interior, I spotted a fellow peering through one of the remaining glass panes on the Lafayette Park side of the restaurant. He caught sight of me and disappeared. A wiry, unshaven white man wearing a flannel shirt then rounded the corner speaking aloud to himself. "I did it; I really did it." He stopped, placed his hands on his hips, rotated his head from side to side and looked at the sky. "Lord have mercy, I don't believe what I just did, but I did it." He again rotated his head and looked at the sky. "What time is it?" he asked himself. He pulled back his sleeve and regarded his wrist.

"How do you like that, I left my watch in my coveralls. They're hanging in the back of the cab. Brand spanking new overalls, brand spanking new watch."

In catching sight of me, the man appeared startled and spoke with intense emotion. "Mister, I'm sorry to bother you, but I've got an emergency on my hands."

Upon hearing the word emergency, I wanted to get involved. The man, out of breath, was facing a true emergency. I held out my hand and turned my head to fend off unnecessary apologies on his part. He needed my help and needed my help fast.

The man looked me up and down then went on. "I locked my tools in my truck. I've got a hammer drill, all my bits. I've got my new electric jig saw, got all my tools in plain view for crying out loud. I've got my work boots in

43

there, my new steel toe work boots and my brand spanking new overalls." The man's eyebrows arched far upward into the center of his forehead.

"It's parked down on Commerce. That's why it took the wind out of me, coming up here like this. I live clear over in Terry Town on the West Bank. I got one hour to get to Terry Town, get my other keys and get back before my men get here, or someone breaks into my truck. I got three men coming this morning, actually four men, four men coming." The man's eyes appeared red as if he had been crying. He was at the end of his rope.

"Mister, I need ten dollars to get across the bridge to Terry Town. I'll give you back thirty. That's how much its worth to me. No," he paused. "I'll give you back forty. Forty. Mister, I can't give you any more than forty, I'm sorry. But I need that ten right this minute."

The man had landed himself in a big pickle, and I could help him even though ten dollars might be a lot of money to lend a perfect stranger. I had already given the most likely delusional Uncle Gambi ten.

Without prompting, the man said, "Follow me; I'll show you the truck." He started back around the corner.

"That's ok," I called out. That was all the proof I needed.

The man stopped, checked his wrist again and threw up his hands. "See that. Left the watch in my truck and I am so used to looking at my watch. Did you see me do that!?"

"Of course, I saw you do that," I said and reached into my pants pocket. The man watched me.

"I know you saw me do that." The man raised his face toward the heavens and cried, "Not this morning, Lord. Not with four men coming; I got four men coming, Jesus. Not this morning."

I could do little not to imagine Moses, or Charlton Heston playing Moses. I handed him the ten. I had answered his prayers.

"Mister, you just saved my life." The man stuffed the bill into his pocket. "I'll meet you right back here. I'll meet you at five. And give you fifty!" I gave him the thumbs up. He pointed at me and said, "I'll see you right here at five."

I watched the unlucky man recede up St. Charles in a tremendous hurry to get back to his truck.

"You just owe me the ten. That's all you owe me," I called out. The man didn't appear to hear me. He had already moved into the middle of the next block.

"This is exactly what I was looking for, real camaraderie," I breathed, turned and entered the Lafayette Hotel.

I found myself within an entrance vestibule of the dimly lit lobby and had to sidestep past a brown couch and two arm chairs, haphazardly arranged, with threadbare upholstery. To my immediate left, chains and a padlock secured the handles of the restaurant door.

A white-bearded man sat in one of these chairs, calf resting on his knee. I had to assure myself that the man was alive as the play of lobby shadow with light inclining through the sooty front window lent the impression of a brooding classic sculpture, the dignity of which could have only been fashioned in an era several hundred years prior. Only a puff of smoke arising from his pipe along with the slightest turn of his head upon my entrance demonstrated proof of animation.

To the rear of the lobby, a chipped red light bulb glowed from a fixture over the open door of an elevator. This elevator was no bigger than a closet. Inside a stool had been bolted to its inner wall.

On the left side of the lobby, behind an old oak counter, stood a pale young man, roughly my age, with a purple scar running from temple to chin on the right side of his face. He had been examining a fingernail when I entered the lobby.

"I had called a few minutes ago concerning a room," I said.

The clerk's expression remained flawlessly void. "How many nights?"

"Just one night. I'm going to look for boarding house lodging tomorrow." I winced; to divulge my ambition to seek boarding house lodging could well be construed as disloyalty to the Lafayette.

The desk clerk pushed a card across the counter. After filling in the registration details, I slid it back toward the man and held my breath: My responses would be subject to scrutiny. I had anticipated these events and rehearsed answers to the numerous and pointed questions bound to be asked in the verification process of signature, identity and intentions within the New Orleans community. No inquiries were forthcoming from the clerk; he held his cards close to his chest, undoubtedly waiting to study each and every notation only after I had left the lobby environs; then conferring with authorities who would insist on him double, perhaps triple checking my submitted information, biding their time while awaiting arrival of FBI and Interpol teletypes.

I would need to prepare myself for that inevitable knock on the door.

The desk clerk arose and stood in front of a wooden board examining various keys hanging on hooks. He moved his hand toward one, hesitated and moved his hand toward another; he lifted this key free of its hook, turned and hit the bell.

A pack of Chesterfields lay on the counter, newly opened, its cellophane wrapper was torn and smudged with red lipstick, remarkably similar to the pack I had purchased a short while before, ripped open by the incisors of the mysterious, full figured woman on Tulane Avenue.

"Do you smoke Chesterfields?" I asked. That we shared the bond of Chesterfields would most likely serve as a considerable ice breaker. I became even more curious about the collection of books this clerk without a doubt stored under the counter to feed the flames of his literary hearth; the uncertainty of their authorship, whether Proust, Lowry or Beat Poet, would provide me with a delicious, if not delirious, smorgasbord of speculation once safely retired within my room.

The desk clerk resumed examining his fingernail as an older black man emerged from small alcove beside the elevator. I wondered what the man had been doing at the moment of the bell's ringing. The man's mouth, expanding into a broad gleaming smile, was incongruous with the dimness of the lobby, as was his faded red waistcoat with golden epaulets. The porter took the key out of the clerk's hand, regarded it and blinked.

"Mmm mm, I'm telling you." He lifted my duffle bag. "I'm telling you," he repeated. I wasn't certain whether he was talking to himself or addressing me. The desk clerk did not acknowledge the man's remarks, his visage that of a Neolithic standing stone.

The porter's smile disappeared quickly, as though some form of mechanical apparatus had been abruptly removed from his oral cavity. He entered the tiny elevator, flicked a light switch and twisted a key. "Uh huh," he remarked. I edged into the elevator alongside him. A whirring noise began.

The porter slowly pulled the outer door closed then even more deliberately dragged the sliding fence across. I listened to the drawn-out sound of the fence rattling into place and wondered if I would have to ride with the porter in this tiny chamber and observe his painstaking actions each and every time I accessed my room. The elevator jerked, shuddered and stopped. The porter sat on the stool for a moment, pulled the fence and door open and said, "Uh-huh."

He picked up my duffle bag and led me out onto the second-floor hallway, just wide enough to allow two people to stand shoulder to shoulder. The porter shuffled down corridors, periodically remarking "Uh huh." His hair, slickened with oil, had been combed up and back. His cheekbones appeared unusually high although, as I studied him, he appeared to have applied some form of makeup as well as sparkling eye liner; in being so adorned, he bore strong resemblance to Little Richard, the rambunctious piano player whom I had become well aware of through the continual viewing of television talk shows in my formative years. Little Richard spoke, sung and played the piano with enormous animation, swung his arms through the air fast and furiously and was given to spontaneous and flamboyant outbursts. I could not imagine this porter doing likewise but wondered if he had attempted to create a likeness to the famous singer as a form of alter ego.

"Do you know *Long Tall Sally*?" I asked and winced; it occurred to me the man might not have known of his uncanny resemblance. Thankfully, the porter did not respond; I hoped he had not heard my question.

We continued to walk for some time through length after length of second-floor hall space. The hotel, when viewed from the street, had not appeared large enough to justify such a duration of travel. I attempted to memorize distinguishing features along the way, stains or cracks on the walls of the corridors, suspecting that we may have passed through the same area more than once. That the hallways were vacant and silent was odd. I heard no scooting of furniture or hawking up of respiratory secretions or sound of canned television laughter, only the creaking of our footfalls. No one appeared to live behind the hundreds of doors along the corridors through which we passed. Any of these rooms could have provided me with adequate and convenient board, yet we continued.

I suspected the desk clerk had deliberately chosen a room of considerable distance from the elevator knowing full well that vacancies existed much closer. And perhaps this same desk clerk was more than adept at wielding isolation as an implement expediting the hotel's psychological manipulations. Much as a water dropper or wire jacket had served the insidious Fu Manchu. Uncle Gambi may well have been right on all his seemingly far-fetched accounts and remained the only sane person I had encountered since my arrival.

The passageways became progressively narrower; we finally arrived at a dead end comprising of three doors angled sharply toward one another. The porter placed the key in the lock of the door on the right. The door was light and flimsy as if made of balsa. I regarded the brass lock jiggling precariously in his hand, constituting no functional lock at all. Assigned a room intimately juxtaposed with two adjacent rooms, I could only be highly suspicious of the scarred desk clerk's motivations and those of the porter.

With a "Mercy," he lifted my duffle bag onto the single chair by the window and held onto its arms, breathing heavily. "Mercy," he said again, wiped his brow with a handkerchief, turned and quite clearly said, "Good Golly Miss Molly."

The porter clearly knew of his resemblance to Little Richard and was now showboating.

The room was bright in contrast to the gray hue of our approach. Sunlight filtered through synthetic velvet curtains. The porter pushed the window open then shuffled over to the bathroom door, reached inside and turned on its light switch. He exclaimed "Uh huh," leaned against the wall and took several deep breaths, bending forward. "Mercy," he gasped, glanced up at me then walked slowly back over to the window. He placed his hands on the sill and peered outside.

"Yeah," he concluded.

The porter was expecting a tip.

I plunged my hands into both pockets and used tactile sense to discern various money groups. Ideally, I would wish to remove a single dollar bill although there remained the possibility of removing the five which I knew had been crumbled alongside my singles. Removing the five would necessitate having to return the five to that same pocket while fumbling afterward for lesser bills. My right eye began to twitch uncontrollably at the prospect of removing stray coins along with various crumbled bills and having to examine, count, and sift in front of the porter.

My worse fear manifested as I removed the five from my pocket. The porter continued to stare calmly out the window, a serene portrait of a lesser Little Richard. I ground my teeth together and drove my hand back into my pocket, removing a fist full of money. Coins dropped onto the carpet with muffled thumps as crumbled bills floated down onto the bed. The porter turned, observed all this, then refocused his attentions out the window.

The outcome was worse than I could have ever have imagined.

I moved forward like a roboton and handed the porter a single then another and another.

His smile lasted a brief instant after which he reached up to tip the brim of an imaginary hat. "It's quieter back here," he said. "Some people like these rooms because they are quiet, you understand." As he closed the door behind him, the porter said, "Nobody listening." I heard him chuckle as he receded down the hall then more faintly add, "I'm telling you."

After a few moments, I peered through the peephole. The porter was no longer present. As the adjacent doors appeared to wrap around the sight glass, I jerked my eye away.

I did not like looking through peepholes; the possibility always remained, however improbable, that a malignant entity might spring forward into its wide-angle view and drive an ice pick through the glass lens piercing the center of my eye. For similar reasons, regarding corners of tables caused me to blink uncontrollably with the prospect of slipping and inadvertently impaling my eye on its converging edges. I could recall always having been sensitive when near sharp objects and their potential for puncturing the ocular globe and extruding its viscera.

Returning to the bed, I sat still and stared at the door, listening for the fumbling of keys or rattling at my lock. Silence ensued. A small night table had been placed beside my bed, across the room a dresser on top of which I noticed a wooden ruler. I examined the cigarette burns on the purple synthetic velvet bedspread; one defect alone was large enough to fit four of my fingers.

I estimated there to be roughly fifty discrete cigarette burns on this bedspread. The mattress cratered deeply at its center. I removed my pants, over shirt and socks, took up my pocket notebook and jotted notes concerning Uncle Gambi's insane discourse. After a short time, greatly fatigued, I placed the notebook on the bedside table in its face up position such that it could be opened and accessed at the merest hint of a need to document.

I lay down, slid my legs underneath the covers, jerked them out immediately and began kicking. I kicked and kicked and kicked the sheets off the end of the bed. The concave indent at the center of the mattress became fully visible; within it lay a pile of sand. Embedded within this pile of sand, protruding like little spring shoots, were pubic hairs. The effect was akin to being doused by scalding water.

I kicked. I kicked and kicked and kicked.

"Someone's been combing their pubic hairs in my bed!" I yelled at the top of my lungs then stood on top of the mattress and brushed myself off as if set upon by fire ants after immersion in a vat of honey. I swept my foot across the sheet, gagging. The pile, little by little, spilled over the edge of the mattress onto the floor. I jumped down from the bed, hurried into the bathroom and washed my feet in the tub. Drying them by the sink with one foot up on the toilet cover, I noticed a gaping hole in the wall under the sink. The hole was big enough for two large rodents to emerge side by side. I stopped drying, took several steps backward and stared into the blackness.

I began to urinate into the defect. My rational was the action would overcome any dormant evil presence residing there while proving to that entity that I wasn't afraid of either the blackness within or the blackness beyond. Urinating into the plaster gash would not hurt or disturb the overall equilibrium of the Lafayette in its present state yet allow me to express myself emotionally during a time of duress.

As my urine stream disappeared into the breach, my mind rekindled a memory of awakening long ago in my childhood home to find myself functioning as if within a walking fugue state. I had arisen from the bed, wandered into our apartment's kitchen, climbed onto the counter and without hesitation, peed into the sink. I then jumped down, removed a raw frankfurter from the refrigerator and ate it, standing in front of the stove. Nothing stirred. My act had gone unrecognized. At that moment, I apprehended that one did not have to pee into a toilet.

The following night I urinated into a wax lined paper sack and threw it down the hallway incinerator. Nothing happened. On the third night, I filled the reservoir of our family humidifier. It ran continuously in the living room with no resultant odor. On the fourth night, I peed out of our eleventh story apartment window with no ramifications. My experiment had concluded as quietly as it began. I had attained a sense of free will and autonomy. Framed within my eleventh story apartment window on West 56th Street, urinating into the Manhattan night. I had chartered a course to become an experimentalist. Now here at the Lafayette Hotel, fifteen years later, I had again urinated into a taboo receptacle and broken a potent spell of fear, reclaiming in the present moment, that essence of vitality and liberation.

Despite the exaltation which arose through this process of magical urination, I regretted my action. Although steeped in scientific rigor, I retained an odd superstition or two. My present state of exhaustion amplified the fear that, were I to attempt a bowel movement while sitting on this toilet situated adjacent to the now violated barrier, rodents might be summoned in demonic rebuttal, swarm from the bowl and claw my hanging scrotum, perineum, and anus to shreds. I backed out of the restroom with eyes trained upon the blackness within this gaping void. Turning to survey the bedspread for any remaining traces of sand and pubic hair, I decided at that instant to seek other accommodations as soon as possible.

Lowered once again onto the mattress, the curtains across the window fluttered; composed of the same material as the bed spread and likewise peppered with cigarette burns, their holes striped the room with undulating cylindrical rays. The lower lid of my right eye ticked rhythmically. As sleep did not come right away, I arose from the bed and retrieved both my pocket notebook and those few pages of the Times-Picayune acquired from the Chesterfield-smoking woman, subsequently modified by Uncle Gambi. I transcribed with great ferocity all that had occurred, including my concerns with the bathroom abyss; I exhausted myself in this manner. Placing the notebook on the nightstand, I took up the newspaper intending to locate a suitable boarding house the following day. My eyelids rose up and down as if born by the warm air currents wafting through the open window.

5
PRODIGIOUS TYPING

I awoke to the sound of constant tapping. Pulling aside the curtain, I studied the light then looked at my watch: twelve forty-five. The tapping soon became recognizable as the distinct characteristics of a typewriter, the typing itself being carried out at an extremely fast rate.

Curiously, the bedspread lay on the floor. My penis slumped outside the front entrance of my tidy whities as if it were a dead soldier. As I was replacing it, a woman's voice cried out, "Yes!"

I jerked my hand away from the underwear door.

The woman yelled more forcefully. "Yes! Lift me. Hurry, lift me with it!" Coming to a full wakeful state, I sat up. The typing ceased. A carriage return bell sounded: *Ding.* The bell sounded again, *ding*, then again, *ding*.

Ding-ding-ding-ding-ding.

"Yes!" She bellowed, voice resonant. My penis, shifting behind its tidy whitie doorway, startled me. My genital acted of its own volition, as a sentient being might.

"Stop! You know it's so difficult for me to be up here. Mother used to lock me up in this very room." The woman's voice sounded familiar. The typing commenced again. I assumed the voice belonged to the operator of the typewriter.

There ensued five minutes of even faster breakneck typing. I stayed still; something instructed me to pay close attention. After a lull, the paper was yanked from the carriage followed by sounds of weeping. A chair scooted; a male voice asked, "Why do you work up here if it's going to bother you?"

"Oh please," she said. "It's not a matter of choice. I have to be here. Where else would I go?" Sobbing continued over the squeak of an advancing typewriter roller.

"This section comprises reflection of the author. The author pretends, you see, inwardly uncomfortable, extremely uncomfortable in fact, traipsing from one relationship to the next in futile attempt to quench desire which she doesn't understand, as if a vampire's bloodlust were displaced. She ends up destroying them all."

My jaw tightened, and my shoulders tensed, rising upward. I remained still.

"Let's see." The carriage returned. "She lost her love and became frustrated to be without one. She doesn't understand the restlessness. Maybe she's bored; she doesn't know. She can't entertain being alone although it was suggested she should be, for the protection of others, and so that she might reflect on her relentless destructive tendencies, on what truths she is not facing. She adored her last man but arranged for his death because he got on her nerves; he made her happy and therefore complacent, which was intolerable and not in keeping with her mission to ride a flaming chariot through the gates of hell. It was too easy, too happy, too soon."

After a silence, the roller turned. The space bar depressed several times, and typing of even greater ferocity recommenced.

The woman yelled, "Take your hands off me!"

I sat up even straighter. I heard a grunt which was followed by another volley of typing. When the woman spoke again, her voice sounded cheerful. "This is just a picaresque fuck book." The male grunted again; the woman brightened further. "The story of a brilliant bitch who is the incarnation of endless want. It's simple, and it is what the fans want."

I shifted my bottom within my tidy whities.

"She meets the man of her dreams who is bent on creating beautiful relationships and destroying them. That's all he can do; all he is destined to do. He's like her double but not exactly." She spoke more softly. "Although I like the chapter when he prevents himself from having his necessary creative time and, arising from the ensuing frustration, goes out and commits murder. He forces himself to live contrary to his true nature and thereby engineers his own rage and provides himself with an endless source of anxiety. This forces him to create out of desperation and the need to escape. She follows him, growing in strength from his sick energy." The woman's voice rose angrily at the end of the sentence followed by a loud crash. I was afraid to move lest the springs on which my bottom sat or the floorboards on which my feet rested, would creak.

The woman's voice did not resume for many minutes. Lulled by the cadence of typing, I closed my eyes and was startled awake an indeterminate time later by a steady low-frequency gurgling. The wall of my room bowed in and out to a rhythmical rasping sound of wood scooting against wood.

"Come on! Quick!" the woman's voice had become loud and clear. I bolted upright and examined my room. "Come on!" She insisted. I stood up involuntarily.

"Let me," she said. "Oh, let me, for God's sakes!" She sounded angry and impatient. Furniture scraped and slammed against the other side of my wall. A paint chip fell; something shattered. The sound of further heavy scooting ensued.

"What's wrong?" she asked. "Now, what's wrong?"

I listened to what could have either been weeping or laughter. The woman inquired, "Why is your holster empty?" I could just hear the man's reply.

"Remember you told me to take out my piece last time? We had it out."

"Well, then where the hell is it? You've been walking around without your piece? What good are you?"

I could not discern further remarks until the woman stated flatly. "You mean to tell me you lost your gun?" Her low-pitched laugh grew in volume, causing the wall to vibrate.

The male voice continued evenly. "We were reading next door. You set the covers on fire." I regarded the bedspread on the floor, my chest tightening. "Maybe that's when I lost it when I was putting out the fire."

"So?" The woman became even more irritated.

"No wait, we were in here." The male voice, insistent, carried the deliberate intonation of an actor reading from a script. "It must be in here somewhere. I always put it in the bedside table drawer." My hand mechanically extended forward as if all movements were being initiated by an unseen servo controller, and pulled open the night table drawer. I had seen a sufficient number of World War II films to understand what lay before me: A forty-five caliber military issue.

"Shore Patrol," I whispered.

There existed the real possibility that someone might intrude into my room; yet, I remained preoccupied with the appearance of the forty-five. I wished nothing more than to lift this forty-five into the air and fire it ten, twenty, thirty times. With difficulty, I released my gaze from the drawer and directed it toward the entrance to my room, more specifically, toward the peephole.

The woman spoke again: "All right, back to work. I've got to finish this chapter."

The door to the adjacent room opened and closed. Footfalls faded with a painstaking lethargy as if the owner had been creating tension by walking more slowly than necessary. I held my breath and clenched my buttocks so as not to provoke squeaking of the mattress springs. After a time, the sound of typewriter keystrokes recommenced along with periodic carriage returns. I remained attentive, seated on the side of my mattress then noticed something odd.

My pocket notebook lay face down on the night table. The ruler, which previously rested atop the bureau, was situated aside my notebook. I did not recall rearranging or moving either.

The irregular orientation of my notebook was bewildering. My consistent practice had been to configure any notebook face up for ease of access; I had organized each in a specific and reproducible manner to facilitate data collection from the upward going emplacement. All inside front covers displayed indices dedicated to current interests while the last three pages always included seminal quotations derived from reviews of literature, science, psychology and philosophy.

To reassure myself, I tossed this current volume open and reviewed its index of relevant topics: *Alcoholic Heroes and Non-Equilibrium Thermodynamics*. I had added both before my departure. The latest, *Pirate Treasure*, had been documented following my conversation with the insane Uncle Gambi. Before replacing the notebook on the table, I browsed other recent selections:

In its distressing nudity, in its light without effulgence…

Into the destructive element, immerse…

I was only twenty-four at the time. My life was already then gloomy, disorderly, and wildly solitary.

I turned the page and noted a new addition to my inventory of seminal terms: *Matelotage.* The word had been written in block capitals and circled. I could not recall transcribing this and flipped several more pages ahead, happening on another unfamiliar entry from the recorded speech subdivision:

There are people alive today who have seen a real treasure chest full of Spanish and French gold…

I had grossly underestimated my degree of exhaustion and attributed my inability to recall these notebook entries to a resultant state of relative amnesia. The longhand was less characteristic of my own but again, given my profound fatigue, penmanship was bound to have suffered. I took up my pen and wrote:

I wonder what frame of mind possessed me to choose this specific detail in that I had chosen to polish the delicate edifices of Byzantium over the mundane task of counting currency.

I closed the notebook slowly and regarded it with some concern. At very least I needed to locate the local public library to clarify this term matelotage. My head swirled with the prospect of library research. Although likely no truth to Uncle Gambi's alleged promise of unfathomable riches, my fatigue had lowered the threshold for finding allure in pirate skullduggery; I huffed its harsh vapors and frankly enjoyed its swirling euphoria.

I raised one hand and solemnly proclaimed, as one might in testifying before a higher court: "I, Rodney Pepper, am confident that neither my father nor mother had ever visited the city of New Orleans nor had they held associations within any buccaneering society." My parents were gentle and private people, not swashbucklers. There may have been merely one or two books of general pirate lore haphazardly placed within their living room library along with a copy of Treasure Island which I had read and enjoyed as a child. And what child wouldn't? The subject of piracy had never been breached yet the man who called himself Uncle Gambi implied that my parents should have fully informed me of my legacy. They had not.

Reconfiguring my notebook into the familiar face up position, I again sat on the side of the bed with hands on both knees. My eyes grew heavy with the cadence of typewriter keystrokes. I thought of my father, who as far as I could remember, had never spoken of his descendants with me. I did recall how he adamantly insisted on preserving his quietude; so much so that he rarely answered the phone. In growing up, I assumed the responsibility of informing his callers that Dad was nowhere to be found even if he had been standing directly behind me. In reviewing all that he had, and had not revealed, I realized I knew little about the man.

Awaking to the sound of loud voices in the hallway, I toppled forward onto the floor, dazed, and lay there; the dim light enclosed me within its cell of cylindrical bars. The sun had receded over the top of the hotel. I listened.

"No one will hear you back here. These rooms are unoccupied." I struggled to my feet as a man called out,

"Shimulo!"

I recognized Uncle Gambi's accent.

"There is no one here to stop us. Perfect."

The second voice belonged to the same man who had counseled the provocative typist on the other side of my wall. He again sounded to be reading from a script. I arose but found my lower extremities had become numb while seated on the bedside. In order to move forward, I swung one leg in front of the other like an Autobot taking its first baby-steps off the assembly line. In this way, I lurched over to the door and peered into the wide-angle lens of the peephole revealing a distorted vision of Uncle Gambi restrained by the same taut-shirted reverse-gunning robber from the Moon Walk bench. The optical effects of the peephole lens further accentuated his biceps. I began to sweat.

As a new sense of righteous indignation welled up, I felt strength return: I had paid for my room in full and therefore was fully entitled to the peace and quiet it offered. My much-needed sleep had been fragmented, fragmented, fragmented. The scene framed within the peephole comprised a gross intrusion. Allowing myself to become filled to the brim with well-deserved entitlement, I stepped backward, sat down on the bed, stamped my foot and exclaimed,

"How do you like that!"

And I didn't care who heard me say it.

Outside the door, Uncle Gambi moaned the now familiar word matelotage.

I flung open the bedside table drawer, grabbed the shore patrol forty-five and strode to the door. Giddy from endogenous catecholamines secreting from every internal glandular orifice, I had difficulty focusing and fumbled with the lock. Uncle Gambi's head repeatedly banged against the peephole, driving its short brass cylinder inward with each impact; it tumbled directly onto the great toe of my left foot.

I hopped up and down and yelled, "Mothering mother-HUMPER!"

Uncle Gambi's hair protruded through the circular opening. "OK, bucko!" the tight-shirted man called out, his voice strained with exertion. I threw the door open, and both the taut shirted man and Uncle Gambi fell forward. Afflicted by spontaneous palsy, I could neither speak nor raise my Shore Patrol Forty-Five but knew that I stood now wearing nothing but tidy whities, stained yellow following the delivery of several anxious jets of urine.

The tight-shirted man regained his balance, stared first at me, then at the gun in my hand and exclaimed, "Oh for Christ sakes!" He released Uncle Gambi, snatched the Shore Patrol Forty-Five and stuck it down the front of his pants. "That's mine, you dickhead. You're supposed to bring your own shit." With that, he turned and left the room.

Uncle Gambi had collapsed in a heap and was breathing heavily, his watch cap laying on the floor of the corridor exposing matted greasy hair. He gripped the frame of the doorway, glared at me with fiery red eyes, and searched his pockets. Noticing the brown bag lying against the opposite wall, he crawled toward it, took the bag in both hands and sat. He grabbed the watch cap and pulled it back over his head. A miniature bottle of rum fell from the package and rolled a short distance away; other bottles clinked inside.

"So, have you found our treasure yet, Pepper?" he asked.

This drunken man had presumed I would be hard at work uncovering a haphazardly imposed and unsubstantiated legacy. I yelled, "Leave me alone!" My exclamation created a valsalva sufficient to provoke several additional spurts of urine from the urethral meatus of my penis. My tidy whities drooped downward from the weight of accumulated fluid. I tugged upward, gripping the elastic to keep them from falling below my knees. Uncle Gambi leaned on his elbow, picked up one of the fallen miniatures and returned it to his paper bag. He sat up and spoke with remarkable clarity.

"The truth is, without my doppelganger, I am unable to locate the chest this time."

The sense of this statement verified the man to be mentally ill, if not floridly so. Most likely the confabulation had been made worse by alcohol consumption. Uncle Gambi had lost all his credibility in stating that he had been in possession of a doppelganger, a literary device, the exploits of which serving to destabilize a fictional protagonist's life while inevitably leading to self-annihilation concurrent with the denouement of plot. A doppelganger represented a symbolic manifestation of extreme psychic conflict and had no basis in reality.

Interestingly enough, while at University, I had been considerably taken up with the study of doppelganger theory. Their reality, akin to zombies, vampires or Santa's elves, suggested that a colorful world of literary fantasy flourished within this lonely man's head. Besides feeling relief, I admitted a small measure of disappointment. As his fantastic delusions became verified, it also undermined the intriguing possibility of pirate ancestry.

Uncle Gambi's fluid and unhesitating manner of speech emphasized that he believed everything he reported. He arose to his feet with some difficulty and said, "My doppelganger and I would place the chest in a new location periodically, always while we had been drinking for several days. We got along very well as long as we were both drunk. Only when sober would conflicts arise. Neither of us would recollect the new whereabouts of the chest, yet we had always been able to locate the clues we had left for ourselves to find. The solutions always become self-evident after no more than a week or two and usually involved straightforward manipulations of high school trigonometry."

Uncle Gambi used the term "self-evident." I was delighted. This had been a favorite phrase of mine while at University, one which I often bandied about with either left or right eyebrow cocked. The man now commanded my full attention.

Uncle Gambi described at length the remarkable and foolhardy process by which he and his doppelganger insulated themselves from usurpers who sought their treasure. The pair reburied the chest during protracted blackout drunkenness and even more remarkably, created clues for each other while in that state. Once sober, they deciphered the symbols and solved the equations, ultimately leading them back to the cache although viewing the unfolding of the search as entertainment. Uncle Gambi was adamant concerning the prospect of my participation and expected me to ferret out solutions to similar clues left in the course of the most recent reburying.

His method did not represent a rational process; the prospect of my involvement was not entertaining at all. Uncle Gambi went on cheerfully:

"We created red herrings for ourselves, misleading information in case outsiders caught wind of what we were doing. The clues would lead us to boxes of novelty items, for instance, initially appearing quite exciting but signifying nothing. How we'd laugh at our miscues, both he and I. This is very difficult to explain, why we would find this so amusing. Each would try to deceive the other, you see, purposefully, the natural inclination of doppelgangers, yet we would not allow ourselves to become frustrated; simply move on to the next deception. You must do the same. I have a tendency to save and collect. My doppelganger was the opposite and liked to pitch things out. He was better equipped to sort out which clues were relevant and which were not. We worked well together."

Uncle Gambi choked on these last words, obviously emotional, paused and inhaled. He asked, "Are you familiar with conformal mapping?"

Despite his drunken state, Uncle Gambi was proving himself convincingly erudite. The term "conformal mapping" had been tossed around the Department of Mathematics hallway like a baseball at spring training.

"I have studied physics," I told him, though uneasy in that confession as I had understood little if anything of what I had studied. I derived far more genuine satisfaction from repeating aloud descriptive terminology utilizing foreign accents, my favorites being German or French. Examining the photographic likenesses of twentieth-century mathematicians and physicists also proved highly rewarding and far more pleasant than attempting to understand their intentions.

Uncle Gambi nodded. "Of course, your father was very proud of this. I admit this is one reason why I agreed to contact you. My rom, the Machwaya, were the astrologers, so I chose mathematics, the language of God. Mathematics has been my natural inclination."

Uncle Gambi spoke hurriedly and with surprising ease of local somatic maps, of modifications to the topology of space-time, and of localized morphological accidents.

"Two spatially disjoint entities could constitute the same being. The concept can be generalized to multi-dimensions, of course. The language of mathematics may be used to conceal, transform, and describe our treasure."

Uncle Gambi implied that he had conferred with my father concerning academic credentialing and suggested that my physics background would enable me to recover his hypothetical wealth. Uncle Gambi's enthusiasm for the mathematical life was frankly contagious; I became intoxicated with the prospect of penning a follow-up notebook entry once business in the hallway had concluded, perhaps creating several nonsensical equations of my own. I looked at Uncle Gambi holding his brown paper bag and became momentarily disoriented from inhaling my own toxic and somewhat confusing intellectual effluvia.

"Each human is defined within a spatial geometry," he went on. "Organic brain substance, contained within the cranial vault, gives rise to an organization, our reality mapped onto two-dimensional space; for instance, onto a page through the impaction of typewriter keys." He lowered his voice. "There is great pressure to conform and distribute these pre-determined mappings, Pepper."

I glanced over my shoulder and felt a sense of bottomless well-being in viewing my pocket notebook on the night table, chock-full of two-dimensional mappings while fully quiescent but forever at the ready in its proper face-up orientation.

"Within the Public Library of this very city, I initially observed my doppelganger as he reviewed the exact mathematics text which I too had sought on that day. We read the identical books and watched identical films. I recognized him immediately and realized how important he would be in my life from that moment on."

Uncle Gambi's tone conveyed a fondness for his doppelganger, who by definition would have served as his saboteur. They had remained, by the sound of it, cherished lovers of the same books. Uncle Gambi described that the two co-gangers had colluded in the reinvestment of their recovered pirate treasure. He characterized his doppelganger as a brilliant and reckless gambler who more than quadrupled their original fortune by repeatedly parlaying the winnings at various racetracks around the country. Betting on horse races did not sound sensible. Then Uncle Gambi said something even odder.

"My doppelganger had been obsessed with his genitals, which were prodigious and of enormous influence." Uncle Gambi crumbled his paper bag. The bottles inside clinked. He changed the subject. "Years ago, I had several of the original coins appraised in the city, an unfortunate choice on my part. Word got out, and I have not seen my doppelganger since."

Uncle Gambi staggered down the hallway as if on the deck of a small boat, speaking over his shoulder. "Your father concealed from you the truth. Bring me the library books tomorrow night, Pepper. Only one will prove significant. We'll have a look together. I should be able to tell immediately. There usually is an assigned unit of measure I plant with which to plot actual distance. Easy. You see, I am practically handing the solution to you."

Uncle Gambi turned the corner; the floorboards creaked once, and everything remained silent. Re-entering the room, I closed the door behind me and stood, not knowing what to do.

I needed to take heroic action and stepped out of my urine stained underwear, holding the pair aloft as Perseus had the writhing head of Medusa. I strode into the restroom and stuffed it into the gaping hole beside the toilet, pushing it far down into the space between the walls. I returned to the living space, picked up the peephole cylinder and replaced that within its orifice then wedged a chair underneath the doorknob. I lifted my duffle onto the bed and thrust my hands inside, pushing them downward through the clothing layers. Like Arthur plucking Excalibur from its stone, I pulled forth a fresh pair of tidy whities. Stepping into both leg holes, I yanked the waistband up over my penis and snapped its elastic with immense satisfaction.

Something was horribly wrong.

I had always remained meticulous in arranging my duffle bag, just as I had been in organizing my pocket notebooks. I had always seen to it that I partitioned the duffel into a comprehensively tiered structure with books occupying the bottom-most strata. Books and clothing never intermingled. Never. I had placed my underwear and socks into a plastic garbage bag for both organizational and sanitary purposes.

The tidy whities, just retrieved, had been *randomly situated* within the bag.

I reinserted my hand and groped more tentatively, summoning the full scope of my tactile acumen: Some supernatural agency had mixed books with socks and underwear. Like the Praying Mantis sensing a predator, I remained still. Despite having been considerably fatigued over the last several hours, I had *not* rummaged within my duffle bag.

I pulled several books from what had previously been the exclusive "underwear and sock section:" Otto Rank's *Beyond Psychology*, Dostoyevsky's *The Double*, Malcolm Lowry's *Under the Volcano*, Rilke's *Letters about Cezanne* and Ilya Prigogine's *Introduction to the Thermodynamics of Irreversible Processes*. I tossed these books onto the bed and regarded them, wishing they could tell me what had transpired. I examined in succession my flimsy door's peephole then its lock then the books again, certain that I had placed them all at the bottom of the duffle just prior to the trip; the bag had not left my side the entire journey.

"No one could have possibly entered my room while I was sleeping and rearranged my duffel's contents," I clarified aloud. "This would have awakened me."

I looked at my watch: four pm. In the waning afternoon light, I pondered the unusual arrangement of objects within the hotel room: my languishing penis, the abnormal configuration of my notebook, the hodgepodge of literature within duffle as well as the unexpected presence of the ruler upon my nightstand. I studied the ruler in particular then regarded my underwear flap. As I sat on the bed, my head gyrated with foreboding. I relived the hallway altercation, my heroic shore patrol forty-five intervention then sat still. Nothing stirred: no creaking, no rattling of keys, the typing had ceased. I picked up the Times-Picayune, already open to the rooms section: At McDonalds, Uncle Gambi had circled an address halfway down the page with my black pen. The ad stated. A second address had been scribbled alongside with a rudimentary drawing of a package with a Napoleon Avenue address. I placed the newspaper down on the floor, stared at it then picked it up again. I threw the paper down on the floor then picked it up one more time. The price quoted in the Prytania ad seemed reasonable. They would not know me there. I could start anew with complete anonymity.

"I will do no such thing as meet Uncle Gambi. His treasure is drunken nonsense." I stood up. "But what if it isn't!?"

It occurred to me that the ten dollars I had given Gambi with the intention of providing him with food had enabled him to purchase alcohol and subsequently made him vulnerable to capture by the clinging shirted Shore Patrol Forty-Five reclaimer. My stomach turned, although there was some sense of consolation in that the ten dollars I had lent to the stranded carpenter in front of the hotel had represented a life-saving boon. Looking at my watch, I realized I had just under an hour to meet this certain-to-be-grateful carpenter.

I took up my notebook and jotted more notes concerning the remarkable delusions of the man who called himself Uncle Gambi. Unable to keep my eyes open, I decided to nap for no more than forty-five minutes.

6
A SIXTY-FIVE DOLLAR ROOM

Having slept straight through the previous afternoon and evening, I felt refreshed yet disappointed in missing my appointment with the previously-locked-out-of-his-truck carpenter. I unfolded my map of New Orleans, located the address circled in the Times-Picayune, refolded and replaced it within my reordered duffle then again regarded my notebook in the reassuring and re-established face-up position. I flipped it open and executed my morning entry:

Whether or not I plunge my hands deep into Uncle Gambi's treasure trove of mathematical obscurity could only be decided after all aspects of his credibility had been subject to rigorous inspection; and this could only be accomplished through inhalation of volatile condensations exuded from the warm moist skin of a library while cradling in both hands her expansive collection of books and lactating the potent colostrum of knowledge.

Invigorated after effusive metaphoring, I trotted downstairs. In passing through the lobby, the desk clerk stepped out from behind his cubicle and followed me into the street, inquiring with uncharacteristic politeness if I might be looking for work. He went on to explain he had switched to the day shift which left the overnight position vacant. Lowering his voice and bringing his head closer to mine, the clerk spoke with a gossipy lilt, whispering that the hotel manager would be conducting interviews the following morning at eight. "If you get here at quarter till, you can be the first." He looked over his shoulder as if he had just transmitted a clandestine secret to a foreign government.

With barest of cocked eyebrow, I offered: "So, my credentials were suitable?"

I knew full well the authorities had completed their review of the hotel registration card and had found my documentation sound. As the clerk feigned incomprehension, I chuckled and lay my hand on his shoulder as it could only be implicitly understood that I was the *shoe-in* for this position. Desk-clerkery embodied a veritable golden egg for the wayward but sincere notebook keeper subsisting on daily rations of dashed hopes and heroic abnegation.

"I'll be here before the cock crows thrice," I told him then sobered abruptly.

The need to amend my language became immediately and abundantly clear. My embellishments were inconsistent with the truncated style of information sharing common among members of the granite-faced desk clerk fraternity, a fraternity within which I would shortly be initiated.

The house was located between an abandoned hotel and a boarded-up automobile salvage garage on Prytania Avenue near the I-90 overpass leading to the Mississippi River Bridge. I stood across the street and studied its structure. Two by fours had been nailed horizontally across the stiles of the louvered door on the left side of the front porch. Planks were missing, and weeds grew where the steps had once been. The floor length windows were tightly shuttered in the *gallerie* above; dark purple streaks from water damage resembled running mascara.

I crouched, removed my pocket notebook and placed it upon my knee. Before proceeding any further, it became essential that I jot down several crucial relationships:

House = Metaphoric Head.

Appearance of Dwelling = Mental State of Inhabitants.

Inhabitants = Various Aspects of Individual.

In more pleasantly pompous cursive, I inquired: *And what psychic agency within dare give rise to such a façade adrip with melancholia?*

Closing the notebook with one hand, I arose to a standing position and held it aloft like the Bolshevik agitator Vladimir Ilyich Lenin might his copy of Marx's *Capital*.

"Yet this is not a world of books!" I cautioned aloud and strode across the street, hoping desperately that a room within this house of obvious mental unrest would be available. Caught up on my sleep, I felt invigorated by the inexorable intrigues of the previous twenty- four hours. Both my expectation and curiosity grew as to the forms this new day's conspiracies would take.

A small girl with black hair and thick dark eyebrows sat in front of a screen door on the right side of the porch taping a Barbie skirt around the waste of a naked and one armed GI Joe. Mucous drooped and jiggled from the girl's nose to wrap around Joe's head. She sniffled, tipped the doll upside down and cleaned his face on her skirt. The little girl then stopped what she was doing and watched me approach. As I stepped onto the curb she began scooting backward, the GI Joe rolling off her lap; he lay on the porch with his skirt wide open, exposing a plastic perineum void of genitals. The girl moved laterally, stood up, slid inside the screen door and secured its latch. She peered down at the GI Joe, looked at me then disappeared into a dim space where crowd applause from a television game show could be heard. A woman arrived and stood behind the screen, hands in her bathrobe pockets. I cleared my throat.

"You had an ad in the paper about a room."

She studied my duffle bag then bowed one cheek outward with her tongue. "You in the service?"

I recalled the suggestion of my Trailways look-alike but hesitated, unsure what the right answer would be in this instance. "Not at the moment. But I was. Now I'm a desk clerk."

The landlady stared down the street. "Well, there are no rooms right now. There might be one opening up tomorrow. There's a man here who hasn't paid his rent." She glanced at me then returned her gaze down the block, pressing a shoulder against the screen. "I'm not sure what I am going to do with him. I may throw his stuff out the front door. He hasn't been around, and his rent was due two days ago. He wears the same dirty old black coat and cap. I don't think he used the shower once."

The landlady was referring to the eccentric Uncle Gambi!

"His room stinks. I'm not even going in there to clean up." The woman's voice rose. "The next tenant is going to have to do that." She lowered her voice and spoke confidentially. "I'll probably just toss the bags out and if he gives me any trouble, call the cops. I'm sick of all the bullshit. And I'll tell you something else; I don't particularly like the man himself." She stopped speaking and pulled the bathrobe more tightly around her. She ran her tongue against the inside of her lips, widening her mouth. I did not understand why she described so familiarly to me the specifics of Uncle Gambi's tenancy as if I had been well acquainted with facts concerning *all the bullshit.*

"Yeah, well, so I should check back tomorrow, Andy?"

For reasons unclear, I had lapsed into a form of Mayberry RFD speak while imagining the landlady as the female embodiment of Sheriff Taylor. I had adapted the momentary persona of deputy Barney Fife. My anus tensed. The woman regarded me without answering, smiled and placed a hand on the screen. She peered down the street, assuming an even more confidential tone. "Why don't you check back tomorrow, there might be something. . ."

As I turned and walked down the steps, a man said something within the house. The landlady called out: "Wait. Did you come in on the Trailways from Tallahassee yesterday morning?"

She inquired so matter-of-factly that I assumed the existence of an extensive network of observers, assigned to street corners throughout the city and active at all hours of the day and night. These operators noted comings and goings, arrivals and departures, reporting all events to the various hotel desk clerks and rooming house landladies.

"Yes, in fact, I did."

"There is one other room available, but I don't think you would want it. I haven't had a chance to get up there to put on new sheets and clean it. It's a room of the sixty-five-dollar kind, I'm afraid."

The landlady addressed me with the tone of a physician informing a family that their loved one's diagnosis had been incurable cancer. Somewhere in the house, a dog yelped in pain; a child shrieked with pleasure, and the landlady turned to yell, "Leave that durn hound alone!" She turned back. "I usually get a twenty-dollar deposit."

Unhooking the latch of the screen door, the woman stepped out onto the porch and stood with hands on her hips, the bathrobe parting. I had wrongly assumed the occupation of rooming house matrons to be the exclusive domain of widows or spinsters advancing in age.

"I wouldn't normally offer rooms that hadn't been made up, but you look Ok. You would probably be more comfortable in the sixty-five-dollar room anyway. The fifty dollar rooms are small."

The landlady's hips were broad. The robe climbed upward and hung over the contours of her pelvis.

"I'll take it," I said.

The landlady cocked her head and stared. "Don't you want to see it first?" She spoke with an unconcealed impatience. I had not thought of asking to see the room first. I hesitated and made an incoherent sound. The landlady's eyes narrowed, and she began to speak hurriedly: "I also have a much bigger and better room for eighty dollars and a suite for a hundred. Couples stay in there usually, but we've had some singles. They're nice and spacious." She squinted and gazed down the block. "I don't know if you would want to spend that much, though." She turned her head and was now squinted directly at me, nearly wincing. "Do you want to spend that much?"

"I'd like to take a look at the sixty-five-dollar kind," I said, whistling the s of sixty.

The landlady led me into a kitchen area. I was alarmed to find there had been others present while we had been conversing.

At the opposite end of the kitchen table, a man wearing a black suit sat holding a coffee cup just in front of his chin. His hair, parted to one side, also jet black, appeared to have had applied either automobile grease or shoe polish. As I stepped into the room, the man placed his coffee cup down on the table with a ratcheting motion and swiveled his head upward to regard me. On a couch directly behind the door sat two teenage girls wearing identical red lipstick and eye make-up. Their heads also swiveled as the man's had, yet swiveled in unison, to examine me briefly then swiveled again, redirecting their attentions toward the television set atop the refrigerator.

The coherent motions I observed within the kitchen of this rooming house made a strong case for the presence of automata. Based on my experience outside the confines of University, life within the novel and life outside the novel correlated, almost exactly; so, with that in mind, couldn't I certainly conclude that every biologic entity within this household to be, in fact, a machine?

"And every machine, a living entity?" I asked, viewing the TV suspiciously.

The man seated at the table turned and spoke to the woman. "What did he just say?"

My eye twitched. I had again misdirected my thoughts aloud. The man took a long drag from a cigarette followed by a longer sip of coffee. His head gyrated downward to study my crotch, much as the woman at the bus depot had done, increased its declination to examine my running shoes, then reset his focus once again into the vacant space over his coffee cup.

A commercial interrupted the television program. One of the girls turned toward me, her expression conveying neither cordiality nor hostility. I characterized her as an adolescent, most likely having reached puberty approximately three to four years previously. I pressed my toes hard against the soles of my running shoes. In answering her stare, I modified my face to resemble a block of unfinished wood, signifying to her that my life had no intrinsic meaning other than my Beingness-as-a-desk-clerk. After a few seconds of this application, my face began to quiver, and my eyes bulged outward. I released my breath suddenly and dashed my gaze toward the floor; there I noticed a cat lolling.

"Come on Princess, come on girl," the girl called to the cat. I could not be sure that there had been any connection between the two events: that is, my noticing the cat and the girl calling it over.

"Get out of the man's way," she added.

Quite pleased at her noting my way to be a *man's way,* I attempted to smile but could not. Thankfully, the game show returned with crowd applause, and the girl's attention returned to the TV. Princess arose, brushed against and around both of my legs then wandered over to the door, sat down and stared at the doorknob. The cat turned briefly to regard the man seated at the table, opened its mouth to hiss, then rotated its head toward the doorknob.

The landlady opened the refrigerator door. On the top shelf, objects had been wrapped in aluminum foil and placed alongside bowls covered with wax paper; two-gallon milk containers, two quarts of RC cola, a carton of eggs rested on the bottom tier while a single item draped with a paper towel had been placed on the middle shelf.

"Everybody uses this refrigerator to keep their food, soda or whatever. Just remember to put your name on your food. Someone might get it by mistake."

The black garbed man held his coffee cup very still in front of his lips and stared straight ahead. I decided at that moment not to store food in the refrigerator.

"You can keep your coffee down here. There's no cooking in the smaller rooms. You can keep your coffee cup in my pantry if you want. There's always a coffee pot on the stove."

"I like a good cup of coffee," I told the landlady.

The landlady moved behind the man seated at the end of the table. She placed a single finger on the left side of his neck, slid it across and off his shoulder. The man pointed at me and said, "He's not Royce." He glanced at the woman, turned to me and said, "You say there's a desk clerk job? Who's hiring?"

"The desk clerk position *had been* available at the Lafayette," I answered.

"They're hiring at the Lafayette? That's interesting." He returned his gaze over the rim of the coffee cup. After a moment, he placed the cup down on the table, twisted in his seat to face the woman and said, "I'm going to go down there, by God. I'm going down there and hire on, praise Jesus, praise God."

I wanted to stamp my foot on the kitchen floor and stamp it hard. I had defined myself as the desk clerk, not this man dressed in undertaker's clothing. I had been the one implying that the position had already been taken yet it was he now *going to go down there and hire on*, suggesting a belief that this job was still available *for the taking* which, in reality, it was but not at all in keeping what I had implied. Perhaps the man in the black suit had been listening all too casually. The position was already filled if the information I had offered had been received and processed; that is, I had told them that I was already working in the capacity of desk clerk at the Lafayette Hotel. Technically, I was not, having yet to interview for the position. But the interviews began tomorrow morning, early, and I would arrive and *be the first one*. I was favored, highly favored for the position in any case, tipped off by my close associate, the existing desk clerk, as to its availability. This was beside the point, maddeningly beside the point. The point was that I fully imagined I already had the desk clerk position and would tell anyone if asked, as I just did, that I was not just a desk clerk, but *the* desk clerk. Of course, this was a lie on my part but just who *did this man think he was*, after hearing me say that I was already a desk clerk, to simply *go down there and hire on?* I would now have to *go down there* earlier than this man in the black suit would *go down there*. I hoped that the man's teeth would inadvertently get kicked in while *going down there*.

I had developed an inexplicable hostility toward the black-suited lodger. The man irritated me to no end, more so than anybody I had met in my life; more so than anyone I had watched on television.

The landlady opened the side door, the cat squeezed out and I was led into a fenced in alley, to my right a locked gate facing Prytania Avenue.

"You come in over there." She pointed at the gate. "You'll have a separate key."

We passed several low-cut doors. A shirtless man sat smoking on the edge of a bed turned and stared. A woman in curlers stood beside him, also smoking. She turned to stare. Neither the man nor the woman nodded or spoke but continued to stare.

I wondered if it was my responsibility to nod first?

On the screen of the small TV at the foot of the bed, a camera panned across the faces of a studio audience. Some members of the audience held hands up to their mouths; others laughed. The audience started to clap. The clapping sounded like a candy wrapper being crinkled.

As we moved toward the rear of the alley, I avoided turning my head to gaze through additional doorways, although maintained my awareness that adults, children, and teenagers continued to sit on their beds or stand beside their TVs, poised and staring.

The integrity of the main house degenerated toward the rear of the compound with numerable sagging wooden staircases and unsupported walkways erected most likely piecemeal over time; stilts had been wedged underneath some rooms and not others. The first landing and its walkway extended around the outside of the house facing Prytania. More stairs broke off and led to other levels.

Thick vegetation grew in spaces between the cottages at the rear of the courtyard. The landlady approached one situated along the fence adjacent to the salvage garage and cupped her hands against its window.

"That man's things are still in there, and I'm already smelling dook from where I'm standing." She turned and raised her voice. "I'm not going in there; I'll tell you that right now."

I sniffed, smelled the *dook* and didn't move any closer. Fingering the key in my pocket, I knew Uncle Gambi had asked me to access this *dook-cottage*. Uncertain whether or not I wished to take further part in his game, I resolved that once my business with the landlady had concluded, I would proceed to the Public Library and investigate all aspects of piracy and pirate legacies.

"He's going to clean his own shit mess up, or I'm calling the law." She shook her head. We continued.

The landlady pulled her robe tight around her and began ascending one of the rickety staircases. As she moved upward, her lower back and buttocks churned at eye level while her shoulders swayed back and forth with each step. Forced to pause and lean against the handrail, I was subject to a momentary fit of vertigo.

The landlady stopped, pointed and said, "The bathroom is up that flight. You share, all right? I don't usually have any trouble, but if a person doesn't clean up after themselves, I'll throw that person out. I'm sick of people messing up my bathroom. I came up here about a week ago, and someone had torn up the commode. I think I know who did it and don't know what that man was looking for in my commode and don't want to know, but I'm fixing to toss his bags out onto the street."

The landlady's voice rose higher as if someone had started to choke her.

"I don't like seeing logs of dook at the bottom of the bowl when I go in there. You can't put paper towel down the commode, and if I smell urine in the tub, you can clean it. I want you to understand that." The landlady was roaring over her shoulder as we started up an even narrower and more unstable stairway which concluded in a walkway serving two doors. By the time she reached the top and stopped in front of the farthest door, she was yelling at the top of her lungs: "SOME WEEKS I WON'T CLEAN IN THERE IF THERE'S DOOK!"

"No, I absolutely clean up," I said. I *slurped* through both the b and the s of *absolutely* like *Sylvester the Cat.* "It would be in my best interest to clean up. I have to rely on the bathroom as well. Why would I want to mess the bathroom up?"

The landlady turned toward the door without replying. The door knob came off in her hand. She replaced it and spoke in a normal tone. "You have to jiggle this one if it doesn't turn right away."

The landlady inserted her key and jiggled the doorknob. The door opened. A double bed took up nearly all space within the room along with a chest of drawers, a bedside table and chair wedged between bed and walls.

Sidestepping, I followed her into the room and recoiled; the effect of the chamber's atmosphere was that of a washcloth laid across my face; a washcloth marinated in distillate of feet, underarm, crotch, urine, vomit and sardine oil. The landlady gagged. Her bathrobe fell open as she stepped over to one of the windows, planted both feet and began knocking the sash upward with the heel of her right hand. Several of the panes of glass had been broken and replaced with cardboard. I leaned against the bedpost, watching her exposed breasts heave with the violence of each upward blow.

A glob of vomitus surged into my mouth; having the viscosity of mashed potato it rolled over my chin, off the top of my duffle and onto the bed. The landlady continued to bang the window. I scooped the material up, hurled it out the open door then wiped my mouth and hands with the bedspread and surveyed the cracked paint, chipped plaster, and rotting wood. I extracted my pocket notebook and transcribed as if I were a ghost:

Gaping holes, exposed pipes, smashed cockroach carcasses concatenating with yellow, brown, amber staining, walls of my temple, Prytania Avenue, the slopes of Parnassus. As Plutarch described the adyton chamber at the temple of Apollo, the inhalation of pneuma emerging from mountain fissures, I, Rodney Pepper, will breathe my room's vapors and seek to recover the omphalos.

I shook my head violently to send these chimeras running back into the forest just as the window opened with a jolt. The slight breeze felt like ice water against my face. I came to my senses and pocketed my notebook. The landlady turned and surveyed the room, hands on her hips, unconcerned that her expansive pubic bush and wide bright orange areolas were fully exposed. After a moment she drew her bathrobe together, tilted her head to one side, and addressed me with renewed irritation.

"You look like you're still in the service with that haircut. You're not still in the service, are you? I don't take military."

Again, recalling the suggestion of my Chesterfield-smoking look-alike, I told the landlady, "Well, I just got out. I *was* in the Navy." I jammed my toes into the bottom of my running shoes; it made no sense to tell her something like that, but it felt good, like scratching an itch.

"If I find out you're still in the military, I'll put your bags on the street."

I followed the landlady's gaze toward the foot of the night table. We regarded a large, dark, moist stain. I smelled alcohol and imagined the former tenant leaning over the side of the bed to vomit a large volume of beer, whiskey, and bile onto the floor before rolling back over and falling asleep.

The landlady yanked the blood-spattered sheets off the bed. Underneath, irregular excavations into the top of the mattress looked to have been performed utilizing small prehistoric tools. Foam stuffing lay scattered on the mattress surface. The urine stains superimposed upon vomit stains superimposed upon beer stains were punctuated by cigarette burns.

Out my window, one could view the alley below and the tin roof of the abandoned automobile junk dealer. On this tin roof, lay beer cans, RC cola cans, potato chip bags, a tennis ball and a miniature bottle of Bacardi rum.

"Both those doors are locked," the landlady said pointing at two doors within the room, one directly behind the head of the bed, the other on the opposite wall beside the closet, more evidence of the rooming house's intricate partitioning. The landlady straightened her posture. "I'll get some air freshener up here. It's a little stuffy."

Already accustomed to its Delphic elixirs, I fingered the contours of notebook and pen within my breast pocket.

"I expect my rent on time," the landlady stated.

"I start my desk clerk job tomorrow," I said.

She frowned. "I already know that. We both heard you say it. I don't know why you would say it again when you already said it once. I'm one for speaking my mind, mister, so I'm not sure why you would say anything at all about what your plans were or why someone like you would be working there. I know you can't be a complete idiot. Only a complete idiot would say that. So there has to be another reason. I'm thinking that has to be the case, but it's none of my business." She hesitated. "Not for nothing but on the chance that you *are* a complete idiot, I think you opened up a can of worms by coming here. There are other rooming houses in New Orleans. You can look them up in the paper. But like I said, that's none of my business just so long as I get my rent on time. I don't want trouble here. If I find out you are up to something, I'm tossing your bags out my front door and calling the law. I don't care who you are." She pressed her finger into my arm and lowered her voice. "But if you come down and pay me, I can give you your keys."

Uncertain by what the outspoken landlady meant about *opening up a can of worms* or, of my choice of rooming houses or, of me potentially being *up to something*, I descended the narrow stairway behind her. Certainly, the contention that I was nothing more than a *complete idiot* was misguided on her part. The outstanding issue of my mistaken identity had prompted this supposition. The misunderstanding would soon be placed behind me. Engaged in legitimate employment, I would blend into my environment. I would transform myself into an unseen feature of the New Orleans woodwork, faithfully representing the veritable line observed upon the inner surface of a tree trunk were it to be sliced vertically; a line created by its xylem tubes, forming the inner structure of wood known as *grain*. The anticipation of blending-in to such an extent as to become grain, the hidden aspect of life's forest, and no longer being subject to stares and speculations, comforted me.

Half-way down the stairs, I noticed the little girl with dark eyebrows again. The girl chased a little boy holding her GI Joe. The GI Joe had become fully unclothed. The girl clutched the little Barbie skirt in one hand and hit the boy on the back of his head with her other fist.

A woman's voice arose from one of the rooms. "You want me to cut a switch?" This woman stepped into view. I stopped my descent on the stairs. The woman shouted at the little girl with unusual vehemence.

The boy dropped the GI Joe. "She can have it," he said and ran into a room.

"Gimme that," the mother picked up the toy and threw it over the fence. It landed on the sheet metal roof of the abandoned salvage garage, clattering briefly. The woman walked back into her apartment. The little girl stared upwards clutching the Barbie skirt.

From my vantage, I could see the naked GI Joe lying with the tennis ball on one side of him, and a miniature bottle of rum on the other.

Returning to the office living area, the sullen bolo tied man and two adolescent girls were no longer present. The landlady handed me a receipt along with two keys and said, "If you need anything just knock on that window right there. That's where I sleep." She smiled. "And you can call me Donna."

I looked through the window the landlady had indicated. Through lace curtains, I dimly discerned a double bed, its covers in violent disarray.

7

THE LIBRARIAN

I lingered in my room of the sixty-five-dollar kind long enough to reconcile the location of the public library on my New Orleans street map and choose a companion book to place in my back pocket. Through tactile inspection, I identified each of the twenty volumes within my duffle bag, all handpicked in preparation for my journey and recently reordered following their curious derangement. Repeatedly withdrawing and plunging my hands inward, similar to kneading dough, I right away was able to identify *Tales of E.T.A. Hoffmann* from its familiar contour. The president of the British Nietzsche Society had admirably translated this particular volume. In the past, having purchased reading material based solely on the merit of cover design, this edition had been chosen for its exquisite front piece, the painting Der Arme Poet, by Carl Spitzweg, depicting a man, the poor poet, night hat on, in repose on a floor bed in the corner of his tiny attic apartment, propped up by pillows, an umbrella over his head, presumably shielding him from a leaky ceiling; The painting comprised a powerful and whimsical vision of how I would imagine ending my days.

After tossing *Tales of E.T.A. Hoffmann* into the air several times, I slid the book into my hip pocket and pulled the thin chamber door closed behind me. I patted my shirt to double check the presence of pocket notebook and pen then let myself out through the side gate. Turning left onto Erato, I made a right onto St. Charles and skirted Lee Circle, passing in front of the YMCA noting its sign displaying the word welcome in ten languages.

Across the street, a ship's wheel had been painted onto the flat wooden exterior of an old building. Several spindles surrounding the wheel were missing; paint had long ago peeled from its facade. In the center of a nearly opacified window, a flickering neon sign advertised Pabst Blue Ribbon Beer. Above the doorway Sailors Welcome had been brushed in continuous cursive configured to resemble rope; its pigment cracked.

The window of the bar resembled a porthole. No one appeared to be going in nor coming out. I wondered if sailors were still welcome and pushed *Tales of E.T.A. Hoffmann* deeper into my hip pocket. Doors of the other nearby bars had been thrown wide open, exposing congregations of older men each holding a can of Dixie beer; all appeared to be ruminating novelists discussing themes, plots, subplots and antiheroes.

In passing an alleyway and hearing voices raised, I noted four men seated with backs against a building. One held a large paper bag in his lap and loudly cried, "Yodelayheehooo!" A fifth man was standing and addressed this yodeling man with a gruff voice, "I said give me the motherfucker. I paid for it!"

"The grateful carpenter!" I exclaimed, thrilled beyond measure. I hurried down the alley. The poor man had certainly been searching everywhere for me and had most likely given up hope for a reunion with no small degree of frustration. I owed him a full apologetic explanation of how I had overslept and therefore could not keep our appointment. The men seated directly in front of him were his workmen, four in number, as he had explained. While approaching, the workman nearest me rolled onto his side, removed his penis from his pants and directed a vigorous stream of urine onto the pavement. I stopped. One of the other men nudged his neighbor and flicked his head in my direction. The grateful carpenter walked toward me. As he passed through an arc of sunlight, a good deal of blood, caked under his nose and atop his lips, became visible. The poor man not only had been locked out of his truck but thereafter suffered some terrible work related injury. My heart went out to him.

"I'm sorry I missed you," I said. The carpenter's memory simply needed a little prompting. The man approached more slowly, tilting his head to one side. I noticed one of his eyes to be swollen and violaceous.

"Spare any change, son? I haven't eaten in two days."

"Remember when you needed the ten to get back to your truck?" I offered." When you were locked out of your truck?"

The man continued to approach without speaking. I felt a sense of unease, turned and walked briskly back toward St. Charles Avenue. The carpenter shouted after me:

"Fuck you, you goddamn little faggot son of a bitch motherfucker!"

I strongly suspected this man's tool box and work truck had never existed, that I had been the victim of a confidence game and that my ten dollars had been used toward the purchase of liquor.

Liquor!

I winced, winced again then again and again and again. I swung my arms like an angry robot all the way to the New Orleans Public Library on Loyola, pulled up short just before entering the building, punched the air and yelled at the top of my lungs:

"That goddamn motherfucking carpenter's teeth need a good kicking!"

Feeling only slightly better, I passed the librarian's desk and glanced at both she and her work area. The woman maintained an upright posture while seated on an old wooden chair. In front of her were three pens aligned parallel to a long yellow legal pad. An old glass inkwell, a well-worn Pink Pearl eraser and what appeared to be an oblong pumice stone sat on the opposite side of the pad as well as a stamp. The librarian's hands set on top of the desk, palms facing downward. She appeared to be waiting and turned her head to follow me with an unusually stern countenance. Her antique gray suit had been buttoned to the chin, concealing her physique. No parasympathetic influence was transmitted. Her hair may have projected a suggestion of red, but its overall color was difficult to ascertain.

I took several inhalations, regaining the necessary composure for investigating piracy as well as doppelgangery. Although ecstatic to once again be present within a large reading room, this one appeared more crowded and boisterous than its equivalent at University; my concentration had already become threatened by several frenzied voices arising from different locations.

"Please be quiet," a woman with long gray hair spoke to a man who also had long gray hair sitting opposite her. The man had been reading aloud to himself.

"Shove it up your ass," the man replied.

"Don't call me names. I'll break your neck," the woman said.

"You couldn't break my neck. I'll snap your fingers like twigs," the man said. The woman arose and walked into the stacks just as another older man limped past me.

"I said I know the left hand of a dog like I know the right hand of a man."

The man paced back and forth in front of the encyclopedias, pumping his right arm and repeating his revelation with violent inflection. The words seemed to convey enormous portent, yet I could not guess the meaning.

I recorded several numbers from the card catalog and moved into the stacks, immediately confronted by a young man licking his index finger again and running it back and forth under his nostrils like a saw. The Dewey Decimal System call numbers at his location corresponded to psychoanalytic theory. In succession, I flinched, recoiled and quivered as a wooden cadence commenced. The library security guard used his knuckles to rap on table tops alongside the heads of dozing patrons. An elderly man raised his voice:

"Second time he did that. He would make a good corporal in the Army. That's a corporal's job."

Trapped within this kaleidoscope of voices, I became disoriented. Whether the voices arose from within or without, I could not ascertain. I sat at one of the vacant seats and arranged the books I had collected so far in front of me. I opened my pocket notebook to note:

Library patrons similar to fish at water's surface feeding on bread crumbs while others driven like horses and lashed by unseen charioteers.

In a much smaller script, I wrote: *I wish I had an acquaintance, someone with whom I could trade books and discuss notebook keeping issues.*

I placed my notebook on the table and sighed. Proceeding with task at hand, I opened book after book, transcribing with increasing abandon, thrilling over this passage and that, word choices and illustrations. Hours passed.

In the midst of copying a particularly harrowing description of pirate torture from of a history entitled *The Buccaneers of America* by Alexander Exquerelin, a hand passed over my shoulder and placed itself upon the book itself. A snake wrapping itself around a hammer as well as the familiar initials ETA were tattooed in the web space between the hand's thumb and index finger. A raspy voice asked, "Curious of pirates, their swearing, and rioting, their oaths, and execration? The reality is far far worse than what described, me bucko."

Without invitation or permission, the man examined the books I had collected. I jerked my head around to examine him. He wore a gold earring and an eye patch; his hair was like black tar washed up on a beach, embedded with shells; his short black beard was entangled with fishing line and hooks of various sizes.

Raven wings for eyes, olive sunburned skin and a voice like barnacled hawser, this man glowed unmistakably with the sulfurous luster of piracy.

"A one-thirty-three, interesting...Several nine-tens...Good. Do you realize we have a one-thirty-nine here? And a one-twenty-seven? One-twenty-seven? I would have truly thought. . . One teens,"

While at once an irrefutable swashbuckler, this stranger's familiarity with the Dewey Decimal system was astounding.

He took up the Exquerelin and pressed his finger directly against the paragraph describing the horrendous practice of woolding. "An invention attributed to Morgan," he growled. "A great man and innovator of atrocity, living in a day when infliction of pain became Art, aye, Art."

My ears perked up at this mysterious man's twice mention of Art, a term introduced to me at University. My initial impression had been that Art constituted a sublimating process; diverting the artist's pervading sense of angst through a constructive occupation while providing a marketable form of entertainment for the consumer. Through formal study, I learned this was not true. Art occupied shelf space on the highest tier of civilization's display case. More importantly, Art had given rise to that very compendium of critical literature to which I deferred; this, as opposed to grappling with the more often obscure and muddled intention of Art itself. Art, prone to misinterpretation, was suspect and therefore lesser than its critical counterpart. When finding myself at a museum, the place where art is housed, I busied myself with careful examination of the curator's cards, placed adjacent to the works themselves. The cards provided marvelous descriptive phrases illustrating what was important and what was not, as well as rendering the appropriate spellings of the artist's name. A glance or two at the actual Art, in whatever form, would usually suffice before moving on to the next card. Through critical study and the reading of curator's cards, I came to appreciate the deadly serious nature of Art, infinitely premeditated and not to be mistaken for entertainment; Art's intention was to be rigorously if not ruthlessly analyzed. Dwelling too closely on the actual artistic image would lead to confusion, vague conclusions and upset.

The man went on: "Nothing's changed, only the technology. The executions display the same cruelty with less artfulness. The Captain favored fire, adorned himself with burning fuses so he would look like a man from hell. He would place these burning fuses between the toes and fingers of his captives. Or he'd strappadoed them!" he said, then paused and added, "Hung them by their thumbs. But woolding was the favorite. They'd wind the rope around a mast to give it strength, you see. This is woolding. The Captain applied this principle to a man's head so as to induce agony beyond measure. As the rope twisted tighter and tighter, the man's eyeballs would fall out onto his cheeks like two freshly laid hen's eggs."

The man's voice trailed off as he took up another one of my selections: *The Double and Psychoanalysis*. He straight away smothered the book with both hands and looked over both shoulders.

"We don't invoke this one-twenty-eight here." His eyes met mine. "We do not discuss or read of it." He placed the book onto a nearby return cart.

"But it's just a literary device," I said.

"Not jussst," he hissed. "Where piracy raises its black standard, the doppelganger heart beats. Most do not recognize their own or deny its existence. When faced with annihilation, it then comes as a complete surprise." He spoke of doppelgangers as had Uncle Gambi, attesting to their flesh and blood tangibility. The confirmation of such esoteric science could only be accessed through the intimate associations within a Public as opposed to a University library.

"The tables aren't safe. Up," he commanded. I arose trembling, reeling, and flinching as if being fired upon by invisible archers. I zig-zagged behind him at a crouch, launching myself up one aisle then down another. The man galloped ahead with his pronounced limp, every measure the peg-legged sailor. He elucidated as he loped; I hung tightly onto every word.

"The Captain was the sweetheart of the lot, the gentlest, kindest man who just about ever lived...by comparison to the French rovers, the uppity bahrstahrds with their extractions carried out upon Spain. Mountbars the Exterminator..." Here the man paused and took a deep breath. "Who would slice open the belly of his captive, reach in to take out a portion of the intestine, nail it to a post then chase his prisoner with a firebrand." The man regarded me with one eye closed, his mouth contorting into a silent snarl. "The bowel would unravel for all to see as he ran about. L'Olunnais would eat the hearts of his disemboweled captives for desert."

This library privateer possessed an intimate and fond comprehension of ancient custom whilst given to an odd form of histrionics of an archaic and displaced quality; this in addition to his physically threatening complexion made him as worrisome as Uncle Gambi had been. As we moved deeper into the stacks, I assessed what lay behind us, were an escape route called for.

"The Spanish," he continued, "were the original torturers of the New World. They would chop off the ears, the noses, the hands then the feet, smear what was left with honey and tie the unfortunate to a tree." He stopped, nodding toward one shelf and muttered, "Here. Nine-ten-forty-five."

Then, he asked an astonishing question: "You like books?"

I wanted to bellow, *I love books more than anything in the world!* I wanted to confess to this man, and do so while rocking back and forth in the posture of Artaud, with arms crossed over my chest in throes of beatific ecstasy; but I could not: My true feelings regarding books were far too frightening to articulate aloud.

"Yes," I said, my arms hanging straight down by my sides.

"Get as many books as you can carry and read of the atrocities that man has committed against man. Read Lafitte's Journal making quite sure you inquire of his trusted Captain Vincent Gambi."

My abdominal muscles contracted. There could be no coincidence in this mention. In light of the man's eye-patch, his bygone phrases and more than intimate knowledge of pirate skullduggery, he undoubtedly shared an incestuous bed with the New Orleans pirate underworld.

"There were accounts passed along over the years, solely mouth to ear, that Captain Gambi's Basque mistress had woolded him near Galveston Bay. She took his entire fortune and went into hiding. This history has been spoken of in no book. They used a nom de guerre. You never had any idea who anyone was. You'll find Dominique You buried in St. Louis number two, the very same who led the expedition to St. Helena to free Napoleon, the same citizen who was as well Jean Lafitte's older brother."

He walked to the end of an aisle, turned and uttered a single word: matelotage. My digestive tract contorted and writhed, sizzling like bacon in a cast iron frying pan. He went on.

"A practice not as respected as it once had been. The world is different, more barbaric, no honor and far less intimate. Do not assume Matelotage represents a careless term. In this day, there rarely could be conceived an equivalent bond between two men. The rights of the matelot had been indissoluble. Matelots sailed together. One worked the deck while the other slept in their shared bunk. Fighting side by side, they nursed one another's wounds and possessed all property mutually. Aye, tread carefully here, note keeper. You will find yourself lost if you don't know your local politics. Know exactly with whom you are conversing and certainly with whom you are bedding with."

My buttocks clenched at the mention of bedding. From the corner of my eye, I caught sight of a man wearing a dark jacket, skirting the end of our aisle. I flinched and pivoted, attempting to view the figure directly. He had disappeared. I turned back to find that the eye-patched historian of atrocity, who had astutely addressed me as note keeper, to have gone as well. Without warning, as I stood in the center of the nine-hundred aisle, books launched themselves upon me like cannon shots, fired by an unseen marksman on the opposite side of the shelves. Thankfully I heard the familiar voice and noted a shock of peppery hair through the newly created gap in the stacks.

"Painful exactions existed for breaking a rule amongst your own. The offender would be stripped naked and forced to run the gauntlet. Fellow crewmen stuck him in the back, shoulder and buttocks with sail needles after which they would throw him into a sugar cask with cockroaches, the cask covered with a blanket; the man left to endure the bayou heat."

Not caring for the implication here, I looked down and picked up one of the fallen texts: *The Journal of Jean Lafitte*, published by the great grandson at the pirate's posthumous request one hundred and five years after his death. I picked up the other books one by one and found them all to concern privateering as it had been practiced in Louisiana, books I had failed to notice previously. The eye-patched man was gone. I understood his intent. Without further debate, I sat down in the aisle and opened the first book. There was no time to waste.

I read of Vincent Gambi, who had smuggled in and out of Grand Terre before its occupation by the Lafittes, who later commanded Lafitte's schooner the Philanthrope then fell out of favor, leaving Barataria for the islands between Caminada and Timbalier Bay. There was no mention of stolen treasure in these accounts nor any description of his death. I repeated the place names loud quietly: Cheniere Caminada, Timbalier Island, Cat Island, Isle Derniere, Bayou Laforche.

Pinpricks arose along the length of my spine as I read of Matelotage, defined as the practice occurring when a buccaneer chooses a comrade, a matelot, and declares the property to be held in common between them. If one had died, the survivor had become the inheritor of the whole. As long as Uncle Gambi was alive, the contract could not be formally enacted. I sat still, considering again how implausible it was that my parents had concealed this legacy. I visualized the faces of my mother and father, placing on each of their heads a pirate hat. I placed a parrot on each shoulder.

"They don't look right," I spoke aloud.

I reviewed accounts of pirate mistresses, women employed by the Lafitte brothers, who accompanied them on treasure burying expeditions. These women lived in extreme fear and seclusion for much of their lives by virtue of merely being suspected of having knowledge of Lafitte treasure knowing Lafitte treasure whereabouts. I felt the burning desire to record these observations and place names, so marvelous in and of themselves. I patted my shirt pocket, recalling having left my notebook alongside *Tales of E.T.A. Hoffmann* at the library table. While hurrying back toward the reading room, I felt intense foreboding, similar to what I imagined a parent might experience in losing sight of their child within a crowded supermarket.

All fears converged into a dreadful reality: My pocket notebook had vanished, as had my *Tales of E.T.A. Hoffmann*! I would have sooner been grilled as a sausage over some ancient Caribbean fire pit than suffer this barbarity: Without pocket notebook, I was left without definition. I stammered and looked around helplessly. The firm ground crumbled away beneath me. The reading room offered no consolation. With trenchant stare, I interrogated every patron, eyebrow arched, and not merely arched but precipitously arched, conveying gross indignation. I served as judge and jury both, awaiting the guilty individual, unable to bear it, to arise screaming and stumbling toward the exit.

An ominous silence descended over the reading room. Even the boisterous insane had dispersed. I did the only thing I could do: I assumed the persona of Madness with a capital M. After placing the mask of Madness upon my face, I began mumbling incoherently. My developing image of self had been obliterated in the split second of robbery. I understood how Artaud felt within his Rodez psychiatric holding cell awaiting electroshock. Bleeding publicly from a psychical stump with no clue as to the whereabouts of my life-affirming-absconded-instruments, my precarious inner homeostasis decayed at an exponential rate. Not only did I *wish* to be *shushed*; I *needed* to be *shushed*.

I raised my voice: "The organ that sins shall be punished; meaning, the offending masturbatory hand shall be smitten!" Several satisfyingly loud *shushes* and *tut-tuts* ensued.

"Even repression can NOT salvage this situation," I bayed Charlton Hestonishly then continued with purposefully provocative whine, an obvious nod to Truman Capote: "I have joined your legions of the lost, starting again at the beginning when only pre-oedipal antecedents of separation exist, namely birth, weaning, and defecation. I am empty, with nothing more to grasp upon arising in the morning, no pages to turn, nothing more to scribble upon, and indeed, nothing more to scribble. My infantile belief in castration had been fully reinstated! Reverberations of past cruelty have not been lost."

The librarian arose from her desk, strode directly to my reading table and stood with her hands clenched in fists against the flanks of her hips. I noted her below the knee support hose, black patent leather shoes and frayed gray woolen suit which contained her bodice; she was buttoned straight up to the chin. Her overall shape was that of an expansive classic vase, contrasted to her threadbare costume. Her clothing appeared uncomfortable to me, and I wondered if her choice was to be so. Phrasing from a curator's card came to mind: ". . . heavy fabric enfolding the body conveys both tensed form and anguished emotion. . ."

Sensing a repressed ally, I informed her, while lisping freely, that my pocket notebook, pen and precious *Tales of E.T.A. Hoffmann* had been stolen.

"In broad daylight," I added.

She replied tersely, without an iota of even veiled sympathy. "You never leave anything unattended. That's your fault. I'm trying to maintain order within the library, a place where people come to read and enjoy that simple pleasure for a few hours. For some, that's all they have. You are disturbing the atmosphere that creates this opportunity and will now have to leave as you are behaving like an infant."

What she said disturbed and embarrassed me. I did not like being considered an infant. With no prospect for nurturing, I moved away from this librarian and recommenced my gesticulations.

"Any of this!" I yelled, making my way toward the door. "None of it is fair in the least!" Some impudent threw a book in my direction which rebounded off the exit sign and onto the floor. I stopped and turned. "I will not be censored. Like an infant, you say? And I suppose you presume this infant to have been hopelessly arrested and insufficiently gratified? Or excessively so? Which is it? Is that what you're suggesting? Perhaps, this infant has been waiting since his infancy for an opportunity to bellow like the heart-stricken moose! And this atmosphere of opportunity, as you call it, has created mine."

Someone laughed derisively. The librarian clapped her hands together, attempting to regain order while standing in front of her desk. In making the sudden clapping motion, a single button from the apex of her gray dress popped from its fastener, making a distinct *tic* upon the library floor. As a result, her collar parted modestly, revealing the flesh of the lower part of her neck. She brought her hand to her mouth as a single wisp of hair detached itself and an associated bobby pin dangled freely above one eyebrow.

Time stood still as I recognized the idiosyncrasies of her costume and bearing which defined her as an individual.

Instead of articulating this, I raised my voice and announced: "My marionette strings have already been cut. Your actuator cannot control me although. . ."

The woman stared in my direction. I had to say something. "Although I do recognize you. In your gray suit, I see the you of you. In your gray suit, with its top button popped, there is more. But the whole thing saddens me. I can bear it no longer. Without my notebook, I have fallen from a precipice. And as I plummet - half heart-stricken moose, half automaton-who-doesn't-know-he's-an-automaton - I find myself with such little time to say those things which I need to say, to you, keeper of books. 'Aye, me hearties, it was Moby Dick that dismasted me, Moby Dick, that brought me to this dead stump that I stand on now.'"

I heard tittering. The moment dispelled. I stamped my foot: "I will not be mocked!"

The librarian called out, "Guard!"

Feeling grossly misunderstood with my incomplete communications, I pushed through the door onto the library steps. Once outside, still unable to edit myself, I kicked the curb. Pain careened up my forefoot. I hopped up and down.

"What are you doing?" The librarian asked, having followed me outside. "What reality do you live in?" She was angry.

I stepped back, lest the woman might hit me. She stood at the top of the steps in her gray suit, and in the sunlight I could better appreciate its well-worn frailty. I looked down at my stained pants and frays along the cuffs. The librarian shifted; as she did, the material of her suit adjusted itself to her form.

"The library is not a stage. The patrons are not actors, not characters."

"Why do you say those things?" I asked, now worried and confused as to why she was taking the trouble to accost me.

"Why?" she raised her voice. "What kind of monster are you? Saying those things in there in front of everybody?" The woman had become unhinged, much as the landlady at Prytania Avenue had in discussing the fouling of her washroom.

"I. . . I'm not a monster." I was feeling ill.

The librarian had suggested that I was some sort of monster. She seemed to be on the verge of tears. I didn't know how I had come to disturb this librarian or this library. Oddly I didn't know why I had addressed the reading room in that way, or why I had said those things to her specifically. I felt as if the librarian and I existed in two different realities as if she were a ghost in her gray suit addressing a person from a different time. I wanted to move away from this librarian; she scared and embarrassed me.

"I don't know what came over me," I said and stepped downward a step. "Sorry. My notebook was stolen. It was as if. . . "

"As if what?" she asked. "I want to know."

I couldn't answer. Now I didn't know why I said those things. I had confused myself. There were too many possibilities, too many choices. And yet, this librarian had seemed to be my ally; she was invested in books.

"As if what?" she insisted. The woman had come outside the library to pointedly and persistently subject me to questioning. I did not know the answers to her questions. She addressed me as if I were someone else. I wondered if she were insane and only masqueraded as a librarian, existing in society by virtue of meticulous attention to detail and order. "We just met. We are strangers," she said.

"No, we," I began then halted. "Wait, I. . ." Of course, I knew that the librarian was a stranger. She was correct, of course. She had unmasked what could be a psychological shortcoming on my part, something which I was denying, on which I would have to reflect upon at some point; just not right now. I turned to examine the traffic on Loyola Avenue. I needed to cross the street and start walking again.

"You have no right," she said.

I staggered away then turned and ran across Loyola Avenue, away from the library. I looked over my shoulder. The librarian continued to stand at the top of the steps, her wisp of hair awry, her bobby pin dangling still, her button still missing.

I had been taken up within an odd frame of mind as if having lost my place in a book I had been reading or as if another book entirely had been placed into my hands when I wasn't looking; a different, perhaps more serious book. I had started reading this different book, somewhere in the middle.

I recalled the porthole window and sailor's welcome sign, the paint peeling off the flat and weathered facade, like Gregory Peck's Ahab, entangled in rigging, fastened to his nemesis, as the whale rose and fell, his arm, all the while, beckoning. Unsteadily, I made my way back to this bar and without further reflection, pushed inward through the door. Groping forward I took the first stool I came to as my eyes had not yet adjusted to the interior gloom. I breathed slowly through my mouth as the smell of stale beer and Pine-Sol was stupefying.

The bar had the form of an L-shape, the foot of this L placed close to the entrance. At the middle stood the same white bearded man I had seen my first morning in the lobby of the Lafayette Hotel, the very same man I had mistaken for a dignified statue. He held a can of Coke and had been speaking to the bartender. The light source shining on only one side of his face came from the row of bottles aligned on the shelf just behind the bartender. The only other patron was a woman with bright red leathery cheeks sitting alone at a table, a single can of Miller set before her; she, in turn, was illuminated intermittently by the scoreboard of a mechanical bowling game which twinkled against the wall.

The bartender walked down to my end of the bar and stood.

"Draft, please."

I had discovered that drinking draft beer at the University tap room had made me feel consistently less anxious while in conversation. As a consequence, I had made it a practice to take at least one to two draft beers before initiating any social interaction. I hadn't needed draft beer otherwise. Recording experimental observations into my pocket notebook, for instance, was calming and did not involve conversing.

I mumbled to myself. "If I could access my pocket notebook, there would be much to record, beginning with the imagined image of a stray dog stopping to lift its leg at the base of the Bodi tree. After doing so, the dog would hunch, arching its back into a U-shaped form, lick its lips and push a steaming fecal snake from its rectum; this snake would forever be forthcoming as Buddha's nose twitched interminably. . ."

In sitting at the end of this Sailor's Welcome bar, I had been provided with a perfect opportunity to be mistaken for someone possessing the neurologic end-stage syndrome of alcoholism. In assuming the role of a brain-addled mumbler, the spectre of the threadbare gray librarian could more easily be forgotten.

"She had served as a lighthouse on the rocky shoreline while I moved farther out into the stormy sea." I mumbled a little louder.

The white-bearded man at the center of the bar slammed his Coke can down and stared at me then resumed his conversation with the bartender, reorienting his head forward. I examined the deeply shadowed corners of his eye and lines inscribed around it, similar to a topographic map. Through the same dim light emerging from behind the bar shining on the one side of his face only, his eye appeared nearly silver and of an extreme clarity.

As the bartender placed the glass of beer in front of me, the door opened, sunlight streamed in, and a hand clapped me hard on the back.

"Look what I found!" The mysterious eye-patched man from the library slammed my *Tales of E.T.A. Hoffmann*, pocket notebook and pen down upon the bar top. Only now he wasn't wearing an eye patch. His eye looked perfectly fine.

"A man wearing the garb of a priest snatched them off your table. He sat outside reading and writing in your little notebook."

Despite feeling euphoric at the return of my precious objects, I held my tampered with pocket notebook at arm's length.

"Seems odd he would do that, don't you think? Out of all the notebooks in the library, he would be fingering yours?"

"Yes, it does seem odd," I said, uneasy with the idea of someone fingering my notebook. The suggestion of someone writing in it caused my sigmoid colon to coil like a boa constrictor in combat with a Nile crocodile.

"I beat this priest on your behalf and regained your books, *atzelari*, then followed you here hobbling on my peg leg." I glanced down. The man's legs appeared normal. "*Kaka zaharra*, I hopped after you as fast as I could. Clump clump clump." The man spoke curiously, citing the sound his purported peg leg made. The man dabbed a drop of blood under his nose with the knuckle of his index finger and regarded it. He then regarded the scratch marks on top of his right hand.

"Thank you," I said and meant this sincerely. I returned my notebook to breast pocket and pulled *Tales of E.T.A. Hoffmann* closer. I had to know to what extent my pocket notebook had been violated but felt uncomfortable commencing a thorough examination under his scrutiny.

"Don't want to lose a book like that," the man said.

I nodded and fidgeted. The man drummed his fingers on the bar; I recalled the porter at the Lafayette dawdling in my room while awaiting his tip. I signaled the bartender by holding two fingers up. After I had done so, the pepper haired man said,

"Do you see the triangle of light under the eye of the subject half way down the bar, on the less illuminated side of his face?"

I looked half way down the bar for a subject. Only the white bearded man was present.

"No longer than his nose and no wider than his eye," he said.

"I. . ." I stammered.

"You appear tough," he said.

I was glad the man had changed the subject. While at University, an acquaintance had once insisted that I resembled no physics major but rather an anthropology grad student!

"And your nose appears Germanic," the man continued. "Obviously a tough German." That he placed so much importance on the appearance of my nose was gratifying. The bridge of my nose had always been flat, and this feature had often been mistaken for a fracture. I found one side of my mouth turning upwards uncontrollably, as Herman Munster's' mouth might have in telling Lilly a fib. "It's been broken," I said.

"Oh *pikutara joan*, you inherited that nasal bone structure."

He knew! "Yes, I suppose it has always been somewhat like that," I conceded, astounded at this man's genetic wherewithal.

"Your people are German," he stated.

As I did not wish to break the enchantment, I said, "There's German on my mother's side."

"So you're a Sockserhause then. *Popatik hartu* by me!" he said, laughing and slapping me on the back. "You've heard of them of course." He gripped my chin, turning my head in both directions until he was satisfied. As I had undergone repeated examinations of my cranial and facial structure, I understood this to be a customary method of greeting others outside the University confines: to take hold of the head and turn it roughly from side to side then palpate its contours.

"I may have heard of them," I said.

"'May have heard of them,' he says, *Alu hori.*" The man chuckled, moving his stool closer to mine. He did not touch his draft beer yet pointed at mine, indicating for me to drink. His nostrils flared. I felt the need to say something.

"My family was from Britain, actually." There was an element of truth in this. I took a sip of my draft beer.

"Cymric Celt then," he said, sniffing. "Otadini maybe. Trace of Picti?" He slapped his knee. "I love the Picts!" He took my hand and gripped it in a soul shake. "They aren't strictly my people, but I love them. You know about the Picts then?" Before I could answer, he slapped the bar. "Aye," he said, "I can see you are no stranger to the Picts, *kabroi.*"

I was thrilled with the man's usage of, "Aye," an expression which pleased me as much as "me bucko." He enunciated the "Aye" gracefully, and I could not help but say, "Ayyyye."

The man regarded me with surprise and repeated, "Aye, *atzelari,* you are indeed Picti." He raised his voice. "*Mutil hori tentelapikoa da!*"

With the brewskis in me, I couldn't help but giggle; the man was speaking gibberish, although his suggestion I was no stranger to Pictidom was immensely gratifying.

With notebook residing safely within breast pocket, security was restored. I had located my place in that even greater book of the world and could now continue reading it.

The brewskis were helping too.

The man still had not yet touched his draft beer but signaled the bartender on my behalf. The bartender questioned me with a look. I nodded happily in affirmation. The bartender exchanged glances with the white-bearded gentleman and pulled down on the tap.

"They fought naked and the Romans, Romans mind you, couldn't handle their tenacity. The Picts were not Aryan, see. Untamed and given to rapine."

With the next draft beer placed in front of me, I suspected that Uncle Gambi had shared many profound and awful truths with me, what I had previously taken for delusion. I lapsed back into reverie and the next time I regarded my glass, it was nearly empty. In University vernacular, I was pounding back the brewskis. That was two in a row! The pepper haired man again signaled, and the bartender appeared in front of me. Envisioning the buxom mother superior drawing in an enormous breath, turning towards her paraclete window and releasing the majestic Climb Every Mountain, I told the bartender, "I'll have another."

"You need to lace your arms with tattoos like the ancients," the remarkable man sitting next to me suggested. He was paraphrasing my very thoughts! With two brew-ha-has and nearly three in me, I wished nothing more than to be tattooed from head to toe like my Pictish ancestors. In fact, I had made note of this desire in the very notebook which had now been returned to me.

"I intend to," I affirmed.

"What's your name?" he asked.

With this the white-haired man in the middle of the bar slammed down his Coke can again and staring at me pointedly. My archaic confidant grabbed my arm and pushed his face almost into mine. "What's your name, Picti?"

"Rodney Pepper." I blurted.

"Pepper," he repeated, appearing to be lost in thought until the next beer arrived.

"Certainly Saxon and something further south…south below the Danube, well below the Danube. . .I wonder, what brings a half Sockserhauser half Picti back to New Orleans?"

I wondered why he assumed that I was returning and wondered what a Sockserhauser was. This man had also most likely mistaken me for someone else entirely. It was gratifying to know that I had an identity and that I was a Sockserhauser and a Pict. I now wanted nothing more but to be associated with a cadre of people and bear their markings. The man cocked his head and pointed at my glass. He realized that I needed another brew-ha-ha before even I did. I held up a finger. I noticed as the bartender poured one more draft the older man in the center of the bar leaned forward and spoke to him quietly. When this draft was placed in front of me, the peg-legged man without the peg leg turned and laughed. I laughed with him.

"Drink *kabroi*!" the man shrieked and pounded the bar. "A Sockserhauser would be finishing a second set already. The bartender would be at the tap continually. A Pict would sit with his head under the tap."

His labile nature caused my heart to beat faster. I gulped my beer.

"Another," he shouted. "Then another and another and another! *Lau garagardo!*"

I was guzzling my brewskis too fast and wanted to leave. I half rose and mumbled, "I've got to meet someone. I was remembering…"

The man's expression became deadly serious. He completed my sentence, "That you had to dig for buried treasure?"

I glanced at the door. The man gripped my arm again, this time tightly, and hissed with even greater intensity. "We have been cut off from our ships, taken from our houses, but now we want to reclaim our home. We want our mother and our father. We want to speak our language. Every child deserves this right."

Feeling an even greater unease by the tone of these pronouncements, I looked toward the bartender and man at the center of the bar, who had stopped their conversation and were staring at us.

"One more," the man yelled. The bartender looked at me; I nodded, and he tipped his beer handle, walked down to the end of the bar and placed the draft in front of me. The man's beer remained untouched. He seemed calmer when speaking or being spoken to and agitated by silence.

I had to say something. "I just got out of the Navy, actually." I tensed the muscles in my jaw and pressed my toes once again into the base of my sneakers. "But I'm looking for work on land now, on land." I spoke much louder than I had intended and became disoriented, fumbling in my pockets. I paid the bartender and tried to think of something else to say. At the library, the man had mentioned the mistress of Vincent Gambi, who had been Basque. Basques played *jai alai* in Florida, so I asked him, "Do you know the Basques?"

The man relaxed, clapping his hands together. He lifted his draft and drained it straight away then wiped his mouth and pointed at me.

"*Bietan jarrai!*" He roared, "You knew all along! You knew from the moment you set your Sockserhause eyes on me. So, it was you who bombed Gernika, of course you knew, *sasikumia. Janzazu kaka!*" He lowered his voice. "I am type O, RH negative."

Mentioning the Basques had been the right thing to say, the right answer. I wanted to goad him on further so I leaned my head forward and knitted my brow to give him the impression I was listening intently. He inhaled deeply and said.

"Sueves in the west, Visigoths in the south, Franks to the North, low and behold Basques are the sole survivors. Below us came *al Tariq* and the *Umayyads*. Visigoths converted, mattered little to *euskaldun*." He paused then raised his voice. "It was *euskaldun* that ambushed the prefect of Brittany, potbellied Charlemagne's nephew, Count Roland, in the mountain pass of Roncesvalles. Little is it known that a Basque blew his horn as Roland lay dead. Aye, Pepper, *Castile-Leon. Reconquista, Pamplona* is restored," he exhaled.

Everything seemed just fine now. I sat back down on my stool. The brewskis were kicking in as if I were back at the University Tap room having one conversation after another concerning the existence of extra-terrestrial intelligence. Everybody was getting along splendidly in the Sailor's Welcome bar. I instinctively looked about for the jukebox. I wanted just one more brew ha-ha as it was all going so well. I backtracked in my head and attempted to count how many brewskis I had poured down my gullet so far when the Basque gripped my hand and squeezed violently, jostling my concentration.

"Aye, *Navarra, Catalonia, Aragon. Euskal herria.* All along the Bay of Biscay they still speak Euskera. It is legal now Pepper. It is the original language spoken before the tower of Babel. Franco could not erase it. *Vitoria-Gasteiz* is our capital. You ask me if I know the Basque, out of all the peoples of the entire world. My name is Erge Laztago. *I zurikin larrua jo.*"

I stepped off my chair again and tried to disengage my hand as his tightening grip hurt.

"Only you know my true name, Erge Laztago. I have never uttered my true name in this city." He glanced at the man in the center of the bar and released my hand.

I felt like kicking my legs out to the side of me then scissoring them back and forth as Dick Van Dyke and his Chimney Sweeps did for Mary Poppins' amusement. I no longer doubted Mr. Laztago. As he was Basque, I could only regard him with a single raised eyebrow, as Spock, of Vulcan heritage, might have. Then he said:

"The last great pirate treasure remains buried, Pepper and it keeps us all alive to know it's still out there and all belongs to the Basques."

Uncle Gambi had bequeathed the buried treasure to me, not to the Basques. Erge was trying to flimflam me. I had already been flimflammed beyond reason. Thankfully, with the brewskis in me, I felt Cincinnati Kiddish, and could chew on my cheroot with only a pair of twos.

Erge looked at his watch. "I would like to trade books. My passion is trading books. I will come to your rooming house immediately. I have history books to trade for your E.T.A. Hoffmann. I went to a great deal of trouble and personal suffering to recover that book because I wanted to trade you for it." He tapped my Hoffmann. "I will trade you all those books you keep in the bottom of your duffle bag for ones I have: Old books of piracy composed of ancient parchment."

Now, this was a marvelous suggestion, to trade books and acquire ancient maps! This was exactly what I had been hoping. I took a triumphant sip of my draft. The beer jetted through my posterior nasopharynx, out my nostrils onto the bar top.

Erge Laztago had more than likely inspected the contents of my pocket notebook!

He implied that I had books stored in the bottom of a duffle bag, yet I had mentioned neither books nor duffle in our conversation. I remained silent, snorting to clear my nose.

"We'll go to your rooming house now," he arose and grabbed my arm. And I had certainly made no mention of a rooming house! This suggestion supported the even stronger possibility that he was trying to hoodwink me. My notations had suggested Uncle Gambi's possessions were at a rooming house, but thankfully, I had cited no address.

"Did you say you were looking for work," a voice interrupted. The bearded man at the center of the bar now stood on the other side of Mr. Laztago.

"Yes, as a matter of fact, I am," I said, sniffling.

"*Zure ama emagaldua da.*" Mr. Laztago continued speaking his gibberish.

The older man ignored him. "You want to work offshore? Most of the kids coming down, do."

"Yes, that's exactly what I had in mind."

"Well, they don't hire in New Orleans. You have to go to Morgan City or Houston. Morgan City is closer. I'd leave town and go up there."

"I'll wait for you out front, *sasikumia*," the Basque let go of my arm, arose and pushed through the door. The older man with the beard was silent and followed the Basque's movements with his sharp, gray eyes until he was outside. He addressed me firmly. "You have a city full of bars, and you come down here. Why are you drinking in a place like this? This is skid row; you realize that? It's dangerous down here."

I could not explain how I was immersing myself simultaneously within the milieus of comedy and tragedy for purposes of self-actualization.

"Skid row?"

The old woman sitting at the table drinking from her can of Pabst Blue Ribbon roared with laughter and spat onto the floor.

"You don't want to get mixed up with people down here." He arose, walked to the door and looked outside. "Your buddy's gone. I would go now if I were you. Walk in the middle of the street." The man returned to his stool and sat. I arose and pushed through the door. It had grown dark outside. The Basque was nowhere in sight.

My destiny had been intertwined with that of Uncle Gambi. Just as he had predicted, predators had appeared claiming other blood lines. I resolved to call my parents at the earliest opportunity and confront them with this issue of a concealed heredity. The brew-brews had added clarity, and I decided that I would provide Uncle Gambi with the solace of his two mathematics books and then rid myself of any further obligation. Then I would choose my own path. Within my pocket, I fingered the cottage door key.

"I will unburden my conscience completely."

First, I needed to obtain a shopping bag in which to carry his books.

8
THE FECAL HOARD

Once outside the bar I removed the molested notebook from my shirt pocket and laid it on the sidewalk as if it were my wounded pet parakeet having just been mauled by the unscrupulous house cat. Outwardly, the notebook appeared no different. I examined each page one by one. An addition to the category of seminal quotations had been written in tidy longhand:

...infinite erectness of sublimity...

This immodest sentence fragment had flagrantly ignored my one immutable tenet: all seminal quotations be expressed with the subject, predicate, and verb. At least a citation of Kierkegaard had been included in parenthesis adjacent to the renegade wording.

My throat tightened: a longer passage had been created following my final entry. With fear and trembling, I read:

Lou-Ann Salome came to the party with Freddy Nietzsche. The tall stranger spotted her in the crowd, walked right up, shook her hand then held onto it. She couldn't stop staring at this stranger because he was wearing a brand-new jet black evangelical suit. Never once letting go of her hand, the stranger led Lou-Ann straight out into the dark woods. Without a word spoken between them, Lou-Ann took hold of a tree trunk with both of her hands. The tree shook as her big heavy titties heaved up and down, fruit falling to the ground with a thump, thump, thump, the tall stranger moving it all up and down and around inside of her as she tore the bark off the tree like some big ole momma bear. The tall stranger couldn't understand what she was shouting, but she kept shouting it into the darkness of the forest in that big deep German accent of hers. When the cameras moved in for their close up, the audience could now see the stranger was an American Evangelist. They rose to their feet, applauding, crying hysterically and yelling their Amens.

I spoke in a robotic monotone: "This faux fiction filth makes no sense at all. I will begin a new notebook and place this one at the bottom of my duffle bag to be thoroughly edited at a later date."

I reread the usurper's passage five more times before closing the book gently and turning my attention to Uncle Gambi's dook cottage. To retrieve and deliver to him the mathematics books requested would rid my conscience of further obligation, and I could get on with life. The risk remained, however, that were the landlady to discover me, she might yell. The possibility of being observed by one of the many children who played in the courtyard was likely; the children would inform their parents; their parents would inform the landlady; the landlady would yell. The landlady had no knowledge or comprehension of my ancestral obligations or the complex issues of matelotage.

I hurried to Canal Street in search of any store which might sell common household items. I stopped in front of the brightly lit Rexall Drugs, seeing an electric alarm clock in its display window. Once inside, I selected from its shelves a loaf of Wonder Bread, a package of Fig Newton's and several cans of sardines. I placed these on the counter and pointed to the alarm clock in the window.

"I want one of those."

"We don't have any more of those," the salesgirl replied.

"Can I have the one in the window?"

"I'll have to charge you full price." She reached behind the cardboard partition and removed the clock from the window display. Without wiping the layer of dust from its top, she placed it directly into a paper bag. While stuffing the cord in, the corner of the clock tore through the bottom of the bag. I tucked the bag under one arm and exited the store. Once outside, I removed my pocket notebook, opened it to the first blank page, wrote *bitch*, underlined it, closed the notebook and made my way back to the rooming house.

Prytania was fog bound. Thankfully, when I arrived, no one was present in the courtyard, and every door was shut. I climbed the narrow stairway, entered my room, plugged in the alarm clock, placed the loaf of bread and sardine cans atop the dresser then slid the Fig Newton's inside the night table drawer. I tucked the folded shopping bag under one arm and tiptoed back down the stairs, wincing with each inadvertent creak of wooden planking. At the bottom, I spread my arms for balance, and like the gentle orangutan waddled with stealth over to the cottage by the fence. I unlocked the door with Gambi's key, stepped inside, and straightened. Unable to take a breath without gagging, I nearly toppled over a lamp in my staggering. The air within Uncle Gambi's cottage was not merely stale. A different species of putrescence was present, more remorseless than that permeating my abode, an odor unlike urine or sweat. Without warning, vomit sprayed from my mouth as if I were the Trevi Fountain in Rome. Clamping my lips shut with one hand, I stood still and inhaled shallowly, just enough to provide minimal oxygenation to my brain.

Not daring to turn on the light, I continued to grope, patting the bed and upturning pillows. I side-stepped over to the closet as the Shaolin novice Kwai Chang had tread upon his rice paper, monitored by Master Po from behind the pillar. Sliding the closet door open, I stared into the dark confines then swept my foot back and forth. In probing like this, something became dislodged and fell forward, striking me in the crotch. I jumped back and whinnied. A small shovel clattered onto the floor. I stood still and listened; nothing stirred outside. The stench in Gambi's cottage remained overpowering, and gagged uncontrollably, feeling my way over to a narrow dresser. In the dim light, my hand brushed against a bottle on its top which rocked back and forth. Fumbling to prevent its fall, I held my breath, sucked in my lips and hunched my shoulders. The bottle rolled off the dresser, and as it did, I brought both hands to my chin, shut my eyes and curled my fingers like a hissing cat. The bottle did not shatter but bounced with a loud, dull *thud*. The faint ray of light through a window slat revealed an old bottle of wine.

Quickly, I opened the drawers of the chest in succession. Within each drawer, a similar bottle rolled toward me, all oblong in shape and without label. As my eyes grew accustomed to the dimness, I saw additional small miniature bottles of Bacardi rum scattered inside these drawers and on the floor around me. I recalled seeing one of these on the roof of the abandoned automobile salvage garage alongside the child's discarded GI Joe. Uncle Gambi must have tossed it over the fence, intentionally or not.

After opening the bottom drawer, I felt as if a rag had been stuffed into my mouth and pushed down my throat. I puffed air into my cheeks to contain the reflexive vomitus once again propelled upward. Dark forms scurried at the base of the drawer, surging over the seething mound.

I instantly understood the material was human feces. I would have to decide my next course of action within seconds; the subsequent maneuver would necessitate full commitment or none at all. My own father's instructions regarding management of a stopped-up toilet was specific: If ever the family commode or the commode at a house at which one visited appeared to be overflowing; if the situation arose such that the toilet bowl's water rose precipitously due to excessive use of paper or a massive stool production, one must immediately and without hesitation plunge one's bare hand into the center of the maelstrom, grasp the obstructing object and pull it forth. After the overflow receded, one could then thoroughly wash with soap and water with little chance of acquiring disease.

The screen door leading to the landlady's kitchen slammed. Startled, I slipped and fell forward, pitching both hands and arms into the middle of the unfathomable dark mire. In doing so, I heard a muffled snap while something at the bottom of the writhing mound bit into my fingers. I jerked my arm upward. Attached to it was the fecally encased mass. The object careened over my shoulder and fell onto the floor with a sonorous thunk as if I had landed a large bottom-feeding game fish.

"I've been bitten!" I bellowed, turning around and around, shaking my mangled hand. The predator released and fell to the floor with a clatter. A drop of dark lotion spattered my cheek as an insect scurried up my sleeve. I jumped up and down, standing on tip toes, sucking in my stomach and shaking my shirt with a clean hand until I heard the insect tap against the floor and scuttle away.

Struggling to suppress further gagging, my nostrils retracted back and upward as much as the accessory muscles of my face would allow. I listened to loud stamping on the wooden porch outside the cottage door.

"Mister, I want you out of my house by tomorrow morning," the landlady yelled. She banged on the door. "I know you're in there, and I know you shit up my bathroom. I can smell your dook from out here, and I have a nose like a beagle. I'll have the Sheriff here by eight-fifteen if you're not out by eight. And I know you're listening. Don't even bother to come out." The stamping receded then the screen door slammed.

Exhaling, I kicked the object which had attached itself to my hand. Listening to the soft metallic clink, I knew the device to be a mousetrap. I shoved the drawer of horrors closed with my foot, picked up the fallen bottle of wine, uncorked it, and poured the alcohol over my hand then swept it across Gambi's bedspread. I repeated the process several more times. With the remainder of the wine, I showered the object laying on the floor enclosed within a plastic bag. Gingerly opening the bag, I removed a small wooden case, untouched by stool.

Life had psychically inserted me into Uncle Gambi's colon. I was a correspondent embedded within the perilous war zone of repression and arrested development. My desire to open Uncle Gambi's hoarded box without delay was immense, yet I did not have the leisure of time. I placed it in my shopping bag and examined the room. Having adjusted to the dimness of the chamber, I took stock of the empty miniature bottles of rum scattered across the floor. I saw the single book stacked atop a night table by the bed. Overcome with the stench, I could not tolerate remaining a moment longer to search for the second volume, reasoning that the chances were good that this one contained the relevant clue toward the location of Uncle Gambi's buried treasure. I placed the book into my shopping bag, dropped the room key onto the bed and closed the door behind me. I moved up the stairs as if I were the 18th Century tubercular ridden romantic poet John Keats wearing winged slippers. I placed the wooden box on my dresser then let myself out through the gate with Gambi's book under one arm.

"I need to be done with all this goddamn shit," I spoke aloud and proceeded into the shadows of Prytania Avenue.

9
UNDER THE OFF RAMP

I stopped a half block away from the I-10 off ramp; a truncated scream sounded as if an animal had been run over somewhere within the space beneath the overpass. No cars were present, only the murk created by shadows, weeds, and concrete support beams.

Having become far too involved in Uncle Gambi's hoarding intrigue, I had a mind to keep this exchange with him as brief as possible. I had arrived at the rendezvous point with a clear conscience, recovering at least one of the books requested under conditions of extreme duress. I had no intention to press this madman for any further details of buried treasure or family legacy. Tomorrow morning I would proceed directly to the Lafayette Hotel, prepared to embrace the romance of desk clerkship until I ceased to draw breath upon this Earth.

No further sounds could be heard from in or around the gloom except for the repetitive moaning of cars traveling along the overhead highway structure leading to and from the Mississippi River Bridge. Serrated metal plates, substituted in sections for road repair, generated short tearing sounds as vehicles passed over. The fog had moved into the city; sound waves underwent multiple reflections with subtle changes in frequency as well as attenuation of amplitude, rendering any accurate determination of direction or distance impossible.

I proceeded cautiously into the immense shadow. Each passing vehicle created loud reverberations, the metal grating under tires sounding as if several crows were cawing in unison. I took several more steps ahead then halted when a loud grunt or, more like an exhalation, arose somewhere in front of me. I peered through the mist and moved deliberately, concentrating my gaze into the area of high grass behind which two metal I-beams crossed. Hearing nothing further, I retreated from under the ramp and stood on one side of a street light. Another man had crossed Prytania a block away; he too paused and seemed to look in the direction whence the disconcerting noises originated.

I walked around the block to the front of the YMCA on Lee Circle and waited a few minutes. With no sign of Uncle Gambi, I returned to Prytania and considered that he might have already left New Orleans, that the Dutchman may have secured him a ship. I decided to make my way back to the rooming house and forget the whole thing. I hesitated in passing once more through the dense fog under the highway even though this was the most direct route. The well-lit return would entail making my way once again to Lee Circle then following St. Charles Avenue uptown to Erato or Thalia. I surveyed the thicket of darkness. Hearing nothing more, I began to move back the way I had come, as quickly as I could. I wanted it done.

The same grunt issued from under the highway structure, this time, louder.

Above me, car brakes squealed. I looked at the underside of the expressway then into the troubling obscurity ahead.

"Hello," I called. Labored panting arose as if someone was attempting to move a heavy object. Edging through the high grass, the rancid odor of my sweat climbed through the humidity. My eyes teared.

Again I offered, "Hello," and heard another breath, this time, a prolonged exhalation. I could not be certain this had been issued in response to my greeting. Gingerly placing one foot in front of another, I bumped against an object, an oblong bottle of wine, without a label, the very same design as the one I had taken up inside the appalling cottage to douse my hands smeared with Uncle Gambi's feces. Several empty miniature bottles of rum also lay scattered throughout the grass.

A distinct scraping arose only several feet away at the base of the nearest highway support.

"Yes? Hello?" I leaned forward and peered through a cluster of thick weeds.

The street lamp provided just enough illumination to outline a man's head. I took an additional step and extended my neck, straining into the gloom. My training in the sciences had not prepared me for what became recognizable under the off ramp. He sat, back propped against the concrete post. Out of instinct, I averted my gaze. His eyeballs bulged yet more than bulged. I turned back and leaned forward again, attempting to focus. His two eyes descended, dangling upon his cheeks grasped only by thin strands of white connective tissue emerging from dark sockets. The pupils of the two disembodied globes met my own, fixed and calm.

A thick wire stretched around both the concrete post and Uncle Gambi's head. On one side of the post, a metal angle iron had been inserted through the cable and twisted several times. I dropped to one knee. His eyeballs had popped from their sockets by the brute force of compression: Woolded!

I lay down and curled myself into a tight fetal posture. I closed my eyes in an attempt to control the violent swirl of darkness and fog. An ant crawled into one ear. I let out a shout. Uncle Gambi grunted. I raised my head. Uncle Gambi inhaled and exhaled several times. I could not be sure if this represented a desperate post-mortem reflex or his true will to live. With the tearing sound of a car passing overhead, Uncle Gambi's leg jerked outward, the tip of his boot kicking me underneath the chin to snap my head back. I pushed myself away and sat. His eyes appeared to be two small light bulbs resting upon his cheeks. He remained still, yielding no suggestion that the last movement had been purposeful. I swatted at the steel bar on the side of his head with one foot, missing the mark repeatedly until tapping it lightly caused the cable to unravel and Uncle Gambi's head to fall forward. His body followed, landing in the grass directly in front of me, the eyes jiggling in the aftermath of descent.

"Matelotage. The treasure will become yours if I die, Rodney Pepper." Uncle Gambi had spoken aloud both my fore and surname.

"What. What? What!?" I emerged from a stupor.

Uncle Gambi's hand shot forward to take hold of my wrist as he inhaled. "I have to get to my ship," he said. "My eyes, they have pulled out my eyes, Pepper." Uncle Gambi was unimaginably alive, his skull compressed, fractured inward with two disengaged eyeballs buoyant upon his cheeks just below their sockets. He addressed me with remarkable clarity: "The two library books, Pepper. Hold them up one by one in front of my eyes slightly below and tilted upward so that I may identify them. Hold them up closely. Move each one slowly up and down so I may see the covers."

"I just have the one." I did as he asked, bracing my hands to stop the uncontrollable trembling. I held the book directly1 in front of his eyes, and as these eyes could not move, I moved the book for him. He remained still, maintaining a tight hold on my wrist. He finally spoke.

"No. You are in danger. We need the other, Pepper. Renee Thom. Mathematical Models of Morphogenesis. In it, the equation, most likely not the measure. Can't remember where I've hidden the measure so you must observe every detail. Focus. Discard nothing."

Uncle Gambi inhaled with a rasp and turned his head slightly as his grip tightened.

"Pepper, replace my eyes."

I choked as if his hands were about my throat.

"Take them in your fingers and push them back into their sockets. Pepper, they are still functional. Replace my eyes. I will then be able to find my ship."

From my medical reading, of obvious paramount concern would be that Uncle Gambi seek the attention of a board-certified ophthalmologist.

"I think a doctor would have to do that," I told him.

"I want you to do it. I trust you." Uncle Gambi's speech was truncated. "Pepper, I remember my brother, your father, standing on the deck of the ship. I was twelve when we crossed. We both became seasick." Rivulets of blood trickled from Uncle Gambi's ears; clear fluid streamed out of both nostrils.

Without thinking, I blurted out, "Where is it then, Uncle Gambi? Where is our treasure?" I fell silent, astounded that I would be capable of asking such a callous question under the circumstances.

Uncle Gambi was still a moment then asked me, "How could you imagine this much pain, Pepper? How could you let this happen? How could you make such choices?" Uncle Gambi's body twitched. The twitches grew in their excursions until both his upper and lower extremities shook violently.

"But I haven't imagined anything."

I hadn't imagined for anything to be inflicted upon Uncle Gambi; I had imagined no pain, nor had I made any choices.

"Find the swallowtail, Pepper! Trust nothing I've said. . ."

Uncle Gambi became gripped by paroxysm after paroxysm of shaking convulsion. The clear fluid now gushed out of both nostrils as his arms straightened and twisted inward, fingers bending backward of their own accord. His head jerked violently one final time. With this force, the two eyeballs simultaneously snapped free from their slim moorings, careened off his cheeks and onto my lap. Uncle Gambi's leg continued to twitch. His upper torso remained still.

Moaning like an animal snared in a trap, I attempted to brush the eyes off my pants. As one adhered to my zipper, I reached down frantically to pluck it free, failed and yanked upwards. The eyeball slipped from my grasp and stuck fast against my forehead. I batted and batted and batted until the sticky globe flew free, its landing marked only by a momentary bending of a grass stem and barely audible *plip*. The other eye had rolled along the ground and halted beside my knee. I scrambled backward, digging my heels into the soil to gain purchase, pushing myself toward the street light, clutching his library book against my chest. Nauseous and unbalanced, I stood and stared into the tall grass. Uncle Gambi's body remained concealed from view as sirens neared. Flashing red lights reflected within the dense medium of the fog. A loud shrill whistle echoed under the interstate as tires screeched above me like birds of prey. The man I had seen earlier staring into the grass stood two blocks down waving toward the approaching police car. I hurried toward the rooming house with the urgency of someone needing to both vomit and evacuate their bowels simultaneously. If seen dawdling in the area, I would be wrongly implicated in this pirate atrocity.

I crossed Prytania and stumbled down the darkened block, peering over my shoulder every few feet. I paused in front of my rooming house long enough to observe the sharper whirling reflections of red and blue lights against the ceiling of fog as the police car pulled under the off ramp. Unable to bear the motion of these colors, I turned to unlock the gate.

10

THE VIGIL

Unable to bear the sight of it, I placed Uncle Gambi's book face down on the bed, Arriving in New Orleans straight out of University, I was unprepared for the city's curriculum of unfathomable hardship and horrendous conclusions to deluded lives. Angry that Uncle Gambi had imposed himself and his violent death upon me, I swept the library text off the bed with the side of my hand. He had allowed himself to be captured by becoming conspicuously drunk with the money I had given him for nourishment.

I should have simply told the woman, *No, you have confused me with someone else, Madame. That person is lying dead in a Tallahassee bus depot. So good day to you.* And with that, I should have returned to the depot, boarded the next bus to New York. Once there, I would have secured the services of a psychiatrist to *get back on track* and continue my University studies. But I had not told the woman that. I had followed the ship's horn to the banks of the Mississippi. Within a short time, *my life had become a living nightmare*, that horror movie catchphrase which I previously assumed to be nothing but hype. I had immersed myself into a boiling cauldron of romance, kicked off both bath slippers, pulled down my urine stained tidy whities and climbed into its scalding water to simmer alongside carrots and onions which I myself had sliced. I was Bugs Bunny. All I needed was a wire brush with which to scrub the remaining flesh off my back so I might cook faster.

Uncle Gambi had been killed using a method practiced by buccaneers of the Spanish Main, giving credence to what I had assumed to be the outrageous and dubious tale of a lonely psychiatric patient. I knew nothing of this man's heritage and apparently, nothing of my own. I had an urge to remove all books contained within my duffle and gather them about me like a blanket. I imagined Uncle Gambi as I had seen him the first time, healthy and upright, smiling, grateful, clutching my hand in both of his. Studying Uncle Gambi's box on the dresser top, I would be strongly inclined, if queried by pirate agents, to deny its existence. I would lie wholeheartedly, telling them I had destroyed it and its contents. I decided right there and then that I would destroy it all, although might hold onto some of his materials a little while longer in order to best decide their manner of disposal.

I needed to put pirate skullduggery out of mind and focus upon my job interview the following day. I switched the bedside lamp off and lay still. After a time, the sound of steady typing arose, co-mingled with a gradually increasing din of rustling and tearing. I entertained two possibilities. Either behind every wall in New Orleans there resided a typist or, what I heard represented white noise oozing from my lacerated id provoked by bearing witness to unspeakable horror. Whichever the case, I allowed myself to be lulled by the rhythm of its *clickity-clack, clickity-clack, return, rustle, rustle.*

After a violent scuffling followed by a volley of claws applied to the wooden surface, I bolted upright. The bed springs creaked once, and the room abruptly fell silent. The typing ceased. Every animal and insect within the boarding house remained poised. After a full minute of stillness, a faint shuffling recommenced behind the loaf of bread on top of my dresser. The typist resumed activity, the sound originating from behind the door at the head of my bed.

I leaned forward and peered through the darkness at the loaf of bread. Dark forms clung to the wrapper and inched inward. Leaning farther still, the springs of my bed creaked once more. The typing abruptly ceased as dark forms scattered like a cannon shot, sliding down the rear of the dresser to thump thump thump at its base like tiny Green Berets at the end of their repel, accompanied by what sounded to be a collective inhalation. Legions of cockroaches retreated within the walls and floorboards as if being sucked through a vacuum hose.

Far more than I could bear under the circumstances, I stood up in the center of my bed and shrieked. Even though the clamor of this retreat diminished, I remained poised for a full five minutes before reaching over to snap on the light. Withdrawing my extremities to the center of the bed, I examined the loaf of bread from a distance. It appeared unmolested.

After another full minute, I extended my arm across space between the bed and dresser to pivot the package with one finger. On the side of the loaf facing the wall had been excavated a tunnel. I jumped down, yanked open the door, grabbed the bread's plastic wrapper and tossed the whole thing across the alley onto the metal roof of the automobile salvage garage. I lowered myself back onto the bed and jerked around to examine the door directly behind the headboard. The typing had not reinitiated.

I recalled the package of Fig Newtons, which I had placed in the night table drawer just before embarking on my horrific outing. Snatching my copy of ETA Hoffmann from under the pillow, I dropped it on the floor between my bed and small closet then stepped down upon it as one might onto a stone in fording a stream. I grabbed a wire coat hanger off the clothes bar and launched myself back onto the bed, rolling to safety as if I had just tossed a hand grenade into a pillbox of Jerries during D-day and was landing on a sand-dune.

Untwisting the coat hanger, I recalled the World War Two American GIs holed up in a cave while Japanese soldiers taunted them in English outside the entrance. A clever Japanese soldier finally asked "Want an egg, Joe?" before rolling a hand grenade into the cave's mouth. Becoming irked that I could not recall the name of the film or if it was a film at all, I hooked the coat hanger wire around the drawer handle and pulled it open. The package of Fig Newtons lay as I had left it. I stood on the mattress leaning this way and that, peering at the package from different angles. With the hanger, I nudged the package and flipped it over. As the drawer was narrow and I could not visualize the rear, I swirled the metal hook against the back panel. As I was reaching downward with the intention of removing the Fig Newtons from the drawer and eating them on the spot, a small mouse wobbled into view with bright red blood spurting rhythmically from one of its eyeballs. My body propelled itself backward off the other side of the bed into the closet as if I had stepped on a third rail. I arose to observe the mouse sniff once then lay still. Blood pooled in the front of the drawer.

I had killed the rodent by inadvertently puncturing its eyeball.

The coat hanger had most likely violated its orbital integrity, accessing an artery. Gripping my forehead, I climbed back onto the bed, blinking uncontrollably from the concatenation of witnessed ocular traumas. I took up my pen and notebook and in keeping with my breadth of despair, began writing over already existing text: To have an eyeball punctured or plucked,

119

to suffer deoculation or evisceration, constitutes the most basic and darkest of prospects. I slammed the notebook shut and gazed at my hands. I was essentially that Roman soldier who had driven the nails through Jesus' palms. Grimacing, I pulled the bedside drawer out with both Fig Newtons and body of mouse inside; I flung the door open and tossed it, along with the coat hanger, onto the roof of the abandoned automobile body shop to join the loaf of bread, the GI Joe and the miniature bottle of rum.

I grabbed my pocket notebook and pried it open as if were a steel trap and noted:

I have perturbed the system with my own measuring instrument.

I pressed the notebook leaves closed and held them close, staring straight ahead until the break of day.

11
INTERVIEW AT THE LAFAYETTE

Overnight my skin had assumed the consistency of a synthetic putty brought close to its melting point. I sat on the edge of the bed palpating the contours of my ocular globes along with their adjacent frontal, maxillary and temporal bony prominences. No lacerations or crepitus were obvious. I made a brief entry in my pocket notebook:

In maintaining a strictly scientific perspective with appropriate clinical distancing, emotional events can have almost no impact whatsoever.

Closing the notebook with militaristic snap, I could now attend to my interview preparations with the cares of the world displaced. I parted the top of my duffle bag, removed and unfolded a deep blue union Big Yank work shirt then smoothed a brown tie against the edge of the dresser. After placing this shirt and tie on, I regarded myself in a small cracked mirror hanging on the door. The collar curled and protruded outward. To cajole the material, it only bowed further, like a sail catching wind. I manually lifted my eyelids and gazed out the cracked pane of glass onto the roof of the abandoned auto shop. Neither the loaf of bread, GI Joe nor rum miniature were anywhere in sight. The overturned drawer remained with the mouse's body in full view resting to one side of the Fig Newtons. The coat hanger sprawled farther up the corrugated rooftop. Reminded of everything, I turned away, sat back down on the bed and vomited between my legs. I now understood the attitude of the previous occupant: It made no difference to the room's demeanor whether I cleaned up this regurgitant puddle or not. I arose, secured the door behind me and descended the outer staircase.

Uncle Gambi's cottage door was flung wide open. I stopped after hearing the squelch and static of a walkie-talkie over the landlady's curses. She had certainly discovered his treasure trove of feces and had called the cops.

The landlady stepped from the cottage door followed by a New Orleans police officer. She dropped a cardboard box filled with empty bottles into a large metal trash container and walked toward her kitchen door, loudly denouncing Uncle Gambi as a perverted lush, then recounted to the officer how he had welshed out on his rent and slathered her property with dook.

Locking the gate behind me, I proceeded onto Prytania. Avenue. In turning up Erato, I had an urge to urinate and entered a half constructed parking lot on the opposite side of the automobile salvage shop. Walking toward the back, I stood in front of a wooden fence post and aimed my penis toward its base. While releasing my distended bladder's volume of urine, I gazed upward at the clear blue sky. My involvement in pirate conniving seemed a remote possibility.

Looking downward, I was startled to find I had been urinating onto the head of a large rat.

The animal remained motionless, inches from my feet. With my penis protruding out my fly, I froze, unsure if a sudden movement with this large rodent in proximity was prudent. The behavior of these creatures when suddenly provoked was not known to me. The rat did not indicate that the day was anything less than pleasant. Its whiskers twitched while sniffing the air.

The rat seemed not to mind in the least that I was peeing on his back.

With a distended abdomen, the rat appeared, if anything, to be enjoying itself. The slight frost covering the adjacent ground suggested the urine might serve as a warming agent, similar to a dip in the Caribbean Sea. I sprayed him further, aiming just behind his ears then shook my penis up and down, zipped up and stepped backward to a safer distance. The rat continued to sniff the morning air.

I noticed shards of bread crust underneath the fence. Remarkably, wedged in a recess, was the Wonder Bread plastic wrapper, remnants of the very loaf I had hurled from my room the night before! Through the wrapper, I saw the familiar torso of the GI Joe. Beside him was the Bacardi miniature, both transported by the heroic rodent from the roof of abandoned garage to his fence post apartment.

Peering closer, I could see the small bottle of rum had been corked.

Containers of this type were generally twist-offs. I could not be certain there was not an object within the bottle itself. I turned my attention to the two characteristic swivel joints attaching GI Joe's hips to his legs. His solid plastic hair parted to one side and clean-shaven face identified him as the model I had possessed as a child before Hasbro introduced beards. For the first time in many years, I spoke a name aloud:

Johnny Jupes.

Johnny Jupes was the name of my imaginary childhood hero. GI Joe could assume the persona of Johnny Jupes and vice versa. As a child, I had removed GI Joe's battle fatigues to lend him the sleek figura of either secret agent or superhero. Without clothing GI Joe became Johnny Jupes, flying over the metropolis of our living room, tilting his body now and then, using x-ray vision to locate enemies under couch cushions and so forth. Johnny Jupes knew what to do. I had assumed Johnny Jupes' persona while socking pillows or kicking couch cushions.

I utilized my mother's tampon inserts with her tampons as GI Joe's hand grenades, telescopes, and mortar launchers. The cotton plug with its string would sail across the living room and explode. Rubble flew from behind the couch. When my parents had guests over to the apartment, my father would remain insistent. "Please, please, please put some clothes on him! Here's another one of your things," he would say, waving a tampon insert. In time, I was forbidden to play with my mother's tampons. The box disappeared from the medicine cabinet.

I had created many stories relating to the exploits of Johnny Jupes. Creating the titles or titling was more important than the stories themselves. Johnny Jupes and the Case of the Sad Woolded Man, I titled aloud.

I had no time to dawdle and set off reemerging onto Erato. I opened my pocket notebook, of course, and composed a poem en route to my interview:

After Morning loaf

Warm shower

Frosty breath

Nose aloft

Sniffing

Can't move

Don't want to.

I snapped the notebook closed like a Japanese fan, turned onto St. Charles Avenue and stood still: Men in flannel shirts shuffled past me, darkness encircling their eyes; gashes, scabs, and sores embedded their faces; while brown dirt caked their boots and jeans. The entire lower St. Charles Avenue appeared blue in its shaded light; I was no longer on a street that lent itself to the composition of frivolous poetry.

A few feet ahead, a door opened, and steam emerged: the sign read Hummingbird Hotel and Restaurant. Through the condensation of the plate glass window, I could discern the backs of men sitting at a lunch counter. Wearing my Union-Made work shirt, I pushed through the door, strode up to the counter and swung my legs over a vacant stool. A woman with a sallow face appeared. I began to speak; she moved away and returned to place a cup of coffee in front of me.

I hadn't said a word only tilted my head imperceptibly.

Surmising that subtle signaling took place at the lunch counter, signaling similar to that transpiring during art auctions, I remained still. The barest eyebrow angulation or slightest twitch of digit delineated between an order of eggs over easy and sunny side up. Glancing down the row of stools, men hunched over their plates and held coffee cups just below the level of their mouths, staring straight ahead. The waitress asked, "Hungry?"

I noted eggs over easy on every plate and answered, "Two fried eggs, over easy. Does that come with toast?" The woman had moved away before I could complete my inquiry. I raised my cup to the level at which the other men had raised theirs, just below the chin. I affixed my stare onto the Bun-O-Matic machine. After a few minutes, I conceded my desire for a large glass of orange juice. Sleepless from a night of atrocity, I wished for a cold orange thirst quencher. Glancing along the counter top, I observed not a single glass of juice. I took another sip of coffee and lowered the cup onto its saucer. I glanced along the counter. The men took their coffee black: Black was the way to take one's coffee.

After a few moments, however, I could tolerate it no longer: In my heart of hearts, I wished that my coffee contained a tad of cream. I reached forward, grabbed the metallic cream container, tilted it over my cup and returned it to its position on the counter as quickly as I could. Glancing once along the row of seats, I noticed the men had continued facing front, all coffee cups poised. They were paying no attention to my actions. I studied my cup. I had not tilted the cream container far enough. No cream had emerged from the pouring spout. I reached forward, took up the container again and tilted it with a greater vigor. Without moving my head, I peered down again, surveying the coffee's surface. A small white cloud spun slowly but had not changed its overall hue. I had poured an inadequate amount. Holding my breath, I reached forward and brought the container toward my cup as my sleeve dragged the fork off the countertop and onto the floor propelling the remainder of the cream in the container onto my lap. In trying to grab my falling fork I tipped my coffee cup onto its side and spilled most of the coffee not only into its saucer but onto the table surface. I ground my jaw together and pressed my toes down painfully into the front of my shoes. The waitress, in one fluid motion, lifted the saucer, poured away its excess, wiped the table, set down a new fork and refilled my cup. Following this, she set my plate of eggs gently in front of me. Glancing at the dark stain to the right of my fly, I winced but nonetheless set about chopping up toast and tearing egg yolks. I gauged how much yolk was absorbed by the toast. While chewing, I regarded the Bun-O-Matic.

In mopping the final streak of egg yolk from my plate, I noticed the Times-Picayune layered in a sales rack by the register. Envisioning Uncle Gambi's eyes sat upon his cheeks, I became momentarily unsteady, losing sight of my vocation as notebook keeper. I could find no rationalization for anything in my life at that instant. The moment passed. However, my equilibrium felt restored, and I purchased one of the newspapers, tucking it under my arm and gained a sense of security in doing so. I paid and emerged into the street. Striding toward me was that very same man who had been seated at the kitchen table of the Prytania Avenue boarding house and had said that he would go down there.

The man threw back his shoulders as he passed me. "A woman with big ole titties runs the hotel. She needs to hire a man to put her in her place, praise God, praise Jesus." This more than irritating man had gone down there and beaten me to the interview apparently. He appeared over-confident, and my step faltered. As I entered the hotel lobby, the scarred desk clerk said, "Just a moment," pulled up the desk's hinged gate, walked into a small alcove and opened a wooden door to enter a back room.

In passing the over-confident ruffian, I considered seeking a different job. I took the pen from my pocket and hurriedly began examining employment ads in my newspaper. *Barman* caught my eye: To work in the milieu of the brewski was on a par with hotel-desk-clerkery. Ample opportunities for exposure to anguish, tribulation, and misery would undoubtedly present. I happily circled the ad, recorded the address in my pocket notebook and was turning to leave when the clerk emerged from the back room.

"Go in through there," he said, then oddly backed away from me as if in fear. Through the door, I passed into a surprisingly spacious room. Behind a very large and sturdy oaken desk at the room's center, sat a woman. To one side of her stood the same tightly shirted man I had seen on the Moon Walk and again upstairs at this hotel struggling with my late Uncle Gambi. He wore a thin black turtleneck and appeared unhappy to see me.

"If you lose your insanity, what do you have left?" the woman had been asking him as I entered. I was certain she had used the word *insanity*.

The man said, "Peace and…." then stopped speaking. He swiveled his torso to face me and pulled away from the desk as a predatory animal might in being surprised during his feeding on a carcass. He moved over to the wall and stood with his arms crossed over his chest.

"Hello, Mr. Pepper, I am Evelyn Razer."

The woman did not smile. My knees gave away. I recognized her as the very female with whom I had collided at the Tulane Avenue Station my first morning. She appeared before me framed amidst a tremendous expanse of black hair with a recently added bride of Frankenstein white streak. She wore two large hoop earrings. A light purple cotton sweater contained her gravitationally dense breasts. Between her breasts, riding on the crest of the sweater's material, sat an enormous cross, perhaps twelve inches long, depicting a writhing, bloodied Christ. My vision abruptly faded as my hands groped to my front, attempting to locate the single wooden chair I had glimpsed in entering the room, positioned in front of her desk. I located it by feel and slid onto the seat, my mouth dry as a medieval parchment.

Recognizing the influence of a rapidly accelerating vasovagal process, I set about attempting to analyze what was transpiring within the office space from a physiologic standpoint: Knowledge of mechanism would prevent further deterioration.

"I need to view her breasts as biological signaling devices announcing fertility," I said, reviewing out loud the genital echo theory, relevant here as it proposed that pendulous breasts provoked excitation in upright male hominids who had formerly felt similarly when gazing at fatty deposits on the female buttocks.

"This could also be a clear-cut case of libidinal fixation," I said, drawing from as many sources as I could. "Excessive attachment to the breast leads to a form of repetition where the ego continues to search for a loss that did not take place."

"What?" Evelyn Razer looked at the man standing by the wall. He shrugged his shoulders.

While my shared inner dialogue was potentially confusing to those present, I was pleased to be speaking out loud. In being confronted by these extreme provocations the quoting of psychoanalytic theory slowed these encroaching malignant vagal and parasympathetic influences considerably.

That I could not comprehend a single word of what I spoke was not only relevant but desirable.

Sounding disgruntled, the woman asked, "Can I have your newspaper, please?" Without waiting for a reply, she leaned forward and removed it from my hands. The tight-shirted man continued to stare. Neither he nor I had said hello. Tapping the eraser of her pencil on the newspaper, she finally broke the silence within the room. As she did so, my lips lost an additional aliquot of moisture.

"Did you read your Times-Picayune this morning, Mr. Pepper?"

I wished to share I had read the want ads while waiting in the lobby but could not formulate mundane speech. The woman unfolded the paper and read aloud, touching each word of the headline with her index finger as she did: "Body of tortured man found under I-10 overpass."

My chest tightened.

"The man, in his mid-sixties, a transient appeared to have been tortured before his death by woolding, a method practiced by ancient buccaneers. Robbery did not appear to be the motive as the man had in his possession several two-hundred-year-old gold coins in addition to a bottle of wine speculated to be worth over one hundred thousand dollars. The assailant may not have realized its value."

She continued to tap the newspaper with her pencil. "You understand for the past two hundred years we have kept all this to ourselves. The Lafitte's no longer fly the Jolly Roger. We no longer live on Cat Island and have no intention of moving back. Lafitte's don't throw beads off floats. We don't go to masked balls. We don't advertise ourselves by..." She tapped the newspaper and said, "Woolding."

Evelyn Razer shifted her posture. "Did you really think that would impress us?" She nodded toward the tight-shirted man. "He would have to go to the library to read about how to do that."

She had assumed that I was the New Orleans woolder! *This felt marvelous.* In the hotel manager's eyes, I was a ruthless woolding pirate. I very much wished that I had been wearing an idiosyncratic piece of clothing such as a pair of patent leather buckle shoes hinting that I was comfortable with my pirate underpinnings and was as unpredictable as a rabid dog. More remarkably, the woman had implied there existed an ancestral pirate society of Lafitte descendants within modern day New Orleans. Uncle Gambi had warned that someone would contact me. I did not completely understand who Evelyn Razer was in regards to this pirate hierarchy yet, given her big desk and swathe of hair, she could only be someone of importance. The notion of a full figured female pirate had great allure while simultaneously provoking physiologic unease.

"The problem is, we are not sure if we actually know who you are," she said and nodded to the tight-shirted man. He unfolded his arms and approached. From his hip pocket, he removed a pair of glasses and put them on. He did not appear exactly academic, but his glasses made me more comfortable. The man moved around me and from various angles conducted a form of evaluation. At one point, he approached particularly close. I jerked my head slightly to the side to get a better view of what he was doing. With this sudden motion, the man gasped, jumping backward and stumbled. The woman chuckled. He appeared annoyed by this and approached again, roughly applying both hands on the top of my head. His palpated my cranium for a full minute, and while he did so, I winced several times although found there to be a pleasant therapeutic aspect to the procedure. He gripped my jaw and chin in one hand and moved my head first laterally then vertically. He stepped back, removed his glasses and said,

"He ain't Royce."

I recalled the man at the boarding house remarking similarly.

"Well, I figured that," the woman answered, clearly irritated. The man shrugged, returned to his position against the wall and folded his arms back across his chest.

"We're confused. . ." She hesitated and glanced at her yellow pad. "You understand that all us Lafittes are phrenologists? We have to be. Every pirate on Barataria had to have an understanding of the facial structure and phrenologic makeup of every other. This is how we maintain security. Mr. Pepper, we're confused about you and confused about the man you killed in that way. Royce did send you, yes?"

Both the large hoop ear-ringed woman and the tight-shirted man glared at me in an unkind manner. I wondered whether telling the truth would be of help or of harm. I found myself able to say, "Yes," having regained the ability to speak to a degree. Yes seemed like the right thing to say, even though yes was a lie.

"You didn't want his wine then?" She asked. With that, it dawned on me this was the woman I had overheard upstairs my first night, the prodigious and aggressive typist. I had not expected to be confronted by this woman, this particular type of woman, this woman whom I had overheard describing her inordinate desires and who typed with lightning speed and presented herself now across an enormous desk with an oceanic expanse of black hair and blood-soaked Jesus writhing on an enormous wooden cross resting atop and between two Virgilian breasts provoking a high amplitude vasovagal symptomatology.

The tight-shirted man had also been present in the room adjacent to mine that first day discussing his missing Shore Patrol Forty-Five. He had accosted me on the Moon Walk earlier then aligned drunken Uncle Gambi's head shortly thereafter within the peephole. Both this man and the woman wore clothing accentuating the contours of their sexual organs. My head began to process slowly like the vertical synch lines dropping down from the top of my family's Zenith black and white television set on which I watched war movies as a child.

There had been a colossal misunderstanding.

"He got drunk on ten bottles of Montrachet, Domain de la Romanée Conti." The woman pronounced these descriptive terms with precise French accentuation.

The turtlenecked man interjected, "At twenty thousand dollars a bottle."

"He also drank the vinegar from a two-hundred-year-old Chateau Lafitte. And those are worth one hundred and sixty thousand dollars, not what they said in the paper." The woman looked at the turtlenecked man and knit her brow. "How would a man living in a shit hole on lower Prytania obtain a one hundred and sixty-thousand-dollar bottle of Lafitte?"

I recalled washing my hands with wine the night previous within Gambi's fetid little cottage and couldn't help but glance at my fingers, still possessed of a faint but unmistakably purple hue. The woman stared at my hands. Uncle Gambi had mentioned the occasional rare wine or brandy.

"Several of these bottles of the Montrachet were found in his room but nothing else. It looked as if someone had come through before the police." She stared at me without blinking.

I had plunged my hands into Uncle Gambi's hoarding drawer yet would not attempt to explain the psychodynamic implication of having done so.

"Its complete elucidation would be well beyond the scope of this interview," I said, completing my thought aloud, pleased with the opportunity to use the phrase well beyond the scope in a sentence.

The woman cocked her head, glanced at the man again and tapped her yellow pad with the pencil. "Yeah, whatever, Mr. Pepper. Listen, I'm successful in what I do, and one of the reasons is that I can smell a rat a mile away."

I recalled the chubby rat on which I peed. Evelyn Razer was a remarkable woman.

"I don't like wasting money on old bottles of wine. I like silver martini shakers polished so you can see your reflection. I like waiters serving me in new uniforms with shining buttons. I like sparkle." She stopped talking for a moment, as if she imagined waiters with shiny buttons, then continued. "We know everybody, Mr. Pepper. The man you killed had informed several people while drunk that he was a descendant of Vincent Gambi, a pirate who stole a considerable portion of Jean and Pierre Lafitte's treasure two hundred years ago. Few people know that this fortune existed in the first place or that this crime ever took place. Over the last hundred and fifty years, the Lafittes had gone to a great deal of trouble to kill Vincent Gambi's descendants along with all their boyfriends and girlfriends." The man against the wall laughed and his shoulder holster, filled with the immense Shore Patrol Forty-Five, flapped against his chest. The man seemed to provide the hotel manager with an audience of sorts, just as Ed McMahon had for Johnny Carson.

"I am telling you this because it sounds like the old man you killed was very wealthy." She spoke more slowly. "You see, until this morning, the Lafitte's never suspected that this treasure existed." The woman arose half-way out of her chair and asked me, "Who are you?" Her breasts swayed ponderously with the exertion. "Are you Royce's twin brother?"

"Yes," I answered without hesitation. It would have been too confusing to explain that he had been an exact look-alike and only through chance, had I met this Chesterfield-smoking, duffle bag guarding assassin and witnessed his violent demise through the bus window in Tallahassee. Privy to dark inner secrets of the New Orleans underworld, I decided to keep kept quiet and play along simply because this was the less stressful alternative at the moment. I felt safer in being considered the woolder. In fact, I felt more than content in being at once the woolder and twin brother to Royce, the hit man. If pressed, I would admit that Royce never used to do his homework as a child. I had and had been referred to as *the good one.*

Evelyn Razer threw her pencil down on the yellow pad. It bounced, hit one of her breasts and snapped in two.

"I had given you specific instructions yet you tortured him? We have guns for this. We prefer gun violence, in fact. You know why? Being so common, it does not call attention to itself. If you had shot him, no one would have cared, and it probably wouldn't have made the newspaper. Royce would know that. As it happened, your stunt made the front page."

In the course of Evelyn Razer's reprimand, my mouth became drier and my tummy more upset. In the ensuing silence, I felt a strong need to both defecate and change the subject.

"I came here for the interview. I want to be a desk clerk," I said. The woman frowned then turned and stared at the tight-shirted man for a full ten seconds. He shrugged, and she turned back to me.

"Are you serious?"

"Yes," I said. I couldn't explain to this woman how much I needed my quiet time in addition to being occasionally splashed with the bow legged high seas hi-jinx of lower St. Charles Avenue. Desk clerking was the perfect profession for an adventurous notebook keeper. And as the New Orleans woolder, I could rest on my laurels to an extent although I realized that the real woolder might appear at some point and become upset I was taking credit for his doings.

"I want to put woolding behind me and settle down to some honest desk clerking." I spoke straight from the heart.

"You want to interview for the desk clerk position?" She asked flatly.

"Yes."

The woman tapped her legal pad again with one of the pencil shards. "OK, whatever. I have interviewed one other applicant today. He doesn't have your pedigree, but then again, that's not what we're looking for at this hotel. What he had was real life experience, and that's all I care about." She sat back down behind the table, pulled a pad of paper out of a drawer and made a notation. "Alright. We are looking to fill a full-time desk clerk position. What hotel experience do you have?"

In applying for the desk clerk position, it did not occur to me that I would be asked about hotel experience.

I hurriedly considered the night I had spent in the hotel itself and the peephole debacle. My heroic Shore Patrol Forty-Five intervention could certainly be construed as hotel experience as was my deft handling of the mound of sand on my bed with the pubic hair sprouts. As I deliberated inwardly, Mrs. Razer's eyes narrowed.

I breathed, "No."

"No?" She frowned, and there ensued another long silence during which I was certain she expected some sort of qualification. I could offer none. Any traces of cordiality faded from her face.

"Then what experience do you have?" she asked flatly. "Except for woolding." She chuckled and glanced at the man in the turtleneck. He, in turn, pointed at her. She fluffed her hair.

The intensity of Mrs. Razor's physical being was focused upon the large wooden cross with its associated blood-soaked Christ figure, inexorably framed and deployed around and within the contour of her measure. I had become markedly distracted by this yet understood what transpired within. In my sub-basement carol at University, through careful study of world religion texts, in particular, the illustrated ones. I had learned that I, Rodney Pepper, constituted a *Smorgasbord of Appetites*. I understood that the quivering genital center of my brain, located in the limbic cortex, would lead me inevitably toward a state of malodorous chaos and dissolution, creating what was known as *hell on earth*. I was resigned to this fate however and the strict fickle imperative of my unopposed id. Experience? I had extensive masturbatory experience. While I could not offer this directly, I asked Evelyn Razer, "Could Malcolm Lowry have chosen not to drink his After-Shave lotion?"

"What did you say?"

I rephrased: "I have been to University."

"I don't give a damn about University. What kind of work experience do you have?"

Her taut shirted muscular protégé, who I now could only assume served as hotel security, cracked his knuckles. The back of my neck itched. I was developing an eczematous rash, intermittently present while attending University whenever exposed to the stress of test taking. I had left my hydrocortisone cream in New York. I ran my hand lightly over my face to ascertain if acne comedomes were forming. I tugged on my ear lobes, checking for sebaceous cysts.

Mrs. Razor continued tapping her pencil on the yellow legal pad. "Do you think you could learn to work a switchboard?"

"I don't know," I replied. In having been a ham radio operator throughout my youth, a switchboard constituted a technically straightforward instrument; aspects of fielding questions, however; that is, the complaints and referrals from various sordid individuals residing within the hotel itself would be problematic. Human interaction made me uneasy, if not overtly ill. I reasoned that I could carry on a form of radio speak with the Lafayette tenants, punctuated by *roger-rogers*, *say-agains*, and *very-fine, very-fines*.

The manager stared at me then at the man standing against the wall. I reconsidered, realizing my background in physics and amateur radio was not insignificant. Wanting to state I could obviously work a switchboard, I opened my mouth but now could not speak. I reached up and pulled my lips apart with two fingers. They had become stuck fast through some rapid bio-psychologically desiccating mechanism. No longer feeling my hands or feet, I mumbled an explanation:

"My Vagus nerve is undoubtedly activating."

I recognized the onset of a vasovagal syncopal event, the mechanism of which I understood through my previous study of medical textbooks. My heart, as predicted, beat at a progressively slower rate while I experienced additional subjective symptoms of coldness and clamminess. I gazed at the beads of liquid forming on the dorsum of my hand.

"Peripheral circulation undergoing vasodilation," I murmured and tried to lift my hand but couldn't. In recollecting this woman's prodigious typing, her shouts, the spontaneous crashing of furniture, the bowing in and out of the walls, my vision dimmed. In further visualizing the eyeballs of Uncle Gambi resting on his cheeks like two freshly laid hen's eggs, I slumped forward slightly. Dimly aware this particular syncopal episode had been triggered by my telling of truth, that is, that I had been honestly unsure whether I could comfortably work a switchboard or not, I now wished to retract this statement and substitute a bold-faced lie which might restore my equilibrium and sense of well-being. In the meantime, the woman was tapping her pencil on the yellow legal tablet. She asked me,

"Do you have a number where we could reach you?"

I expelled a flatulent at the moment of her question. Recalling the eggs I had eaten for breakfast at the Hummingbird, I inhaled deeply. My mouth turned downward of its own accord as my head jolted backward with each reflexive sniff and inhalation of my sulfurous stench. The tight-shirted agent of security shifted slightly and produced a remarkably loud and sustained low-frequency reply approximated phonetically as *blababbabbbabbbabbbablab*. He then regarded me with no amusement whatsoever. The woman appeared oblivious to either of us despite both of our emissions having resonated unmistakably throughout the interview chamber.

Sweat cascaded down my forehead and along the side of my chest wall as I attempted to address her question, speaking slowly and sounding as though I were underwater.

"I don't think....there's any real way..." Mrs. Razor cocked her head and frowned. "You can actually get...in...touch...with...me."

Evelyn Razor leaned backward in her chair. I recalled TV and film episodes in the course of which an actor pitched to the board, usually leaning forward with his hands placed firmly on the conference table and garnished the promotion. That was how to achieve success! I wanted this job, and needed to turn the tide in my favor; I had to say something to convince this woman that I, Rodney Pepper, was an experienced and callous woolder who could manhandle a switchboard and that doing so would be, as a physics professor might say, trivial.

"All I ask is a chansh." I could not control my lisping. I winced and groped in front of me, hands attempting to retract my words as they left my mouth, at the same time pushing and pulling my tongue which protruded like a dry piece of beef jerky. To secure the job, my next sentence must be forceful, without significant production of spittle. I played what I knew to be my trump card.

"I have experience with this hotel. I know this hotel. I am familiar with this hotel."

As soon as the words left my mouth, I lost sight of my trump card. There was something to the idea of knowing the hotel, but as my brain was inadequately oxygenated, I had not flushed the notion out or brought it to a logical conclusion. I needed to lie down, or I was certain to fall from the chair. I utilized this opportunity to show her what I was made of. The hotel manager surely must have understood that physiologic events within me were progressing rapidly. I would demonstrate to her that I could hold on until loss of consciousness, similar to a marine at Paris Island boot camp supporting a telephone pole while standing knee deep in swamp water.

"I ashk....jusht give me a channnssshhh," I said and gracefully moved off the edge of the chair and onto the floor, maintaining the convincing appearance, with one eyebrow cocked, that this was a most natural thing in the world.

"I have to lie downsh for a momentsh." While unable to control my lisping, I managed quite competently to curl up in the fetal position directly beside my chair. As my vision closed in and all became dark, I knew I had timed my descent admirably. My silky-smooth manner of losing consciousness would surely count for points toward securing the much sought after desk clerk position. And then, by way of putting a capital V on Victory, at the moment just before completely releasing myself into blackness, my second trump card appeared. And I played it. With eyes closed, laying comfortably alongside my chair, I stated,

"I jusht gotsh out of jhuh Navy. I was a deshk clerksh in the Navy..."

"Jesus Christ," I barely heard Mrs. Razor exclaim, as if she were speaking on the other side of a waterfall. "I cannot fucking. . ."

I heard a voice say, "He's getting a little color back now." I opened my eyes. The old man with the white beard peered down at me.

"Aww, he's all right." he said, chuckled and lit his pipe. I had been placed in one of the lobby chairs, apparently. The scarred hotel desk clerk was also staring down at me. He handed me my newspaper. I arose, clothing drenched in sweat.

As perfusion restored itself to my cerebral cortex, I felt there was no better time to snag the elusive barman position than now. Quite pleased that I had garnered this significant interviewing experience, I felt I could sell myself in almost any capacity.

"I think the whole problem was that I didn't have a nice big glass of OJ at the Hummingbird."

With that, I walked out of the lobby door and hurried down St. Charles. I had no cause to doubt myself, any longer. It was the barman's life for me. As everything had coalesced perfectly, I winked at an old man stumbling out of one of the lower St. Charles cocktail lounges and told him,

"I'll be swimming in a lake of broken dreams. before you can say Peter Cottontail!"

I heard a shout and lurched forward as if hit by a graviton beam. A block away, Mrs. Razer, stood on the sidewalk under the Lafayette awning. She waved at me, and as she did so, the surrounding buildings bowed in and out as if time and space were warping. I turned and hurried onward to my next interview, sticking index fingers into both ear canals and humming.

12
THE LEOTARD

When I arrived at the North Rampart address, a pale and unshaven man had been pushing a set of batten shutters against the exterior wall. I stood and watched him grab chairs off tables and flip them upright, followed by stools along the bar top. He moved back to the doorway bringing with him a bucket which he dropped onto the sidewalk in front of me, with a loud *clank*. Inside the bucket was a mop.

My response would normally have been to flinch: I did not flinch. My nervous system had assumed a refractory state attenuating any startle responses; the conditions bringing this about arose in the aftermath of my Lafayette Hotel interview during which I had been subject to an overload of sensory and psychosexual inputs.

Certain that the man would have noticed that I had not budged in response to the percussion of his bucket, I allowed myself a James Bondian drawing back of the mouth: The interview for barman had begun. Odd Job had been defeated at Fort Knox. First impressions were crucial. I was sure that I had made a good one; the outer world, rife with startling noises, remained at peace with my inner Kwai Chang.

I realized that while this administrator would not have strictly expected my arrival, placing the ad in the Times-Picayune heralded the commencement of barman interviewing. Most likely the first interviewee to arrive, I could only interpret the timing of the mop and bucket's clatter as an interviewing prompt.

This bartender fully expected me to take the mop out of the bucket and clean the sidewalk.

I did exactly that and did so with wide energetic sweeping motions.

"What the fuck are you doing?" The man strode up to me, snatched the mop from my hands and slammed it down into the bucket. I wondered why he appeared so upset as I had passed the taking-initiative portion of his test with flying colors.

I noted there had been no water in the bucket. I chuckled and pointed.

"Water, right?"

"What do you want?" the man asked gruffly then turned and entered the bar. I followed him inside.

"There was an ad in the paper about the barman position."

The bartender disappeared into a back room. Smelling Ajax, I sneezed, then placed three quarters in the cigarette machine and pulled the handle underneath the Chesterfield box. In my walk over to North Rampart, I had resolved to conduct the entire barman interview with a Chesterfield balanced precariously on my bottom lip and make a point of frequently laughing while exhaling all the while making casual *fuff-fuff-fuffing* sounds.

I sat on one of the newly upturned stools and placed my Chesterfields on the bar top. The man emerged with a bucket filled with ice and emptied it into a chest under the beer taps. The bartender's forearm had a tattoo of a hula girl.

"So you're here for the barman job, is that right?" He walked into the back room again.

I very much wanted a hula girl tattoo.

As soon as the thought entered my mind, I flinched. My startle response had returned, this time, provoked by the crinkling of a wrapper commencing to one side of me. I recoiled back, imagining an insect or rodent might have alighted on the bar top.

A hand and forearm, tattooed with haphazard ciphers, ill-drawn crosses and body parts rested on the counter beside my own. I had heard neither footfall nor scooting of any bar stool. And no one other than the bartender had been present at my arrival.

Seated next to me was the same dark-jacketed man from the Prytania Avenue boarding house, the man who had confidently strode past me having usurped the Lafayette Hotel desk clerk position previously earmarked for only me. This same man now began to unwrap my newly purchased pack of Chesterfields without even a hello. He wore the same black garb, the only alteration being that his sleeves were rolled up.

I did not like this new coincidence.

The tattooed intruder had no business arriving at my second job interview let alone meddling in the first. I judged him roughly to be my same age, a few inches taller with thicker bone structure. He shared my brown hair and brown eyes but was by no means my look-alike. He removed a cigarette from my pack and placed it in his mouth. Black and blue discoloration were visible surrounding one eye; I recalled the Basque's story in the Sailor's Welcome bar, that while retrieving my notebook, he had beaten a man wearing the garb of a priest. The man seated alongside me could indeed be mistaken for a false minister.

"You work here?" the tattooed despot asked, striking a match.

"No," I said with unconcealed irritation, obviously engaged in conversation with my future boss. There could be no room for distraction.

"You here for the barman job?" The intruder persisted. Simultaneous to his query the bartender posed a question from the back room which I could not hear. I strained to listen but heard only scraping.

Having missed an interview question as the result of this man seated beside me, I blurted, "Oh fuck it all to goddamn hell," turned and hissed, "Yessssss."

I projected my voice toward the back room: "I just came by to interview. I just got out of the Army." I neither winced nor flexed my toes against shoe bottoms. I had grown comfortable lying. In fact, since my previous vasovagal episode, I was mightily emboldened to lie at every opportunity life offered me.

"Lie like there's no tomorrow," I had vowed aloud during the walk over.

I could only express obvious annoyance at the unexpected presence of the intruding meddler seated alongside me, a meddler who did not hide his interest in what transpired between myself and the bar official.

My interviewer, likely equivalent to a full Colonel in the ranks of the barman hierarchy, emerged from the back holding an ice pick. I blinked rapidly in recognition of this implement and the psychopathology of its possibility. I turned my head away: Its point posed an immediate ocular threat.

"What did you do in the Service?" the bartender asked. As I wracked my brain trying to imagine a job one might hold in the Army, the man sitting next to me whispered, "You know they found a body under the I-90 off ramp early this morning. You hear what happened to him?"

"Please, one moment," I fended off the interruption. My mind strained to recall military recruiting brochures I had collected as a child.

"He was woolded," the intruder continued.

"What?" I was momentarily alarmed and distracted in again hearing the archaic usage of the verb to woolde. Yet, I was quite sure I knew a little something about woolding that this man didn't. My mouth turned upwards on one side as I was happy, quite happy, that I knew more than he did about woolding and I was not at all abashed to convey this knowledge with a characteristic Herman Munsterish upturning of the lip.

"Herman Munster? I didn't get that. What was your job in the service?" the bartender repeated the question, leaning around the doorway. I had unintentionally concluded my inner thought process aloud. I must have spoken the name Herman Munster while arranging the expression on my mouth. The intruder sitting next to me guffawed.

"That bartender is hung over like a fucking mangy dog. You want to work for *him*? Look at his face." My barstool neighbor was speaking loud enough for the bartender to hear. I recalled my father having mentioned serving in the Signal Corps.

"Signals," I called out.

"You know what woolding is?" the infuriating intruder asked, moving his mouth closer to my ear.

"Why don't you get a job with the phone company or something? They're hiring," the bartender returned from the back and poured a bucket of chipped ice into an aluminum chest then carried the entire chest behind the bar.

"You know what woolding is?" the intruder repeated.

"Woolding. Yes, I do know a little something about woolding; quite a bit, in fact." I spoke curtly, on the verge of telling the obnoxious man that I had been acknowledged in underground circles to be The Woolder. He interrupted me.

"Uh huh. Give me another one of them Chesterfields."

"I was a radio operator," I called out to the bartender. "I can send and receive Morse code at thirty words a minute." I padded my resume. I could only comfortably receive at fifteen words per minute on the ham frequencies.

"I heard that he claimed to know where millions of dollars in pirate treasure was," the intruder said. "But no one's sure if that's true. Everybody in New Orleans is looking for the man who last spoke with him."

As I knew that person was me, I continued to feel special. Within the pirate circle, I was famous if not infamous. I glanced at the oaf's hand. Crosses, penises, and breasts, all dripping with blood comprised a disturbing yet admirable campaign advertisement for a governorship run on the sociopath ticket.

"Well?" The bartender stuck his head out the door again.

"I want to be a barman!" I called out. The bartender emerged from the back room with a case of beer and a small black piece of fabric.

"Try this on. It's the only one I have for now. The last guy quit and took the whole fucking drawer. Use the back." He tossed the cloth to me and continued to unload beer into the ice chest.

I entered the back room then emerged a moment later to confirm that I understood him correctly. "Is it that you want me to wear this?"

"That's a Roger Roger. Isn't that what they say in the Signal Corps?" The bartender turned and continued loading the beer.

"Just put on the leotard you big pussy!" the tattooed intruder called out.

"Why don't you mind your own business," I answered.

"What?" the bartender asked me.

"What?" I asked.

The bartender shook his head and murmured something. The intruder snickered. I went into the back room and put on the leotard. My underwear became visible beneath and just outside the elastic border of the tard, crumpling at the crotch, my arms and armpits fully revealed. I dawdled in the back room for several minutes examining myself at different angles in the mirror.

I resembled Alfalfa as he had appeared in the Little Rascals episode dressed as a ballerina while attending Darla's dance school.

I began to itch.

The leotard most likely had not been washed since the last barman wore it. Mites of various species had laid their eggs throughout the material, eggs which may have hatched.

I tore the leotard off and feverishly brushed myself off as if having been doused with gasoline and set on fire. I put on my pants and shirt. Recalled my studies of the French Quarter guide books. I spoke aloud my conclusion, unconcerned that someone might hear me.

"So in lieu of tipping, the clientele would bugger the barman in his mite infested leotard?"

I emerged from the back, communicating through the use of an impetuous gait that I knew full well what was what. The bartender leaned on the bar, smoking a cigarette; it was unclear whether he had been talking to the tattooed menace or not. Both appeared carefree.

"Like I said, the phone company's hiring." The bartender spoke without looking up.

My pack of Chesterfields had found their way into the intruder's front pocket.

"Can I have my cigarettes, please," I demanded

"These are my fucking cigarettes. I didn't take your cigarettes," the bartender snarled.

"No, I am talking to him," I said.

"What?" the bartender asked.

The intruder removed a few cigarettes from my pack and tossed it to me. I left the bar with the perception I had again been manipulated and undermined although relieved that I would not become a barman which I now knew to be synonymous with an object to be groped while wearing a leotard. I stormed out disillusioned. The more-than-irritating-man followed me.

"You're not going to take the job? I would go back in there, put on the fucking leotard, work for a week then rob that asshole's cash register. Or quit then rob his cash register. Whatever. I don't have to put on any leotard because I got the job at the Lafayette to fall back on." I turned and walked rapidly along St. Peter. He followed me, speaking closely into my ear:

I know the left hand of a dog like I know the right hand of a man.

The deranged library patron had spoken those very words, words which I had then recorded in my pocket notebook. This black-garbed scoundrel had stolen ETA Hoffmann! And he was the author of that puerile, stomach-turning, lustful intrigue forever marring my fragile pocket notebook.

"I had my interview at the Lafayette this morning," he said.

"Oh, I'm already well aware of that," I said, increasing my pace and humming to myself.

"Razer told me I did extremely well. She used that very phrase. 'Extremely well.' What did she say to you?" he asked. My legs felt flimsy; I wobbled.

"She said she would be contacting me," I told him over my shoulder.

"She didn't say that to me. To me, she said, 'I'm impressed with what I see.' She looked me up and down. She sized me up." The devil continued to strut down St. Peter. I had enough of his petty squabbles and gossip and turned up Bourbon.

I suspected that my mistaken identity might not be a boon. I had erred in not vehemently denying to all concerned when presumed to be the New Orleans Woolder. I should have gone to the police the night of Uncle Gambi's brutal demise and explained everything. But I had not.

God forbid that I would have to prove my woolding fortitude. I had enough to worry about simply as a notebook keeper.

13
PHONING HOME

After the Barman debacle, I made my way to the nearest pay phone on the corner of Rampart and Canal. I inserted two dollars and twenty cents in change and dialed the number for my parents.

"It's him! It's him!" My mother shouted, "Dad! Pick up!"

I heard a click and a scrape. Without waiting for my father's voice, I asked, "Am I descended from pirates?"

My mother said, "Oh Noooo. Of course not. Dad?"

"No. .no." My father's speech was barely audible.

"Dad?" I asked. "Am I descended from pirates?"

"Are you ok?" my mother asked. "We are so glad you called. We were watching the news and heard about that poor man they found under that highway. It's on national news. He had very expensive wine which the muggers didn't even know about…"

"He was woolded." I interrupted.

"Woolded," my father murmured. "Gee Gods."

"Do you know what woolding is, Dad?" I asked.

"No, I don't know what that is," he said.

I could barely hear my father.

"No, I don't think he does. You don't know what woolding is, do you, Dad?" My mother asked. She often repeated questions.

"No…" my father answered.

"Are you ok?" my mother asked.

"Do I have an uncle that you have not told me about, an Uncle Gambi?"

"Why did you ask that, Rodney?" my mother asked. "Why did you ask that? You've never asked that before."

"Do you know the name Vincent Gambi, Dad?" I asked.

"Oh no no, we don't," my mother answered.

"I was asking Dad. Gambi, do you know that name, Dad?"

"No, I don't," he answered softly.

"It's an unusual name; I'll say that," my mother added. "Very unusual. Are you ok? You sound so tired. He sounds so tired, doesn't he, Dad?"

"Maybe he wants to come back home," my father said.

"Oh yes, just come back." My mother's voice rose. "It's not worth it, Roo." I cringed. Roo was a childhood nickname, certainly not in keeping with a moniker one might assign a sought after pirate hit-man who had recently woolded or allegedly woolded a freebooter under the I-10 expressway. "They say that New Orleans is the murder capital of the United States now. It just took over as the murder capital of the country from Washington DC."

"Gee Gods," my father mumbled.

"And that man was woolded. Did you ever hear of that, Dad? Woolding. I haven't. It sounds like torture. I don't even know what that is but if it's torture I can't bear to listen. I can't bear torture of any kind."

"Dad. Do you have a brother?" I asked.

"No, he does not," my mother's voice rose further. "There's just some old uncle who was locked away years ago. Completely insane, wasn't he Dad?"

My father mumbled something else which I could not hear. I was not told I had an insane uncle.

"No, Dad, he was insane," my mother insisted. "That's why we never told you, Roo. He had died before you were born. We lost track of him, didn't we, Dad?"

I slammed the phone down. If my ancestors were from a pirate bloodline, my mother and father were not admitting it. I would have preferred one of them to have simply said, 'Here is your great uncle's blood-stained bandana. The time has come for you to put it on.'

I returned to my Prytania Avenue boarding house and sat on the edge of my bed. I contemplated Gambi's case for a moment, grabbed the Times-Picayune and turned to the employment section. A large ad in the center of the page read *Tack Welder, will train, $4.75 an hour, Avondale shipyards*. With various intonations, I repeated the job description Tack Welder aloud for several minutes. I began to feel better when a loud knocking shattered my repose.

"Rodney Pepper!" The landlady's voice called out. "You have a phone call."

I cracked the door and examined the landlady in her bathrobe. "You have a phone call downstairs, Rodney. A woman from the Lafayette Hotel. She said you would know who she was." She pushed a finger into my arm through the crack in the door and added, "She said it was important." I followed the landlady downstairs to the kitchen. She handed me the phone, moved to the doorway and stood, examining her fingernails.

"Rodney! It's Evelyn Razer. I'm sorry our interview ended so abruptly. Just a minute." She covered the mouthpiece, and I heard loud muffled voices. She uncovered the mouthpiece and spoke hurriedly. "You saw me, didn't you? Waving at you after the interview? I had a glass of water. Well, I've got terrific news. Hope you're sitting down. You got the job, Rodney Pepper. So congratulations. I was impressed. No, really. I've been thinking of the initiative you demonstrated with the woodling." Evelyn Razer's breathy accents transmitted an auricular disequilibrium sufficient enough to tilt the axis of the refrigerator with respect to the kitchen floor. I held on to the counter top.

"The Lafitte's like that, Rodney Pepper. We haven't seen that kind of innovation in a long time."

My lips became dry, and I felt myself listing to one side, as if on the Titanic. I grabbed the kitchen chair. The landlady pushed herself away from the doorway with a puzzled look on her face. I lowered myself into the chair and kept a firm hold on the table.

"You can start tomorrow. Room and board included. You'll be staying in your old room. And we may just have more woolding for you to do from time to time; you were so good at it."

Evelyn Razer referred to my old room at her hotel as if it represented a pleasant childhood memory; The chamber, rife with pubic debris, cigarette burns on flammable bedspreads and gaping gashes in the wall, had created nothing but bottomless anxiety.

The tonality and breathy intensity of Evelyn Razer's voice served to distort my spatial orientation. Relieved not to be in her presence for the duration of the phone conversation, I would have otherwise been forced to relive the violent warping of curved space-time. The telephone reproduction of her vocalizations created only minor perturbations. In considering what Evelyn Razer represented, either symbolically or literally, any physicist worth their salt would be prompted to ask the fundamental question: What is mass?

I cocked an eyebrow and declared: "I got another job."

"I was afraid of that." She covered the mouthpiece. I could hear her say something to the effect that he got another job followed by angry muddled speech. She uncovered the phone. "You didn't sell yourself short I hope?"

"Well, I'm going to work at Avondale shipyards. Tackwelder. Just had an interview."

"Just had an interview?" she paused. "Avondale shipyards? You just had an interview?" She covered the mouthpiece, and I heard laughter. She uncovered the mouthpiece. "You know then you have to go over the Huey P. Long to get there. Do you have a car?"

"No."

"Listen I have the perfect solution. Do you want to work offshore, Rodney Pepper?"

The old man in the porthole bar had used that same term: Offshore.

"I do accounting work for a company just past the Huey Long, in Kenner. If you are willing to travel out to the Avondale shipyards, then take this address down. I'll let Eddie know that you're coming. He's the personnel manager and we know each other. We need to take care of our own, Rodney Pepper."

I opened my pocket notebook to its third to last page, a page reserved for practical matters. I scribbled the address of this company complete with Evelyn Razer's directions.

She then said, "Maybe I'll run into you, and we could have a cocktail together. I know I'd like that."

"Sure, that would be . . . sure."

I imagined Evelyn Razer seated inside the University tap room, her vast expanse of hair and hooped earrings attracting a congress of writers and rabid intellectuals. I pushed through the crowd holding two tropical drinks each with their little paper umbrellas and stood alongside her.

"OK then," she said.

Just before hanging up, Evelyn Razer made a sound as if an unseen force had knocked the wind out of her. I stared at the receiver. After hearing the dial tone, I placed the handset back into its cradle.

"You sure do change jobs a lot," the landlady said, still standing in the door frame. Her bathrobe had parted while she had been listening. "I don't care what job you do, just so long as I get my rent on time." The landlady remained standing in the doorway, and I was forced to slide past her, my arm brushing against her hip. She said, "You know where to find me if you need me."

These repeated exposures to female form and vocalizations provoked sustained disequilibrium, and I veered off to one side in walking the length of the alley. Once back in my room, the vertigo subsided and was replaced, curiously, with an unbridled resolve. Seizing Gambi's box from the dresser top, I flung it open and dumped the contents onto my fetid bed. Out spilled sheets of paper populated with nothing but line after line of mathematical equation and calculation. The handwriting, small and meticulous, had been penned in a black ink without a single cross-out or revision. I flipped hurriedly to the final page. The calculations continued right off the end with no obvious final determination.

Imprinted upon an additional folio was an engineering diagram depicting what appeared to be an antiquated device reminiscent of a Da Vinci machine, consisting of a wire frame, a system of turnbuckles, and two large sack-like structures. Differential equations and vectors neatly annotated its contours. Initially appearing to be a buoyancy device; upon closer examination, I realized the design proposed a form of industrial brassiere designed to harness enormous breasts.

On the bed lay scattered many well-worn ticket stubs associated with bets placed at various race tracks throughout the country: Belmont, Saratoga, Pimlico and Churchill Downs. There were many different wagers: Trifectas, Quinellas, Win, Place, and Show. The bets had all been large: One thousand dollars to win, ten-thousand-dollar daily double, five thousand dollars to place and so forth. I added the sums represented by the sampling of tickets; nearly five hundred thousand dollars had been wagered overall. Uncle Gambi had related how his doppelganger and he had worked on a system for predicting the outcome of horse races, purporting this had successfully been applied to increase the value of the original pirate fortune.

I felt disappointment after examining the box; its contents had proved far more mundane than I had anticipated without bringing me any closer to the treasure's whereabouts.

The box and its contents represented a dead end, merely evidence for Uncle Gambi's hoarding behavior and not much else.

Uncle Gambi had mentioned the possibility of dead ends, but I had not taken this literally. Were it that my life to be a tedious novel in which little transpired, the reader would have already closed the book and returned it to its dusty shelf; or placed it atop the john and taken up a tabloid. The newspaper would at least have provided them with the immediate payoff of a sensational headline or two.

The betting tickets gave credence to a good deal of what I had previously assumed to constitute far-fetched alcohol inspired nonsense from an author who claimed close affiliation with a prodigiously genitaled, horse race handicapping doppelganger; the stubs provided proof for his precarious investment strategies. I stared at the tickets, sitting on the bed feeling for the first time to be far from home, and uncertain of who was telling the truth and who wasn't.

I stamped my foot: "Fuck it all to goddamn hell! Imagine opening the magical pirate box you've been expecting only to find a handful of old expired betting slips."

I had not counted on the postponement of success. The treasure should have been mine by now. I trusted that no further detours, dead ends or disappointments would arise. Treasure hunting had proved unexpectedly precarious. There was also no guarantee that one could make a living doing it.

14
THE TRAINEE

I took the streetcar to its last stop then boarded the Kenner Local at Carrollton and Claiborne. With the windows jammed open, the passengers stared ahead, fanning themselves with newspapers. The bus creaked and swayed from side to side as though we rode atop an Indian elephant. I disembarked at the large blighted intersection under the Huey Long and walked along Jefferson Highway as instructed until I noticed the sign for International Petroleum Positioning. As soon as I entered the lobby, a secretary behind the reception desk asked, "Rodney Pepper?"

"I don't have an appointment and am not in an ideal position to present my credentials yet I believe. . ."

She interrupted. "I'll call Eddie."

Right away, a door opened off the lobby, and a man stepped out holding a glass of water. His hair had been blow-dried to the extent it appeared sculpted from bronze. He extended his free hand and said, "Rodney. We've been expecting you." He handed me the glass of water.

"Thank you," I said. "I don't have an appointment, and I am not in a position to present my credentials, yet I believe. . ."

Eddie cut me off with a friendly nod and said, "Evelyn told me everything." He led me into a small office and indicated that I should take a seat. Eddie right away tapped the pitcher of water on his desk. "There's more where that came from so just say the word, and I'll top off your glass."

I nodded and took a sip. Eddie continued.

"Excellent. I.P.P. is an offshore oil service company providing equipment and personnel toward the navigation and positioning of survey vessels, pipe laying barges and drilling ships as well as other specialized radio surveying operations. Do you follow me so far?"

On the desk lay a copy of QST magazine, the American Radio Relay League's Amateur Radio Journal. Eddie, the personnel manager, was a ham radio operator, as was I! More than delighted, I utilized Morse code to phonetically sound out the radiotelegraphic R: *Dih Dah Dit.*

Eddie would surely understand this to mean Received Ok, as did I.

I added *Dihdihdihdih dihdih* which represented the letter H followed by the letter I, the widely accepted practice for abbreviating a radiotelegraphic laugh. Eddie smiled conspiratorially, and I gave him the thumbs up.

"In the course of eight weeks, you and seven others will receive classroom instruction on the theory and practice of radio positioning. Its basis is geometry, specifically the principle of triangulation. Positioning measurements are taken utilizing modern techniques of radio frequency transmission and reception. Two base stations must be set up on land. The vessel is equipped with a receiver-transmitter-computer which communicates with the base stations and utilizes their signals to obtain a position. The accuracy of the triangulation is within two to three meters, and that's an acceptable tolerance facilitating the location of oil deposits, drilling sights, and underwater wellheads. You will learn to operate systems such as Navcomp, Maxiran, Raydist and Loran C. Does this sound interesting to you, Rodney?"

Dah Dih Dah Dih.

I had answered by way of a radiotelegraphic C, the universally acceptable abbreviation for affirmative. Eddie had been addressing me in a no-nonsense technical manner, the idiom of which I appreciated both while at University studying physics and as a ham radio operator. Eddie had gained my respect and trust. Relieved beyond measure to have found myself once again immersed in a predictable world of radio operation with its procedures and protocols; piracy, murder, and mayhem must take a back seat.

Electronic radio navigation jargon, like a glass of warm chocolate milk, had an immensely consoling effect, so much so that I could no longer focus on Eddie's exposition. As I sipped water from the glass, I became internally preoccupied with the utilization of Morse code to spell various names: I spelled my name, Eddie's name and of course, Evelyn Razer's name.

Eddie paused, and I seized the opportunity to spell out *In the destructive element immerse*, an obvious wink at Joseph Conrad. I transmitted the Morse code at ten words per minute, the speed with which Eddie was bound to comfortably receive:

Dih dih - Dah Dit Dah-dih dih dih dih-dit. . . .

Eddie interrupted me. "That's Morse code, isn't it?"

Dah dih dah dih.

I tapped the QST magazine on his desk and chuckled as one ham would to another.

"Oh, this isn't mine. I'm holding mail for one of our engineers while he's away. But that's interesting you know Morse code. We don't require it for the job if that's what you were getting at?"

"No, I was. . ."

Eddie scratched his nose and said, "But that's good, though. I wish I knew Morse Code. I'd like to spell things out behind people's backs sometimes; you know what I mean?" Eddie chuckled.

"I know *exactly* what you mean," I said and chuckled. Eddie had made me feel comfortable; my speaking to him in Morse Code was not viewed at all a faux pas; entirely the opposite: it seemed to have garnered me enormous favor.

Eddie held up a large poster board on which had been diagrammed the representation of a seismic boat towing a cable. At the base of the poster, antenna towers were drawn with lightning bolts depicting radio signals emerging from their apices. My head swiveled from side to side, examining, the boat, its cable, the two radio towers and their lightning bolts. Eddie remained behind the poster then peered around one side. The notion of working offshore and becoming a navigator caused my mouth to fill up with saliva to the extent that it cascaded over my chin. Eddie, being an observant personnel manager, handed me a Kleenex.

After an indeterminate time, Eddie stopped speaking and examined me. I could not be sure if he had asked me further questions. To test the waters, I made a noise by blowing air through one of my nostrils. Eddie seemed encouraged by this and asked, "Soo, again, Rodney. . . Would you be interested in working on a boat?"

Having jumped the gun on too many questions since my arrival, I took the time to consider this one in all its aspects. I began with my own reference point of the sea: Gilligan's Island, the Minnow and its three-hour tour. As soon as I envisioned the portraits of the Skipper, Mary Ann, Ginger, and Thurston Howell the Third appearing in its opening credits, I found there was no need to proceed any further. My answer for Eddie was succinct:

"The weather started getting rough; the tiny ship was tossed."

Eddie asked, "I'm sorry?"

I paraphrased: "I want to work on boats." With that, like Robin Hood, I had split the Sheriff of Nottingham's arrow. Eddie nodded and put away his poster. He withdrew a sheet of paper from one of two stacks on top of his desk, affixed it to a clipboard and handed it to me: I.P.P. Medical Information Record.

"One thing I have to ask you and this is just a formality. We have to ask everybody this." Eddie chuckled. "Do you have a problem with sea sickness?"

Years previously, I recalled having accompanied my aunt and uncle on a large cruise ship. I had vomited before the vessel left its pier. I vomited continually for the duration of the voyage. At that age, I had been predisposed to violent motion sickness. Any aberrant movements provoked the symptoms. The possibility I had not fully outgrown this tendency was remote.

And how could this not be the case; the sea had become, by simply listening to Eddie's job description, not only my vocation but my wind jamming ham radio concubine.

During my University studies, I recalled experiencing intervals of protracted nausea and vomiting which extended over several days. The relevance of this could be discounted here as the response only became manifest after ingesting many draft beers combined with the repeated inhalation of various hybrid strains of combusted marijuana. I had dutifully examined the nuances of nausea along with its physiologic implications, visiting the University Medical School library to do so. I enameled myself with the knowledge of vestibular physiology, inner ear anatomy and the various vomiting centers of the brain-stem; this proved to have a protective effect. I could, without qualm, assure Eddie, were he to press me for further details of my history, that I had complete control over my vestibulo-ocular reflex. I could tell him I had done my homework, and then some.

"No, none whatsoever," I said, shaking my head and grinning.

Eddie grinned back at me, and we shared a good chuckle.

"Like I said, I have to ask everyone this. We had a few people go through the classroom training then get out there and find....they have a problem. We really can't afford to hire anyone who gets seasick."

Continuing to chuckle, I wiped a whimsical tear from the outer canthus of my right eye while simultaneously shaking my head in collusion with this astute personnel manager.

"Oh no, I don't have a problem with that, but I can see though...how there could be problems with some."

My profound motion sickness proclivities of the past would not affect my ability to function aboard a ship in the present. I had found my mythological dream job; to have it compromised if not nullified by a tendency to become motion sick would be unfair beyond what was reasonable to expect from life. As I had been subject to a disproportionate amount of unfairness since my arrival in the Crescent City, I could put this unlikely possibility safely out of my mind.

So there would be no misunderstanding regarding my intention, orientation, and commitment, I explained to Eddie, "I vow to have no mistress other than the sea." I allowed myself to cock the left eyebrow at the severest of angles and insist,

"I require the sea as others need food to eat or water to drink."

I stopped speaking. A low-pitched laugh vibrated the entire seat of my chair while propagating upward through my buttocks and base of my scrotum. Clearly visible out the open doorway, pressing herself against the receptionist's counter, like a Dallas Cowboy linebacker blitzing the Green Bay quarterback, stood Evelyn Razer. The personnel room, along with the entire I.P.P. complex, became subject to an extreme torque. I gripped my chair and lurched to one side as Captain Kirk had done on numerous occasions, traveling at warp speed while making the necessary turns to outmaneuver Klingon destroyers.

Mrs. Razer wore bright red lipstick and a scarf barely containing her vast expanse of hair. Blood pooled in my lower extremities, decreasing circulation to central organ systems. I forced myself to look away, scooting my chair so Mrs. Razer would no longer be visible. I pretended to sneeze and in doing so, covered my face with both hands. Within moments my mouth felt as if I had just emerged from a week in the Sahara without water. Eddie handed me a Kleenex, arose and closed the door. He poured me another glass of water and placed it into my hands.

"Evelyn Razer, as I think you already know, serves as our company accountant."

Eddie examined me carefully as I drank. Weakened considerably, I supported the glass with both hands, gulping and slurping, thankful to have remained conscious. Eddie picked a piece of lint off his sleeve and let it fall to the floor. I gasped, "Thank you," and handed him my empty glass which he filled instantly and handed back. I continued to hydrate as Mrs. Razer's deep laughter drilled through the thickness of our door like a large bore auger.

Both Eddie and I turned to regard his flimsy wall, the sole barrier separating us from the lobby space in which Evelyn Razer stood. I had no doubt Eddie, like me, sensed her to be the equivalent of a neutron star spinning at its characteristic seven hundred and sixteen times per second while pulsing highly penetrable x-ray emissions outward, agitating not merely I.P.P. and its employees but the entire Jefferson Highway industrial complex.

Mrs. Razer had undoubtedly discussed my interview at the Lafayette with the personnel manager at great length. Based upon that discussion, Eddie likely had scotch taped my name to the inside of his desk drawer as a storekeeper scotch taped stolen credit card numbers or names of check forgers on the side of his cash register. Eddie knew that I was prone to fainting spells and had offered me a glass of water on my arrival in the supposition I would become vertiginous during my interview, slip from the personnel office chair and lapse into unconsciousness as I had at the Lafayette. Only Mrs. Razer and precisely she, the Teutonic vixen of hotel-dom, could have alerted Eddie to that possibility, undoubtedly laughing long and lustily as she did; informing him that my lips would desiccate before his very eyes. And perhaps they had counted on that happening, and that Eddie had even looked forward to it; he had wanted very much to see all this transpire for himself. Who else would be interested in witnessing anomalous interviewing phenomena but the Bronzed Blow Dried Eddie, personnel manager for I.P.P., who otherwise conducted mundane interviews day in day out, week after week after week?

Despite my suspicion of collusion, Eddie had proved himself to be in possession of considerable psychological acumen. I would welcome him as my own psychiatrist were I to require one, which I didn't. He made me feel at ease. I had an urge to tell Eddie everything, the whole truth, to reveal to him my deepest fears; namely, that I could barely admit to myself that I, Rodney Pepper, was not only markedly introspective by nature but could well be highly susceptible to seasickness. Moreover, I would become seasick at the mere suggestion of becoming seasick. As if reading my thoughts, Sigmund Eddie then confessed something remarkable:

"I was one of those trainees, Rodney. That's why I'm in personnel. At one time I wanted to work offshore, just like you. But after the first week on that training boat, I told them, 'get me off this fucking thing.'" Eddie chuckled. I chuckled too. His speech, admirably laced with profanity, candidly unveiled himself and his shortcomings.

"I was vomiting over the side from the minute I got up to the minute I climbed back into my rack. Couldn't take it. It was a turning point in my life. Why someone would purposefully subject themselves to that, I asked myself. Yeah, I wanted to be an overseas operator, but I couldn't physically do the work. So why would I lie about who I was? A person who goes ahead and chooses a life course knowing it would make them sick must be some super freak."

I wanted to give Eddie a hug and tell him everything would be ok. Eddie had come to terms with his demons, accepted his lot and embodied the self-actualized man.

"I know exactly what you mean," I said, feigning self-actualization myself. I pointed at Eddie.

"You're one of the few," Eddie chuckled. "We live for the good times, right?"

"Oh, and how!" I chuckled as well

"We just want to be comfortable, not uncomfortable. So again, no problem with sea sickness? I'd hate to see you end up like me out there or be embarking on a life of misery."

"Oh no. All I want to do, Eddie, is to live for the good times," I insisted, deciding against telling Eddie the truth. Telling the truth would be too difficult. There was too much explaining to do.

"Good. Just had to get that out of the way. I always ask the question twice. Some people are embarrassed to tell me the truth on the first go around. It's psychology."

"Oh no, that's one thing I would not lie about," I told him emphatically and shook my head. "Who wants to live a life of lies?"

I knew full well that I had also not checked the box on skin conditions, even though I had developed severe eczematous eruptions in the past, usually when subjected to life stressors. Had I checked that box, I would have been obligated to jot a short note in the margin qualifying these rashes manifested more frequently on hips and upper thighs, while only occasionally appearing on the hands. In fact, I had checked no boxes on the company health form, implying that I remained in perfect health. I handed the form back to Eddie, which he slid into a Manila envelope, placed that envelope into a folder, made a single tick mark on a clipboard and informed me that training would begin the following Monday.

"Congratulations, you are now a navigator trainee, Rodney Pepper."

As I had once overheard a Business Major remark at University, *I had nailed the interview.*

In riding the Kenner Local back to the Carrollton stop, I gazed unabashedly around me, meeting glances, winking liberally, neither taking offense nor giving any, all in keeping with my new status as navigator trainee.

A young woman who had run for the bus just before the Huey Long sat across the aisle from me and recrossed her legs periodically. With each crossing and recrossing, my eyes were pulled, as if gripped by tongs, to focus upon and gather light from her extremely thick ankles.

I removed my pocket notebook and transcribed - *as if gripped by tongs* - diagonally across a blank page.

The girl self-consciously picked at an adorable imaginary blemish and peered at me shyly. I slid the notebook deep into my breast pocket and had difficulty uncoupling my eyes from her ankles, thick as Doric columns. I redirected my gaze upon her face which carried a familiarity difficult to pinpoint. Her chest and upper body were unusually developed however and provoked uncertain undulations within my viscera. As it happened, both she and I disembarked from the Kenner local and simultaneously boarded the streetcar. Our embarking and disembarking gave rise to a sense of mechanical reassurance.

Noting that the throw switch over the streetcar conductor's head had been labeled using the large stenciled lettering ON/OFF, I took out my notebook and with confident strokes of the pen observed:

There was simplicity in the two contacts of the switch, the on and the off. The device resided in the domain of action, facilitating the passage of high current. The street car either had power or it didn't.

I felt myself to be part of the whole, to be integrated, at once trainee, navigator and notebook keeper. In this, I felt lonely and added,

Is there anyone in this city, anyone at all, who would be true, who might recognize the me of me?

After this transcription, I spied the same girl with her unusually thick ankles, who had once again sat across the aisle from me. I maintained my pen in hand and notebook in the open orientation: While the set of psychoanalytic analogies and substitutions included notebook and pen, this girl was most likely not aware of the fundamental transferability of pen to penis and notebook to vagina.

As I glanced, she glanced. . . in my direction.

At once navigator and trainee, I returned her glances without flinching. And in my unflinching state, I became emboldened to further glance at her and she, in turn, at me. We glanced back and forth as if we were two mechanically coupled servo mechanisms. The girl remained innocent while I, the navigator, remained worldly. I carelessly went about penning observations:

So timid, so inexperienced, lips ripening to the point of rupture. Yet, she was rather broad shouldered and tautly thick ankled, in a disarmingly charming way.

I had a thing for this girl and pocketed my notebook hurriedly lest my flamboyant yet virile notebook keeping be observed and misunderstood as a form of namby-pamby voyeurism which it was *not.*

The street car slowed to a stop before Napoleon Avenue. The girl arose, passed me a final look then disembarked, her thick ankles drawing me upward as they simultaneously sucked all the air out of the streetcar through its open door. Compelled to arise, I twisted around the center pole once, dragging my toe then propelling forward as I had never propelled forward before, past the driver, past the ON/OFF switch, finding myself standing on the ground beside the tracks before realizing that I had even moved.

I had been transformed into an ancient warrior sporting a bronze muscle cuirass and elaborately adorned helmet from the apex of which protruded a red feather no less than two feet in length. The steel greave on my left leg and copper armbands, wound in the form of serpents, spoke of menacing prowess and combat know-how. No material covered my buttocks except for a single strap of leather flung between cheeks to join an iron codpiece bulging out to several times the actual girth of my member.

"This girl is a paragon of innocence," I whispered and felt the natural obligation to thrust myself upon her as would a despicably erect forest stag. I heard a woman exclaim *Oh look he's going after her* as she peered out the window of the streetcar. I winked and called out in the baritone voice of the Roman Centurion:

"HABE ME EXCUSATUM!"

Having learned a smattering of Latin in secondary school, my alter ego found it appropriate to utilize this knowledge to it full extent. Yet the phrase went unheeded as the girl disappeared behind the rear of the streetcar. I sprinted to the spot I had last seen her and raised my hand to forehead, scanning the streets.

"Ahh, of course," I breathed. The girl was bounding gracefully across St. Charles. I had no idea what I wanted to say or do but with hands on hips, I announced,

"MIHI NOMEN EST DE RODENEIA!"

The girl did not stop. She glanced over her shoulder an instant before entering a large drug store at the intersection. Simultaneous to the glance, she pushed her rump upward into the air as a doe might in smelling the pheromones of the fornicating forest buck-cum-Roman-Centurion. I strode across St. Charles and as well entered the store, swinging my shoulders back and forth, a more than mildly irritated Victor Mature. She innocently fingered a bauble in the middle of one aisle before catching sight of me then scurried away. I strode up one row and down the next, dragging a virtual steel Phallus, which produced its own phantasmal *clank, clank, clanking.*

"Excuse me," I called out, in English, so as to be understood, and arose onto tiptoes. She turned up another aisle; I changed directions and headed her off at stationary, concerned, were I to become more aggressive, that she might swoon. Being a navigator trainee, I could not predict what I might do next, what course my unconscious assertions might take. Perhaps, I thought, an aggressive baritone aria might suffice, and sang:

"Deh, vieni alla finestra, o mio tesoro. . ."

Thankfully, there was no further need for song as we nearly collided at the stool softener section. She drew in a frightened breath, as expected and I set about mollifying her.

"Please. I'm sorry. I don't wish to bother you. I just. . .You're so pretty that I just had to get off that street car."

She said nothing, turned and walked away. I followed.

"I'd like to get your phone number then I won't bother you. I probably won't even call you to tell you the truth. What's your name?"

"Rhone," she said.

"What?"

She stopped, stamped her foot and repeated, "Rhone!" Her stamp threw me off guard, but only slightly. She had become more impetuous than frightened.

"Dare I ask how old you are?"

"Fifteen," she said.

Legally too young, This was wrong. Dead wrong. I regarded her thick ankles, however, and fumbled for words.

"I just got out of the. . .well." I couldn't decide which lie to tell her first. "I'm twenty." Of course, I was twenty-two.

"That shouldn't matter," she said flatly, stepped closer, looking down the aisle then over my shoulder. She took a ball point pen from its hook and removed the wrapper. She lifted a notebook off the shelf, wrote her name on one of its pages, tore that off and handed it over. She put both notebook and pen in her pocket, turned and walked out of the store.

In being so anxious, Rhone had been unaware she had inadvertently shoplifted.

"I'm a navigator," I called out after her and stood at the end of the aisle for a few minutes looking at the piece of paper with her number written on it. I walked up to the counter and said, "A friend of mine took a notebook and pen, and I was going to pay for it. She had to leave. I'd also like one of those packs of...." I paused, scanning the brands. I didn't see Chesterfields. I said, "Kents."

Kents sounded like a bland, no-nonsense cigarette. I recall my father had smoked them. I took a matchbook as well.

Once outside the store, I tore open the Kents with my teeth, lit one and staggered backward, once again the smoke stinging my eyes. I persisted in the smoking of the Kent however and swaggered toward the downtown area. I relived, again and again, my heroic leap from the streetcar and recalled the phrase of the observing passenger: *Oh look, he's going after her.*

"That shouldn't matter," I repeated Rhone's words aloud, recalling how she had trembled.

I considered the vague robotic aspects of our encounter regarding my actions and hers and the influence of her ankles. The sudden impetus to disembark the streetcar implied an unseen controlling entity with its own agenda applying hidden leavers and pulleys. Granted that my actions were rash and spontaneous, this robotic aspect was disconcerting. I quickly reassured myself that all was as it seemed, dismissing the thought I had been manipulated and busied my mind envisioning Rhone's trembling hand laying upon the home telephone while holding her other hand over mouth like a Japanese schoolgirl anticipating even the remotest possibility of a call from me.

I would go to a bar, have several drinks then consider calling Rhone some more. I would imagine her sitting beside the phone, imagine her waiting with trembling hand over her mouth.

I chose the Flamingo on St. Charles where I had overheard a heavily tattooed woman call a man a bitch in front of several parked motorcycles, a markedly intriguing advertisement. In seating myself at the bar, I noted everybody had placed their cigarette packs directly in front of them. I removed my Kents and placed them on the counter directly in front of me. The other bar patrons squinted and inhaled, so I squinted and inhaled. Thrilled to be simultaneously in possession of a new profession, a new girlfriend and a new pack of Kents, I ordered several rum and cokes in succession. Halfway through my fifth drink, a forearm appeared adjacent to mine, a forearm tattooed with that same amalgam of absentmindedly scrawled circles, crosses and stars belonging to the wretched tormentor living under my boarding house roof.

"I'm looking for work," he stated.

"What about the Lafayette?" I shot back. He reached upward and rubbed the material of my Big Yank work shirt collar between his fingers and asked.

"What kind of work do you do now?"

"I work offshore."

"Offshore? That's what I do."

Having become worldly in a short period, I knew he had spoken much too quickly. The man was trying to bamboozle someone who had repeatedly been bamboozled and therefore savvy to all manner of bamboozling. And in any case, I was the one who worked offshore not him.

"What company do you work for?" he asked.

"I.P.P," I said, grimaced and tightened my shoulders. Not only had I had answered too quickly but had volunteered accurate information to a nefarious scourge, inviting calamity.

"I.P.P. I heard of them. Are they hiring?"

I hesitated and mumbled, "Yes, I think so."

"What kind of work is it?"

"Boats."

The tattooed terror stared straight ahead and fidgeted. He asked quietly, "Would there be any problem hiring someone with a prison record?"

I had read books by and about convicts and had been waiting for this opportunity.

"Oh, you did a bit? I don't know how much your pedigree counts, Jim. It's a stomp down trickhouse. One of the mackmen is a juicy stone mama." I was alluding to Mrs. Razer. "You have to deal with this stallion, baby, you understand, and the choked up Johnnies she keeps in her stable. Everybody in the company is busting their nuts for this foxy lady, Jack. Go on down and find a stump to fit your rump and come on with them. Now I'm no ditty-bopper, and I went down and didn't come up no zeros neither. I don't know what their policy is about the ice box...uh." I asked him, "So, you been to Soledad or where?"

"Angola. Buy me a drink," the monster said. He picked up my Kents and placed one in his mouth before putting the entire pack into his pocket. I winced. He was bullying again, asserting his prison dominance. I should not have used prison lingo. He might have interpreted that as the rustling of a Norton Anthology Elizabethan hoop skirt.

"I can't," I lied. "I don't have any money. I drank it up. I'd like my pack of Kents back, please."

The ex-con nodded, took my glass and asked, "Can I have a sip of yours then?" Without waiting for a reply, he drained my glass. If this had occurred in Angola, I would have been obligated to spear one of his eyeballs with my fork and eat it in front of the guards and other inmates to save face. I glanced at the open door of the bar and was certain that I could outrun him. After having five rum and cokes in succession, I felt an odd sense of relaxed kinship and said. "Angola? That country club?"

His upper lip pulled back revealing his gums and rather large teeth.

"Easy Butch," I said, sensing no danger.

"What did you call me?" He turned and faced me, puffing out his chest.

"Didn't you ever watch the Little Rascals?" The rum and cokes allowed my mind to remain placid as a cool mountain lake.

He blinked once. "Yeah, I watched the Rascals at Industrial School in California." He tilted my glass and chewed an ice cube. I went on.

"You remember the one when Butch was chasing Alfalfa, and they wound up…"

"Dancing with the ballerinas," he said, completing my thought precisely.

"I lied," I admitted. "I have four dollars left. Two more," I told the bartender then turned to him and confessed, "I sometimes feel like Alfalfa. And I bet you assume the persona of the Butch archetype, the juvenile offender."

He jabbed a finger into my chest. "And you're getting your personality yanked by the rooster sitting on top of the box you're hiding in?"

"Exactly," I said. The usurping demon referred to Alfalfa's trademark, a long strand of hair which stood straight up from the top of his head, referred to as his personality. The tattooed ex-con finished his rum and coke in one gulp. "I need a reference. I need your name." He reached over and took a pen from behind the bar. "Ready."

I hesitated then said, "Johnny Jupes." I had given the Butch archetype the name of my childhood alter ego.

He stared at me for a longer moment then asked, "How do you spell that?"

"Johnny Jupes. J-U-P-E-S. Jupes." I observed the menace carefully transcribe the fictional name onto his napkin. He did so with his tongue protruding slightly. He folded the napkin and placed it with his pen into a pocket. He turned and walked out of the bar.

My Alfalfa had put one over on his Butch. In imagining the marauder telling Eddie that Johnny Jupes had recommended him for the job, I laughed; the first time I had laughed since arriving in New Orleans. My laughed crescendoed, and not un-demonically so.

15
NEIGHBORS ON THE RIGHT, LEFT AND CENTER

Remaining in my room until the first day of work, I emerged only to purchase several cans of tuna and place Uncle Gambi's overdue book, Complex Analysis, into the library drop box. I had not bothered to examine its contents and wished only to rid myself of memories and influences associated with that horrid night. The deceased himself had advised the book held no relevance while implying that the second, unfound volume, authored by one Renee Thom, apparently contained the relevant equation. I had no inclination to seek it out.

While the nightmare of the previous week had softened in impact, a new preoccupation replaced it: Aberrant noises and voices arose periodically behind the two locked doors of my bed chamber.

Sitting at the foot of my bed, I stared first at the door to my immediate right then had to swivel and examine the portal behind my back board. Beyond the former, a full-time tenant resided. Beyond the latter, I was not altogether sure; its emanations were not of a conventional sort and inferred human presence only in the self-limited flurries of late night typing superimposed upon a background of evangelical radio programming.

Whenever my neighbor on the right entered the room, vibrations of his heavy footfalls rattled my bed's headboard. Each day, I recorded the time this occurred on a chart created specifically for this purpose within my pocket notebook. His evening arrival was heralded by the emission of a loud flatulent growing from the low throaty growl of a wolf to the high-pitched whine of a puppy; a puppy then abruptly strangled. A flurry of footfalls followed his entrance flatus; the window sash was shoved upward.

Following one evening's arrival, as a result of a particularly aggressive window thrusting, the mirror over my own bureau bounced free of its hook and crashed to the floor. The occupant on the right grunted. Just as I could hear each and every movement in his room, as well as every gaseous emission, so could he most likely hear my local investigations and eructations. Every night, upon his return, I closed my notebook, turned off the light and remained still. I did not wish to disturb or modify the behavior of this neighbor on the right, only to monitor him closely as he carried out his leisure activities. His belief, perhaps, of not being monitored, allowed him to mutter comfortably or unleash a torrent of flatulence if moved to do so. Each evening, in silence, I cracked open my pocket notebook and made precise, clandestine note of it all.

My neighbor on the right went to work at seven in the morning, returning by eight in the evening; his window slid up, his TV turned on and channels changed *snap-snap-snap* until he settled upon a favorite comedy. Shoes thumped, one after another, onto the floor followed by socks pulled off, each with a grunt. In the ensuing hours, laughter arose periodically from the TV audience and my neighbor himself.

The stillness of my observational state superimposed itself upon the daily torpor within the Prytania Avenue rooming house; I sweated profusely while monitoring my neighbor's activities.

Brother, you shouldn't have done that, he would say or, look at him.

One morning I ran into this neighbor on the right as he ascended the stairs to the bathroom. He smiled with a cordiality that seemed to suggest that he well realized I inhabited the adjacent room and that I was behaving appropriately. I speculated whether this neighbor on the right had also been enthusiastically listening through our partitioning door and had amused himself by monitoring my opening of tuna fish cans or my creeping from the bed to the window. His smile was not imposing or indicative of a desire to make further contact. I appreciated this; we subsequently had no formal interaction.

The face of my neighbor on the right had been thoughtful and suggested an intellectual bent, which was puzzling. Did the man's long working hours necessitate him continuously watching TV as opposed to reading? Or did he read while watching television and embody the squelched Nietzschean Overman, trapped within an urban environment not of his choosing? The neighbor watched TV for two sometimes three consecutive hours before falling asleep. I noted that on Sunday, he awoke and watched TV the whole day. Pills rattling in plastic containers accompanied the TV canned laughter. The exuberance of my notebook keeping in monitoring his activity duplicated that of a naturalist living within a Borneo tree house amidst a rare species of orangutan.

My toiletries entailed leaving my room, locking the door behind me, descending a flight of wooden stairs, walking in front of several doorways, ascending another set of stairs, entering the communal bathroom and locking that door; I then set about performing routines of showering, brushing teeth and washing face. The sink, toilet and shower stall, puddled, dabbed and smeared with urine and sprinkled with all manner of sedimented filth and roach entrails made bathing an exercise necessitating exquisite coordination. To put on underwear and trousers after showering while standing on one foot, that one foot balanced on a flip flop without allowing one's pant leg to brush against the mildewed shower curtain, urine ridden toilet seat or diarrhea smeared floor, required an austere temperament and no small measure of physical dexterity. In performing these rituals, I came to understand the landlady's disgust with the state of her lavatory and peered out my window into the alley, regarding each tenant in an attempt to glean from a facial expression which might be most likely to have left their feces at the bottom of the commode basin without flushing.

Of the tenant in the room behind my headboard, there arose sounds to suggest human occupancy on only one occasion. On that evening, a Pentecostal revival service played loudly on this occupant's radio, the broadcast preacher speaking, shouting and mumbling continually while his congregation hurled out Amens, Praise Jesuses, and Halleluiahs.

Jes-uss! The radio preacher shouted.

Gee-zusss! The behind the headboard occupant repeated.

The radio congregation sounded to be a collective beast, groaning and clamoring as if having been sprayed en masse with cold water.

Hummmuh hummmuh hummuh Church-Uh. Gotuh go tuh church-uh!!! Haaa! The radio minister screamed.

Church-uh…hummuh hummuh hummuh…Church-uh the occupant behind the headboard repeated.

The radio congregation made a coordinated noise to suggest a finger had been thrust up each and every one of their rectums simultaneously.

Bee-ell-zee-bubb-uh the radio preacher intoned.

Beeee-ell-zee-bubbb-uhhh! the occupant repeated with his own embellishment.

The radio congregation went wild and began repeating the many variations of Jesus's name: Hay-suse! Oh, Jesus! Sweet Hay-suse!

Haysuse! The occupant behind the headboard had answered in the midst of this frenzy.

Taken up in this pandemonium, I called out Haysuse!

There followed a cessation of all sound. The neighbor's radio was switched off. I remained deathly still in hearing no movement within the chamber behind my headboard. Not a single muscle fiber contracted for an entire hour.

After that, I made the acquaintance of another neighbor, my neighbor on the left. His door was located directly adjacent to my own at the top of the outer staircase and stayed open. He could be found sitting on his bed every single time I passed and always looked up to regard me. Once, I glanced inward and nodded. With this, he stood, came to the door and said, "I like to party." My neighbor on the left gripped my hands in a soul shake. "I come all the way from Mobile." I nodded. He said, "Let's blow one right this minute," then leaned over the railing of our staircase and said, "Party, yeah…parteee." I longed to return to my lodging at that point but sat on my neighbor's bed as we watched TV and listened to his tape deck. His room was smaller than mine. I speculated it to be one of the fifty-dollar kind. The room was constructed tightly around his double bed and a TV stand. He asked me often, "You don't have any tapes, do you?" He added, "I'm getting tired of mine."

Having just returned from reviewing Kierkegaard's notebooks, I had been making lists of his capitalized words for my notebook's capitalized word section. The resultant paucity of speech may have caused my neighbor on the left to become uneasy as he arose from his bed every few minutes to walk outside and call down, "Hey, anybody around?" Eventually, somebody appeared in the alley. "Hey, we're partying up here. What's going on?"

"Nothing." I recognized the voice of the teenage female I had encountered in the kitchen my first day.

"We're partying up here," my neighbor on the left offered.

"Listening to some rock and roll?" she asked.

"Yeah, if you want to party with us, come up. The door's open." The fellow returned and nudged me. "There's some nookie downstairs I be wanting to fuck." He laughed, and I laughed. He whipped his hair to and fro then adjusted the volume of his tape deck upward to the point where the speaker rattled. He continued to whip his hair to and fro for many minutes. I contributed nothing to the partying. I could have picked up the tempo on imaginary bass or imaginary high hat cymbal but remained motionless. At some point, my neighbor on the left stopped his slashing motions and walked out the door.

"I've got to check out this piece of nookie downstairs. You can stay if you want."

I was happy our session had concluded, went straight to the restroom, urinated and decided to call Rhone, the apple of my eye. As I was descending the stairway, a voice called from behind:

"Johnny Jupes!"

I turned and recognized Butch, my rum and coke guzzling underminer! His hair was wet and partly neatly to one side, his face scrubbed. He wore a button-down shirt, the sleeves buttoned at the wrists, concealing his haphazard array of tattoos. I tried to hurry down the steps, but the fellow followed me closely and asked, "What was all that shrieking I heard in your room a few nights ago? You had a girl in there?"

"What?" I pretended not to hear. He was referring to the night of Uncle

Gambi's woolding when the roaches had scattered, and I had inadvertently cried out.

"You got that door behind your headboard, right? I got a door behind my headboard too."

The Butch archetype had been that pretend minister who practiced aloud his praise Jesuses along with the Holy Roller radio congregation!

"I'm writing sermons, so I need my quiet. Evelyn Razer gave me a typewriter. She thinks I've got potential. She told me that. So I'm busy and don't need to listen to you shrieking at all hours of the night. I already have to listen to you turning the pages of your books. The scratch of your pen keeps me awake. I hear you open up your cans of tuna fish and crinkle your wrappers. I know you're not asleep because your springs don't creak. You just lay there. You don't even whack off."

This remark confirmed that as I listened, others were listening. I trusted however that unlike the Lafayette, these others had not been moving in and out of my chamber as I slept, taking anatomic measurements and other liberties while rifling through my delicate reading materials. The Butch archetype lowered his voice to a whisper,

"I don't pay rent, and I know everything that goes on in this place. I'm servicing the landlady."

As we approached the landlady's window, he ducked down and waddled underneath so as not to be seen. He opened the gate then turned and said, "Donna put me upstairs after her old man got back."

He implied to have been previously sleeping in the bed with the sheets in violent disarray.

"This is his white shirt and black pants. Tomorrow morning I go over to I.P.P. and hire on. Tonight I got a date with a fifteen-year-old, praise God."

Rhone, the apple of my eye, was fifteen. The coincidence provoked a momentary quivering of my lower lip.

"Do I look like a television evangelist?" He opened his arms and turned around. He had buttoned the white shirt up to the collar. "Look how much taller I am than you," he said.

I returned to my room and sat.

I did not like that this man lived in a room behind the door at the head of my bed nor did I appreciate that he applied for the same jobs as I; nor did I care for his volleys of high-speed typing on a typewriter purportedly given to him by Evelyn Razer. I refused to believe this: Notebook keeping and everything extending from its purview endured as my vocation and my vocation alone. I had not invited him nor anyone else to intrude upon me. I did not wish to be eavesdropped upon nor did I wish to remain perfectly still in my room at all times of the day and night. And if I had a mind to utilize the personal pronoun I at the start of every single sentence I wrote, I would do so.

At that moment, loud banging commenced from behind the headboard, as if my very thoughts were overheard: My inner and outer worlds circled one another like two boxers vying for a title belt in the center ring.

Knott

16
LUNCH BREAK AT THE PLANTATION

I chose Michael Foucault's dissertation Madness and Civilization as a companion for my first training day. Having recently reread it for the third time with little comprehension, I wished to write a review. Fortunate enough to find a seat on the Kenner Local, I straight away removed my pocket notebook, created a book review module and proceeded with my entry:

In rereading Foucault's histories, I passed from an easy wandering existence of undifferentiated experience through the gates of his asylum in Vichy territory well before the time of my own birth. I was greeted at the door by Dr. Gaston Ferdière who right away assigned me a diagnosis. Immensely reassuring, his diagnosis explained so much about what 'made me tick.' The facility itself also lent considerable comfort, as if I had been set down within an enormous restroom stall, its door securely fastened. I could scribble on the walls to my heart's content while relocating the Loose Stool of Unreason away from the prying eyes and sniffing nostrils of society. No. I followed the motion of my author's fragrant scented 'censer of phrasing' down torchlit passageways. All was well, until he, for no reason other than malice that I could tell, shackled me within a dungeon of connectivity and seared the letter M deep into the flesh of my forehead with his flamboyant branding iron forged in some secret wordery by smithies bearing University degrees and wearing nothing but black leather chaps. Indelibly labeled as Mad with a capital M, I came to be trapped, unclothed, within the walls of not only the said author's narrative but within my own, no possession other than his obscure text. As I remained interned within this asylum, receiving treatments for my affliction, I came to comprehend the simple joy of tossing the slim volume up in the air while striking various provocative poses after each and every catch. I feigned intelligence through a great display of lip pursing and eyebrow cocking. If caught I was lashed mercilessly and appropriately, and made to confess, again and again, that I was ill; and not only ill, but MENTALLY ILL.

Pleased with the insight my book review offered, I took its success to be a sign that my luck had changed.

Each trainee smoked a different brand of cigarette. The trainee who chose the seat to my left smoked Winstons but more significantly, carried with him a book, the only trainee other than myself to do so. He placed the book face down on our table. I was unable to judge by its shape whether it fell into the classic or philosophic genre. Before leaving University, I had fully anticipated encountering individuals of like interests with whom I would be challenged through debate, discourse, and literary recitation. During one of the breaks, this trainee turned the mysterious book over.

Following my hire at International Petroleum Positioning, I forgot all notions of my matelotage with its concurrent responsibilities of a Lafitte Lieutenant. I focused all of my attention on the romance of radio position navigation and revisiting in memory the trembling Rhone with her tree trunk ankles and upturned iron buttocks. The contents of Uncle Gambi's box had proved uninspiring while the vision of his horrible woolded visage had all but faded. The murder and mayhem of the previous week seemed unlikely to have taken place and until that moment, I had almost discarded it as fiction. Viewing the book's title was equivalent to being awakened by a prodding cutlass while standing on a thin wooden plank, hands tied behind my back with hammerhead sharks circling below. The title was Search for Pirate Treasure!

Each trainee had had to introduce himself. I learned this treasure hunting classmate was Kerry Kelly from Austin, Texas. I observed him carefully from that moment on and recruited appropriate extraocular muscles to expedite lateral gaze excursions. With thinning hair and cowboy boots, he continually shifted in his chair and wiped his forehead. He arose periodically, paced to the window, gazed out onto Jefferson Highway and lit Winston after Winston.

Except for Kerry Kelly and myself, all the trainees had been recently discharged from the Navy and had grown up, not in the University milieu, but on destroyers and aircraft carriers sailing the world's oceans. I wished that I too had grown up on the high seas and decided that I would pretend I had. No one would know the difference. In the course of our first lunch break, one of the trainees inquired, "Where did you work before this?"

"I worked for the railroad," I said without hesitation, hitching up my belt and grinding my teeth together. I did not wish to be considered an outsider because of my notebook keeping propensity. I had read Soldier of Fortune

Magazine while riding the Trailways bus to New Orleans and nearly offered myself as a mercenary recently returned from the Congo. At the precise moment of inquiry, however, I envisioned a haggard man wearing an engineer's cap clutching a dented lunchbox within which was only a pint of rye whiskey. The trainees gathered about me, nodded and appeared satisfied. Kerry Kelly, however, carried an odd expression on his face.

I wondered if he suspected that I was fibbing.

Once again I had been thrust into a classroom milieu and understood the subtleties, behavioral or otherwise, of this environs. Two instructors, who mostly remained in a small office adjacent to our training room, conducted the schooling. The facility was situated in a separate building, part of a small strip mall of office space next to the main I.P.P. corporate building.

Grady Ranger, the chief instructor, sat at a desk with his back to a large window. He maintained an upright posture and went running during his lunch hour. He shook his head whimsically at the negligence of the trainees, in particular, our inability to answer questions in class. While in the office, he conscientiously examined and shuffled papers about his desk with a posture remaining far straighter than that of Earl Short, the other instructor. Grady Ranger held a familiarity for me, a resemblance I could not put my finger on. Grady Ranger would occasionally stare at me for no obvious reason, and in passing seemed to be on the verge of speaking but did not do so.

The instructors changed the location of their desks several times during the first two days. Earl Short, for instance, moved his desk outside their office, sat in the alcove for several hours then moved it back. The two instructors did not appear to interact much with one another nor did they appear to be particularly busy. Earl Short had confirmed this in a remark he made initially: "The I.P.P. instructors had the easiest fucking job in the goddamn world, and the bloody trainees had the second easiest."

Grady Ranger had interjected, "I wouldn't go so far as to say that, Earl."

At this retort, Earl Short had taken a drag from his cigarette and squinted in Grady Ranger's direction then blew smoke upward.

With both instructors seated, their room became cramped to the extent that a trainee was forced to stand in the doorway to conduct business. Earl Short placed his desk facing the wall and away from Grady Ranger. He worked out of the main building but had been reassigned to help Grady Ranger six months previously as there had been more trainees hired than expected. Earl Short had taught three training cycles yet had not been reassigned back to the main building, where he preferred working. He did not appear to get along with Grady Ranger and gave the impression he was uneasy at times.

Earl Short's brow remained knit to the extent that it always appeared as if he were on the verge of tears. At any given moment, Earl Short was either inhaling deeply from, or in the process of stubbing out a cigarette. Earl Short stubbed out his cigarettes in a slow, methodical manner, twisting them while simultaneously subjecting the ashtray to a severe scrutiny. Earl Short squinted while both inhaling and stubbing. He did not shake his head nor raise his voice nor smile as did Grady Ranger.

Grady Ranger did not smoke and could frequently be observed arranging a set of wooden blocks on his desk. A similar set of wooden blocks was present on Earl Short's desk although the latter never touched them. Grady Ranger explained operating procedure while Earl Short discussed the breakdown of navigation circuitry and hardware repair.

On the first day of training, Earl Short had announced that after our first three weeks of classroom instruction, the trainees would travel to Pascagoula, Mississippi and board a training boat which would then simulate the operation of a seismic vessel at sea. I smiled and nodded along with the others, recalling my omission on the company health form regarding an uncertain tendency to become sea sick. I remained unconcerned; this training cruise was several weeks away. I could comfortably put out of my mind the possibility of becoming incapacitatingly seasick.

Earl Short rendered his description of the navigation equipment's electronics in a flat monotone. He explained: "You aren't expected to know fuck all about the individual goddamn components but should fucking well be able to swap the bloody circuit boards *out*." The trainees smoked cigarettes and wrote down everything Earl Short said on yellow legal pads the school had provided.

On the third day of our first week, Grady Ranger posed a question to the class concerning contour maps. I had noted that the trainees derived a certain amount of satisfaction in competing for correct answers whenever questions were posed. At University I did not answer questions in the classroom setting. In fact, I did not participate at all. Likewise, I had remained silent within the I.P.P. classroom. On this occasion, as no one in the class responded, Grady Ranger moved directly in front of me and leaned forward, placing his hands on his knees.

"You were a physics major. You should know this. Come on, Rodney. I know you can do it."

I ground my jaw and pressed my toes deep into the front of my sneakers: My fellow trainees would now know that I was not a railroad man. With head bowed, I responded: "Differences in lane-count between two adjacent pairs of stations are plotted on a map as a family of hyperbolas."

Several trainees leaned forward and stared along the length of the table. Others exhaled cigarette smoke silently toward the ceiling. Grady Ranger seemed satisfied by my response. Earl Short stood against the wall and squinted. He inhaled deeply and blew smoke through his nostrils. Louis, who had been in the Navy for six years before his hire at I.P.P., whispered urgently. "Physics? You did physics, man. Shit, physics. That's...hard shit, man."

At our break, as the trainees were walking out to the parking lot, Earl Short stepped out of his office, grabbed my arm and called Louis over. He pushed his bottom lip outward to allow smoke to ascend, ever so slowly, enveloping himself in a haze. Within the cloud, he spoke. "Louis, why don't you take Rodney out and show him where the lunch wagon is. Show him the old plantation."

"Do you think that is particularly wise?" Grady Ranger asked, placing both of his hands flat on his desk and glaring at Earl Short. I looked first at Earl Short then at Grady Ranger. Earl Short did not respond. Louis regarded Earl Short and pulled on his mustache.

Earl Short said, "Seems that Grady is looking out for you, Rodney. But no, Grady, I thought it would be fun for Rodney to ride in Louis' pick up. Take his mind off of all that goddamn physics."

Grady Ranger coughed, rearranged his work blocks and said, "Physics is exactly what his mind should stay focused on. And if he wants to think about physics, Earl, then he should be allowed to think about physics. If anything he needs to be challenged and focus more. I would like to take him under my wing. Rodney can help me with the navigation problem sets. Now just remember men, we're starting back at one pm sharp."

Earl Short regarded Grady Ranger and squinted. I followed Louis outside.

Earl Short was correct in his assumption I would be pleased to ride in a pickup truck. I had never ridden in one. As soon as I climbed into the cab, however, to steer the subject away from physics, of which I had a great interest in but very little understanding, I asked Louis, "What was the Navy like?"

Louis regarded me out of the corner of his eye, shook his head and chuckled. He reached up and pulled at his mustache, not speaking for many moments then said,

"You can get a woman to stay with you the whole night in the Philippines for a bottle of Prell, man."

I tried to recall the appearance of Prell.

"It's sad, man. Prell." Louis pulled at his mustache then asked, "Do you smoke, man?"

Louis was asking me if I smoked marijuana. I poised, hands aloft, Flamenco jacket tightly corseted, castanet's lightly clicking, black boots rapidly stamping, then tossed my head back and flung my jacket against the floor.

"Yes, I smoke."

From a nearby luncheonette, we bought two fried oyster Po boy sandwiches and two Budweiser longneck beers. We drove to River Road and parked the truck in front of an old plantation house which Louis explained had burned to the ground several years previously. Only the foundation, its stone walls, and several charred beams remained. As soon as he stopped the truck, Louis removed a large marijuana cigarette from his pocket and lit it.

Louis and I were smoking marijuana and drinking beer on our lunch hour. I realized that upon return to our training facility, I would be considerably impaired and subject to Grady Ranger's technical inquiries and wholesome scrutiny.

Despite these concerns, I inhaled deeply from Louis' marijuana cigarette, wishing only to escape the painful stigma of my University physics background. After what seemed like several minutes, I thought: *I am so stoned I have ceased to function as a trainee. Grady Ranger will undoubtedly return from his lunch hour jog just as Louis and myself will return from our lunch hour pot smoking and beer drinking. Grady Ranger consumed no alcohol. Grady Ranger studied calculus during the evening at the University of New Orleans working toward a degree. Grady Ranger was an authority figure. Grady Ranger was on the side of good and everything descent in the world. My mother would describe Grady Ranger as wholesome. I couldn't possibly let Grady Ranger know that I was stoned, couldn't possibly let him know, man. I would have to play it cool, man, real cool when Grady Ranger was around.*

I fell easily into the vernacular of Louis, utilizing his favorite vocative - man - at every opportunity within my impaired internal mind speak.

As we stood amidst the ruins of the Plantation, surrounded by willow trees, Louis pulled on his mustache and asked, "Have you seen that Lady Mrs. Razer yet, man?"

His question freaked me out, man, as I had not only seen Mrs. Razer but had been interviewed by her. The question freaked me out because I had associated Mrs. Razer, the Lafitte descendant, man, with her very large gravitationally dense bosoms which precipitated desiccation of my oral mucosa. I did not share these thoughts with Louis but was glad, man, real glad, man, that Mrs. Razer's bosoms were very very heavy. And that woman, Mrs. Razer, had hinted that we might even have a drink together, man.

I asked Louis, "Man, who is she, man? Who is that woman, man?" I couldn't help but ask Louis more questions regarding Evelyn Razer. "I have seen her all over the place, man, and I mean all over the place. Just who is she, man, Mrs. Razer? She was in payroll during my orientation then I saw her outside the door in personnel and Eddie, the personnel man said, 'That's Evelyn Razer, man,' just like that. Everybody knows her, man. Everybody sees her coming from a mile away. This woman, man, this woman I've seen all over the place. Just who is she? That's what I would like to know."

I continued to enjoy the prefacing and suffixing of my sentences with - man - however I could not inform Louis of my Lafayette interview, of my matelotage or, of my tragically woolded Uncle Gambi, even though I wanted to blabber about everything that had happened to me from the time when I was born until now, man.

Louis picked at his mustache and asked, "You don't know who that lady is, man?"

I counter-asked, "No, man, who is she?"

"I don't believe you don't know who she is, man. You don't know who she is, man?"

"No, who is Mrs. Razer, man? Who is she, man? Who is that woman?" I fired questions as if I were Gene Hackman playing Popeye Doyle in the French Connection.

"She's head of payroll, man. You have to tell her where you want your paychecks sent." Louis tugged on his mustache.

Louis and I stood in the midst of an old Plantation, which had burned down some time ago. The sun was warm.

Louis said, "She's got the biggest knockers of any woman I've ever seen in my life, man."

Louis had created a Hegelian Synthesis along the dialectical pathway to Godhead with Evelyn Razer's right breast the thesis, her left, the antithesis.

Louis continued to tug on his mustache as we walked slowly back toward the truck. "I've never seen knockers like hers, even in Australia, man," he said.

"Were you in Australia, man?" I asked.

He nodded. "In the Navy, man, and the women there are beautiful. These tall blond women. All these big beautiful women. I'm telling you. They're all like that. These big blonds, man."

"They got big boobs. Big boobs?" Words were being shoveled out of my mouth as if stoking coal on the Wabash Cannonball. My eyes closed for a moment then opened.

"Yeah, man, some of these big blond Australian women have the biggest knockers in the world, man."

These were sweeping generalizations, but I believed them all to be true. They would have to be tested in a rigorous manner, subjected to anthropologic scrutiny using any testicle means necessary.

I whinnied aloud: I had meant to think using-any-statistical-means-necessary but said instead, you know what.

"I'm high as a kite," I murmured.

"I lived off the base for a year, man, in Australia, lived with one of them, man. Six feet tall. They love Americans, man. Australia. Fucking Australia, man." Louis shook his head for a full minute as he recalled the tall blonds of Australia. I maintained my respectful silence and titled inwardly: Johnny Jupes and the Golden Knockers of Australia.

Louis said, "In Australia, they call a fag a *pooftah*. He regarded me and pulled his mustache. I became unsettled by this and shifted in my seat: *Walt Whitman wore a rakish hat. He was a pooftah. Marcel Proust lay down in bed when he wrote books. He was a pooftah. Michel Foucault wrote Madness and Civilization. He was a pooftah. Henry James wrote a novel in which he created a character named Caspar Goodwood, an American, who I had been instructed at University represented a walking penis. Caspar Goodwood wanted to have heterosexual relations with another character, Isabel Archer, who was also an American. Yet Henry James was a pooftah. Herman Melville wrote Moby Dick, one of my favorite novels. He was a pooftah. Sartre wrote a very long book about Jean Genet, who wrote his novel Our Lady of the Flowers on rolls of brown paper while in prison. As soon as he finished the first draft, a guard burned the paper, so he wrote it again on brown paper. Jean Genet was a pooftah. At University fraternity parties, I had noted that to assume a comfortable place within the American fraternal society, one had to, at some point, make fun of pooftahs, thereby implying that one wasn't one whether one was or wasn't. I wondered how many pooftahs themselves made fun of other pooftahs as if to imply that they weren't pooftahs when they actually were? The word pooftah, having repeated it ten times in succession, ceased to have any meaning for me.*

'Ayz uh pooftah.' Louis imitated an Australian accent. He chuckled and shook his head. "A pooftah, man…"

I weakly repeated, "Ayz uh pooftah" and gazed out the passenger window of Louis' truck. *Johnny Jupes and the Squawking Birds of Byzantium*, I titled and swallowed, realizing that Grady Ranger was most likely transcribing the afternoon's assignment onto the blackboard at that moment. As we drove back, Louis recounted how he would become stoned on ships while in the Navy.

"Whitey, man. Whitey used to…"

Louis went on about Whitey. I didn't listen for a few moments as waves of stoned-out- of-my-mind-ness washed over me in addition to concerns of how-am-I-going-to-function-as-a-Trainee. I pulled on my own imaginary mustache.

"The officers, man. I know for a fact that some of them were cool, but you couldn't hang out with them. No way. Even the Chief, man. If he caught you…" The truck bounced along the road, and I stopped listening to him again for a few more minutes.

"….I know he smelled something that time, man. I know he did…" I felt the warmth of the sun and again began listening to Louis' tales of getting high aboard naval vessels.

"….then in walks this ensign, man, a fucking ensign, man, and we had just lit up this big bone, man…."

I envisioned the surprise of the electronic techs as the ensign walked in. Louis described how the electronic technicians had pulled out numerous electronic modules before smoking and had their equipment laying on the floor to lend the appearance of diligence. Louis described the ensign standing in front of the sailors and making small talk. He described how the sailors had choked and coughed then finally exhaled after the ensign left.

"The ensign knew we were holding our breath, man but he just kept right on talking. He was secretly busting our chops, man."

After a time Louis seemed to speak to himself, enwrapped in memories of his Navy days.

"We used to climb the mast, man. We were ETs, man. I was checked out on all the weapon control systems. I worked on the Sparrow, man. It was a Mark twenty-five or, no," he stopped talking and pulled at his mustache then spoke more hurriedly, "a ninety-two, man. No, I take that back, it was a twenty-five. . .aw, I forget, man, but I worked on all of it." Louis pulled at his mustache. "You know what SATCOMM is, man?"

"No," I said.

"OE 82? You don't know what SATCOMM is?"

I wanted to join the Navy after the lunch break. I wanted to know what SATCOMM was. SATCOMM sounded like a ham radio abbreviation.

"One day Whitey and me, man - this was when the ship was in port - one day we went up onto the mast, right behind the SPS antenna, man. The big long range antenna. I mean they weren't using it, it wasn't turned on or anything like that. I mean you would have to be on my ship to know what I'm talking about, man. We were sitting right behind the forty. There were all kinds of antennas, man, up there. We had the mark thirty-five, for the five-inch gun. That's radar. We had SPS ten. We had SLQs, man. You've heard of them, haven't you?"

I couldn't move my mouth.

"They're countermeasure systems, man. We had the thirty-two. We had gunfire control up there. We had Radome, man. I was checked out on all of it. The Chief knew it cold, but I worked on it. Whitey and I went up there, I still remember it, tripping our brains out, man. We sat up there in the sun, man. We had ASROC, you know what that is, don't you?"

"No."

I felt like I didn't know anything about anything.

"I heard of it," I added feebly. Gunk had encased my lips. As we pulled into the parking lot in front of the training facility, I scratched the tops of my hands. I remained in the truck, unable to move.

"Anti-Submarine Rocket is what it stands for. It fires out of this box, man," Louis had gotten out of his truck and was speaking to me through the passenger window. I was somehow able to get out of the truck and follow Louis into the training facility.

"We had a five-inch gun on the bow. That's a thirty-eight caliber," Louis said over his shoulder as Earl Short emerged from the instructor's office. He looked at me then looked at Louis. He blew cigarette smoke out of the side of his mouth and said,

"Pepper, get your ass over to the main building. Don Canyon wants to see you." Earl Short turned and walked back into his office. Mr. Canyon, we had been informed, was the president and owner of both Canyon Fleet, a supply boat company, and International Petroleum Positioning.

"Oh shit, man, I wouldn't want to be in your shoes," Louis said, pulling on his mustache. "I bet you'd sooner try to disprove relativity theory to Einstein than talk to the CEO right now."

Louis turned and walked back into the classroom.

17
DON CANYON

Within the administration lavatory, I lowered my head under the faucet, filled my mouth, rinsed and spat several times. Pushing and pulling the skin around my eyes, I threw several handfuls of water against my face and stared into the mirror.

Standing in the hallway outside Mr. Canyon's office, I heard what sounded like the whir of a blender and an unmistakable reverberating laugh. The door swung inward. There stood Evelyn Razer, tightly fitted in a gray business suit, her white cotton blouse displacing the lapels of her jacket to either side. At the instant of the door's opening, Evelyn Razer's head had been thrown back, her mouth widening to the extent that I could have placed a pack of Chesterfields within it, possibly two packs.

"Rodney," Mrs. Razer winked. "We've met of course." She had woven her hair on the back of her head into a bun, lifting it away from and exposing a thick, sinewy neck.

At that moment, I wondered if I had fallen in love with Evelyn Razer.

I found myself once again in front of a large desk, this time, made of steel, behind which a man stood drinking from a glass pitcher. His free hand, balled into a fist, was held against his hip, elbow bent at ninety degrees. The man's head tilted farther and farther back as he drank, Adam's apple jerking with each swallow. Thick froth dripped from his chin onto both shirt and trousers while splashing the papers on his desk. Mrs. Razer moved forward with a Kleenex and dabbed the drops of liquid hanging from the pitcher's lip. The man concluded his drinking with a loud *slarp* then equally as loudly exclaimed, *Ahhhhh*, after which he forcefully twisted the container back into its base sitting on the desk.

Lowering myself down onto the wooden chair placed in front of his enormous steel desk, I regarded the rim of foam around Mr. Canyon's mouth. He stood square-jawed and unflinching, a millionaire many times over. Mr. Canyon turned his attention to the stack of papers in front of him. My job application, visible on top, had been spattered by droplets from the shake.

"Do you know Yul Brynner, Pepper?" Mr. Canyon asked.

"Yes, I do," I answered.

Things seemed to proceed smoothly.

Mr. Canyon inhaled deeply, drawing up his chest. He placed both hands on his hips and swiveled his head to the right. Only his eyes turned to regard me. Maintaining this posture, he asked, "Of course, you know who I am, don't you?"

I wished to say, 'yes, of course, I know who you are, Mr. Canyon,' but I couldn't. Who Mr. Canyon was pretending to be was not obvious.

"I'm not sure but…"

I needed more time to think.

"Of course, you do," Mrs. Razer playfully slapped me on the shoulder. "Of course, you do," she repeated with more urgency, now motioning with her eyes to again look toward Mr. Canyon. Through my study of literary criticism at University, I had become versed on subtleties of psychological inference and subtextual body language within a novel's narrative which was synonymous with the narrative of life.

In being stoned-out-of-my-mind, I was not only having difficulty analyzing Evelyn Razer's prompts but having difficulty analyzing everything taking place within the office.

She said, "Don't think, Rodney, respond. Don taught me that. He wants you to respond to his pose with what you know. Feel it." Evelyn Razer was trying to help, but I was beyond help.

"I think I feel it. I think I do. I think I can." I said.

"If you don't know something, don't goddamn say that you do." Mr.

Canyon spoke with annoyance. "I'm Ramses, King of the goddamn Pharaohs. This should have been obvious to you. This is my goddamn Ramses pose. Should have been an easy one, Pepper."

"I see what you mean. No, I see what you mean. I should have gotten that one." I pointed at Mr. Canyon even though his pose made no sense to me. He was not smiling. Mrs. Razer's expression had also become less cordial.

"That's how this company makes me feel, Pepper, like a goddamn Yul Brynner playing Ramses. We understand your family is connected to the entertainment industry so I assumed you would immediately know that pose," Mr. Canyon regarded Evelyn Razer with unconcealed disappointment.

Mr. Canyon was not pleased. His Ramses, King of the Pharaoh's pose was obvious now but why could it have not been obvious a moment ago? Why-not-then-why-not-then-why-not-then?

My body was becoming itchy. I scratched my elbow. My lips felt like tree bark.

"I.P.P. is not contracted by the goddamn entertainment industry. The fact of the matter is, we serve the Offshore Oil Industry. I am like your surrogate father, Pepper. I have essentially taken the place of your biological father. From now on, say what you mean or don't say anything." I nodded. My eyes darted to the wide expanse of Evelyn Razer's lips then jerked downward to her fulminating breasts, careened over to Mr. Canyon's bicep then back to Mrs. Razer's thighs framed within her charcoal gray slacks. As I could not find a neutral ocular orientation, my gaze ultimately arrived at the base of Don Canyon's milkshake blender, awash with foam.

"And let's get something straight right off the goddamn bat, Pepper. There is only one reason that I would fire an employee at I.P.P. and that's for goddamn treasure hunting. This is something Eddie won't tell you but I will. I've never fired an alcoholic, but I've fired treasure hunters."

An urgent fullness arose within my rectum and my itching intensified. I scratched both elbows simultaneously with opposite hands, panting, mouth open.

In having been matelotaged and inexorably beholden to recover and care for the treasure of Vincent Gambi, I could not reconcile that treasure hunting was forbidden within the company, my company. This rule created a considerable conflict.

"I don't care if there are a million dollars in treasure sunken in Barataria Bay; while you are working for this company, you will not pursue it. If I discover treasure maps on a trainee's person, I will confiscate them, and they will become the property of I.P.P."

How much information had Evelyn Razer shared with Don Canyon regarding my ancestry? And was it legal to confiscate treasure maps from a trainee?

"The riches would not be technically yours, Pepper." Don Canyon hesitated then said, "You know the Lafitte's were great patriots. If it were not for them…"

"Andrew Jackson would have been defeated at Chalmette," Evelyn Razer completed his sentence. They both nodded. Evelyn Razer gave me the thumbs up sign. I swallowed hard.

At their whim, Don Canyon and Evelyn Razer, my surrogate parents, jerked on a wooden control bar to which my arms and legs had been attached by strings.

"That's right; all those goddamn riches would be the property of. . ."

Mr. Canyon stumbled with his words. Evelyn Razer nodded encouragingly, prompting him as she had prompted me:

"Just say it, Say it out loud, Don. Let it out."

"The riches would become the property of I.P.P. making it my goddamn property and, of course," He looked at Evelyn Razer, "the property of the goddamn Lafitte family as they had a. . . ."

"Treaty," Evelyn Razer completed his sentence again then grabbed Don Canyon's bicep and squeezed.

Don Canyon turned. "You know our President Reagan strikes numerous poses."

Evelyn Razer said, "Oh does he ever, just like you do, Don."

Don Canyon had made an observation concerning Presidential posturing as if it naturally followed from his previous statement. I could not glean how it did. I remained confused yet continued to nod enthusiastically, wishing that the C.E.O. remain pleased. Pleasing the C.E.O. seemed like the natural thing to do and want to do. Yet it sounded as though Mr. Canyon, my surrogate father, inferred that my treasure would become the property of I.P.P., and this was not in my best interest. The treasure was my treasure. I looked from Evelyn Razer to Don Canyon, grateful that my inner dialogue was being carried out in silence which wasn't always the case.

"What we're talking about is Patriotism, Pepper," Don Canyon said. "Our goddamn Commander-in-Chief would know exactly what I'm up to. And what an audience he has. The entire country. You know he loves it."

"Loves it," Evelyn Razer seconded.

"Look at me, Evelyn. Just look at me. I am going to allow myself to imagine a goddamn audience looking at me."

"I'm looking, Don," Evelyn Razer said.

"Pepper, you look at me too," Mr. Canyon ordered.

I nearly said I'm looking too, Don but Mr. Canyon had already continued.

"Evelyn knows that I don't like to keep anything on my goddamn desk other than what I need. I need the goddamn telephone, a goddamn blender, a goddamn pad of paper and a goddamn pen. I also need my work blocks or my metal bar." Evelyn Razer pointed to each object on his desk after Don Canyon named it.

"And I don't take goddamn vacations. You get a taste of vacation and that taste changes your perspective. I prefer not to know what vacation tastes like. I chew on work if I need to chew on something. It's leathery, like an overcooked steak, but it's edible. If I have nothing to do, I go to my steel bar." He picked up the steel bar on his desk and strained for a moment, trying to bend it. He put it down. "Or my work blocks." He picked up an assembly of wood cut in various shapes which fit together to form the word work. He rearranged the blocks. "I've had these goddamn wooden work modules issued to each of my employees stationed at their goddamn desks."

Mr. Canyon sounded somewhat disjointed and required periodic refocusing by Evelyn Razer. I wondered if Don Canyon was also stoned out of his mind, as was I.

"But why would he be?" I inadvertently asked myself out loud and winced.

My inner bathroom stall door had been kicked open revealing that my tidy whities had been pulled down around my ankles, genitals exposed, a log of dook hanging from my rectum.

"Don't mumble, Pepper. If you have something to say, say it. I'm not afraid to say just about goddamn anything," Don Canyon said.

"No, you're not, Don." Evelyn Razer looked at me, nodding, and said, "He's not, Rodney."

Mr. Canyon picked up his phone and dialed a number. With his ear to the receiver, he told me, "You must know by now, Pepper. This company retains deep ties to the Navy."

"The Navy contracted Don's company for all their submarine trials in the sixties," Mrs. Razer said. "God, I was just a baby then." She paused, fanning herself. "I think I'm having hot flashes just thinking about all that."

Mrs. Razer slowly removed her jacket. She tossed it over one shoulder and smoothed the front of her blouse. Her nipples displaced its material like two high tension ceramic standoff insulators.

The Jodrell Bank array of radio telescopes remained silent in the magnitude of their design, poised and listening for extra-terrestrial intelligence. I was being heated from within as if hovering adjacent to a quasar, directly exposed to intense bursts of microwave frequency electromagnetic radiation.

Don Canyon handed me the phone. I flinched in hearing the man's voice.

A naval recruiter had pestered me week in, week out for my entire University tenure. Ironically I had been stoned-out-of-my-mind as I was presently one Saturday night in my freshman year. I had filled out a small postage prepaid card displaying the photographic likeness of a nuclear submarine, strongly inclined at that moment to make a career in the nuclear submarine service of the United States Navy. I had torn the card from its perforations on the announcement board, checked several boxes and placed it into a mailbox. I had then forgotten about it entirely until Chief Petty Officer Deckley called a week later. He called every week after that and never stopped calling.

"I'm no longer in recruitment, Pepper," Chief Petty Officer Deckley began.

I could not conceive what this was about and did not wish to be involved in any further conspiracies. Functioning as a trainee proved more than enough. Maintaining one's composure at work while stoned-out-of-my-mind, for instance, filled my plate completely.

"I am Naval Intelligence now, Pepper. I will be contacting you shortly. That is all." A dial tone ensued. I handed the phone back to Don Canyon, feeling as though I had just eaten a baby's diaper.

"Treasure hunting is more serious than you realize," Don Canyon said. "This is why I asked you to come see us, today. It's not to worry you, but. . ."

"Oh no," I interrupted. "This is A LOT more serious," I said. I knew what Don Canyon wanted to hear. I could not help but bellow certain words. "I've learned my lesson, AND HOW!"

"I'm glad to hear you say that, Pepper and I'll tell you why. The man killed under the expressway the other day had been an employee here. I hired him about twenty years ago as a goddamn engineer. It turns out he had lied. I caught him using company equipment for personal gain and treasure hunting. Had a gambling problem too and I suspected him of homosexuality. Smart man, Evelyn, I believe you knew the man's friend?"

"Yes, I did." She answered, winked at me then stroked the side of her neck with one finger.

"They were both homosexuals from what I understand. But I will say, he designed some of our base station antennas which we still use. He designed our dual parabolic dish relay station."

I understood the brassiere-like device on the back of Gambi's mathematical documents was a prototype sketch of a dual parabolic dish antenna and constituted I.P.P. company property. Having it in my possession placed me within the apex of the maelstrom, with the eye of this storm blinking rapidly.

Don Canyon pressed his index finger down upon my milkshake-stained application. "Focus, Pepper. You have a goddamn degree in Physics. Thinking a couple of years of gaining real experience in the field?" He looked at Mrs. Razer then picked up a rubber ring from his desk. He squeezed it. "Thinking of management?" Mrs. Razer placed her hand on my shoulder then motioned toward Mr. Canyon.

The correct answer was clearly yes. I said, "Yes!"

"Good," Evelyn Razer said, nodded to Don Canyon and pointed at me. "And going for a masters? That's what Grady Ranger is doing. You know Grady is doing that, don't you Don?"

Mr. Canyon appeared irritated at this mention of Grady Ranger. "I know Grady is going for a masters. I am well aware that Grady is going for a masters, Evelyn."

Mrs. Razer gave me an exaggerated nod and pointed in my direction. "Don, Rodney, and Grady have such a lot in common, don't you think. Grady being a double major. Then there's Rodney and his physics."

"What does that have to do with running a company?" Don Canyon mumbled. Evelyn Razer stared at Don Canyon with her hands on her hips. He ran his hand through his hair and looked out the window. Evelyn Razer spoke again.

"I think they would make a good team, part of the I.P.P. family, like brothers, but I'm thinking more than brothers, Don. Once Grady gets back to his natural self, it will all be fine. I just can't help being the little matchmaker, Don, you know that. Oh, I have plans for you, Rodney

Pepper. God, I'm so excited." She clapped her hands together.

Evelyn Razer had plans for Grady Ranger and myself. I was excited to be part of the I.PP. family structure although was unsure why she mentioned Grady Ranger and myself as she did. I was unsure whether I wished to be Grady Ranger's brother let alone being more than a brother.

Clearly and irrevocably on the I.P.P. career tract, the immense pressure to emulate Grady Ranger had become daunting although the notion of re-enrolling at University to pursue my masters degree was like a pacifier dipped in warm milk and honey. Treasure hunting must be stricken from my new company advancement agenda. The commitment to management would necessitate discretion with whom I shared the *me of me*. I would be forced to bottle my voracious penchant for Egon Schiele's masturbatory self-portraits, for instance, as well as his splendid renderings of salacious women. I would maintain a state of political camouflage, make ambiguous statements at I.P.P. cocktail parties all the while nodding and agreeing with every one of Don Canyon's principles, laughing uproariously at his jokes while attempting to emulate each and every one of his poses, giving my personal opinions voice only when the lavatory stall door had been closed and tightly latched.

I glanced in turn at Mr. Canyon and Mrs. Razer, my corporate Father and Mother. "Dad" had been talking about what it meant to be human.

". . . As humans, we have our flaws and holes in our armor. Treasure hunting is a good example of a goddamn hole. We plug that kind of hole at I.P.P. We act out in other ways if we have to. We choose different goddamn vices. Alcohol, for instance. Alcohol I one hundred per cent support. I have developed my personal outlets, as you can see." I nodded enthusiastically. "I have become familiar with a great many famous movie moments and have developed poses which arise out of these timeless events" Mr. Canyon was revealing a great deal about how he thought and how he lived.

"Don is just so good at them, Rodney," Evelyn Razer added. "He's shown me some that take my breath away. I literally can't breathe after he's done. We all have our evil hidden little pleasures, don't we, Rodney? It could be anything from typing one's novel at high speeds to, oh, I don't know, perhaps overhearing someone typing their novel at high speeds." She slapped me playfully. My heart accelerated.

I was receiving unconscious input from my autonomic nervous system. With her mention of high-speed typing, I could not be sure that incestuous boundaries had not been crossed between surrogate mother and surrogate son. A prohibitive quivering commenced at the base of my perineum.

"It's cold in here. Just look at me, boys," Evelyn Razer announced. Her nipples rose against the material of her cotton blouse like freshly baked blueberry muffins taken out of the oven. "And I'm not doing anything, am I Don?"

Both Don Canyon and I stopped speaking. I gripped the armrests of my chair as the room tilted. Evelyn Razer replaced her jacket, smoothing its material by stroking downward with both hands.

Mr. Canyon pointed at Evelyn Razer. "Pepper, you know she does all my accounting as well as manages several hotels. She can handle just about anything I throw at her. She won't say it but I will. She hates being stereotyped. Resents it. Men don't see past her goddamn breasts. They identify who she is by those two big goddamn heavy breasts of hers. I've known Evelyn since she developed her secondary sex characteristics. Imagine what that was like for a thirteen-year-old to suddenly have stripper's breasts and what effect that had on the men around her."

Evelyn Razer fluffed her hair and said, "Thank you, Don."

Don Canyon brought both fists upward directly in front of his face with forearms touching. He slowly lowered his arms to chest level and said, "Evelyn, I know you know this one. I'll let you tell Pepper."

"Rodney, that's what Yul Brynner did when the Red Sea swallowed up his army and Charlton Heston got away. Brynner saw his army being swallowed up and he struck that pose exactly like Don is doing it."

Mr. Canyon performed the movement again. "Then he lashed his horse and rode away." Don Canyon picked up the phone. "I'll tell Earl Short to give you a basic electronics test."

The interview concluded, and I returned to the school building with every intention of building a future at I.P.P. I stopped in the parking lot, took out my notebook and wrote:

I will become wholesome and true blue even if it's contrary to my nature or even if it kills me.

As soon as I entered the training facility, Earl Short handed me a basic electronics test and turned his back. Afterward, I was called into the instructor's office. Earl inhaled deeply from a cigarette, squinted, and pressed that cigarette hard into his already overflowing ashtray.

"Despite your goddamn Physics background you don't know fuck-all, am I right?"

Earl Short continued grinding out his cigarette, twisting and turning it slowly. I stood in the doorway.

"You basically failed the fucker, Pepper," he said.

Grady Ranger turned and spoke, "Yes, Rodney, you could have done better. I know you could have. And next time, you will. But the important thing was you made a good impression on Mr. Canyon. You pleased him; I could tell from the tone of his voice. He asked that you be given one of the company cars to use. A car could come in handy if you need to go to the library or the bookstore. These trips would be permitted as they pertain to your education. I will show you where you can find the bookstores."

Earl Short swiveled around in his chair, leaned back with hands behind his head and interrupted Grady Ranger. "Kerry Kelly lives downtown. Maybe you two can ride together." Grady Ranger stared at Earl Short for a moment, aligned a stack of papers, moved a pencil from one side of his desk to the other. He took up Don Canyon's work blocks and began manipulating them.

"I think he meant for Rodney to have the car for his own use."

Earl Short said nothing to this and called Kerry Kelly into the office. He spoke to him deliberately, as he had with Louis, "Why don't you take Pepper under your wing and keep him out of trouble." Earl Short continued to ground out his cigarette as he squinted at Kerry Kelly. Kerry Kelly looked from Earl Short to me and nodded.

Grady Ranger looked at me oddly, seemingly arrested in mid thought while cradling the work blocks in his outstretched palm.

"I guess that's about it, Pepper," Earl Short said. "We're pretty busy in here." Earl Short tossed his lighter open and regarded the flame. He closed the lighter then opened it and looked at the flame again. He closed his lighter and placed another cigarette in his mouth. He then opened his lighter and moved his head forward.

18
NAVAL INTELLIGENCE

Kerry Kelly took the keys out of my hand and said, "I'll drive."

Grady Ranger had intended for me to use the company car until Earl Short had opened his big mouth.

I would have very much wished to make side trips bookstores and libraries as Grady Ranger had suggested, and make these trips all by myself. This would now not be the case. Earl Short told Kerry Kelly to take me under his wing just as Earl Short had asked Louis to show me the plantation. Show him the plantation was synonymous with getting the trainee stoned out of his mind then, sending him over to the CEO's office to be interrogated and exposed as a treasure hunter. I gazed out the company car window at the passing industrial landscapes along Jefferson Highway. Could I trust anyone? Could I trust even myself?

The marijuana smoking had addled my brain, and I had the munchies. Normally, as I had learned at University, symptoms could be controlled to an extent by consuming a quart of strawberry ice cream sitting in front of the common room television set. I became imbued with a craving to transcribe internal dialogue. With trembling hand, I removed my pocket notebook and placed it onto the top of my right thigh. I uncapped my pen. Kerry Kelly looked over and asked,

"What's that?"

I slid both notebook and pen back into my shirt pocket. "Just a notebook," I said. Kerry Kelly nodded.

Since arriving at the Tulane Avenue Trailways Depot, I had become not only paranoid but immensely paranoid; my pocket notebook, a Conduit of Truth and my trusted colleague, had repeatedly been ravaged. The calling of notebook keeper had proved more precarious than I could ever have anticipated.

As we drove toward the center of the city, Kerry Kelly told me he had worked for the Southern Pacific Railroad as a truck driver and described an accident during which he had sustained an injury. He pointed to the upper portion of his face and informed me he had been waiting for his lawyer to call him regarding a settlement. I felt the need to interrupt.

"I'm sorry. Did something," I hesitated, "Poke you in the eye?"

"A sharp piece of metal cut right into my eyeball, cat."

The high amplitude myoclonic tic arising because of this conjured image caused my neck flexors to contract violently; my forehead slammed downward against the dashboard. The glove compartment opened. Kelly Kelly asked,

"Are you ok, cat?"

"Yes, fine. That was psychological."

My profoundly intimate and complex relationship with the ocular uncanny was too complex to elucidate at the moment. I hardly understood it myself.

Kerry Kelly went on, "He's settled for five thousand, I think. But I had to mail my entire paycheck to Houston for my alimony. I can give you whatever as soon as we get our checks. Sixty would do it." He spoke softly. "And I'm going to need the car for the night. I'll leave it in front of your place."

Even though Kerry Kelly lay his treasure hunting book conspicuously between our seats, I did not inquire of its implication. I could tolerate no further implications of any sort.

After borrowing the sixty dollars, Kerry Kelly dropped me off in front of my Prytania Avenue rooming house. I had decided in our ride back from work to sequester myself within my rank bedroom and remain deathly still for the remainder of the day. After opening the door to my room, however, I stood still, looking at the debris.

I could well have been an archivist having discovered an overlooked box of world war two photographs gathering dust in a museum closet and be looking upon the remains of Dresden, in February 1945, as it had never been seen before.

My clothing, shook from the duffle bag without a morsel of sensitivity, comprised a tossed salad with underwear and t-shirts laying in several of the mildewed and vomit-ridden puddles. Books lay strewn about the room in sickening postures. I knelt, as any parent would, hands hovering over yet not touching, my Norton Anthology of English Literature. She lay violated, unspeakably so, in the middle of the bed, pages bent back at inhuman angles, her face slashed with a haphazard graffiti. The bandit had depicted a small penis protruding from the middle of Queen Victoria's hoop skirt; a bubble emerged from her mouth inside of which was scrawled: *I'm Rodney Pepper*. My hands trembled, expressing the inexpressible. Likewise, Camus' *Myth of Sisyphus* rest on the pillow, cover shattered by an infantile cartoon imagining Sisyphus pushing a large rock uphill with his own three-foot long phallus.

"God fucking dammit to goddamn shit fucking hell!" I bellowed.

Thankfully, Uncle Gambi's box had fallen onto the floor, slid underneath the bed and lay unmolested. In searching through the horribly scattered materials, it became evident that one of my pocket notebooks containing important expositions and elucidations concerning Camus, Nietzsche, Proust, and Kierkegaard, had gone missing. Other volumes were unaccounted for. I took two stairs at a time down to the alley and knocked frantically upon the landlady's door. She stared at me through the screen as I explained, in a single breath, that someone had burglarized my room and that my books had been scattered higgledy-piggledy. She remained silent, her face gradually hardening as her eyes narrowed. She asked,

"Well let me ask you this. Do you know anything about what happened to my commode? Someone stopped it up."

"No. I'm a navigator. I've been at work."

"I found pages of somebody's notebook and some paperbacks in there." Her voice began to rise. "And I know you read."

She disappeared behind the screen, continuing to speak with increasing volume. "A friend of mine said you read more than anyone in this place.

Do you know anything about this?" She returned and pressed a sodden page of printed text against the screen. I leaned forward and recognized the page to be an extraction from Dostoevsky's The Double, my most cherished of the cherished.

"Someone's been wiping themselves with pages from this book. I buy toilet paper, mister." The timber of her voice approached that of a near shriek. "I'm not saying you did it. I just want to say that there's a roll of toilet paper in the dispenser, so nobody has to wipe themselves with books. Books plug up my commode, see."

I was deeply offended.

"I would never wipe myself with books. Never!"

"I'm not saying you did it."

"I always use TP."

"I know you've read this book. And I can tell when somebody is lying."

The landlady possessed the acumen of a bloodhound; and in the presence of her inordinately wide pelvis upon which her bathrobe hung, I admitted, "Yes, I read that book. It's a classic, but I didn't wipe with it. I couldn't wipe with it. You don't understand the relationship I have with my books. Even if I were in the woods, I would not use that book. I would try and find leaves."

"And another thing," she continued. "I'm going to find whoever's been writing in a notebook here. On one page covered in dook, someone had written that I speak in what they called the black idiom but that I'm white. Someone's been writing about me speaking in an idiom, and I'm going to find out who that person is."

I mashed my toes deeply into the base of my shoes. My observation had been intended to remain private; this woman's vernacular of speech was of no interest to anyone but myself, a patois incongruous with her appearance as was that of the Irish Channel resident who I recognized could easily be mistaken for one born and bred in Brooklyn. The landlady needed to appreciate that careless speculation comprised the way of the notebook; I was reluctant to explain this as she continued to be markedly agitated.

Returning to my room, I sat on the edge of the bed to contemplate all that had transpired, overwhelmed by its entirety. I could only draw comfort through imagining the innocent thick-ankled Rhone fleeing from me down a drugstore aisle.

Yet even that reverie was compromised; for as soon as Rhone's figura stepped out onto my mind's darkened playhouse stage, it became enveloped in shadow, a monstrous special effect subsuming her entirely, recognizable as the striking silhouette of the far more worldly actress, Evelyn Razer, the capable I.P.P. accountant, for whom I was fighting the forbidden urge to LOVE!

"Oh dear GOD!" I shouted and pulled at my clothing, struggling for air. The cadence of her typewriter welled within my brain like summer crickets, throttling me like a snare drum tattoo played with bayonets instead of drumsticks.

My reverie was interrupted by the arrival of my neighbor on my right with the usual rattling of keys and jarred opening of his door. From this neighbor's chamber, his usual slow *blappity blap* of a flatulent was truncated by an uncharacteristic *gasp*. I sat down on my scavenged mattress and listened. Something out of the ordinary was transpiring. My neighbor on the right's door had opened, the occupant had pooted yet there had been no opening of his window, nor thumping of shoes nor grunts which accompanied his tugging-off-of-socks. Hollow plastic containers fell onto his floor one after another. The springs of my neighbors' bed creaked once, followed by quiet sobbing. His TV remained silent.

Another disturbance arose just outside; my neighbor on the left was speaking aloud: "They got my tape player."

I opened my door. My neighbor of the left had been addressing somebody in the alley then turned to me. "They got all my tapes and my TV." He stood with his arms by his sides, staring into his room. "Looks like I'll be heading home."

Both my neighbors on the right and left had been burglarized, likely by the same thief who had ransacked all the rooms. After shutting the door, I gathered my belongings, closing my books and smoothing my tidy whities, returning all to my duffle bag.

After only five minutes, I flinched as there came a loud rap upon my chamber door. I open it. My heart increased dramatically in rate: a United States Naval Officer stood just outside my room with a briefcase handcuffed to one of his wrists.

Having watched innumerable television shows depicting drill sergeants inspecting soldiers lined up alongside bunk ends within boot camp barracks, I knew that regulation shoes were inevitably polished, and pant leg creases folded like paper. No lint was ever apparent. Ties were aligned as if by plumb line. This Naval Officer was not anticipating inspection. Possessed of a prominent and disconcerting bulbous red nose, he stood before me licking his lips in a curious manner. His hands shook markedly. The sheen of his left sided regulation patent leather shoe was marred by what appeared to be a dollop of mustard. His protruding abdomen strained the brass buttons of his regulation shirt. The collar looked to have been dipped in ketchup.

My chest tightened as the name tag clearly read: Chief Petty Officer Deckley. I opened the door fully. He stepped into the room and spoke.

"You have been on our radar for some time now, Pepper. And what I am referencing is an issue of national security which falls one rat's hair short of treason. And treason, you probably know, is why a man gets sent to Leavenworth. We have a vast intelligence gathering network and knew the instant that your room was being ransacked. I was deployed forthwith."

I wasn't sure if I followed the logic in his introduction although the idiosyncratic speech patterns convincingly replicated that of an agent representing a bona fide intelligence gathering organization.

Chief Petty Officer Deckley was undoubtedly for real. As my eleventh-grade science fair project entailed the reception of weather satellite data, I knew enough about intelligence gathering to be convinced of this.

I sat back down on the bed, my legs rubber bands. Chief Deckley continued.

"They will try you in a military court. And we don't follow the same rules, Pepper. But don't worry yet. And that's a *guarded yet*, son." He placed his Naval briefcase upon my recently ransacked bed. "This is what you call a preliminary investigation. I am what you might consider your good cop. I know you've watched a lot of TV so I know that you know what I mean by that."

"Of course," I said, feeling extremely lucky to have watched a lot of TV.

Chief Deckley snapped the locks of the briefcase open one by one then lifted its lid and removed a stack of photographs from a folder marked top secret.

The first photograph depicted me and Uncle Gambi seated at the McDonald's on Canal Street. Uncle Gambi had been leaning across the table speaking with his mouth open and clearly full of Egg McMuffin at the moment of his photographing. Orange juice dripped from his chin.

"Who is this?" Chief Deckley asked and pointed, not to Uncle Gambi, but to my own likeness.

I regarded Chief Deckley to confirm I had correctly interpreted his query. Chief Deckley remained poised regarding the photograph with the severest of expressions, index finger outstretched and directed, without ambiguity, toward my likeness. Chief Deckley was proving himself to be a savvy government interrogator: Pre-requisite to beginning his investigation, Chief Deckley obviously wished to confirm whether I knew who I was.

Hesitating, I said, "That is me, or rather, that is I." Unsure of the appropriate usage in the context of rendering such testimony to this representative of the military court system, I admitted: "I made need clarification Chief Petty Officer, as far as protocol is concerned. Don Canyon has instructed me on the imperative of precision communication. I am attempting to uphold that standard."

Chief Deckley reassured me. "What you need to do at this juncture is take a couple of Hindu cleansing breaths or what have you. You're doing just fine, son." He snapped the next photograph out, this one taken at the public library depicting the Basque and I standing in the middle of a reference aisle, the former grimacing while wearing his eye patch.

"Who is that?" Chief Deckley asked, again directing his finger toward me

"Me or rather, 'tis I, Rodney Pepper." I winced, feeling my grammatical floundering was bringing me one step closer to the Leavenworth front gate. Chief Deckley nodded, put the photographs away and asked,

"Did Mr. Gambi or the other man attempt to pass any so called documents to you?"

I wondered whether he already knew the answer. I glanced at the box just protruding under the bed.

"Yes," I answered. "I have what looks like so called equations."

Chief Deckley leaned forward. "Did you attempt to solve these so-called equations?"

"No. I have taken a course in partial differential equations but nothing beyond that."

"That's enough to get you into trouble," Chief Deckley said. "Son, don't even try to manipulate these so called equations. I don't pretend to understand what this man did. I am only acting as a liaison for the United States Government as I was acquainted with your background. They sent me because it avoids embarrassing lights and sirens. All I can say is that we have reason to believe. . ." He paused and inhaled.

I had heard the expression, *We have reason to believe,* spoken on numerous television police dramas. Officer Deckley was clearly the real McCoy. Only, he wasn't reading from any script. My skin was becoming clammy fast.

". . . that he may have derived certain equations which, when solved under certain boundary conditions..." He stopped again. "I am not allowed to comment on this case any further. My duty is to inform you that in solving or even reviewing these equations you may be putting your life and the lives of other in danger. This information has been passed on to me by top ranking naval pencil pushers in Bethesda. To be honest with you, they had to call in Japanese Scientists."

"They're good," I stated.

"Oh, they're more than good." he spoke quietly. I nodded, and Chief Deckley continued.

"As soon as we learned of Mr. Gambi's presence, I was called to the war room."

I realized that Chief Petty Officer Deckley was most assuredly in disguise here, dressed as a ruffled infantryman but undoubtedly, once within the war room at the Pentagon, would be adorned in military dress blues sporting painstakingly hand polished buttons and mirrored shoes.

"What confounded us was Mr. Gambi's portrayal of himself as some pirate ancestor of yours along with his pretense of being your uncle. We realized he was simply well read. He spent inordinate amounts of time at the library."

The rooming house had been staked out; the agents had used ear plugs and alligator clips, disassembling pipe fixtures by way of expediting the retrieval of my pocket notebook's torn and wiped-with-dook stained pages. Carefully synthesized reconstituting chemicals would have been applied, drop by drop, while they wore rubber gloves and breathing apparatus.

"He sought you out to communicate this classified information when he realized himself to be a target for assassination. If we had gotten to him first, he would have been placed in a military forensic unit. Gambi had been classified as criminally insane by Bethesda psychiatric."

The lump in my throat became immobile.

"We have reason to believe that he had communicated to you certain encoded instructions. Intelligence noted he used the code word treasure in the past to refer to materials which the director is just now starting to refer to as Weapons of Mass Destruction. You are going to be hearing that term more and more in coming years, Pepper, I'll guar-ohn-tee that. And Pepper, make no mistake, if, in the course of this interview, I so deem it necessary, the President will be sequestered at Camp David and Air Force One will be deployed."

No longer able to coordinate my pharyngeal muscles to swallow, I took shallow breaths as the Chief lowered his voice to a whisper.

"Pepper, I have been your friend and ally throughout this investigation. I was the one, if you recall, to whom you related your interest in a Nuclear Submarine career. Believe it or not, that patriotic intent was what stalled your immediate arrest and incarceration at Leavenworth."

My abdomen became distended. I felt the urgent need to expel the entire contents of my bowels because I was innocent of any wrongdoing. My participation in treasonous activities had been inadvertent and unintended.

I noted that Chief Petty Officer Deckley, envoy from the Pentagon, was sweating profusely. A yellowish hue superimposed itself upon on his regulation khaki brown shirt in and around both armpits: Axillary rings of demarcation due to the highly acidic nature of his sebaceous secretions. I assumed the Chief operated continually under highly stressful conditions, serving the intelligence-gathering branch of government.

"Were Mr. Gambi's equations to fall into the hands of a primitive technological society and solved by that society, even using numerical techniques, this could create a significant threat to freedom and democracy." Chief Deckley hesitated and ran his hands through his hair. "We request at this time all documents in your possession relating to Mr. Gambi's work in any way be handed over to the United States Government."

There had to be much more to Chief Deckley than met the eye. The United States Government had sent him as a sole envoy regarding a matter of National Security. I decided right then and there that I would cooperate yet was simultaneously faced with an ethical conflict similar to what I imagined a journalist might face in being asked to divulge an unnamed source. I had been matelotaged and imprinted with an image of a woolded man's visage just as the baby bird views the worm hanging from his mother's beak. A pirate's responsibility resided outside the scope of government.

In outwardly agreeing to contribute all the notes, I could feel both patriotic and in the government's good graces. I would ideally wish to withhold one or two of the documents, of no interest to anybody, for my private perusal and titivation, like a keepsake. Although this would not be easily accomplished under Chief Petty Officer Deckley's eagle eye.

"You can have the mathematical documents," I declared, bent forward and gathered up Uncle Gambi's box. I removed the pages of equations and handed them to Chief Petty Officer Deckley then shut the box. His smile became immense. I had pleased him and in doing so, had pleased the United States government.

"We might even consider the matter closed if these documents pan out," Deckley stated. The pressure in my rectum and lower bowel decreased. "Any additional clues he may have passed along becomes the property of the U.S. government."

Chief Petty Officer Deckley added, "And I almost called you soldier."

He snapped his briefcase closed, nodded curtly, turned and left. I swelled with pride when the door closed: I felt very much like a soldier and knew that I could pose as one with my haircut. In fact, I essentially was a soldier, in the good graces of both company and nation. Inwardly I had doubts, however, knowing myself to have resided within a veritable feeding frenzy of compounded lies and confusions. On one hand, I liked the idea of being a soldier and dying for company and nation but on the other, I liked the idea of being a pirate with the lucrative prospect of digging up a treasure chest and keeping all the doubloons for myself.

In the midst of this inner debate, an image of an innocent yet thick ankled Rhone asserted itself, goosestepping onto the tarmac of my mind's Stalinesque parade ground, dressed in frayed combat leotard and carrying a Kalashnikov. This "Rhone" would need to be interrogated. I would be forced to chain her thick ankles to two equally thick posts driven deep into the ground. She would undoubtedly yank impetuously at her restraints.

Entangled, if not enmeshed, within this fancy, barely able to see straight and sweating profusely, I stumbled into the YMCA on Lee Circle, placed several coins into the lobby pay phone and dialed Rhone's number.

19
MEIN DOPPELGANGER

"Rhone? This is Rodney Pepper. I chased after you. . ."

"I remember." Rhone's voice was deeper than I recalled.

"I wondered if you wanted to go out on a DATE?"

I inadvertently bellowed the word date.

"We going down to the Quarter?" She asked flatly.

"No. I thought we might go to AUDUBON PARK."

I had again inadvertently bellowed.

My head swam. I felt justified in my bellowing as it remained imperative, as she was fifteen, that my communication be firm regarding the planning of a safe agenda with no ifs, ands or buts. No going down to the Quarter, for instance. Rhone needed to be steered her away from those havens of villainy which were as familiar to me now as my own childhood bedroom. For it was I, Rodney Pepper, who symbolically accompanied Dionysus on his escapades, not she; I who shared ancient knowledge, not the nubile Rhone. How she had shivered in the course of my animal pursuit through the drug store. Rhone had little experience with boys, much like an awkward but thick-ankled doe.

With the phone cradled against my ear, I removed my pocket notebook and, with lips markedly pursed, sketch a Grecian Satyr, part man, part beast, ears and tail of a goat, typically found in a state of high arousal. I gazed at my rendering and allowed myself to repurse my lips, hearing the satyr's hooves clattering upon French Quarter pavement. I closed the book and returned it to my breast pocket.

Bars were out of the question. Rhone might think she wanted to go to a bar or have some notion in her head as to what all that was about but the reality was, Rhone had no conception of what all that was about. Most likely alcohol had never passed her lips nor would it ever occur to her to try it. I would have to supervise her.

Oddly, in considering myself in this supervisory role, there commenced a familiar compression of subtunical venular plexuses between the tunica albuginea and peripheral sinusoids of my penis.

"Venous outflow is being reduced," I said.

"What?" Rhone asked.

"Oh no. I was just. . ." I chuckled, having been caught off guard in the midst of an oracular utterance, in this instance concerning a physiologic process. I tried to explain: "You see, the word oracle comes from the Latin verb ōrāre meaning to speak."

Rhone let out a considerable sigh for seemingly no particular reason then asked, "OK, WHEN?"

I had to hold the receiver away from my ear and stuttered, "What about tomorrow morning?" The morning seemed like a good time of day for our date as its soft light would render the shadowy silhouette of the forest satyr easier to bear were she to catch sight of it.

"Morning?"

"Yeah, maybe we could drive out to the Lakefront or something." I added one of Kerry Kelly's "or somethings." Kerry Kelly had described the numerous restaurants overlooking Lake Pontchartrain in which you could eat oysters and crawfish all day long.

"Maybe we can eat oysters or crawfish or something," I suggested, borrowing Kerry Kelly's Texas drawl.

"I can't understand what you're saying. You're mumbling. Why are you talking like that?" Rhone sounded impatient.

I wasn't prepared for the tone of Rhone's questioning and repeated, "The Lakefront. Maybe eat oysters or…"

Rhone interrupted. "Then you need to pick me up at the entrance to Audubon Park at eleven tomorrow. I have to go. There's someone here." As she was hanging up the phone, it sounded like the wind had been knocked out of her, oddly similar to the conclusion of my phone conversation with Evelyn Razer. In Rhone's case, the sound was undoubtedly created by a profound release of tension. I imagined her staring helplessly at the phone in its cradle, vaguely touching her sinewy neck, confused by what she was feeling. Clearly, no one had arrived. I continued to chuckle and muse of the delightfully timid but thick-ankled Rhone as I strolled about the Uptown area for several hours enjoying the sensation of my vaguely tumescent penis pressing against the material of my pant leg.

"Like the mythical stag in the forest of Dean," I noted aloud. As the sun set, I realized an early bed would be prudent. "I do not wish my face to appear drawn and macabre to the easily frightened Rhone," I announced and turned back toward the rooming house.

As I reached the gate, a figure stepped from the shadows of the abandoned automobile salvage garage. "Is this yours?" Cradled in the palm of the menacing preacher's hand was my pocket notebook, an unspoken admission that this Antichrist had been the Prytania Avenue rooming house burglar. Overjoyed to see my notebook, I reached out to retrieve it.

The marauder withdrew his hand, flipped the notebook open and said, "Not so fast. I added my own story." He thumbed through my notebook's terrified pages with a disconcerting familiarity, making it clear by his manner he had read its entire contents and contributed his own addenda. He began walking and read aloud. I followed him, waiting for an opportunity to snatch the book from his hand.

'The rhino is charging! My gun is jammed!' Rodney Pepper cries.

In clearly having become the protagonist in a sordid narrative penned by this false author, I alternatively began wincing then flinching, in rapid succession.

"Hem rolls to one side as the rhino gouges Pepper in the groin."

This instigating minister had obviously read my homages to Papa

Hemingway and was attempting a futile parody.

"Hem drives back into town with Pepper laying in the back seat of his Land Rover, blood spurting out of his severed femoral artery like red jizum. Hem stops the Rover in front of the town cantina. When he pulls up on the hand break, it shrieks like a dog being crushed under a truck tire. As blood pumps steadily from his artery, Pepper watches Pappa through the bar's window. Pappa lights a cigarette while feeding a fresh piece of paper into his typewriter roller. Realizing that Papa had forgotten all about him laying outside in the Land Rover bleeding to death, Pepper's head rolls over onto his other shoulder in despair. His gaze becomes fixed through the window of an old hotel across the street. The curtains are swept aside momentarily by a gust of hot air, and there Evelyn Razer straddles a man pounding him like a diesel-powered pile driver. Pepper watches as she comes, lunging backward into the air like a salmon leaping up the river. At that moment Pepper exsanguinates, and his heart stops.

The vision of Evelyn Razer frozen in mid-air through the open window of that hotel is what Pepper sees for all of eternity. Rodney Pepper lives in the ninth layer of hell for the murders he had committed during his short, miserable life. The Reverend Johnny Jupes brought Pepper in, his ankles shackled, and God gave him a big reward."

The demon handed me my notebook, puffed out his chest and announced,

"Now that's writing."

"No. That's shit. SHIT!" I screamed. This man was deluding himself. What he had written was not true. "IT'S NOT TRUE!" I yelled. I was very upset that he was a writer at all. "AT ALL!" I shrieked at him.

The man continued calmly: "I showed both my stories and your stories to Mrs. Razer. She liked mine and said I could write fuck books and make big money if I concentrated. She types up her sex stories real fast and sells them like hotcakes. That's how she gets money to buy real estate. She's going to teach me everything she knows."

I was appalled that my private missives had been on display! In particular, appalled they had been on display to this woman who allegedly typed pornography at high speeds. For one, I could not accept his contention that

Evelyn Razer wrote simply pornography. Had James Joyce or D.H. Lawrence been endowed with enormous breasts, Evelyn Razer would undoubtedly be crowned their logical modern successor. Throughout history, literature had often been mistaken for pornography and more than wrongly subject to censorship. And I could only be extremely curious as to what Evelyn Razer thought of my own speculative musings, of my writings, if you will.

Apparently, this dilettante was not afraid to directly ask her opinion of what he boldly deigned to describe as his stories.

The menace poked me in the center of my chest. "I needed three or four sets of evangelism suits, and you give me my own name as a reference?" He alluded to that very clever prank on my part, that is, providing him with the name of my childhood alter ego, Johnny Jupes, as a personal reference. He appeared hurt by this. I honestly did not quite understand what he meant in saying, my own name.

"I was halfway through the application with this Eddie blow dry fucker, and I didn't think he was even going to check my record until I mentioned the fact that I know somebody that works at the company. He says 'Oh, what's their name?' And when I give him the name Johnny Jupes, he gets up and walks out the door. Then Jack Lalane comes in a few minutes later and says there is no one working at the company by that name. Then Eddie comes back in and says he was sorry, but he can't hire me. See, I just thought you gave me my own name because we're doppelgangers. It made sense at the time. I didn't even ask Razer or Donna what your real name was. I never thought you would lie about that. But I should have known better; you lied about everything else."

"Your name is Johnny Jupes?" I asked, dumbfounded. Johnny Jupes, the name of a fictitious creation from childhood was actually his name. And I was quite certain I had just heard Johnny Jupes define us as doppelgangers.

This man, arising from a flaming hell of the uncanny, handed me a document from the state parole board. "Johnny Jupes," had been typed above his photograph. The letter constituted an introduction to prospective employees. He quickly withdrew the document and said, "I don't like working on the water anyway."

I also had inwardly referred to Eddie as Blow Dried Eddie.

"I needed the work. I didn't tell him that me and you were doppelgangers because I respect that. You can't tell anybody that."

Uncle Gambi had spoken about doppelgangers, and now this fellow insisted on being my very own. I understood. The man had stolen my notebooks and read what I had written regarding both the denizens of the library and doppelgangers and now expected me to believe that he was my doppelganger.

"You stole my pocket notebook and read about doppelgangers," I stated. I wanted to add bitch but refrained in doing so as he was bigger than I, and unpredictably violent.

"I don't need to read your pocket notebook. I bought a box of my own and filled four this morning. I fill one and as soon as I finish that one want to fill another one. I need twice as many notebooks as you do."

I squirmed slightly in the face of his apparent proclivity toward insatiable notebook keeping.

"I don't trust you with all the lying you do, telling Donna that you had been in the Navy then telling that bartender that you had been in the Army then passing yourself off to Mrs. Razer as some kind of pirate. When you lie like that you deserve anything and everything that comes your way." He spat on the sidewalk. "Once you open that door, the hounds of hell will come running in. And mark my words, they will hide in your house and feed on you when they hunger."

Johnny Jupes resembled no Christian priest I had become familiar with through my more than comprehensive assimilation of Sunday morning television programming.

"I heard talk of this treasure. I want in on that." He poked me in the chest like a real bully. "I want your matelotage turned over to me. That's what I want. I'm one of the powerful people, and I'll be needing that matelotage. I'll be needing big money for my career in television evangelism."

I stared at him, flared both nostrils and kept them flared. There was no ambiguity in my message: Johnny Jupes had no concept of what a true matelotage implied or entailed. A matelotage was not something one would need. A matelotage is not a commodity to be transferred indiscriminately. Uncle Gambi's matelotage could only be bequeathed to me through birthright. While we weren't matelots in the strict sense, it was most appropriate that things worked out the way they did, most appropriate.

"New Orleans is a doppelganger destination." Johnny Jupes lowered his voice. "Where people are partying, you have a much higher incidence of psychic dysfunction." This man, who made the assumption of doppelgangery and who never attended University, presumed to lecture me on the unconscious! "I could not believe my doppelganger had come up weak, like a chump," he said. "I'm embarrassed to be my doppelganger, to tell you the truth. I don't want to be seen with you, but I have accepted that undermining you is just my job. Someone's got to do it."

Having been thoroughly flimflammed since my arrival in New Orleans, I was savvy with regard to all manner of fraud. What he proposed reeked of another attempt at a staggering dupe. I could not and would not fall for the same trick three times in succession. People from New Orleans had been telling me nonsense since my arrival, and there was an expectation I would swallow every last crumb of idiocy at every single meal.

"The bartender didn't see me sitting there last week, right? That's because I'm your doppelganger. I'm invisible when I'm subverting you, and I was subverting you back then, don't you even understand that?"

"Oh I understand doppelganger subversion quite well, Mister Jupes," I exclaimed testily. I could not agree or disagree. I had no idea if the manager of the leotard bar had seen him or not. I examined Johnny Jupes' face.

I could not fathom how anyone might attempt to swindle another by posing as their doppelganger. Such a ploy would be unthinkable, akin to robbing Fort Knox by ringing the buzzer at its front gate then announcing "pizza delivery" over the intercom.

Such a con man would have no hope for success on a career-criminal track. The myriad of movies on the subject made it clear that the confidence man must be grounded in the real world and harbor a profound understanding of human nature to successfully apply his trade. The rube must be near imbecilic or an extremist in new age occult movements in order to play into such a proposition. Regarding this tattooed counterfeit doppelganger, I seriously doubted he would have the necessary combination of imagination and gall to attempt such a gambit. I could only agree with his uncanny premise provisionally, concluding this man believed himself to be my doppelganger as an act of true self-deception. At the same token, I felt a smidgen of excitement of even the remotest possibility of having a flesh and blood doppelganger.

But at the same time, I resented it! I stamped my foot.

"I'm self-taught," the bastard continued. "I read everything they had at the Tulane library: Freud, Jung, Erikson, Rank, Ehrenzweig and Maslow. I have all the coeds I want whenever I want. I need to know it all for my TV career. Evangelists have a lot of women, and they need to know how to handle them. I go to Tri-Delt parties and ask them to meet me in the library during the day. They talk to each other and know about me, so they show up and give me hand and blow jobs." He hesitated and looked momentarily confused. "I can't stop. I'm all sexed up."

Johnny Jupes was overly genital-centric, much as Uncle Gambi had described the tendency of his own doppelganger. In Johnny Jupes' case, his insight was skewed and his expectations unrealistic. While purporting to be an evangelist, he did not sound Christian in the least. I did not debate he was pathologically self-seeking but my actual doppelganger? Preposterous!

"See, you were at your job interview, and there I was, undermining everything you did. That's just the way it works. You can't fight that. I was just doing my job bringing about your downfall and reaping the benefits. You can't blame me one minute."

"Oh, is that the way it works? I know the way it works," I snapped. "Two substantives? Double Walker? Psychic projection? Unresolved anxieties? Narcissistic self-preservation? Taboo objects? Autoeroticism? Living castration? And I suppose you know Other is spelled with a capital O, Mister Jupes, Mister Big Pants, Mister Self-Study?" I found myself inexorably drawn into his pettiness as if I were caught up in a bottomless vortex, my chalice filling up with malice the longer I remained in his presence. If I had a leather glove at that moment, I would have slapped, and not only slapped but bitch slapped, Johnny Jupes across the face with it. Better acquainted with machinations of doppelgangery than I? Whilst it was I, not he, the University-Trained Ganger, who knew full well how to subject hypothesis to rigorous inspection. No, my doppelganger had come up weak not the other way around and how maddening it was in considering this criminal minister might be more of an intellectual than I, and through self-study nonetheless, amply rewarded, by the sound of it, with rampant sexual favor.

I would have to locate all of Otto Rank's psychoanalytic treatises once back at the library and subject them to inside-out scrutiny, front and back covers included.

"I already know you are going to help me because I have been reading your little notebooks telling of you and your stupid experiments," he stated.

I stared at Johnny Jupes, my mouth dry as a tobacco leaf. He had violated my pocket notebooks again and again and again.

"You're autodestructing no matter what I do. You don't need a doppelganger to help you. I'm flesh and blood. You're a pocket notebook."

Mein doppelganger! I shrieked inwardly. *He was no sham!*

"These pirate assholes think you woolded that Uncle Gambi of yours when I know for a fact that you didn't." He smiled. "But as far as I'm concerned you did. You told me so yourself. I'll testify you did, and you'll go to prison for that if I decide that you should."

My doppelganger Johnny Jupes was implying he was the New Orleans woolder as well as demonstrating himself to be the embodiment of evil, chasing me as if within a nightmare. That others might confuse the two of us or that I might be discovered to be in possession of a previously concealed undermining side, was nauseating and embarrassing. That at times I might appear to the world as the devilish Johnny Jupes and vice versa, that our faces would transform from Rodney Pepper to Johnny Jupes then back to Rodney Pepper, was a premise I could not accept.

Rodney Pepper, the Monster of Metairie, I titled, imagining the Times-

Picayune headlines.

"Your uncle approached me," he said. "He wanted to pay me with wine, but I don't drink wine. He wanted me to go up to some house on Napoleon and pick up his package. The little woman who owned the place wouldn't open the door. She looked at me through a crack in the door and told me her husband was the deputy sheriff and all this shit, and that the law could get there in three minutes. I just turned around and went back to your sorry-ass uncle's room and took a nice big shit in his clothes drawer. I called it my package delivery."

"The bottom drawer?"

I had immersed my hand in a mound of my own doppelganger's feces!

"He was afraid of me after that and didn't come back to the rooming house. I found him, though. He would have told me about any treasure, but he didn't. I asked him 'Where's the treasure!? Where's the treasure?!' Then you killed him. You woolded him."

"Wait? Did you take his book?"

"What?"

"There were two books. Did you take one of them?"

Johnny Jupes poked me in the chest. "Yeah. I used it to wipe myself; is that alright with you? But it was filled with shit anyway as far as I'm concerned. I may have glanced at it."

"What happened to it?" I asked.

Johnny Jupes stared at me without answering then said, "I think Donna may have taken it back to the library with one of her kids' books. Missing a few pages, though. I wiped myself with a whole lot of other books. Your books."

Appalled, I walked away, on the verge of tears. He followed me closely, hissing in my ear. "I will make your life a living hell if you don't give me what I want. If you don't give me what I want, I'll puncture your eyeballs with one of your own ballpoint pens." He took the ballpoint pen out of my pocket and mimed the action of sticking a pin into a balloon. I winced and blinked several times. He pocketed the pen. I had written several discourses on ocular disruption and assumed that he had read them all.

This demonic optician wanted my matelotage, but Johnny Jupes would not get my matelotage. Uncle Gambi had pushed my head down at the McDonalds counter, not Johnny Jupes' head.

My doppelganger laughed and announced, "I'm going over to the Lafayette now. Razer said she would teach me to work the switchboard. I just come back from her daughter's, or at least, that's what she calls herself."

I stumbled away as he laughed demonically. I ran around the corner just out of sight and slumped down against a building, taking out my pocket notebook as if it were a radio and I was calling in an air-strike on my own coordinates.

Genitals, I wrote, underscored the word twice and let my hand drop, exhausted. Genitals would be placed into the Capitalized-Words-of-Great-Import section of my notebook alongside Godhead. I then wrote *Heavy Breasts* but immediately tore the page out, crumbled it into a ball and threw it onto the sidewalk. I replaced the notebook in my pocket, breathing heavily.

My only consolation was, in having become legitimately despondent through the experience of all this SHIT, I was finally living.

I stumbled all the way back to my rooming house and sat on the edge of my bed inhaling the room's ambient odors.

How had I provoked the deployment of this unworldly hell-hound? If my ego had not truly been disintegrating, which I didn't feel it had been, then why would a caustic three-dimensional entity have any reason to pursue me? I tried recalling Gambi's words as he had described certain mappings regarding mathematical principles describing doppelganger manifestations and multiple ganger iterations.

But I could not recall: I had not been paying attention!

I tried to compose myself and review the facts: My doppelganger interacts with people as do I. Yet as far as I could tell, we lead separate lives. He aspired to television evangelism, a profession of no interest to me. Under whose unconscious control then were our destinies being shaped? Did additional manifestations of psychic discontent live and breathe in and around New Orleans beside doppelgangers? Trippelgangers, for instance? Watching and waiting for an opportunity to manifest and wreak three times the chaos? And of further duplications? Could two, three, four, five manifestations of a single individual walk, talk and drink simultaneously to all the others carrying on within different Bourbon Street bars? Or lesser ranks within the psychic infantry? Fecal hoarders, nipple fixators, penis-enviers, the foot soldiers serving as cannon fodder for the capricious psychoanalytic Generals drinking Schnapps in their gaudy tents, far from the site of conflict. And God forbid that I were to stumble upon my very own anima, my inner priestess and female personification of the unconscious, smoking a cigarette, flaunting her boa, thighs barely contained within torn stockings, strutting north dangerously, across Governor Nicholls, across Barracks, across Esplanade!

I lay back down on my rodent gnawed mattress and stared at the water marks on the ceiling as if they were gypsy tea leaves.

20
RHONE

I parked near the Audubon Park entrance on St. Charles and tapped the gas gauge. The instrument was malfunctioning; the needle had not moved from its resting position on the far left side of the gauge since I had activated the car's ignition. Rhone stood a short distance away looking at her watch. I opened the door, raised my hand and had to squint. Sunlight shined upon Rhone's ankles.

My foot caught the edge of the curb and I lurched forward. Rhone watched me then looked away. To redirect her attention, I loudly posed the question:

"Is there anything wrong, Rhone!?"

I had spoken much louder than intended and winced. A *good morning, Rhone* or a *hey, hey cat*, as Kerry Kelly might have said, would have served as a more appropriate preliminary greeting.

From a distance, Rhone appeared taller and more broad in the shoulder than I had recalled. Curiously, she wore a snug fitting skirt decorated with purple tiger stripes. Black garter belt snaps attached her stockings, calling attention to her legs and of course ankles which appeared even sturdier than at the first meeting. I again neglected to pay attention to foot placement; the tip of my sneaker snagged a protruding brick. This time, I did not stumble but was propelled over to one side, emergently applying both palms against the ground. I arose triumphantly holding my bleeding palms aloft.

"Her appearance smacks of the uncanny," I called out, pointing at Rhone and approaching her with Robert Mitchumish nonchalance. I trusted Rhone would find my addressing her in the third person to be quite clever while serving as an ice breaker and segue into my recollection of a pocket notebook sketch made several weeks previously. With little contemplation and for no particular reason, I had dashed off a drawing of a robust woman dressed nearly identically to Rhone. I began to relate this to her with the intention of exploring subtexts of the uncanny:

"You know, I had rather spontaneously sketched this image of a large boned, quite muscular. . ."

Rhone regarded me without smiling. I stopped speaking, reconsidering my intentions. Her dress probably represented nothing more than an odd coincidence. Rhone had clearly borrowed her mother's clothing and made herself up without permission, not realizing all the choices had been adorably inappropriate for her age.

As we walked through the park, I had difficulty thinking of things to say to Rhone and found myself repeatedly inquiring if there was anything wrong. I told her I had little money to spend on our date but told her not to be scared. After I had told her a second time I had little money and not to be scared, she turned and stated in a deep voice,

"You said you were going to take me to the Lakefront and get me toasted."

I had *not* told Rhone I would get her toasted. Momentarily confused by the suggestion, I stammered,

"I have a car."

"I want to drive then," she said.

"Do you have a driver's license?" I asked, concerned with the legalities in being the responsible party.

"I'll just steer. You do the gas and brake."

As soon as Rhone saw the car she stopped and placed her hand over her mouth. "I know this car. You're driving me to the lakefront in a fucking I.P.P. company car?" She stamped her foot. "I like new things that shine. I don't like dirty old company cars."

Curiously, Evelyn Razer had used a similar expression during my interview at the Lafayette Hotel. I started the engine and tapped the gas gauge once more. The needle did not move above empty, still indicating a malfunction. Kerry Kelly, who had last driven the car, would surely have filled the tank.

"Wow, how do you know that this was an I.P.P. company car, Rhone?"

She stamped her foot. "Why are you asking me so many questions? You're frying my brain. Can't you just be cool."

To placate the suddenly testy and aggressive Rhone, I allowed her to steer while I pushed the accelerator and break. We sat side by side, her thick ankles visible and rubbing against my pants leg. I could not consider them at this time, fully preoccupied with the precarious driving arrangement. Rhone was calm, engrossed in the process of maneuvering. She drove well, making several turns and merges with appropriate use of turn signal. She instructed me occasionally to slow down or apply the brake. We drove in silence. After a time I was forced to admit, "I don't know where we are."

She said, "We take Carrollton to Wisner. You make a left onto Robert E Lee. I usually cut up Canal to get onto Lakeshore. I'm practically out there every day." Rhone steered with one hand and possessed a surprisingly good knowledge of the city roads.

I began to ask her how she could possibly get out to the Lakefront every day while attending to her busy school schedule when she blurted out, "I'm bored," and jerked the wheel from side to side causing the car to swerve across the median line. After a few moments of this, she announced, "I have to get ready." Without warning, she let go of the wheel to remove a small pocket mirror from her purse. She began carefully examining herself turning her head from side to side. I regained control of the vehicle nearly losing bowel and bladder control.

Once out at the Lakefront, Rhone managed to steer us to the front entrance of a large restaurant. She opened the door before the vehicle had come to a complete stop, got out and began climbing a set of stairs to an upper deck facility. I parked the car as fast as I was safely able being quite concerned that Rhone was under the legal drinking age. I would certainly have to accompany her every step of the way.

Oddly, the bouncer gave Rhone a high five and nodded her through while neglecting to check any form of identification. He barred my passage and took an inordinate time to examine my credentials. As he was doing so, I followed Rhone with my eyes as she strolled along the bar swinging her purse in small circles.

Rhone was fully un-escorted and very deliberately examining each patron one by one.

The older men turned to stare blatantly while a Coast Guardsman took her by the wrist and spoke directly into her ear. Rhone laughed. He laughed.

I wished Rhone would just calm down!

The bouncer finally returned my driver's license. I hurried inside.

"You don't have to do that," she said.

"Do what?"

"Trot like that. Buy me a Penis Colossus."

"What?"

"That means buy me a Pina Colada," she said. "It's a joke?"

"It's only eleven o'clock in the morning," I reminded her.

"You don't have to have one." She walked over to the railing overlooking Lake Pontchartrain. I followed her a few steps then returned to the bar. I calculated having spent eleven dollars in total: ten for the drinks, one for the bartender's tip. It left me with thirty-nine dollars until payday after the money Kerry Kelly had borrowed.

Rhone had been looking down over the railing toward the water as I arrived holding a tropical drink in each hand. She turned toward me with her face in hands. I peered over the railing at a very large and fast looking speed boat tied up on the level below. On its bow a woman lay on her stomach, sunbathing. The straps of her bathing suit top lay on either side of her chest; her breasts bulged and spread out underneath her. A heavily tattooed man climbed into the cockpit of the boat with two drinks from the bar on the lower level. At his arrival, the woman propped herself up on her elbows. With an aching sensation in my abdomen, I recognized the man kneeling beside the woman to be Johnny Jupes!

As the woman tilted her head to one side, the sensation of recognition was equivalent to being lifted up by the ears: The indomitable businesswoman Evelyn Razor, at once Lafayette hotel manager and I.P.P. accountant! I nearly plummeted over the railing with the abrupt onset of vertigo. Gripping the rail, I watched as Johnny Jupes placed the two drinks down on the deck and began rubbing suntan lotion on her back. With one fluid movement, he reached around and smeared suntan lotion over both breasts, lifting her up and back in doing so.

"Take me the fuck home," Rhone said, clearly upset by my doppelganger's graphic lotioning, something an underage girl should never ever have to witness.

I followed her, unable to stop asking, "What's wrong Rhone? Rhone? Rhone?"

"That big fucking oaf!" she sobbed, turned and roughly grabbed one of the drinks from my hands. She swallowed the entire Pina Colada in one pull then hurled the glass over the rail far out into Lake Pontchartrain.

Rhone had an unusually good throwing arm for a fifteen-year-old girl.

I looked around anxiously. Rhone had destroyed restaurant property in a moment of indiscretion.

"He's just a big walking penis," she shrieked, tears streaming down her face. "And I love him!" She nearly knocked me over as she walked past then turned and bellowed, "You act like you're seventy fucking years old." The men at the bar guffawed, but I could not help but trot after her. At the gate, the bouncer would not let me leave with my drink. I left it on a railing and had to skip to make up the ground she had already covered.

"What's wrong? What's wrong, Rhone? Rhone, what's wrong?" I could not stop asking her. "What's wrong? What's wrong Rhone? Rhone? Rhone? Rhone, what's wrong?"

Rhone did not respond. Once in the car, she crossed her arms over her chest and stared out the window.

My world had imploded around me like a Sun having run out of hydrogen.

No longer the knight with a feather protruding majestically from the apex of my helmet, I had become roadkill, the corpse of a peacock hanging limply off the side of a shovel.

Before starting the car, I took out my pocket notebook and created a subheading entitled *self-deprecation*, underlined it and wrote:

Package of skinless chicken breasts, expiration date long passed, stacked carelessly in the refrigerator section.

I closed the notebook. Rhone had not even noticed. I became compelled to ask, "What's wrong Rhone? Did I do something wrong? Rhone? Rhone? RHONE?"

I bellowed her name in despair. It had all gone so well on the street car and then, in the drug store. With ego disintegrating, I spoke like an automaton: "I had been so penis-gourdish. Just where is your Papua New Guinea Man now? Perhaps I should simply DEOCULATE MYSELF!"

Rhone turned and spoke angrily. "De-what? What are you talking about now? I can never understand what you are saying. You talk to yourself in gibberish half the time. What are you talking about?" She shrieked in my face: "DON'T YOU REALIZE THAT WAS MY FUCKING MOTHER BACK THERE?"

"Your fucking mother is Evelyn Razor?!"

The magnitude of the coincidence was akin to Sigmund Freud, Franz Kafka, and Friedrich Nietzsche becoming stuck in a single revolving door while emerging from the same Prague Department store, each carrying the same colored hat box!

"Take me to the Quarter. I'm going drinking." Rhone said, raised her knee and kicked the dashboard. The glove compartment handle cracked. She continued to kick it repeatedly until the handle broke off. She then placed her leg up onto the dash; her skirt fell back revealing the side of an unusually taut and somewhat hairy left buttock. Her ankles were thick, as Redwoods. We drove in silence for a few minutes then she said, "You think you just followed the scared little girl into that Napoleon Avenue drug store all by yourself?"

I recalled the streetcar and Rhone's frightened expression.

"Drop me off on Rampart," she said.

"Rhone, what's wrong? What's wrong Rhone?" I asked.

"My mother is getting suntan lotion rubbed all over her back by some new....lover boy? And you ask what's wrong what's wrong what's WRONG?" Rhone yelled then sobbed. I felt like holding Rhone and caressing Rhone. We shared disillusionment. I tried to grab Rhone's hand. She flung it away.

"Fuck off!" she screamed with a voice that sounded much deeper and scarier than previously.

I knew she didn't mean that.

"Yeah, I know," I commiserated. "He's my doppelganger."

She stopped sobbing and asked, "He's your fucking what?"

"My doppelganger." I had to make her understand and trust me. "I thought that doppelgangers weren't real, but they are. Your mother hired him while he was already subverting me."

"Johnny? He works for my mother. He's bullshitting you." She was quiet for a moment and looked out the window. "He told me he wanted to fuck me so bad."

Maddening to hear that Johnny Jupes had spoken to Rhone in that way, I stamped my foot against the floorboard. She glared at me defiantly then turned and stared out the window with her arms crossed.

"They all looked in your stupid notebooks while you were sleeping," she said. "So did I. We all did. Why do you think I'm dressed like this? I saw your drawing and just thought I'd go for it. But this is what I do; I'm a. . ."

Rhone stopped speaking abruptly.

My suspicions concerning the placement of my pocket notebook the first day at the Lafayette had been correct. Both notebook and person had been measured and analyzed.

"Even though I was pretending, you got off that streetcar and came after me. We all like that so I let you chase me." She looked at her fingernails. "And I thought you were the one that woolded Gambi at the time." She looked at me almost mournfully for a brief moment; her expression hardened. "I'm doing you a big fucking favor with this next piece of advice. No one else is going to tell you the truth. You should take your stupid notebooks and leave New Orleans. None of this is any of your business. You're a chump."

I became quite upset that Rhone considered me a chump, much more so than I had been when that inhumane doppelganger hottie Johnny Jupes had labeled me such. Rhone's opinion mattered more than his.

"Are you an idiot?" she asked.

I was confused now. "No, I . . ."

"Are you going to spend the rest of your life forcing a round peg into a square hole? You go on and on about shit hoarding and despondency. Are you kidding me? They were all laughing, but I wasn't. It made me fucking depressed. I had to leave the room. I think your head's not only stuck up your ass but has made its way up to the top, came out your mouth and is floating about two hundred feet in the air like a balloon waiting to be popped."

Rhone doubted me, and this was devastating. Yet her similes held me spellbound. I swallowed and continued to listen. She went on.

"You have heavy aspects of Neptune in your natal chart, and there are only two choices if you want to disimpact the shit up your ass like you say you want to."

Rhone had read notes from my *Disimpaction subcategory*!

"One way through it is true love, which I can tell you right now you won't find anytime soon, and if you do, you won't be able to comprehend that it's standing right in front of you." She was silent for a moment. "The other way is traveling up your mother's snatch with a mining helmet on, going back the way you came in."

At this suggestion, I could only look at her oddly. She became even more impatient.

"Underworld journey?" She stared hard, her voice deepening to an alarming degree. "Holy Grail? You're worse than Percival. You're like some dipshit who goes back to the castle like twenty times and by the time you ask the right question, the king's died of old age, and nobody gives a fuck. The guards see you coming and say, 'Oh shit, it's him' because you're always tripping over your sword or falling backward into the moat. To them, you're comic relief. I might be the only one who sees that it's your fucking life on the line, Rodney Pepper, you dip-shit." Rhone bit a fingernail and looked out the window.

I found myself developing a much bigger thing; she was inordinately clever and to an extent complex in addition to being big boned and thick-ankled.

"Thank you," I said. "Thank you, Rhone, thank you. Thank you. Thank you, Rhone."

In thanking Rhone uncontrollably, I winced then flinched then winced then flinched. I noticed the upper part of her thigh to be hairier than the lower part. She bit another fingernail and continued.

"The only reason that you aren't dead yet is that you know where our treasure is. Well, that and there's another aspect to all this that is totally fucked up. My mother really wants to get you hooked up. The whole thing turns my stomach to tell you the truth, and that's hard to do. I don't even want to talk about it but lucky you! The only thing I can say is that there's at least one person in New Orleans who cares about you. I guess I have some competition." Rhone laughed and didn't stop for a full minute. I did not understand the joke nor conceive of whom my secret benefactor might be. We passed Louis Armstrong Park on North Rampart Street; the car's engine stalled abruptly. I tapped the gas gauge.

"What's wrong?" Rhone asked.

"I'm not sure. I think the car is out of gas." I had only seen people run out of gas on Leave It to Beaver.

"Out of gas? You think? You don't know?"

Rhone opened the door and slammed it. She began walking. I got out of the car and trotted beside her.

"What's the matter, Rhone?" I asked. She stopped and stamped her foot.

"You're like a big square brown package sitting in the middle of the road waiting to get run over. It's even painful for me to look at you."

"I can't leave the car. It's the company car, your mother's company."

"Well then don't you think you had better stay with it? They'll fire your ass so fast that it will make your wooden head spin like a top." She walked away and called over her shoulder, "If you stay in New Orleans it's your fault, and you deserve everything that happens to you."

I knew she couldn't mean that. She had just been too upset in seeing her mother with her new lover boy, my dastardly doppelganger, and had taken it all out on me. I could not understand how my date had become so botched-up and that I ended up getting a lecture.

Rhone turned, took a few steps back toward me and said, "I would go out with you if you find the treasure, and if you grew your hair longer. I would party with you then." She suddenly pushed her large knee between my legs and lifted me up in the air. My left testicle became crushed. I yelped, withdrew the one leg in pain and hopped up and down. Rhone said,

"It's not your fault, but nobody cares whether you're a cripple or a freak."

With that, Rhone turned and strolled away swinging her purse. I gazed at her and realized that I would have to spend half of my remaining money on gas for the company car then request an advance on my paycheck. This would necessitate a visit to Evelyn Razer, Rhone's mother, in the I.P.P. payroll department. After observing her breasts being lotioned and lifted, I was concerned that once in her presence, I might not be able to articulate aloud what I needed. I would have to write it all down beforehand, hand her the sheet of paper and sit down immediately.

21
EVICTED!

Lowry's *Under the Volcano* lay face down on the sidewalk in front of the boarding house; pages bent like wings of a fallen sparrow. My clothing and my books, all recently repacked meticulously within my duffle bag, had been scattered along Prytania Avenue in front of the rooming house. The landlady, standing behind the screen door, began shouting.

"I'm sick of all your lying bullshit. My commode flooded over and broke through my ceiling, Mister!"

I could only produce clucking noises as I set about collecting my belongings; this was the third time my duffle bag had been transgressed.

"I know you know what I'm talking about, and I know you didn't stop it up while you were sleepwalking, Mister. And I know you never been in the Service either. Johnny told me everything about your perverted shit. He told me you were the one who shitted up my cottage. So I did a little digging in all your filth and found that trashy diary of yours. Just pick up all your garbage and GIT, or I'm calling the law."

My knees gave way: My doppelganger had exposed me. This landlady needed to know that my pocket notebook was not merely a diary but a carefully transcribed collection of empiric data. To my further horror, as she stood inside the screen door, she began reading both loudly and offhandedly from one of my most cherished notebooks.

"The landlady speaks in a curious incongruous vernacular when she angers, which is often. She raises her voice so the whole facility may hear her thoughts. She is wholly concerned with the status of her commode and becomes quite enraged when it is tampered with or soiled."

She stopped reading and yelled, "You dirty little son of a bitch! I'm trying to make things nice for you and the others, and this is the thanks I get?"

I could not vindicate myself as what had transpired was clear cut skullduggerizing at the hands of Johnny Jupes. Trying to explain it all to this already enraged woman might very well make things worse. I surveyed the fresh pairs of underwear marred with footprints; t-shirts draped over rotting fence posts and orphaned books sprawled between parked cars. My duffle bag had been tossed directly off the porch onto the sidewalk without securing its clasp!

The landlady continued to read passages from the notebook while I, like the Van Gogh potato picker, bent forward and continued gathering my defiled items.

"There is no justification for my memories. I'm spiraling downward on a worm gear, transferred from cog to cog on an endlessly interconnected gear train."

"No!" I yelled. "That's my private business!"

"Don't even think of threatening me." She shouted back. The figure of a man, shirtless with a blond mustache appeared beside her in the doorway. He took a bite from an apple, making a loud *crunck*. He stared at me pointedly then disappeared into the kitchen.

"I might show this to the law!" she called out. "It's got evidence!"

I wanted my pocket notebook back. The landlady continued to read.

"I sit in my smelly room and stare at scraps of paper, my legacy of solitude, self-examination, and self-doubt. I occasionally arise and peel trepidation and anxiety from the walls. I am thoroughly an impostor and can barely live with this knowledge."

"No!" I cried.

"I had perturbed the system with my own measuring instrument, my very own purple prepuced, lollygagging Parisian with his beret; circumcised to resemble a German foot soldier. He remained drunk the entire occupation while real existentialists made careful notations. The bell tinkles as the bumbling infantryman, holding rifle clumsily over one shoulder, enters the Byzantine shop to turn left then right then left again, knocking golden birds off their golden perches. Blah blah blah. This gets boring fast." She skipped a few pages and continued: "My memories sadden and delight. Blah blah blah. Boring." She scanned my notebook quickly.

It WASN'T boring. The landlady was simply taking it all out of context! If she read any of it out loud, then she should read ALL of it out loud.

I listened, numb and denuded of psychic skin!

"And how easily am I distracted….Blah blah blah…Oh, and here it is, girls." She cleared her throat and glanced behind her. "I look at the women. I look at their faces and at their breasts, their shoulders, arms, forearms, and fingers. I look at the breadth of their hips and their thick ankles and their big feet. I can't stop looking. I can't tear my eyes away. I don't know what to do." The landlady held her head and laughed.

"I watch the landlady's eyes for above all else. She remains wholly contained within her eyes. Behind these gems, she guards something precious, a self she rarely shares, a self she cannot share."

The landlady stopped reading and bit her lip. She opened the screen door, drew her bathrobe tightly around her and approached with long angry strides, carrying a newspaper in one hand, my notebook in the other. I fully expected to be struck.

"And I'm not even going to read this piece of smut out loud. Right here, read THAT you little cocksucker!" She pounded her finger at the notebook page upon which someone had written in block capitals:

YOU ARE IN OVER YOUR FOOL HEAD AND NOW YOU ARE GOING TO GET YOURSELF KILLED BECAUSE YOU BELIEVE EVERYTHING THEY SAY. GIT OUT OF NEW ORLEANS! THERE ARE THINGS YOU DON'T UNDERSTAND.

The landlady gripped my arm as her womanly lips brushed against my cheek. "Here's your deposit money back, Mister." She pressed both money and notebook against the palm of my hand and squeezed, then handed me the folded portion of newspaper upon which Uncle Gambi had scribbled an address. She whispered, "You should know that preacher is no good for either of us. You're in danger with the likes of him and that woman you were talking to on the phone from what he said. I have to protect my girls, Mister. I sold the place. Got my asking price too and I'm getting the hell out. They said they want to turn it into a parking lot. They can be my guest." She paused. "What you said about my eyes. I never thought anybody would ever see me. Be good to yourself, Mister."

She raised her voice and shouted: "Now git, you perverted little son of a bitch! And WAKE UP!"

I heard laughter from behind the screen door. I turned and walked back to the company car cradling my belongings in both arms. I sat in the driver's seat, examining the room ads in the copy of the Times-Picayune and the address circled in pencil. With my returned deposit money, I now had one hundred and eight dollars to my name.

22
MRS. GOLD'S LIVING ROOM TABLE

Given the repeated exposures and derisions of the day with the sun now setting, the contents of Uncle Gambi's box residing somewhere within this large house on Napoleon Avenue mattered little. I only hoped that a room would be available. After ringing the bell, a small silhouette appeared behind the curtains hanging just inside the front door's glass panel. A shrill voice called out, "Who is there?"

"I am responding to your ad in the paper."

"What do you do?"

"I work offshore. I'm a navigator."

"Yes, this is good. I'm Mrs. Gold." The door cracked open, its chain remaining in place. A short woman wearing large round glasses examined me from head to toe.

"Yes, OK, you look all right. We only take clean people who have jobs. I have a very nice house. I have a son, maybe older than you. He's a doctor in Houston, Texas." She examined me carefully another time, cocked her head to one side and said, "He's a very busy man, and when he comes to visit me, he needs quiet to rest."

"Yes."

"He's always busy."

"Yes."

"My husband is a deputy sheriff. If there is trouble, the police are here in three minutes. They all know who he is."

I shook my head up and down, wanting nothing more to do with trouble.

"I have a very nice room downstairs. You would like very much to stay there; I know this." The woman stepped out the front door and closed it behind her. She guided me back down the front steps, continuing to speak as we walked around the side of the house.

"The entire police department, God forbid if they should come, would be here in three minutes. Three minutes, God forbid should there be a problem." She unlocked a small door. I followed her inside, having to duck under the door jamb.

"See, you have your own entrance."

In contrast to my previous quarters, the sterility of this new environment was equivalent to that of a bone marrow transplant unit. The room, odorless, possessed clean wood paneling and intact window panes. Not a stain was visible on any surface.

"I do not allow visitors," Mrs. Gold went on. "No visitors. House rule. No." She held up her hand as if I were protesting. "I'm sorry. No visitors. The room is one hundred and five dollars a week." She held her hand up. "This is the usual rent. You look clean, so I will let it go for one hundred dollars. Nowhere in the city will you find a room like this." She shook her head. "Very rare. I clean the rooms myself. One hundred dollars. This is a very good deal. A very good deal."

The landlady led me through a second door on the opposite wall of the room directly into a basement area. Six other rooms were constructed around the perimeter of the space, each possessing wood paneling along with similar outer and inner doors. All inner doors opened into the communal basement expanse. A single set of wooden stairs at its center ascended into the house.

"This is where everybody lives." Mrs. Gold waved her hand across the basement then pointed at the stairs. "The boarders are not allowed up the staircase." She pointed to a washer and dryer. "I cannot permit you to use the washer and dryer. There is a laundry mat very very near." She opened another small door. "This is the wash room and shower. I keep it very clean. I do not allow paper towel in the bowl. This is very important. You see, I have the signs placed to remind you." She pointed to a large piece of paper taped to the middle of the mirror over the sink. The sign occluded the surface of the mirror. Mrs. Gold looked at her watch.

"Please, I have somebody coming to see the room in one half hour. I will rent it to you for one hundred dollars since you are here first. Usually this room, this room is a very nice room, goes for one hundred and five dollars." She guided me back into the room and patted the mattress. "You see, very clean. I clean every day. If there is something out of place, I will know. Maybe one year ago I had to ask a man to leave, but usually, I have no problems." She then took my arm and pulled me down to the level of her head. "My husband is a deputy for the sheriff. He's a deputy." She threw up her hands and looked at her watch again. "Please, they are coming soon and may very well take this room out from under you." The landlady tilted her head to one side and regarded me.

"OK, I'll take it."

"Yes, you are very smart. You will not find another room like this." She flipped through several pages on a receipt pad and began writing. "That is one hundred six dollars and thirty cents a week that you pay me now," she said.

"I thought you said one hundred?"

"I did not add tax." She began writing again and spoke simultaneously. "Tax is the law. Tax is only six dollars."

To pay her what amounted to nearly all the money in my possession, I had to remove my socks, accessing a concealed twenty-dollar bill then locate a specific pair of tidy whities at the base of my duffle which concealed several tens. Mrs. Gold observed me do this, and held the bills as I presented them to her on a piece of Kleenex she had removed from her dress pocket.

"I will write a receipt. Come with me." She climbed the forbidden stairwell while speaking over her shoulder. "Just this one time do we do this. After that, the door stays locked." Mrs. Gold rattled a set of keys and opened the door. I followed her into a living room cluttered with antique furniture.

"Stand over there please." She indicated a table on which there were many packages and letters. I spotted a large rectangular box, adorned with colorful stamps postmarked Seville, Spain. The handwriting belonged to my late Uncle Gambi. Postmarked three months previously, it had been addressed to PAM Dirac, the very package he had solicited my own doppelganger to retrieve, the package which had incited Johnny Jupes, in frustration, to evacuate his bowels into the chest of drawers which I had subsequently accessed.

"I would pick up mail here?" I asked.

Mrs. Gold stared at me. "You are going to get mail? If you could get your mail sent to the post office, that would be better." She looked at me. "I charge for receiving letters and packages so the post office might be better. But you don't come up here looking for letters. Up here is where we live. The door is always locked and bolted. This is the only time a tenant comes up here when I write the receipt. Down there is where the borders stay. If there is an emergency you must knock but I prefer if you come to the front door. If you think you have a letter, you come to the front door and knock. I will then check. If you do have mail, I must collect one dollar for each letter before I give it to you." She hesitated. "Five dollars for each package. I only charge twenty-five cents per postcard." She chuckled. "Tell your friends that the secret is to send you postcards."

23
THE SWALLOWTAIL SINGULARITY

Having glimpsed Uncle Gambi's package laying on Mrs. Gold's living room table, I returned to my new quarters feeling bound by duty to fulfill the mandate of my matelotage. I placed my duffle bag in the corner and ducked under the doorway to make my way back to the New Orleans Public Library. With two dollars left in my pocket, all hopes and physiologic well-being depended entirely upon finding Uncle Gambi's treasure as soon as possible.

My first order of business became inquiring at the reading desk whether or not Uncle Gambi's book had been returned. I approached the same gray jacketed librarian who had previously followed me onto the library steps. She regarded me sternly and did not respond to my inquiry. During this uncomfortable silence, I studied the woman's face. I had not taken the time to do this, recognizing patterns in its structure, idiosyncratic for her. She had become recognizable to me, imprinted and familiar, if not dear, unlike other faces. Her features carried the suggestion of neither beauty nor ugliness; her imperfections irrelevant. Nor was I swept up in sexual allure or provocation. She kept her body covered by her gray uniform. The librarian, in the waning light of day, was recognizable for who she was: the librarian in the worn gray suit. I became embarrassed and saddened. She sat behind her desk as if composed within a painting.

I had no place in disturbing her. She was not trying to flimflam me, perhaps the only person in the city who had not tried. I had a sense that she had been flimflammed to a degree and bore a considerable weariness if not resignation. The librarian, unaware of my thoughts, finally spoke.

"Yes. *Mathematical Models of Morphogenesis* was placed in the book drop with six months unpaid overdue fines and additional damage fees. Feces were on several of its torn pages. I had to reconstruct the book after a complete sanitizing."

The librarian regarded me as if I had been the one who had torn and fecalized its pages. My doppelganger had done so. I could not explain this.

"I don't know anything about that. I only wish to find this particular book."

"Very few people would be interested in that book. It has been checked out twice since it arrival at the library. I've seen you here before. You're the noisemaker," she stated. I could not tell if she was using sarcasm in her tone.

With that, I backed away into the shadowy anonymity of the stacks and surveyed the reading room; its appearance lent no indication that either madman or doppelganger was present. I went about my work without interruptions. Comfortably surrounded by books once again, I inspected text after text within the five hundred section, the domain of the natural sciences and mathematics. I could not locate the Thom volume, so I gathered any others with notations in the margins; in almost all cases the handwriting belonged to my now deceased and long lost blood relative, Uncle Gambi.

I tried to recall details of conversations which took place between myself and this tragic man before and during our breakfast at McDonalds, while outside my door at the Lafayette Hotel and lastly, under the I-90 overpass before his final convulsion. I stood up, sat down, stood up, sat down. I picked up the pace of my research knowing and hoping that the solution, as Uncle Gambi had suggested, would soon become evident. I transformed myself effectively into an alien intelligence whose task it was to absorb the entire knowledge of Earth's civilization in a matter of hours for transmission back to a mother ship residing on the far side of the moon. My eyebrows cocked, double cocked and thrice cocked as I blinked at faster and faster rates of speed, reading of the new science of chaos, of periodically kicked rotators and of regular and irregular motions influencing conservative systems. Within a book chapter entitled *Self Similarity*, Uncle Gambi's notations were found along every margin. Several pages had been torn from its binding.

"Take the Feigenbaum route to chaos," he had written aside a passage describing scaling behavior at the transition to chaos, governed by universal constants. I dutifully copied the Feigenbaum number into my pocket notebook then wrote,

Made uneasy by the pitchfork bifurcation resulting in two stable points within what is referred to as f2 space, I now examine the Liapunov exponent, the order parameter. I must inquire if an inferred relationship could possibly exist between it and the Kolmogorov entropy with additional alliance to the Hausdorff equation.

I sat back. The passage constituted a complete codswallop of jargon and obscure mathematical meaning, Yet I could not stop bandying the terms about as well as the associated names of mathematicians; I continued to take copious notes regardless of these shortcomings in comprehension.

The pace of my breakneck note taking faltered as I became overtaken by a growing suspicion, if not fear that I would not be able to understand or even recognize these clues which Uncle Gambi had provided; even if they turned around and bit me in the ass. I whispered a question in inner dialogue, a question too painful to articulate at any significant volume within myself: What if I were to FAIL?

I flipped a few pages ahead in my present notebook and created a section entitled *Bitter Truths*. I numbered the first entry *One*.

(1) In order to succeed in the world of treasure hunters, I would have to remain disciplined. That is, I would have to become a person different from the one who I was, without SO many fundamental shortcomings of character. The understanding of mathematical principles does NOT arise from reading aloud proofs with theatrical panache, applying decorative moles to one's cheek or being adorned in exquisite combinations of velvets, furs, silks, laces, cottons and taffetas.

I stopped writing. One entry had to suffice. I could bear no more bitter truths about myself. I ripped this page containing the single bitter truth from its binder, balled it up and flung it into a trash bin under the table. I flipped a few more pages ahead and scrawled diagonally across a page.

What EXACTLY is relevant and what isn't? Could it ALL prove irrelevant? Could my notebook entries be viewed by everyone except myself as flippant poppycock, constituting a monumental self-deception leading nowhere while suggesting that I actually was The Madman himself wandering the streets, gesticulating to a non-existent God?

I tore this second notebook page out and hurled it into the same bin shared by its ugly sister. Surveying the reading room while arriving at this impasse of self-doubt, I felt the criminal thrill-seeking urge to be shushed; and not merely an urge: I felt the *need* to be shushed.

I spoke aloud at conversant volume: "I fancy myself one of the new breed of string theory proponents, pushing my infinitely dimensional scientific phallus into the gaping vagina of blind faith."

Several loud satisfying shushes ensued. The librarian immediately arose from her desk, walked across the reading room and slapped a book down in front of me.

"You can look at this on condition you stop announcing your inner thought processes. It is becoming tedious. Otherwise, you'll have to leave the library." Her hand remained on top of the book. I glimpsed the name Thom through the web space of her fingers.

"Yes, of course. I'll stop." I looked at the librarian carefully. She appeared sad, tired and not amused. Without further comment, she walked away.

I knew it would be nearly impossible to stop announcing my thought processes. I suspected the librarian realized that. Somehow, it was sad that she did.

I turned my attention toward the book and in seeing the title, blinked as if an insect had landed directly on the surface of my cornea and was proceeding to clean itself thoroughly: *Mathematical Models of Morphogenesis*. I turned pages frantically, halting at a chapter entitled, *Catastrophes of Bifurcation* and noting the chart *Singularities of co-rank one*. As I turned one more page, my eyes fell upon the diagram labeled The Swallowtail Singularity.

I recalled Uncle Gambi's final epileptic-driven outburst: *Find the swallowtail!*

Next to this diagram, a handwritten notation had been created within the margin: *Examine parallel plane five units from vertex of tail along St. Charles Avenue. General Lee defined as unit normal at point of intersection of plane curve, move to one of two cusps.*

I read and reread Uncle Gambi's message while holding my breath.

Carefully examining the polynomial function generating the shape of the singularity itself, I realized this was the mathematically derived treasure map I had been looking for. Within my notebook I labeled a rendering of the swallowtail function as Diagram One then added, Uncle Gambi had provided units of measurement by defining General Lee statue as the unit normal. Uncle Gambi intended to take the curve projected onto a particular intersecting surface defined as the distance from the vertex and use that curve, with its corresponding dimensions in unit-General-Lee-lengths, as the map.

I understood that I would have to plot this function to scale on a modern map of New Orleans to locate the positions of the swallowtail cusps. I flipped a few pages ahead and labeled a new heading *The Wonderful Rewards of Life*, underlined this four times and wrote: *The reward for performing my tedious and previously unwelcome high school geometry homework proved to be nothing less than a treasure chest laden with golden doubloons!*

I was both overjoyed and reassured that rewards were manifesting. I had recently become concerned with the possibility that no rewards would be offered in life; that it resembled nothing more than a confidence game advancing hollow promises with little or no payoff, the equivalent of traveling along a nearly endless highway with toll booths situated every few miles.

I inquired after the availability of tracing paper at the information desk. The librarian opened a drawer, thrust toward me a single sheet and slammed the drawer closed. Without looking up, she continued to make notations on her desktop collection of papers and notebooks. While curious, I could not pause, having my work to attend.

I laid out a coordinate grid upon one of the New Orleans street maps then found the dimensions of the statue in an architectural monograph within the special books collection. Upon this same document, there appeared faint pencil drawings similar to those adjacent to Thom's swallowtail function, confirming that I was precisely following Uncle Gambi's drunken logic. As the guard announced library closing. I hurriedly plotted the two swallowtail locations. Each of the cusps lay along a line defined by Calliope Street. Without hesitation, I snapped my notebook closed and set out. Unable to control my elation, I paused and said thank you to the grey-suited librarian. She did not raise her head or acknowledge this; I could not help but linger at the door, turn and gaze back at her, feeling that perhaps we could be friends. As I pushed through the doors onto Tulane Avenue, I was uncertain if I ever had a true friend or what that would feel like.

Shaking off this odd distraction, I made my way directly to the plotted set of coordinates representing the first cusp. The mapping placed me in the middle of the intersection at Calliope and Baronne, clearly not the location of a recently buried treasure. I slumped against a parked car, feeling the same sense of dread experienced while at University in receiving a lower than expected test grade. At that precise moment, however, my attention became diverted toward a remarkable disturbance in the middle of the next block. I scrambled inside a recessed doorway to garner the best vantage possible while remaining unseen.

Chief Petty Officer Deckley of United States Naval Intelligence braced himself against the wall of a building and was jetting urine in a centrifugal fashion. His regulation naval khaki pants were stained green over both knees; his belly protruded through an unbuttoned flowery shirt. Even more astonishing than this government liason's presence and sodden deportment, was the appearance of my doppelganger, Johnny Jupes, dodging the Chief's haphazard spray while desperately attempting to lend him support. Jupes followed while the Chief argued with the air itself, lunging forward and throwing a right hook before lurching into a parked car. Chief Deckley bounced off the car, careening off the sidewalk into the street; Johnny Jupes followed him while attempting to maintain hold of one shoulder. The Chief tossed his arm to one side and barked, "I don't pay you for that! I pay you for information! The fuck good you are…"

My doppelganger, boaster of prodigious genitals and manly exploit, hung his head and followed the Naval Officer like an obedient puppy; serving, by the looks of it, as some form of lackey!

Chief Petty Officer Deckley stopped in the middle of Calliope, convulsed and vomited, staggered backward then continued retching while braced against a parking meter with ribbons of yellow and blood tinged fluid jiggled just underneath his chin. The Chief nearly toppled over yet flung Johnny Jupes' hand away once again and pointed to a door across the street. Above this door, I could just read a small hand written sign: Dixie Beer.

"We need a drink to become men again!" Chief Petty Officer Deckley roared and stumbled off the curb to pick unseen objects out of the air, at first delicately, then, with growing alarm. He turned in circles, urgently brushing himself, the movements intensifying to where as he appeared to be fending off an attack of locusts, culminating in a wild thrashing of arms and violent slaps against his head. As soon as the attack commenced, it stopped.

The Chief now dug both hands deeply into his pockets, losing his balance in the process. Johnny Jupes leaped forward once again attempting to prop him up. As the Chief removed a hand from one pocket, loose cigarettes, spare change, and business cards spilled onto the pavement. He attempted to place one of the cigarettes in his mouth yet as the hand shook so violently, it fell. The Chief then abruptly crossed Calliope directly into the path of a pick-up truck. Johnny Jupes had to run forward, pushing him out of the way. The truck slammed on its brakes and swerved around the pair as they disappeared through the door of the bar. More than astonished, I quickly moved forward to pick up one of the fallen business cards and examine it.

David Deckley, Private Investigator - Infidelity, Surveillance, Disguise

Chief Petty Officer Deckley, Military Intelligence, was one and the same as David Deckley, the drunk Private Investigator: I have been deceived again. Johnny Jupes continued to appear at in-congruent points in time and space, dragging me further into a hellish black hole of subversion. With the latest charade unmasked and what it implied uncertain, my resolve to locate Uncle Gambi's treasure only intensified.

Holding the traced mapping in front of me, I continued toward the second plotted point, approaching the I-10 expressway underpass as I had before on that horrid night and once again inched through the tall grass toward that same steel off ramp support beam. In kicking a Bacardi miniature, I looked toward my feet. Where the beam met soil, I saw the distinct scratch in the form of a swallowtail singularity.

Unlike my first visit, I was now almost impatient and from my back pocket snatched the copy of Foucault's Madness and Civilization, which I had been reading for the fourth time, and began to dig, using the spine of the book as a spade. The soil proved loose and very shortly a smooth wooden surface was apparent. I cleared more dirt away and recognized a bird, a swallow, carved into a cedar lid. Realizing the box was far too small to represent a treasure chest, I slapped my palm against the soil.

Recalling that an answer key had been provided within the appendix of most University Science textbooks and that I had found it particularly convenient to read my study questions at the end of any given chapter then refer to the answer key for solutions to problems which were particularly difficult or taking an inordinate amount of time to solve. Uncle Gambi had not provided me with his answer key. He was dead, and I was on my own with more work to be done, more revisions, more editing, more thinking. The process seemed endless. Why was I being tormented in this manner? What was I missing? Jerking and tensing my shoulders as a car shrieked overhead on the I-10 expressway, the serrated metal plates once again reverberated like crows.

I tossed Foucault into the vacant hole, kicked dirt over it with the side of my shoe and walked back to my new lodgings on Napoleon Avenue. I sat trembling on the edge of my small but clean bed, pulled the lid off the small cedar box and examined its contents.

An old Bible lay on top. I flipped through its pages impatiently. Seeing nothing unusual, I stored it in my duffle bag, pushing it downward toward the base, well past my strata of recently reordered underwear. I removed several scraps of paper covering what appeared to be a collection of maps. These random snippets consisted of receipts; the first two from Swiss banks, one dated 1942, of five million pound sterling; the other dated 1967, fifty million pound sterling while the third and fourth had been handwritten in a meticulous calligraphy: *Cent bouteilles Montrachet, Domaine de la Romanée Conti, Cinquante cinq mille dollars and Sept bouteilles Château Lafite Rothschild, 1945, Cent Mille dollars.*

This merely confirmed what I knew: Uncle Gambi had guzzled several hundred thousand dollar bottles of wine as if they had been cheap liquor store rotgut.

I examined the maps underneath one by one, spanning several centuries by the looks of it, documenting historic layouts of both the city of New

Orleans and Southern Louisiana. Each bore separate and diverse notations, penned by what had been many hands over time.

I looked at the oldest, entitled *The Course of Mississippi River from Bayagoulas to the Sea*. The cartographer had included several landmarks annotated in English at a later date: *Fort la Boulage*, the first settlement; *Point a la Hache; Detour des Praquemines; Bayou du Mardi Gras; La Potence a Picard*, Second tree; First tree had been originally *called L'Arbre a la Bouleilee; Pass a Serigny*.

I could not be certain what this signified. The documents were pleasing to the eye. South Pass had been scribbled in English as had Mud Cape just above an original designation of *Cabode Lodo*. Chandeleur and Breton Sounds had also been written in English along the coastal area. In more careful script was penned *Shallow water cover'd with many small islands which are but little known*.

Above this, an island had been circled and labelled *L'aux Chats* with the English notation Cats Island circled beside it. An X had been placed over this Cat Island with yet another English addition: *Chest relocated here from Cheniere Caminada, 1893*.

I glanced at the gap under my basement door for a sign of shadow or footfall, bundled the maps up and shoved them under my pillow. The documents appeared to represent treasure maps. Or, they had once served as treasure maps, describing the relocation of Vincent Gambi's stolen money over centuries; money transformed, invested and reinvested.

I possessed goddamn treasure maps.

A small leather pouch remained in the corner of the box. Undoing its leather drawstring, with thumb and forefinger I removed several dull yellow cylinders and placed them on the bed. Brushing one of the smaller lumps with my sleeve, a faint engraving became visible. I knew from my library review that I held several gold escudos, pieces of eight, which had been subject to the elements over time.

I returned everything to the swallowtail box, shut its lid and lay awake, envisioning in succession the Basque's trenchant stare, my doppelganger's jailhouse tattoos, the freight train breasts of Evelyn Razer, the lawn sprinkler penis of the charlatan Chief Petty Officer Deckley and the milk shake mustache of CEO Don Canyon. All would give their incisor teeth to examine what resided in my brigand safe house on Napoleon Avenue!

Yet something important was still missing.

My eye ticked ticked ticked in time to the clock on my night table until dawn broke with the barking of dogs. Uncle Gambi's treasure was buried somewhere in New Orleans, and I imagined Earl Short's voice: *Despite having a box full of goddamn treasure maps, you still don't really know fuck all, do you, Pepper?*

24
DOUBLE SNAKE BITES

Kerry Kelly dropped his book, *Dig for Pirate Treasure*, onto the table and nudged it with the side of his hand until it abutted my legal sized yellow notepad. I could do little not to shout at the top of my lungs: Under my seat are treasure maps and a pouch filled to the brim with goddamn golden doubloons! I had transported the contents of the swallowtail box to work in a small backpack, reluctant to leave anything unattended within my rooming house.

Grady Ranger had been more wont of late to linger in front of our desk, pointedly directing technical questions toward me and challenging the issue of my reluctance to answer aloud in class. He sensed this apparently and had even gone so far as to quip in passing: "Just drawing you out of that impenetrable shell of yours, Pepper." Interestingly enough, each time Grady Ranger approached our desk, Kerry Kelly lifted my yellow pad and slid his treasure hunting book underneath. Kerry Kelly indicated that he wished to keep all treasure hunting agendas between himself and I. His reading choice had been so profoundly serendipitous, however, that I suspected yet another subterfuge. I ignored the possibility; I could no longer bear the responsibility of a Lafitte Lieutenant alone. I needed to trust someone with my Swallowtail box filled with its corsair's secrets. So desperate was I to convey this that I opened my pocket notebook, placed it on my knee just below desk level and wrote:

The pressure to locate Gambi's treasure had become imbued with the same insistence as that commonly recognized just prior to the passing of a baseball sized rock hard stool. As I metaphorically pushed the baseball sized stool out, diaphoretic within my psychic restroom stall, I sorely needed the aid of a sympathetic labor coach, someone to stand alongside and shout: 'PUSH, Rodney Pepper, PUSH!'

Glancing up, I scooted my chair back abruptly, nearly tipping over backward. Grady Ranger had placed both of his hands on our table and was leaning far forward, staring directly at me, inches from my face.

"Do you want to share what you're writing in that little notebook of yours, Rodney?"

The other trainees peered along the table; I stopped breathing.

Were I to read this passage aloud, I was risking a far greater exposure not only as a physics major but as a notebook keeper preoccupied with metaphors of impacted stool and its passing; there would be no appreciation for the many hours of study I had spent seated at my sub-basement University Library carol extracting symbolic meaning and associations related to fecal release; the view of stool as gift, for instance, a present under the tree as it were; the gift to be released with sufficient love and withheld when no love was offered; feces as currency, similar to the golden doubloons residing in my treasure pouch, which I had come to realize, had been withheld by my miserly Uncle Gambi, giving him, I imagined, the same sense of control a major league baseball pitcher would feel in wielding a masterfully thrown curve ball.

I flinched and shut my eyes tightly in imagining a ball of stool hurled across the strike zone as ninety miles an hour.

Stool related metaphor jumbled my thinking.

I stammered nonsensically when Kerry Kelly interrupted: "No, Grady. Rodney was just trying to help me understand the calibration procedure. I asked him to write down the equation for me; that's all."

Grady Ranger slowly pushed himself away from the table. I exhaled.

"Well, we're not discussing calibration at the moment, but it's nice to see you are cooperating. Earl, I like that. You see. The trainees are cooperating. I told you they would."

Earl Short, standing by the door, did not respond, having enveloped himself in a cloud of his exhaled cigarette smoke, his eyes barely discernible and narrowed to an even greater degree than usual. I sensed Earl Short knew I had not been writing about calibration issues.

Pretending to scratch my buttocks, I slid the notebook back into my hip pocket. My thoughts after that became entirely taken up in how I might hint to Kerry Kelly of our coinciding worlds. As if of a single mind, Kerry Kelly pulled me aside after lunch and quietly suggested we make our way after work to the old Blacksmith's Shop in the French Quarter for a round of double snake bites.

I now had no doubt that Kerry Kelly retained the same impacted stool of privateering mystery within his own cognitive-rectal vault and likewise needed it passed.

Thrilled beyond measure to have formed a treasure seeking confederacy, I confessed to having no money for even a single Snake Bite. Without hesitation, Kerry Kelly handed me a twenty dollar bill.

"I never forget a favor, Cat. I'm like that."

The money represented a Godsend with capital G. I had spent my last two dollars that morning on a package of Yodels and carton of chocolate milk. I wondered where Kerry Kelly could have acquired the twenty after attesting to his bankruptcy only a few days prior while urgently needing to borrow sixty dollars. As if anticipating this doubt, Kerry explained that his lawyer had called and wired a portion of the money which the railroad company owed him due to his ocular injury.

Driving toward the French Quarter after work, Kerry Kelly spoke of his roommate, a man named Danny Shane whom he said had been drinking up their rent money. "Danny drinks a bottle of gin a day," Kerry Kelly said. He described this man as someone who would turn it at the drop of a hat and was the fastest man to turn it than anybody he had ever known and that included the Gypsy Jokers. Kerry Kelly had become afraid to accompany his roommate on outings as violence would inevitably erupt. Kerry Kelly explained that Danny Shane's drinking had gotten to the point where he would "go to the grocery store intending on buying milk for the baby then come out with a pint of gin in the bag." Kerry Kelly explained that they had worked together on the harbor tugs several years prior and had become close.

Although unsure why he shared this information, I became exhilarated by

Kerry Kelly's description of Danny Shane, both concerning the man's senseless drinking and that he constituted the-fastest-man- to-turn-it-that-Kerry-Kelly-had-ever-known-and-that-included-the-Gypsy-Jokers.

I reassured Kerry Kelly: "Malcolm Lowry drank his after shave and still kept chronicling, and I mean, he chronicled everything."

While not acknowledging my homage, Kerry Kelly seemed to have something else in mind, continuing his histories with strange insistence. He explained that Danny's wife served as a school administrator, that her nickname was The Costa Rican, and that she too was possessed of unusual violent inclination as was her brother. Danny Shane had met the woman while in the state loony bin and ever since their release, had remained devoted to her.

"The Costa Rican wants to build a new school," Kerry Kelly finally stated, drumming his fingers on the steering wheel. He turned and studied me for no apparent reason. I could not comprehend how the aspirations of building a school related to me. I realized that Kerry Kelly was unloading and that he simply needed to vent, a practice much encouraged at University while serving as the basis for much psychoanalytic discovery.

Kerry Kelly then explained that The Old Blacksmith Shop had been constructed by the Lafitte brothers as a front for large-scale smuggling operations. Relieved to find myself within a sanctuary for transgressors, I was provoked more than ever to unburden myself of all that pertained to the toll which my matelotage had extracted. Kerry Kelly was unaware that the waters of this Louisiana treasure cabal into which he was about to wade had a perilous undertow.

We sat at one of the candlelit tables near the front door. Kerry Kelly ordered a round of double snake bites. He explained that Schnapps was a type of brandy, and had been served as refreshment for French marauders in Lafitte's day. Finishing the snake bites, Kerry Kelly straight away ordered two rum and cokes. I removed from the backpack Uncle Gambi's pouch and his maps. Placing the items on the table between us, I undid the thong of the little sack.

Kerry Kelly's eyes flared in the candlelight as I placed the golden clump of weathered doubloons between us. He covered it with his hands, leaned forward and in a hushed voice insisted we move over to a table next to the stone wall in the most recessed part of the bar.

Once reseated, he whispered, "People are funny about this kind of thing, Cat." I recounted my tale of Uncle Gambi and all incidents following our initial meeting. Kerry Kelly lit cigarette after cigarette, his lighter *snit snit snitting* repeatedly. He, again and again, removed the clump of gold from its sack to turn it over in his hands while I described the process of my research leading to the discovery of the cedar box under the I-10 expressway. Kerry Kelly let his cigarette burn down to its filter until I reached the conclusion.

"Have you told anyone else? You didn't go to the police?"

This had to be asked; a question asked in every TV crime show ever produced. I answered as every character had answered: "No."

I recounted my meetings with both Don Canyon and the drunken confidence man Chief Petty Officer Deckley. I told Kerry Kelly everything, withholding only details with regard my doppelganger as this comprised the deepest layers of my forbidden psyche.

Kerry Kelly nodded and began, "Yeah, I heard all about. . ." then discontinued this thought and performed a cigarette smokers trick: Inhaling, he let smoke seep from his nostrils to sweep it up into his mouth then, as a finale, blow several perfect smoke rings.

"What I was going to say, I had heard about your Uncle Gambi. He worked for I.P.P. about the time Danny's father was killed." He went on to explain that his roommate Danny Shane's father was Bob Shane. "You can ask any of the old-timers about Bob Shane. He founded the company with Don Canyon. Died about fifteen years ago when Danny was a teenager. Bob Shane was a diver and in the treasure hunting business. Danny told me his father got a hold of some old maps and may have found a wreck somewhere off Timbalier Island. Had gone out to shoot a magnetometer line in a small boat and his body was found by the Coast Guard in Barataria a few days later. Cord tied around his head." Kerry Kelly drew his two hands slowly apart in a tightening gesture.

"Woolded," I whispered.

Kerry Kelly nodded. "Same thing happened to the Costa Rican's sister."

"Woolded?"

Kerry Kelly didn't answer but by way of reply ordered two double rum and cokes with lime.

I was glad he had and hoped the next would be a goddamn triple.

This was the perfect juncture to remove the bundle of maps and lay them on the table between us. The first document we examined had been drawn up by L.W. Brown, City Engineer in 1895 and labeled Present Drainage System. There followed inscriptions for drainage machines and rain gauges. Another document in this group was entitled, General Map, Parish of New Orleans: Report of the Advisory Board on Drainage, 1895. Numerous drainage machines were depicted: the Dublin machine, the Melpomene machine, the Bienville machine. I read directly from a handwritten notation: The Rampart Street was twenty-five feet above sea level while the river was thirty-seven feet at high water.

Kerry Kelly tapped the chart with his index finger. "Cat, you bury anything in New Orleans, you have to know its water table. You bury anything where a hurricane lands, and it'll end up in the river."

We examined the several Coastal Charts published by the National Ocean Service: Dog Keys Pass to Waveland; Barataria and Bayou Lafourche Waterways; Waveland to Catahoula Bay; Southern part of Laguna Madre.

"Barataria" Kerry Kelly repeated aloud and swirled his ice cubes.

There was also Norman's Plan of New Orleans, dated 1854. Kerry Kelly pointed out, "The city was organized into districts and wards, cat." He pointed. "See? The spelling of Prytania was *Prytanee*; Lee Circle was Tivoli Circle." He became very excited and lowered his head over the map. "That area in the tenth ward, see that, in the Fourth District, it's circled. And that's an X right there, Cat, right on Adele Street."

It all reeked of treasure, and we both knew it. We were on the right track, both of us half-lit moving throttle down towards fully-lit. After the round of double snake bites and double rum drinks, Uncle Gambi's legacy seemed well within our grasp.

I repeated well within our grasp internally, swirled my ice cubes as well then turned to an older map, dated 1815, which bore the name of a Mr. Maspero of New Orleans alongside of which was inscribed the name of the City Surveyor, Joseph Tanefse. I crunched my ice cube now.

"This is history, Cat," Kerry Kelly said. "See that." He pointed: Surrounding an area labeled *Nouvelle Orleans*, which I knew to represent the French Quarter, was *Faubourg St. Marie*; *Faubourg Solet* extended into the uptown area. Just over *Faubourg St. Marie*, between *Rue Girod* and *Rue Poidras*, was penned another X, while the ink beside it, once a comment, had run, obscuring another ancient clue.

We regarded the Plan of the City of New Orleans and Adjacent Plantations. Compiled in accordance with an ordinance of the Illustrious Ministry and Royal Charter, Twenty-four, December, Seventeen ninety-eight, drawn by Alex Debrunner of New Orleans; the scale was in *Toesas*. Beside the scale notation, hand written in modern English was the comment: One Toesa equaled five feet six and seven tenths inches.

"Wait," Kerry Kelly murmured. "See that slaughter house, near the river, between St. Ann and Dumaine? It's been circled in ball point pen. That's recent. And there's a piece of this map missing." A carefully scissored omission, the edges freshly cut and unfrayed, had been extracted from the original map, possibly within the time frame during which Uncle Gambi had reburied his fortune.

"That missing area includes Jackson Square, a cat and everything below it, right down to the river." Kerry Kelly stared at me and asked, "Do you know how heavy those iron treasure chests are, Cat? I'm talking just the chest."

As if in unspoken agreement, I folded the maps and placed them in my backpack. Our research had concluded, and after that, we immersed in speculation. I had not considered the logistics of actually removing a treasure chest from the ground. My bias had favored the theoretical, assuming that the physical treasure itself, repeatedly recovered and transformed, as Uncle Gambi had inferred, had already been transformed conveniently into more portable currency or symbolic wealth such as Bonds or stocks.

"It would take four men to carry the chest even if it was a third of the way full with gold doubloons. They had to bolt those chests to the decks of their ships." Kerry Kelly showed no squeamishness regarding speculating of treasure chests filled to the brim with golden doubloons.

"People are funny about treasure, Cat. It causes all kinds of problems. You're probably already in a lot of trouble. You don't know the people down here, Cat. There's a lot of old blood."

I recalled the old blood I had seen that had dried on the face of the ungrateful carpenter as he staggered toward me menacingly and said, "I know all about old blood."

Kerry Kelly blew smoke upward, looking straight ahead. I glanced over my shoulder. The bar had emptied. I sipped my double rum and coke through its cocktail straw, drawing in my cheeks as I did. I squeezed more lime into the glass and let the rind float on top of the ice cubes. Kerry Kelly removed a large knife from his belt, broke the clump of old coins in half then reached into his pocket and counted out eight twenty dollar bills.

"Here's the money I owe you as well as a deposit on this. I know an old sea Captain I can trust with this." He placed half of a clump in his pocket, returned the other half into the pouch and handed it back to me. Kerry Kelly appeared pained and said, "Some people in this city would kill you if they knew you had these maps. You can hold them, or I can hold them for you. But if I were you, I'd be thinking about getting out of town." Kerry lowered his voice further, glancing at the bartender. "What I mean to say, I wouldn't want to see anything happen to you. I just wouldn't trust anybody, cat." Kerry Kelly looked me in the eye at this. "Your Uncle Gambi was right. If you're serious about shipping out, you should find the Dutchman. If anybody can help you get a ship, the Dutchman can. He hangs out up around Lee Circle. I've been thinking about shipping out myself."

In the flickering candlelight of Lafitte's Blacksmith Shop, filled with snake bites and rum, I considered finding the Dutchman and shipping out. I also considered joining the Navy, then considered joining the Marines, then considered getting a tattoo across my entire back illustrating a muscular woman with large breasts crucified atop a Rock of Ages.

I crunched my ice cubes as Kerry leaned back in his chair and looked at his hands. "I thought about firing the Dutchman up myself and getting the hell out of rum city. . .."

I understood. Kerry Kelly had been offering me a sincere warning, implying that I could ship out thereby back out of our search for the treasure and implied that I had a choice. I deeply appreciated his gesture yet was certain the warning did not apply to me. Head swimming as I drained my double rum and coke, much had been clarified. For one, I was immortal. Nothing could hurt me.

"Listen," I announced; "We're partners." Kerry Kelly had introduced me to the French Quarter with its sunrises on bar-stools. The Quarter had become at once my notebook keeping abbey and monkdom, a mythical land of Cockaigne. And in this mythical land, who else could I choose as my shipmate but Kerry Kelly from Austin, Texas? I extended my hand.

"I just want you to know I'm not the kind of people who will stab you in the back. But there are some who will." He too drained his rum and coke in one gulp and extended his hand.

With tears welling in the corner of both eyes, I made up my mind right then and there to buy Kerry Kelly a pocket notebook and pen.

The following day Kerry Kelly borrowed some of the money he had given me back and after work, we visited several bars, speaking quietly at corner tables of how we might spend our treasure money. We drove our company car out to the lakefront and strolled past the sailboat dealerships.

"I'd like one of those Bertrams," Kerry Kelly spoke longingly. "Get me a Bertram and tie it up down in South Padre Island. A Bertram is a little more expensive, but it's what I like. The same goes for Barbados rum."

We drove back to the Quarter and visited all of the nautical stores. Kerry Kelly examined every memento on their shelves, fingering the books and inquiring of the prices. We ordered shot after shot of rum, tequila or Schnapps in bars en route to these shops, speculating endlessly and buying nothing. Kerry Kelly never once requested to study the maps nor did he query me further concerning the details of my story. We did this day after day. I offered no embellishments or follow-ups, cherishing our practice of going down to the Quarter and throwing aside the world of analysis and rigorous inspection, aside all responsibility in fact, to witness the sun come up on a bar stool again and again then reel out into the street fully lit after our morning omelette at Mollys viewing the Quarter's batten shutters extending the lengths of Decatur, Chartres, Royal, Bourbon, Dauphin and Burgundy.

"If I were a Captain," Kerry Kelly would go on, "I would run a tight crew. If my mate didn't want to get high and hang out, I would order him: 'Get high motherfucker!'"

I liked the idea of pot smoking day and night with my crew and sailing stoned-out-of-our-minds, or, a far better idea, never leaving the dock in the first place.

Kerry Kelly insisted, "I just want you to know that I'm the kind of people that doesn't forget a favor, Cat. I'm telling you that right now. I'll always pay back my debts. Years may go by. I may be in another state. But if I get the money and know where you are, I'll mail it. That's how I am, cat."

I gladly spent all my money on oysters, beer, and rum as it assisted our endless notioning. Kerry Kelly ordered his shot of Barbados Gold rum upon arrival at every bar, repeating his adage: It's a little more expensive, but it's what I like.

The more Kerry Kelly and I drank, the more Kerry Kelly and I wanted to drink. My chronically knit brow began to unfurl at long last. I had, over my years of study, a tendency to regard people with the severest of tight-knit gazes and suspected that my foreboding countenance caused sober individuals to become agitated. The current release of tension was so pleasant that I debated whether a continual regimen of rum was called for to expedite that welcome sense of ease in proximity to my fellow man.

My face felt a whole lost less sore now. Becoming unfettered by extremes of contemplation and the anxiety it engendered was something I had not previously experienced.

I found that the more Kerry Kelly and I engaged in speculation, the farther we departed from the actual interpretation of Uncle Gambi's ciphers. At some level perhaps we both realized there might have been nothing to work out, that the maps signified nothing and their final solution might not be evident even after subjecting the material to diligent analysis, which we had planned on doing, at some point.

Whenever doubts such as these crossed my mind, I simply ordered up another round of double snake bites.

25
THE COMMUNAL LIVING SPACE

While the accommodations at Mrs. Gold's boarding house were agreeable, its audio-visual characteristics proved just as unsettling as the issue of organic decay had been on Prytania Avenue. The gaping keyhole of my inner door, for instance, served as an ocular gateway between my chamber and the communal basement; to prevent visual intrusion, I stuffed tissue paper into the hole. Similarly, I sealed the three-inch gap below the door with a folded towel.

Transmission of sound into my enclosure occurred without attenuation. I maintained as I had in the past, a motionless vigil on the edge of my bed with pocket notebook and pen poised for transcription at all times. The tenants at Mrs. Golds were a social lot and kept their basement doors open. My basement door, in contrast, remained tightly secure with my duffle bag, containing weighty but necessary literary compendiums, wedged tightly against it.

Recalling that my doppelganger overheard even the barest rustle of bedsheets from his position behind the wall abutting my Prytania Avenue bed, all proceedings within my new living area were conducted in painstaking quietude, similar to the maintenance of vows within a Cistercian order. At one point, I overheard Mrs. Gold alerting another lodger to my presence behind "the door next to the john," informing him I was "a young fellow who worked offshore," and that I "was a very nice boy." She encouraged the man to make friends with me, "since you both work on ships." The man had grunted in response then chuckled. After that, I crept about with greater care, emerging only very late at night to utilize shower, commode, and sink. Always before doing so, I would remove toilet paper from its keyhole and confirm the basement's vacant status.

My inner door and that of the lavatory were at right angles to one another; with each use, this lavatory door swung open and crashed against the inner door, inciting an immediate startle response. The opening of the bathroom door suggested my own basement door was being opened simultaneously. With each displacement of lavatory latch, I bolted upright in bed or, if already standing, I threw myself upon any maps or books I had been studying until the illusion of encroachment had been dispelled. Even though capable of cognitively distinguishing the spatial orientation of the two doors and their inevitable interaction, I could not convince my limbic brain that faceless pariahs were not continually attempting to force entry into my apartment.

Perhaps of more significant issue was the derangement of the lavatory door and resultant percussion serving to interrupt my masturbatory practices: Each thump of wood expedited a flurry of Kleenex, a snap of underwear elastic, and a hiss of rapidly deflating penis. After that, I would be stricken by a catalepsy lasting several minutes. Observing this response, I added an appropriate axiom in the speculative science section of my current pocket notebook:

The fear of being exposed while masturbating is sufficiently primordial so as to be transcribed within our genetic code.

Subject to the precise acoustics of fellow lodgers attending their toiletries, I found myself an audience to a medley of flatulence. Resigning myself to the task of naming and cataloging them, I created subdivisions within the organizational schema of my pocket notebooks. Several distinct classifications were more frequently represented: *Rippling Whiners, Snorting Pigs, Forty Four Magnums, Molotov Cocktails and Wheezing Bjeezuses.* My genuine appreciation for the diversity of farts at this boarding house was akin to the entomologist's sense of wonder in happening upon several rare but distinct species of butterfly within his own back yard.

When painful grunts and groans arose, followed by the dismal blip of a single dingleberry dropped or, flatulent accompanied by no splash whatsoever, the fears and despondencies with which Hippocrates had defined *Melanchiolia*, consumed my being. My heart softened on behalf of its sufferer. The *pips, pops, sniffs, snoffs, wet ones* and *squealers*, in contrast, caused my whole rib cage to expand mirthfully and contract, forcing me at times to pinch my nostrils closed and puff out my cheeks to suppress further paroxysms; in these instances, my middle ear inevitably received undue pressures which mechanically deformed the communicating inner ear chambers with their associated semicircular canals, initiating waves of unremitting vertigo.

The farts of the man who worked on ships, sounded like gunshots or more accurately, shotgun blasts, occurring directly after his lowering of the toilet seat. Easy to identify by heavy footfalls and the conspicuous flapping of flip flops, this sailor's flatus preceded the dropping of dense stool. These expulsions were a prelude to a booming-ka-chunk-of-shit. Each of his evictions was so forceful as to render flatulent and splash as one frightening Nagasaki-like apocalypse of water and noise, indiscernible in its components.

I dutifully transcribed all observations regarding the Napoleon Avenue boarding house into my pocket notebook. Note taking ceased in hearing the toilet bowl lid lower. All reading and writing materials were placed to one side; concentration became futile as I waited patiently, arms crossed over my chest. The acoustics were such that the toilet, with lodger seated upon it, might as well have been situated a foot from my bed.

Far more disrupting than this intrusion of sound were the dimensions of the rooming house doorways and its bathroom fixtures. The measurement from floor to ceiling within our rooms and basement area was uniformly six and a half feet. The doorways had been cut at just over five feet allowing Mrs. Gold's four-foot, ten-inch frame to pass unimpeded. The curses of lodgers, as they scraped and buffeted the tops of their heads against the low laying structures, could be heard continually.

The shower fixture consisted of a pipe extending from the base of the bathtub concluding in a nozzle at only four feet of height. Rigidly attached, the nozzle could not be turned or swiveled to increase the angle of its water jet. The average proportioned shower taker was forced to squat on their knees to come fully under the water stream. A plastic curtain, drawn along a circular track, encompassed the participant and confined them. The diameter of the track, barely the width of a typical adult male pelvis, pushed the curtain against the occupant's skin as if animated and predatory. Writhing in disgust, I shifted, ducked and dipped, overhearing fellow lodgers likewise cursing and groaning, one after another, fumbling and falling within the shower curtain tract. This configuration, of Mrs. Golds' design, comprised some form of either purposeful or inadvertent debasement which her lodgers came to resent collectively.

No greater vehemence was expressed regarding the dimensions of the living environment than that of the two men who had moved in the day after I. In overhearing Mrs. Gold explain their rental agreement; I deduced the pair were father and son, both employed as waiters at a well-known French Quarter restaurant. One of them always remained at the boarding house while the other worked; similar in spirit to the concept of matelot in the old days of sailing. It didn't take long before I could identify, through the aggressive intonation of their cursing, whenever one of them had made his way into the basement space. I braced for both the inevitable thump of forehead against bathroom door frame and subsequent violent retaliation. Either the basement wall, bathroom door or my own inner portal was slapped or kicked en route, producing a jarring impact. In understanding the source of their anger, I could take no offense. The lodgers all felt similarly. I initially experienced a kinship with the father and son in that regard.

Any compassion I held for them, however, was not only dispelled but transformed into weighty suspicion after a single disturbing observation.

After returning from the training school each day, I had taken to eating at the Bonanza Steakhouse on the corner of St. Charles Avenue, generally strolling down Napoleon in the late afternoon as the sun was setting to observe the waves of yellow light crashing over its black and white tiled floor. That same sunlight split in frequency as it shone through the three glass vessels set upon each table: the steak sauce, the ketchup, and the Worcestershire. Floating within this warm kaleidoscope, patrons brought forks to their mouths and placed slices of beef or delicately buttered mounds of mashed potatoes onto protruding tongues, drawing them inward, lolling the fare first to the right then to the left. The eyes of these masticators remained fixed ahead, half focused on some internal marker as their mandibular muscles grew taut then relaxed, taut then relaxed. Many solitary individuals such as myself cast their eyes around the restaurant as they chewed, reviewing who was sitting by the window and who by the salad bar. Each regarded their baked potato then set about peeling the foil with an enormous anticipation.

On an evening toward the end of my first week at the Napoleon Avenue residence, I entered the restaurant alcove and drew up short. Through the glass pane, I observed Johnny Jupes, my abominable doppelganger, seated alongside my father and son neighbors. I lingered behind the pay phone peering at these three men smoking cigarettes and engaging in what appeared to be a conversation of much relevance. My doppelganger wore a new black suit with a white shirt buttoned up to the collar and a wide-brimmed black hat similar to what an Amish grandfather might wear. In his left hand, he clutched a large black Bible. The father and son were both dressed in their restaurant tuxedos which I had observed them consistently wear while entering and exiting the boarding house. At one point, the son, standing in front of the table, presented an idea to his father and Johnny Jupes, gesturing angrily. The father grabbed him by the shoulder and pushed him into a seat. Afterward, their heads bent forward while Johnny Jupes offered some form of clarification concluding with him pointing at his watch and sliding an envelope across the table. The father examined its contents with the son peering over his shoulder. The father nodded and placed the envelope in his jacket pocket. As all three arose, I let myself out the alcove door and sprinted up the block to stand behind a tree and observe the group leave the steakhouse. Johnny Jupes turned and sauntered up St. Charles Avenue. The father and son stood on the corner while the former examined his watch and shoved the son into the street; he pointed in the direction of our boarding house. The son argued for several seconds then walked slowly in my direction.

The son then did something odd.

Cutting behind the steak house, he stood in front of its trash dumpster, pushed the lid upwards and thrust his entire jacket sleeve inside. He removed a discarded can of tomato paste and quite deliberately rubbed his shirt against its rim after which he threw the can back into the dumpster. He turned to proceed back up Napoleon. I walked ahead, keeping within the shadows, filled with significant unease in having witnessed these new associations.

While leaving my room the following morning, the son appeared just ahead of me. Without prompting, he turned and stared. I nodded. He did not return the nod but made the sound produced when particulate matter is sucked between teeth. I nodded again. The son did not return my second nod.

After work that same day, Kerry Kelly suggested that we have a tequila at Johnny White's bar in the French Quarter. I cherished any opportunity to have another what-would-we-do-with-all-that-treasure-discussion. Kerry Kelly described Johnny Whites as the place where all the Quarter people went to drink after work and a bar where people turn it at the drop of a hat.

I welcomed the prospect of drinking tequila to enable further speculations concerning the spoils of treasure, with the additional possibility of observing someone turn it at the drop of a hat; this was preferable to remaining within the troublesome environment of my rooming house with its latest hidden agendas and low-lying ceilings.

As soon as I sat down at the bar, I caught sight of the son, dressed in his familiar soiled restaurant tuxedo, playing cards by himself at a table against the back wall. As he had not yet recognized me, I made an adjustment to my posture, arching my back like a cat and peering over Kerry Kelly's shoulder. The son drank from a Dixie Beer bottle and dealt himself hand after hand of solitaire. I told Kerry I had forgotten my wallet back at the rooming house and hurried away without explanation.

Curious and alarmed, I returned the following evening, this time alone, to observe, not the son but the father, seated at the same table, playing cards and drinking soda water.

Neither the son nor the father appeared to work at a restaurant.

Each returned to the boarding house every evening following an afternoon of playing cards at the rear of Johnny Whites, feigning fatigue and commenting on the fictitious aspects of their employment. I tried to imagine what the pair might accomplish through biding their time at the Napoleon Avenue residence in this way, involved in some unknown form of malignant collusion with my ubiquitous doppelganger Johnny Jupes.

Henceforth, I listened more intently to the father and son's guarded conversations on the opposite side of my wall. They behaved cautiously; the more heated their debate, the farther they moved into their room; the father frequently raised the volume of their TV which drowned out many of these exchanges. When the son's anger erupted, the father offered explanations and appeasements; these were followed by heavy footfalls and sounds of furniture toppling over. Occasionally the father's voice became raised and strained with abrupt and severe admonishments. The son usually remained silent afterward. When not arguing, the father spent most of his time watching TV while the son roamed about their room complaining.

"Keep your goddamn head on your shoulders," or, "We can't afford to lose our heads," the father would say.

Besides this new preoccupation, my mind again became addled by the mysterious postmarked box from Seville, which remained sitting on the table at the top of the stairs. Vincent Gambi, my ancient benefactor, would have kicked in Mrs. Gold's forbidden door by now and taken the package without paying her handling fee or even asking permission. I often removed the maps from my duffle bag and viewed their barely legible notations which I knew represented the poignant record of an ongoing process which began nearly two centuries prior. I gazed at the void in the one map and could only be concerned that Uncle Gambi, in his final drunken state, may have discarded this key and had been rendered incapable of providing any intelligible clue at all which would lend these documents an historical relevance of any kind. The possibility that the Lafitte treasure, undoubtedly buried somewhere, might be lost forever, was maddening to consider.

My attention, however, shifted to a new concern, or rather, an old one.

A week before the start of the practical phase of instruction, Earl Short recounted the history of our training vessel, the Yul Brenner:

"The Yul fucking Brynner's keel was laid by the goddamn Erie Concrete and Steel Supply Company in 1942. It was commissioned by the Navy a year later. The Navy designated it a fucking self-propelled lighter and the Brynner was issued a bloody YF hull number. She was built entirely of hard-assed steel, one hundred fucking feet long, seven and a half fucking foot draft and a twenty-seven fucking foot beam, displacing three hundred fucking tons with a full-assed load. The Brynner was originally designed for carrying bloody fucking ordnance up and down the Atlantic. Here, just aft of the goddamn forecastle this mast and boom were originally constructed to lift five fucking tons. In 1950 the vessel was transferred and recommissioned by the bloody Coast Guard. They hauled its ass in to be refitted in Curtis Bay, Maryland as some god forsaken buoy tender and salvage vessel. It was issued some other chickenshit WLM hull number. In '62, the vessel was decommissioned and sold to the cheap asses at Stegner Marine salvage. They fitted an A-frame over the fantail in Morgan City. In 1975 someone came up with the bright fucking idea of repainting the hull, so it was winched out of the Harvey Canal, and her ass stayed out of the water for four years, too bloody expensive to operate until Don Canyon paid for her sex change operation and she was named the goddamn M/V Yul Brenner." Earl Short winked at Grady Ranger and continued. "At Avondale, its cargo hold, forward of the goddamn wheelhouse, was divided into compartments. The fucking galley was expanded and its sorry-assed crew quarters were moved forward. This useless five fucking ton boom was removed on the forward deck while a big-ass cargo container was fitted onto the starboard side. I.P.P outfitted the motherfucker with navigational equipment and partitioned a container to provide more sorry-ass quarters for the instructors. The other half was turned into your goddamn Nav shack."

Earl Short stared at me and spoke slowly: "The training vessel operates with half its bloody salt water ballast and shows a shit load of freeboard. It's wide, Pepper, and bobs like a goddamn cork. We use it because it interfuckingacts with even moderate goddamn seas to simulate the worst motherfucking conditions you might encounter as the radio position operator aboard any godforfuckingsaken seismic vessel on the planet."

Earl Short did little to hide his inference I might develop a problem with sea sickness while aboard the Yul Brynner. His concluding remarks were transmitted with the same psychically damaging intensity as Ravel's theme from Bolero repeated for the ninth time. I had to place my head down on the table after his announcement as an unpleasant swimming sensation commenced.

From that moment, time proceeded relentlessly toward embarkation; the close of each day was marked with a resounding dread, as hollow and as sonorous as if an iron bolt had been dropped into an empty metal bucket. In the midst of classroom instruction I experienced subtle cardiac and respiratory disturbances; finding myself periodically overcome with slow whirling progressing to abdominal bloating, peripheral numbness, paresthesias, palpitations and dryness of the mouth, all culminating in a sense of cataclysmic doom.

Each day Grady Ranger took me to one side and inquired after my well-being. Gripping my arm and standing within such proximity, I could feel his breath upon my neck. He asked, "Are you ok? I noticed that you color was a little off," or, "So how's it going?" as if I were ill. He became unusually insistent that he show me each and every returned calculus homework assignment, all marked with an A+.

"If you have time, I would like you to review my homework," he said.

Grady Ranger strove to instill a sense of welcome within the company. He was a nice man, and always nice to me, concluding each work day by saying, "Well, take care; we'll be thinking about you," as if I might be a family member leaving on a trip.

Earl Short made inquiries in his own manner: "Finding anything besides a hangover, Pepper?" or, "How's things in the pipe dream department?" He would continue to squint and did not appear to expect a response.

On the Friday before our training cruise, I visited the medical school library at Tulane to gain an understanding of the precise physiologic mechanism of motion sickness. I chose several neurology textbooks for my review. Through visualization of physiologic and spatial interactions, I aimed to exert a precise real-time control over the vestibular center of my brain. The assurance that an intellectual understanding of the mechanism would allow me to control my symptoms proved comforting.

Seasickness arises from conflicting sensory cues; I read then copied the sentence into a general notebook page; I recopied it into a seminal quotation category as a special entry even though it represented formulation of empiric science. I paraphrased out loud:

"Below deck, upon a ship at sea, the sailor's eyes would measure stability while the vestibular sensors of the inner ear detect accelerations due to the motion of the boat upon the water. A conflict arose when there was a failure to match input from various equilibrium systems."

The librarian shushed me. I examined her. A University librarian, she too wore a floor length cut of dress as had her Public counterpart although without the impression of it being frayed; the black cotton material was pressed, its large white buttons clean and sharply demarcated; stray threads were not obvious. She wore a white bow in her hair, precisely affixed. The dress, while appearing recently purchased and of better caliber than that worn by the public librarian, similarly did not accentuate her body curvature. What's more, the faces of the two librarians bore a striking resemblance in their degree of melancholy if not resignation. I could not attribute these characteristics to all librarians, however, only to the two I had encountered. I wondered if they knew one another. I could not make a sufficient commitment toward understanding what these two women represented for me or why they even provoked such consideration along with an accompanying sense of unease. I felt there was something I had not been told about the two of them. I decided that I would attempt to offer the University librarian at least some form of explanation as to what I was doing. I stood in front of her desk and explained,

"I am here to master my vestibular apparatus, the transducer of linear and angular motion stimuli."

The librarian stared at me with the same silent severity as had her public compliment.

I said, "After my studies here, I will be able to tend my vestibular apparatus as a mechanic tends to his fine-tuned performance carburetor."

The librarian slammed her ledger closed. I returned to my table and commenced my study by reading of psychosomatic etiologies, noting phrases such as excess anxiety and hysterical personality. I flicked a few pages ahead and read of egocentric attitudes, exhibitionism, dramatics and suggestibility.

I did not like this book, arose and placed it several tables away. Returning to my seat, I took up the next neurology textbook and read of desensitization therapy which the Air Force had offered many of its pilots in the nineteen fifties and sixties.

I would place myself on a military regimen, each day exposing myself to cross-coupled stimuli of progressively increasing intensity.

I studied the photograph of a man strapped to a metal seat, the notorious Barany Chair, which was rotated by hand, a device capable of completing ten turns in twenty seconds. Afterward, the subject was examined for evidence of nystagmus, the number of times the eye would oscillate laterally. I turned the page and viewed a photograph of a man taken immediately following the conclusion of the experiment. My library chair was tipped backward with the force of reflexive recognition; the back of my head contacted the medical school library floor with a loud TANK!

The photograph had revealed the post-experimental subject's upper torso awash in his own frothy vomit. The Air Force man's head had subsequently hung limply upon on his chest, with the appearance of having lost consciousness. Like the combat foot soldier heroically rising to a standing position despite having taken shrapnel to the head, I forced myself to fixate upon the image, and stammered: ". . .have to keep conditioning, conditioning, conditioning."

I rubbed the back of my head while the librarian stared at me. I issued toward her a reassuring thumbs up and continued in the spirit of tenacious self-sacrifice, this time as if I were a Navy Seal attempting to tie an underwater clove hitch, swimming amidst a school of flesh-eating piranha. I turned to the next page presenting a photograph of the legendary optokinetic drum within which the subject sat motionless - the enclosure itself spun around him.

I contorted at the sight of the ghastly barbecue spit, its subject strapped to a narrow table turned by a handle around its long axis resulting in highly stimulating otolithic provocation. The photograph, black and white, taken in the 1950's, depicting a physician scientist turning the spit with his cropped military style haircut. Another physician scientist, hair cut similarly, stood alongside the first making notes on a clipboard. Both wore floor length white lab coats with several pens protruding from breast pockets.

I moaned and partially regurgitated into my mouth reviewing a description of the haunted swing in which the room enclosing a stationary observer swung around its participant. I read of vertical oscillators and modified lifts then happened upon an image of an experimental chair fabricated purely of angle iron. The subject was photographed strapped against the bare steel bars, head and neck affixed rigidly while an additional apparatus resembling a fishhook dangled in front of his face, spinning wildly. A scientist sat behind an electronic console turning a single large knob.

I had reached my limit and slammed the book of vestibular experimentation shut, breathing rapidly. Knowing I could not quit, I flung the book open, and again and again and again gazed at its photographs, in particular, bade myself to linger upon, above all the other images, the quintessential man's head slumped forward and resting upon onto his vomit drenched chest. My eyes ticked uncontrollably.

I scanned the text regarding a surgical cure and read it aloud as if I were Dylan Thomas lamenting lost youth: "The removal of the entire cerebellum confers. . . . immunity."

I flipped to the glossary; my eyes fell straight away upon the term avalanche phenomena. At that instant a hand bearing bright red nail polish reached over the top of my head and slapped the book closed. A heavy and somewhat moist object applied enormous pressure to the occipital area of my cranium, pushing my face downward into the table. Acute unremitting vertigo commenced as the nail-polished hand took up my pen, and drew an X on a blank notebook page.

An all-too-familiar voice breathed into my ear: "You are here. X marks the spot."

I gurgled.

"You are a sketch yet to be colored," she said. "The sketch needs color to define its borders. Do not place your first color unless you are with me. Meet me tonight at Tyler's Beer Garden and I'll show you this first color."

The pressure abated. I frantically looked over my shoulder to observe Evelyn Razer exiting the library wearing a white feathered boa and a leopard spotted skirt, head tilted back, laughing. The librarian glared at her then at me until I arose and reeled out the fire door, setting off its alarm.

26
A COCKTAIL WITH EVELYN RAZER

Evelyn Razer squeezed into a sequined gown, appeared in the doorway of Tyler's Beer Garden and waved at me. When she tilted her head back and began to laugh, the ice cubes in my rum and coke rattled as if a large truck was passing by outside. She continued to laugh as she moved toward the bar, swinging her purse in circles as her daughter Rhone had done, only in larger circles. She sat on the stool next to mine.

The bartender remarked, "Look who's here."

She asked him, "Do I know you?"

The bartender shrugged, poured Bacardi into a glass and placed it in front of her.

I did not like the way the bartender had looked at Evelyn Razer or the way he had poured her a drink without first asking what she wanted.

Evelyn Razer glanced at me, tilted her head backward, and laughed again. The ice cubes in my glass tinkled. The propagation of Evelyn Razer's laughter within the closed system of the bar created a resonant condition resulting in the significant vibration of objects not rigidly affixed to the building's foundation.

"I just love getting out," she said and lit a Chesterfield. She held the cigarette in her right hand and snapped the middle finger of her left hand against her thumb, keeping time with the music playing on the jukebox. She rolled her wrist with each snap, the practice of beatniks and jazz aficionados.

I found myself unable to speak yet was able to observe her undulate as she sat. Occasionally she whipped her substantial assemblage of hair around to crack it like a whip, emphasizing various turns in the music. She craned her neck and appeared to be looking for someone. I wanted to ask her who was it that she was looking for, but I could not speak. She recognized several people in the bar and waved to them. She leaned over the bar and conversed with the bartender. I strained my ears in an attempt to hear what she was saying to this bartender but could not. From time to time, she turned and winked at me.

After several minutes, still unable to formulate spoken word, I arose and made my way to the restroom. Within the comfort of the latched enclosure, I removed my pocket notebook and in a bold unrestrained cursive, wrote:

Ponderous brains suspended within enormous scientific glass beakers, exert action at a distance, modulating my limbus as Kirk had been telepathically controlled by Sargon after answering the distress call from a lifeless planet. They speak in strong clear voices without moving their lips as the counsel of beings had communicated with the astronaut in Beneath the Planet of the Apes.

I closed the notebook and returned to the bar, my underarms saturated in sweat. As soon as I sat down, she said,

"You just made a notebook entry, didn't you?"

Evelyn Razer knew.

I recalled Uncle Gambi's warning: She will insert herself into your head, and you will have to extract her with pliers. She had somehow inserted herself into my head, but Uncle Gambi had otherwise been overly paranoid. I certainly did not wish to extract her with pliers. I did not wish to extract her at all.

I studied Evelyn Razer's large diameter hoop earrings and wished to return immediately to the confines of the restroom, erect an important subdivision within my current notebook, and entitle it Speculative Symbolism. The first entry would be Large Hoop Earrings. As I arose to do so, Evelyn Razer scooted her stool closer to mine and said,

"No more, Rodney. You're wearing me out. Your ideas are coming so fast and heavy I frankly need time to rest, Mr. Pepper. Dear God. Just sit and don't think. Love this music, don't you? Just love it."

Evelyn Razer knew.

She enunciated the word *it* directly into my right ear. I flinched and sat back down, vertiginous. She drained her drink and said, "We have to pretend, don't we, that we are someone else for their benefit out there. I take care of the kid, take care of the hotel. That's all I do, take care of that stinking shit hole of a hotel. I don't want to do it anymore. You're looking at a woman who is fed up."

She slammed her glass down onto the bar. The bartender poured her another rum.

"All I do is work and take care of my kid. Big handful. Constantly in trouble. Lies about everything. Can't trust a word she says. Not a word. But that's what we do, right? We have no choice." She was referring to Rhone, of course, and it didn't surprise me in the least to hear that she was a consummate liar. I felt relieved. Nothing of what Rhone had told me could be true, nothing about myself, about my hopeless journey or with regard to her mother, this competent woman who sat before me. Rhone had implied that her mother wanted nothing more than to extract the whereabouts of Uncle Gambi's buried treasure and cared about nothing else. How more wrong could Rhone have been. Evelyn Razer was sharing with me, confessing as if I were her most trusted confidant, a priest but more than a priest.

I had an urge to whip my hair around like Evelyn Razer had been whipping hers. My hair was too short to whip. I could only move my head around and around, like a helicopter rotor.

"We walk a thin line, don't we? On one side, the inner; on the other, the outer. God forbid we stray too far in either direction. Am I reading you right? Can you feel me turning your pages?"

"Yes," I said but thought Oh God, yes and would have said, "Oh God, yes" aloud but could only manage single word utterances. I had been stricken with the usual expressive aphasia and regarded her dreamily.

Evelyn Razer placed both hands at the base of her spine and arched backward, nearly shoving me off my bar stool with her left breast. She reached across and grabbed the bartender playfully by his tie and pulled him over the bar.

"I want a Penis Colossus," she said. Curiously this was the same quip her daughter Rhone had made at the lakefront bar. I then observed Mrs. Razer kiss the bartender full on the mouth, placing her tongue on his tongue. I resented the attention she was paying the bartender; resented it bitterly.

I raked the bartenders face with my psychic cat's claws.

She turned to me and whispered, "You were feeling anger, just then, weren't you? He means nothing. Nothing. You hear me? I'm trying to make you jealous. Succeeding right? Feeling it? Me too. Anybody that so much as glances at you I want to dismember them with a rusty can opener. I needed for you to be jealous. I just don't want to share you. That's my problem."

She knew.

I felt the weight of the world drop from my shoulders. Evelyn Razer wanted me to be jealous. And I had been. She swirled her drink and said, "Both my kids call me selfish and self-centered but what am I going to do, right? It's the writing life I crave, that we crave, am I right? Did I read you right?"

Evelyn Razer was reading me like an airport paperback. I felt her fingers turning my pages.

"Your notebook gives your miserable life meaning, doesn't it? Mine too. We're not like others. And speaking of jealousy. There is no more of a jealous mistress than the notebook. Am I right? Am I?"

"Yes," I said.

"We both know how ruthless she is, don't we?"

"Yes," I said again. She was right. The notebook was female. "Yes," I repeated.

"I've tried to fit in, Rodney; expectations of happy home, two car garage. Failed. Doesn't work. Can't work. I could have pretended. Could have. But no. Wanted it all. Cake and eat it too. Left a trail of bodies." She gripped my arm and whispered. "Rodney I'm so ashamed. I killed so many but then again, none of them knew any better. How could they? How could I? I absolved myself of responsibility and guilt long ago."

As I could only offer a single word in reply, I chose the word, "I," the first word in her last sentence.

"I. Exactly." She understood as she resided in my mind.

I listened.

"I didn't know any better half the time. Just dove right in without my bathing cap." She laughed at her joke, and I laughed too as if it were my joke. I was able to laugh now, so I laughed more than I probably should have as this was something I could do. Laughing was something that I could do so I laughed and laughed and laughed. She went on.

"I would rather have time to write, but they get in the way, don't they? That's the way it always is with our sort of commitment. I know you understand, with all those little notebooks tucked away in that big duffle bag of yours. I saw you go to the john and knew what you were up to. Was it about me? Were you writing about me?"

"Yes," I said.

"Or was it about a part of me?" She arched her back.

"Yes," I said but thought, Oh God, yes.

"I can see you're just starting out on your little path of destruction. How exciting is that?" she asked. I wanted to say *very exciting* but couldn't as I couldn't speak.

"I find it just so hard to let go of material things, and the flesh, of course; oh, and all those attachments to friends and family. Keeps a tight grip, doesn't it?" She again enunciated "it" into my ear. I flinched. She knew precisely how to enunciate *it*.

"The problem was I looked eighteen by the time I was twelve. That's how it all started. I didn't know a thing. You never do. But I made him pay. I made them all pay. They're still paying if they aren't dead. After that, my world was like Dresden, every day. Carpet bombing. Do you know Dresden?"

Did I know Dresden? We were so much alike!

I nodded vigorously. She went on. She needed to talk. I sipped my drink and listened to her talk.

"I flew the bombers. Blew them all to smithereens. He became obsessed just like they all did. I just let him. Used it to my advantage. We both know that's wicked, but it's also ok, isn't it? If I get exactly what I want?"

"Yes," I said. I believed her, the way she said it, that it was ok. She had convinced me, her world view. She was preaching to the choir.

She fluffed her hair. "You see, I'm telling you everything. Everything. Then I'll probably have to kill you, right?" She laughed, and I laughed. I laughed and laughed and laughed.

She rose from her stool and said, "Enough. Come. I have to pee." She took my hand and moved through the crowd, yanking me forward. I almost fell. She looked around as she moved; she seemed to be looking for someone. I wondered who it was.

"I treat myself," she said over her shoulder. "Once a week. I wouldn't do anything at all were it not for this one night. So I go out, have a few drinks and listen to music then go back to the hotel. That's it. That's my life."

She opened the door of the restroom and spoke over her shoulder. "You're still going to be here when I come out, aren't you?" The door cracked against my forehead as it closed. I listened to her thick stream of urine then turned my head as there was a commotion. I paid no attention. I heard a flush. The restroom door opened.

"I feel I can talk to you, Rodney Pepper." She hesitated and looked at her watch, appearing displeased. I wanted to ask her if there was anything wrong but I couldn't. I was glad I couldn't speak in this instance as I might continue to ask her if there was anything wrong and would not stop asking her if there was anything wrong. An air current transported the odor from an underarm and thrust it upward through my anterior nasopharynx as if I were undergoing a lobotomy by the infamous Dr. Freeman with his pioneering leucotome. I sneezed.

"Uh oh," Evelyn Razer said. I wiped mucous away from my upper lip and followed her gaze at Johnny Jupes pushing his way through the crowd toward us. In one hand he held a large butcher knife. He tipped over a chair and appeared upset.

"Rodney, you had better defend yourself. I didn't know he would be here, honestly. I had no idea." She touched one of her breasts.

"I'll show you what a television evangelist is, by God, Praise Jesus," Johnny Jupes yelled. As he yelled, however, a tall blond woman arose from a nearby table and pulled him down to the floor by the hair. She struck him with her fist once, struck him twice and then a third time. With the heel of her shoe, she came down on his hand holding the knife. Johnny Jupes shrieked and began crawling toward the door. The woman tore the blond wig from her head and raised it above her head solemnly like the Statue of Liberty holding her torch.

The woman holding the blond wig above her head was Grady Ranger!

Evelyn Razer said. "Jesus. Rodney, we have to leave. Now." She pulled me toward the bar as Grady Ranger pushed his way between the tables towards us. "I'm sorry. He never comes here. He doesn't even drink." I knew Grady Ranger didn't drink. Nor did he smoke cigarettes.

Grady Ranger stood in front of us holding his blond wig in one hand and said, "I'm disappointed in you, Rodney Pepper."

That was exactly what I thought Grady Ranger would say. I felt disappointed in myself. But I didn't know why.

"Can we not do this here, Grady." Evelyn Razer said, bit a fingernail and gazed over her shoulder and around the bar. She appeared bored. Grady Ranger continued.

"I asked if you could have a look at my calculus assignments and you said sure. I waited and waited and waited. You obviously don't have time for that. But you have the time for this. And this is not healthy." He pointed at my rum and coke. "You have a training cruise coming up first thing next week. You need to get early beds."

Grady Ranger was right. I should get early beds. I also knew I needed to begin my vestibular conditioning. But I couldn't right this minute as I was too drunk.

"Grady. Please," Evelyn Razer said. "We're on the same page, honey. Just not the right time." She touched his face. "I have it under control."

"What do you have under control? My life? Your life? His life? And when is the right time, Evelyn? It's never the right time. And meanwhile, my life is going by, my life."

I wondered if Grady Ranger had just as big a crush as I had on Evelyn Razer and had gone to great lengths to dress up as a woman to spy on her? I wondered if Grady Ranger experienced the same gamut of emotions as I did?

Grady Ranger certainly never appeared this upset in the classroom even though the trainees sorely tried his patience. Earl Short, on the other hand, said that he "couldn't give a flying goddamn fuck what any of us did." Maybe this was why he steered clear of Grady Ranger because Grady Ranger cared just too damn much.

Grady Ranger said. "You steal everything. Imagine how I feel for one minute? Can you even try to imagine? Are you capable? No, you can't. You're incapable. And did it ever occur to you that this is why I might have done what I did?"

"No, I'm not buying that," Evelyn Razer said. "You are not laying that guilt trip on me."

"I've got news for you. I've made my decision. I'm going back."

"When did you decide this?"

"What, not congratulations? Not, I'll support you whatever you decide? When did you decide this? Is that all you can say? When did you decide this?"

Evelyn Razer threw up her hands. "Not now, Grady. I'm happy for you."

"Really? I will be who I am regardless of you or my father. And I'm going to be one hell of a woman, and I'm going to make some man very happy one day." Grady Ranger put a hand on my shoulder and added, "God willing."

Grady Ranger turned and strode out of Tylers holding the wig. Evelyn Razer shrugged and said, "He used to do that all-the-time."

I had regained my ability to formulate speech and asked "Do you two? Are you?"

"No no. God no. Not in that way. You don't know? It's such a long story but not now. Grady has always been like this. Over the top. He doesn't come across that way at work but trust me, he gets bent out of shape and imagines things. I don't know what to say to him half the time. But right now Grady Ranger isn't your problem. I'm your problem, Rodney Pepper." She pushed me playfully. I laughed then stopped laughing. Evelyn Razer appeared lost in thought.

"He could be your problem, though . ." She paused. "I just can't deal with any of that at the moment. Never think about your past, Rodney Pepper. It's too painful. And if you are going to be successful, never think about anybody but yourself." She stood up and stated, "My car is up the block. We need to get something straight before we can start making wedding plans, right? Come." She took my hand.

Evelyn Razer wanted to marry me!

"It's just so dangerous to express ourselves honestly, isn't it? We have to reality check constantly, don't we? Where am I? Is this real? We have too many responsibilities and have learned there are things we want more than carnal pleasure. So we compromise, right?" Evelyn Razer lowered her voice to a whisper as we walked along Magazine. She took my arm in hers and pressed her breast against it until my hand and forearm became numb from the impaired circulation. "You know I was going to be a philosophy major at Tulane but went into business and never looked back. Raising a kid; had to be practical. Oh, I've always dabbled in the sexual drama. Started out as a hobby, a way of escaping my miserable life."

Evelyn Razer wanted to marry me!

"So I type. That's about the only thing that gives me hope. If I didn't have my typewriter, I would dry up, Rodney. Dry up." She bit her lip and asked, "Did you hear my typing?"

"Your typing overwhelmed me." I could not help but confess to her; I had to confess to her. "It overwhelmed me," I repeated. She lay a finger on my lower lip.

"We're on the same page. And while we're on the same page, I have another wicked confession to make. I read your pocket notebook."

"You did?" I wanted her to have read my pocket notebook, in its entirety, even my lists of Capitalized Words and Seminal Quotations.

"The first morning, and after that, all I wanted was for you to hear me type." She pushed me playfully against a parked car. "That was all right, wasn't it? I was so curious since you refused to play by the rules. So after I read and understood you, all I wanted was for you to hear me type."

"You type so fast," I said.

"Touch type."

"Did you take a class?"

We were hitting it off incredibly as if our cells shared the same mitochondria.

"Self-taught. Oh God, Rodney, you don't know how much I wanted you for my desk clerk. I was killed when I heard about your other interview. Killed. You see, I never go out. Once a week at most. I don't date. Haven't been with anybody in years, Rodney, years. Please don't get me wrong. I'll take a back rub from that doppelganger of yours once in a blue moon but nothing more. But only because he's the closest I could get to you."

"You knew he was my doppelganger?"

"Oh please. My strength has always been my intuition. I should have been a psychologist."

I recalled Johnny Jupes reaching down and spreading lotion around Evelyn

Razer's already oiled breasts. She probably had not realized his hands had touched her. My doppelganger had been overstepping his bounds. I could no longer believe a word he said, ever. And aside from that, he tried to murder me tonight.

"You goddamn son of a bitch!" I yelled aloud.

"Your inner becoming your outer?"

Oh, she knew.

"Yes!" I cried out. "Yes! Yes, yes, yes, YES!"

My inner and outer voice could as well have been a notebook entry and all because of Evelyn Razer, Evelyn Razer, Evelyn Razer. She was very much the introvert as was I, a modern-day Emily Dickinson sequestered in her paraclete, writing desperately, viewing the world only through slanting rays of light framed within dingy back rooms of the Lafayette. What a false impression the world had of her, assuming because of her manner, her stereotyped physique, and fashion choices that she was promiscuous. There had been rumors about Dickinson too, but all of these rumors had been complete balderdash. Neither Emily Dickinson nor Evelyn Razer were sexual in the least.

I wanted to marry the chaste Evelyn Razer. I imagined our wedding night; her enormous brassiere draped over the bedpost. I would stay up all night long gazing at it hanging there.

"You have to proceed with your matelotage, Rodney Pepper. He chose you as his matelot. Treasure hunting is in our blood, isn't it? I saw from the moment you stepped into my office that you were not desk clerk material with that blackness in your eyes."

I wanted to rush to the mirror and observe that blackness she observed. I would curb the strong urge to make faces.

"Confession: I played along. I knew you would never have the patience to work the switchboard. That's why I'm general manager. I can smell it and taste it."

Evelyn Razer made ample use of her senses.

"The treasure is all yours, just remember that. You deserve it all," she said. "Trust your instincts."

Evelyn Razer was helping me actualize my untethered proclivity for piracy, encouraging it even.

"We'll both be careful and suspicious of anybody who approaches you, won't we?" Her nipple touched my elbow. Others had given me the same advice, but she was the only one really looking out for me.

"Yes." I slurped inadvertently.

"It's decided. I'm going to become your accountant," she stated. "No charge. You're going to be rich as hell, but the very first thing I'm going to need is that manifest. That way I'll have a full an accurate sense of your Fortune. Your Uncle stole the manifest from Seville, did he tell you? He told one of my bellhops that when he had been drinking. Gambi and his doppelganger were so irresponsible and both sexually promiscuous, especially that big fucking doppelganger of his. We knew each other. . ." She paused and touched her hair. "But you are so different. You are a quiet businessman. That's why Grady likes you. But as your accountant, I need for you to bring me the manifest to calculate your income tax. We don't want to be audited, now do we?" She ran her hand through my hair.

Evelyn Razer and I were now together, engaged to be married by the sound of it as well as being business partners. I did not understand tax laws in Louisiana but respected her commitment and hard work on my behalf. Evelyn Razer was protecting my interests.

"God, she's competent," I could not help but speak out loud.

"I like that touch, referring to me in the third person. Didn't think I'd notice? You handle the treasure. I'll handle the paperwork. Honestly, we make a great team. But treasure, first and foremost. That's your job. He must have buried it somewhere in the city. Left clues? Am I right? Is that what you think too or did he tell you? I trust what you think, you know. Oh God, I'm so vulnerable, just hold me." Her breasts pressed against my neck, impairing cerebral blood flow to an extent. While we were holding each other, she said, "No one knows I'm Lafitte, just you."

I seemed to recall the taut shirted man was privy to this and Uncle Gambi had mentioned something about this claim. She was continuing, I had to listen.

"I get all dressed up to go out, and no one sees me but you. How do I look, Rodney? Do I look ok?" She stepped back, turned and gazed at me over one shoulder. "Am I still ok?" I stammered, but she had stopped and was now opening the passenger door of a silver sports car. "This is my Porsche. I need to show you something at the hotel."

I smelled leather as Evelyn Razer violently shifted gears. We rode in silence at high speed to the rear entrance of the Lafayette Hotel where she led me into a service elevator, still sharing secrets. "Sometimes I ask myself, 'What's the point? All this. What's the fucking point?' Oh God, listen to me. I wouldn't talk like this with anybody else but you, Rodney Pepper."

"I understand 'what's the point. I keep a copy of Camus' *Myth of Sisyphus* in my duffle bag," I said. We entered another small elevator. She pushed a button and knocked me against the wall with her right breast as she turned.

"Honestly, sometimes all I want to do is hold a penis between my legs, a penis the size of my arm at least. I don't know why I think that because it's over as soon as it begins, just like life. It all cycles back and forth, doesn't it? I don't ask myself why. We don't like uncomfortable facts, do we?. We do anything we can to avoid them, don't we? Isn't that what Camus did? Was he the one that said it was all meaningless shit until we die and then there's nothing? Wasn't he the one? No penis, just some worm crawling out of a decaying orifice?"

I drew a sharp breath. Evelyn Razer was speaking to me figuratively. The big penis of which she spoke was a metaphor. I wanted to tell her that Camus concluded Sisyphus was a happy man, but we had arrived at our floor, and she walked from the elevator.

I followed her along the same hallway through which I had followed the bellhop who resembled Little Richard. She led me once again to the same doorless corridor concluding in three doors. She removed a set of keys from her purse.

"My Nom de Plume is Jickey," she said. "And this is where I write."

"Jickey," I repeated and followed her through the middle door. She moved over to a plain wooden desk upon which sat a typewriter. She yanked open the desk drawer and removed what appeared to be an old parchment. She read.

"'Today, fifth, October 1806, it has been agreed and fixed between us, privateer, Captain, Officers and Crew of the Corsair called Le Philanthrope as follows, to wit:'"

"'Article one. Half of all that is captured will belong to the privateer. . .' That's all I need to read, Rodney. You know of course, who the Captain of the Philanthrope was, your relative Vincent Gambi. The Philanthrope was the only schooner absent from Barataria during the capture in 1814. He was a coward and a traitor, not a man of honor."

Without warning, Evelyn Razer pushed me backward against the wall and gripped me tightly around the throat, pushing me downward. "Bitch, I'm trapped in this fucking place."

Evelyn had called me a bitch. She had a nose for danger.

"I have my own dreams!" she shouted angrily. I looked downward toward her crotch, noting her garter strap stretching tautly. I was afraid that it might snap and thwap my testicles. One of the straps of her dress came off, and a breast emerged like a blue whale through the arctic fog. Sweat dripped from its nipple into my eye. I blinked. The sweat stung. Just as abruptly she loosened her grip, pulled herself off of me and stood breathing like a large bear. I stood.

"We have to turn the page," she said matter-of-factly. "Vincent Gambi, under the Lafitte Charter had plundered more than twenty-five Spanish vessels and took everything. I know this to be true but can't confirm it without the archival records. Otherwise, it would all legally be mine as a direct descendant. That's the law."

"That's the law," I repeated back, watching a dollop of sweat drop downward from the nipple of her still exposed breast.

"That's the law," she repeated. I recalled the package from Seville still residing in Mrs. Gold's living room. I needed to get the package for Evelyn Razer. She was my accountant and my fiance.

"Most of it was originally buried on Cheniere Caminada with a few sites left around the southern part of the state. A thousand people were killed on Cheniere in the 1893 hurricane. All human clues disappeared. A few of the original Gambi people escaped to the mainland sometime after and moved the treasure. They must have buried upwards of fifteen million dollars in gold and silver, that's weight value only," she spoke as she replaced her breast. "The coins would fetch far more, sold individually. All of it represented thirty million dollars as far as I know. I know he invested some of it. There were rumors that it had all been consolidated. Twenty years ago the man you woolded turned up with some very detailed maps and tries to sell several Spanish *eight-real* coins to a jeweler in the Quarter."

I wanted to sit and watch Evelyn Razer as she typed, as she went about conducting her business.

"I want to watch you," I interrupted her. I couldn't help myself.

"Oh, I know you do. I got that."

"No, but I really want to watch you."

"I want to watch you too. I want to watch you dig deep into the ground with your shovel. I want to watch you lift the treasure chest over your head. I'll clap."

"Sometimes I don't know if you're speaking figuratively or not." I was blisteringly honest, but she was preoccupied with the treasure, and I needed a smidgen more of reassurance at that moment. I needed to know *the her of her*.

"Both. Both." Evelyn Razer was reassuring and clarifying while remaining mysterious.

"If you find our treasure we'll all be lined up Basin Street just waiting for you. All of us. Are you kidding? You could take your pick. But you won't have to. I already have someone lined up."

I could take my pick; she had said. I had no reason to disbelieve her. But I didn't want to take my pick. I wanted Evelyn Razer.

"I want only you," I blurted. I moved forward and pursed my lips. She turned her head slightly, and I kissed the side of her nostril. She jerked her head back.

Something bothered me, and I didn't know what. I ignored whatever it was that was bothering me and wanted nothing more than to drink all night long with Evelyn Razer sitting next to me on a bar stool.

"Not here," she said. "This is where I write."

"Let's go down to the Quarter and watch the sun come up on a bar stool, Evelyn." I took her hand and pulled. She stood fast.

I wanted to eat scrambled eggs with her in the morning, looking across the table at her while our warm apocrine glands evinced sweat reeking of rum.

"Work tomorrow, Rodney. We'll talk." She closed the door. I stared at the door knob, hallway silent as a church. I stood, encompassed by the three doors at the end of the hallway at the Lafayette.

I wondered what Evelyn Razer was doing inside her room.

"I want to know everything about you," I said and listened. I imagined she was poised behind the door, listening as well. I walked a few steps, turned and said. "I am being dragged back down the hall back toward you." I shuffled my feet to impress upon her that I was being dragged. I listened and still heard nothing.

I was expressing what I felt. The hallway felt safe as if I were seated comfortably within a restroom stall where I could pantomime to my heart's content.

"You're a popular woman with men because you're very very attractive." I smelled her on me and sniffed.

Typing commenced behind the middle door. Evelyn Razer was at work. As if I were within the very casing of a grand piano, each keystroke felt to be tapping on the narrow border between my scrotum and anus. I knelt, opened the pocket notebook, and composed a poem:

I want to sing and desperately sing,

A morning song.

To crane my neck

Receiving vomit

From mother's beak.

Featherless wings

Peeking over the side

At the big drop.

I closed my notebook and stood, feeling inanimate, like an urn, then announced, "I'm going to go down to the Quarter." I listened for a response. There was no pause in her typing. "I'm going to watch the sun come up on a bar stool." The typing continued. I walked down the hallway and listened to my own vacant footfalls.

27
SUNDAY MORNING AT SEA

Someone had just come and sat down across the table. I had ordered eggs and was seated by the window at Mollys. My inner voice was drunk.

"I have a mind to go over and fire up ole Cap Norris."

I looked up. Kerry Kelly. I looked down; my eggs, on a plate, two over easy, knife in right hand, slicing across the yolk; the orange color pooling on top of my white plate. Knife across the egg white, all white, initially, everybody writing about white, God with a capital G, separating one fried egg from the other, then, flipping the one, onto a piece of toast and taking a bite. I see the orange yolk on my white plate, examine the proportion of orange to white, divine but forgot any and all possibility and opened my mouth. I did not know who Cap Norris was or understand fire up. I ate my egg, now on top of my toast, bite by bite, dripping orange yolk onto my white plate.

"I've been doing a lot of thinking, cat." Kerry Kelly said. I chewed my buttered toast, my eggs, chewed but couldn't taste. I held the food in my mouth, trying to taste but couldn't.

"I was thinking about going over and firing up ole Cap Norris."

It was Sunday morning. Kerry Kelly had already said he was thinking about that.

"I would be surprised if he wasn't up."

I chewed my eggs and looked out the window of Mollys onto Toulouse. I felt sad. The street, drenched in darkness moments before had dried out in the light. I sipped my coke, shook the glass and watched the ice move then stop, still not tasting. I noticed the bread basket and took a roll, mopped egg yolk, placed it in my mouth with two fingers yet still couldn't taste the roll or the yolk but chewed nevertheless.

"He used to be a tanker captain. He hurt his back in an accident up in

297

Alaska and retired on disability. The Cap was never good after that. You look at him now and wouldn't believe his actual age."

I pushed the roll around the plate, mopping up any yolk I could.

Kerry Kelly and I went into the street where I saw angles and corners, rows of long batten shutters, closed, stretching all the way to Esplanade, blue. Rilke spoke of blue in his letters concerning Cezanne.

Nothing blue.

"What, Cat?" Kerry Kelly asked. I had said nothing, or, assumed I had. I couldn't speak, only think: *suddenly-morning-blue, behind-the-batten-shutters-blue, sharp-morning-blue, endless-gutter-before-the-street-cleaner-blue.*

Two people carried newspapers. Newspapers. A long haired man sat in a doorway, a woman next to him; they stopped speaking as we passed, watching us and not watching nicely; the blue gone as quickly as the light had come. I looked at yellow paint chips on wood frames and the smear of light brown dog shit on the pavement. We walked around corners and down streets until Kerry Kelly stopped. He pressed a button. The apartment complex, not of wrought iron but renovation and shingle, and not romantic. A shade drew to one side. A gate opened with a buzz. I followed Kerry Kelly into the first apartment where behind a mahogany bar sat a man with a dirty white beard who continued peering around the curtain into the courtyard. He pulled the shade down only after we had closed the door. With the shade down, his face now appeared gray. Nautical mementos were stacked on a small set of shelves against the far wall and on the bar, a gallon of vodka. In front of the bar, one foot resting on the lower leg of a stool was a man with chiseled face and hair cut straight across his forehead.

"Well, b'god!" The bearded man sounded like a movie pirate. I understood that we were firing up Captain Norris. The man with his hair cut straight across his forehead hugged Kerry Kelly as if he were a long lost brother.

"Whatever you do, don't tell the Costa Rican I jumped ship. If she knew I was on the beach, she'd kill us all." The man looked at Captain Norris then at Kerry Kelly then at me. "She'd kill us all," he repeated.

Kerry Kelly told me Dan Shane had a half finished tattoo because he had turned it with the tattoo artist before they were finished: Standing before me was Danny Shane, the fastest man to turn it of anybody Kerry had ever met and that included the Gypsy Jokers.

"You know I wouldn't bring over a chump." Kerry Kelly said. He repeated, "I wouldn't bring over a chump."

Rhone had called me a chump.

"I was telling Rodney this morning that I.P.P. is a secure job, but it's not my idea of shipping out," Kerry Kelly said. I didn't remember Kerry Kelly saying that. I didn't think Kerry Kelly had said that.

"If you had an opportunity, you would drag up in a heartbeat, wouldn't you Kerry?" Dan Shane asked.

"Hell yes," Kerry Kelly answered.

"If you're this man's buddy, this man right here, then you must be ok," Dan Shane said. "Kerry, I want you to look at this seadog right here. Doesn't he look good?" Dan Shane nodded toward the bearded Captain then turned. "Doesn't he look good?" Captain Norris looked deathly gray. He had been injured in Alaska and retired on disability. "We've been drinking vodka all night long." Dan Shane stepped toward me and asked, "Donny, if something came up, if we found you a ship, you'd drag up in a heartbeat wouldn't you?" Dan Shane had called me Donny.

"I would drag up in a heartbeat," I said.

"You know Kerry and me were the best deckhands that ever worked the harbor tugs. They all loved us. They all loved us, didn't they, Kerry?"

Kerry Kelly turned and said, "They loved us, cat."

"Norris, the skipper on the Bonnie Lady, loved us. He loved us because he knew we would do anything for him. We worked with him down off Main Pass. Kerry, you remember that time we were out on the back deck when that buoy line got tangled in the tires? Thirty-five, forty foot swells with at least a ten-foot sea on top of that and the skipper just says, 'one of you boys go cut that cable loose.' The man knew we would do anything."

Kerry said, "I wasn't going over that rail for any paycheck that night, cap. It wasn't that I was scared, it's that I somehow knew. . ."

I was listening as I had never listened before, to Danny Shane, Kerry Kelly and Ole Cap Norris telling sea stories. Sea stories! And the Ole Cap said b'god; he interspersed his sentences with b'gods with bgod's WITH B'GODS!

"A man would have been lost if he fell over the side that night, Norris," Dan Shane said. "There would have been no hope, Donny so I don't blame Kerry. He told me he knew, and I believed that he knew and that his time had come. We both knew it. Kerry would have disappeared in the current. But we were drifting down on a platform and dragging the anchor with us. Somebody had to get over that side. You remember, Kelly? Head first, over the side, like this!" Dan Shane climbed onto the bar and leaned over the side. I caught the rocking bottle of vodka. Captain Norris and Kerry Kelly removed their glasses.

"Kelly had me by the ankles. Come on Kerry, grab my ankles, I want to show Norris and Donny."

Kerry Kelly held on to Dan Shane's ankles as he leaned forward farther over the edge of the bar. We had all been drinking rum and tequila and vodka all night long and were now reliving that stormy night at sea on the Bonnie Lady.

"His ankles were slipping, I remember that," Kerry Kelly said. "His ankles were slowly slipping."

I finished my glass of vodka ahead of the others and braced myself with one hand against the wall. The room spun once then stopped.

Dan Shane spoke with his head laying on the carpet. "Kerry's absolutely right. My ankles were slipping out of his hands. The sea was washing over both of us, Norris. You know how it is."

"We both could have drowned without falling overboard, Cap."

"Kerry's right. Forty foot swells and that anchor buoy must have weighed three-quarters of a ton, jumping around three feet from my head, like a seven hundred pound cork. And whenever the buoy slammed against the boat I'd yell back at Kerry, 'pull me in, Kerry!'" Dan Shane pulled himself up to the level of the bar. "Donny, that buoy could have popped my head like a grape. But somebody had to do it." Dan Shane dropped back over to the side of the bar while Kerry Kelly held his ankles.

"All I had in my hands was a red fire ax to cut through the steel cable."

Kerry Kelly's arms shook in holding Danny Shane over the bar. Danny Shane arched his back while making ax chopping motions. "I kept shouting back at Kerry, 'Don't let me loose, Kerry! Whatever you do, don't let me loose!' You remember me shouting that over and over and over and over, Kerry?"

"Cap, I had his ankles, but I could feel my hands going numb."

"Don't let loose, whatever you do, don't let loose, Kerry!" Dan shouted.

"Whatever you do, don't let loose," I repeated. I dare not breathe.

Kerry Kelly could not hold Danny Shane any longer and dropped him onto the carpet. Dan Shane stood and said, "You know what I'm going to do? I'm going to throw the Costa Rican a party. That's what we'll do. Invite everybody."

The sea story now over, Dan Shane was speaking about something else.

"Everybody will be there when she walks through the door. Kerry, I'm counting on you to make sure everybody shows up. When she walks through that door, the lost treasure chest is going to be sitting right in the middle of the living room with all its jewels hanging over the side. That's going to be the very first thing she sees when she walks through the door. Everybody will stand up and just start clapping. She'll open the door, and everybody will just stand up and clap."

Dan Shane was describing a lost treasure chest. In the eye of Dan Shane's mind, my lost treasure chest was sitting in the middle of his living room. Dan Shane, the fastest man to turn it that Kerry Kelly ever met and that included the Gypsy Jokers, had put it there. Dan Shane clapped. He looked at the other two men then nodded to me. I clapped several times then stopped. Neither Kerry Kelly nor Captain Norris clapped. Dan Shane had referred my matelotaged treasure chest to the middle of his mind's living room. Dan Shane suggested that my matelotaged treasure chest was not mine but the property of his wife, the Costa Rican. I had not yet imagined opening the treasure chest in my mind, yet he had already opened it in his. Everybody in Dan Shane's mind was looking at the jewels hanging over its sides. I wanted to open the chest by myself and look at the jewels hanging over the side by myself, dig my hands in by myself and throw doubloons up in the air by myself, all by myself, not in anybody else's living room.

Dan Shane said, "You know, Donny, the Costa Rican is descended from one of the original pirate lines, and there's a buried treasure out there that's rightfully hers. These two men right here know that the Costa Rican has a heart of gold, Donny. Pure gold."

"That she does, b'god." The Ole Cap nodded.

"All she wants to do is to get her auntie's treasure back and build a school. That's all she wants to do. Build a school. She doesn't want to spend the money on herself. She's one in a million."

Danny Shane refilled all the glasses and took a drink. The half-gallon bottle of vodka was almost empty. "Donny, reach underneath the bar and get another bottle of this turpentine. Everybody wants more, don't they?" Danny Shane glared at me. "You want more, don't you Donny? You want more? Don't you?"

"I want more. More," I said. Dan Shane glared at me. My knees wobbled because Dan Shane moved toward me: Dan Shane was the fastest man to turn that Kerry Kelly had ever met, and that included the Gypsy Jokers. I took one step backward.

Dan Shane stopped and said, "Tell us a story."

"I attended a George Thoroughgood concert the evening before a calculus midterm and had to be carried out of the auditorium's restroom covered in my own vomitus. They asked me what drugs I had been taking, but I had just been drinking beer, just beer. They wouldn't believe me. I said just beer, but they kept asking me what drugs had I been taking. They told me I was white as the porcelain toilet I was holding. I vomited the entire night until the time of the examination at nine the next morning. I vomited once just before entering the exam room then once during its course but had managed to finish the test and score above the mean." I stopped telling my hero's tale and hiccoughed. Kerry Kelly said,

"Tell them about the man you met your first day in town, the man who said he was your Uncle Gambi."

"Yes-b'god," the Captain roared. "Uncle Gambi!"

Dan Shane stopped moving toward me and shook his finger at Kerry. "Uncle Gambi! That was the story Kerry was telling me. I loved that story about Uncle Gambi."

The men's faces became solemn. They were preparing to listen. I began at the beginning: "I was wandering around down by the moonwalk and sat on a bench to watch the tugs. I noticed there was a man squatting over on the grass who I had seen a few minutes before at the bus station."

Kerry interrupted. "Said he spoke like he was from Europe somewhere, Cap; said he was shipping out; said he was going to find the Dutchman."

Kerry Kelly was telling part of my story and covering a lot of ground. I didn't want him to tell the tale.

"The Dutchman, b'god. Well then, sounds like he was going to find himself a ship. I bet I even knew the bastard."

"Norris knew the man, I'll bet," Dan Shane interrupted. "If anybody would know him, this man right here would."

"I was sitting there watching the tugs. . ." I began again.

"The man wanted you to get his books and his bags out of his room and meet him under the overpass." Kerry Kelly interrupted again. "Right, Cat?"

"Why did he want you to do that, Donny?" Danny Shane looked from Kerry Kelly to Captain Norris to me.

"He said there were people looking for him," Kerry Kelly said. They had asked me to tell them the story and Kerry Kelly was telling it.

I wanted to tell it.

"What did you see under the overpass, Donny?"

Dan Shane was jumping way ahead. There was so much build up before that, so many necessary details to make the impact of the woolding all the more startling. The story was an intricate one and had to be told properly.

"What in hell did you see under there?" Dan Shane insisted.

"Well, first I had to go into his room…" I looked at their faces and knew what they wanted to hear. "In his room, I found his case underneath a mound of feces."

"He means shit." Kerry Kelly clarified. "He had shit all over the case in the drawer."

I meant to say shit but said feces instead. I winced then twitched. The Captain roared and hammered the bar with his fist. "B'god the bloody bastard shit all over his bloody map case. Then what happened b'god?" The Old Cap loved my story. I wanted to tell more of it but tell it my way.

"Map case? Did you say map case? Are you saying that there were maps?" Dan Shane exclaimed. I mentioned nothing about maps. Kerry Kelly must have already told them about the maps.

"Treasure maps!" I yelled before anyone else could interrupt me. I knew they were worthless treasure maps, but I wanted to yell it out nonetheless. I hiccoughed.

"Treasure maps, b'god!!!" The Captain hammered his fist on the bar and laughed.

"This is great. I haven't heard this man laugh like that in a long time, Donny. He had treasure maps, and you had to pull them out from a drawer full of shit with your bare hands then clean them with priceless wine."

Kerry Kelly had already told them the whole story. Thankfully, I had revealed nothing to him about my doppelganger at the Lafitte's Blacksmith Bar, nothing concerning my doppelganger and how he took his vengeful shit upon Uncle Gambi's map case or why. This would have complicated the tale, unnecessarily so.

I couldn't stop hiccoughing.

Kerry Kelly said, "He said that they squeezed the skull of that man under the Interstate until his eyeballs popped out of their sockets."

"You saw your Uncle Gambi's eyeballs, Donny?"

I hiccoughed.

"That's the old way, Cap," Kerry Kelly added.

"I am beginning to love Donny, Kerry," Dan Shane clapped me on the shoulder. "He was quiet before, now listen to what he's telling us."

I hiccoughed again.

"You have to get rid of those fucking hiccoughs, Donny. Here." Dan filled a glass to the brim with vodka. "Just drink that down without breathing. That's how I get rid of them."

I drank the vodka and felt a strong desire to go back and embellish my tale. "I was just sitting down there on the moon walk watching the tugs, the fuggin' tugs when it all started." At University, I had taken careful note of the descriptive term fuggin' in Norman Mailer's manly novel of war. I had heard no one utter fuggin' so I was employing it now. With the glass of vodka in me, I wanted to bandy the adjective fuggin' around like Norman Mailer's sergeant had, fuggin' this and fuggin' that.

"Were you watching tugs or push boats?" Dan Shane asked, and put down his glass of vodka. "I bet they were fucking push boats."

"They were fuggin' push boats." I nearly said goddamn fuggin' push boats but edited myself. I was editing and embellishing all at the same time.

"No, there's an important difference. Have you ever worked on a push boat?"

Danny Shane spoke deliberately. I was confused why he focused on the difference between tug boats and push boats. Kerry Kelly had told me about push boats. That's how I knew about push boats. And I had watched them push. I had watched them push the Lyke's Line ship around the Algiers bend.

"So do you work on the tugs, Donny?" Danny Shane asked.

Danny Shane knew I worked with Kerry Kelly at I.P. P. I didn't work on the tugs and didn't know why Danny Shane was asking me that question or why he was moving toward me now. Danny Shane became very serious very quickly. He took another step forward.

I stepped backward and said, "No."

"That's what I thought. No. Then how can you tell the difference?"

The Captain and Kerry Kelly put their glasses down on the bar. Danny Shane stared at me. I thought I could tell the difference between a push boat and a tugboat. I thought I could, but I didn't know what to tell Danny Shane at that moment.

I hiccoughed.

Kerry Kelly snickered; the Captain slapped the bar and said, "Bygod, it's his bloody hiccoughs. That's his problem, Danny!"

Dan Shane pointed at Captain Norris. "You're right Norris. That's Donny's whole problem, his goddamn hiccoughs!" I felt happier because Dan Shane was happier and was glad I had a hiccoughing problem.

"The reason I was asking, Donny, is because working the push boats in the harbor is a goddamn dangerous job. Whoever has to grab a hold of that toothpick and take up those wires. You know now, some of my seamen won't even do it. I have to do that part. You can have a tow of fifteen loads, and you got to wire all of them. They're afraid of falling between the barges when they take up on the ratchet. Many men have been crushed to death or worse. When those winches start up, and those cables start to tighten, I have to jump in to get a hold of that toothpick and give it one or two more pulls until you can hear the wire making that noise."

"Those cables will snap," Kerry Kelly said. "As soon as you get that shackle on, you had better start running."

"Running won't help you if they part, b'god," the Captain stated.

"Listen to him," Dan Shane said, pointing at the Captain. "When those cables break they come scuttling back up that deck as fast as a bullet."

"You remember when they tightened up, Kerry? You can hear them tightening, Donny."

Dan Shane formed two fists and moved his hands apart, his voice changing from a lower to higher frequency:

Jjuh jjuh jjuh jjuh jjuh juh juh juh.

"You haven't heard anything until you've heard one of those damn cables tightening up right beside your ear."

jjuh jjuh juh juh juh.

"And you have no way of knowing if one is going to break or one is going to hold." Kerry Kelly said.

"It happened to a seaman of mine. Cut him in half-b'god!"

Dan Shane continued to imitate the sound of cables tightening while drawing his tightened fists apart. His knuckles turned white,

Jjuh jjuh jjuh jjuh jjuh juh.

Dan Shane smashed his hands together. I jumped into the air. The Captain said, "A man never hears the wire that kills him b'god."

A man never hears the wire that kills him.

I groped for my notebook but at that moment Dan Shane said, "The three of us could easily handle the Yul Brynner."

Dan Shane had mentioned the name of the I.P.P. training vessel.

"What we need are your charts, Donny. Bring everything on board the training boat with you. We'll do the rest."

Dan Shane looked from Norris to Kerry Kelly and shook his fists, laughing.

"We're going to hijack the goddamn Yul Brynner, Donny, bring her over to Cat Island and grab that treasure chest once and for all!"

I attempted to focus and understand what Dan Shane had just said. A great deal of marvelous storytelling had taken place until that point, and I had become very woozy after my last hiccough-curing-glass-of-vodka.

"If you had a chance to hunt for pirate treasure, you'd take it, wouldn't you? If you had the chance to sail on a ship that flies the Jolly Roger, you'd take it wouldn't you, Donny? When I was your age…What are you, about eighteen?"

I nodded. I was twenty-two.

"When I was eighteen, I would have given anything to help my three old pirate uncles hijack the I.P.P. training boat."

Dan Shane's planning was getting out of hand. Even with the last big glass of vodka in me, I was certain no treasure still existed on Cat Island. The treasure had been moved one hundred years ago.

"We'll give some kind of signal. We have to come up with some kind of signal." Dan Shane clapped his hands together and announced: "I know. A faint whippoorwill call!" Dan Shane placed his hands to his mouth. "*Coo coooo, coo cooo.* When you hear that sound, Kerry, that means you and Donny take the Brynner. Donny you'll have to arm yourself. Get their goddamn fire ax or better yet; we can give you Norris' forty-five. That might be better. They might not pay any attention to you otherwise."

Norris interrupted. "Has he ever fired a forty-five, b'god?"

"Have you ever fired a forty-five, Donny?"

I recalled my tidy whities standoff in the Lafayette hotel room.

"Hell yes," I said.

Dan Shane turned to Captain Norris and shrugged.

"I think we should leave the gun here-b'god. The Coasties might send that cutter they got down in Brownsville."

"The Durable," Kerry Kelly said.

"God, the Durable," Dan hit his forehead with his fist. "They'll send the Durable and blow us out of the water," Dan said laughing and slapped me on the back. I felt as if I was submerged under water and the three men were talking on the surface.

"They got a fifty on the Durable, a three inch fifty and two or three machine guns-b'god," the Captain raised his eyebrows. "They got a patrol boat in Mobile that has a twenty millimeter and one or two machine guns. They got a patrol boat in Pascagoula. I don't know what she carries."

"Hell, they got the Point Spencer tied up in the Navigation Channel right this minute," Kerry Kelly said, jerking his thumb over his shoulder.

"They got a fifty caliber on that," Norris said.

"My buddy over there told me they fired forty rounds into a boat off Grand Isle last November," Kerry Kelly said.

"Did you hear that, Donny? Forty rounds from a fifty caliber. And that was just pot. We'll have endangered the lives of the crew so they'll blow us out of the water." Danny Shane clapped his hands together excitedly.

I stood and held onto the bar. "I'm going for a quick stroll." Without waiting for a response, I walked out the door into the bright sunlight. The prospect of hijacking Don Canyon's training vessel, the Yul Brynner, and sailing it to an ancient, obsolete burial ground provoked an extreme giddiness which subsided the farther I moved away from the pirate's lair.

"I'll ask Mrs. Gold for that goddamn package from Seville," I said, feeling not a shred of anxiety. A man stopped wiping a shop window and turned as I told him, "With Evelyn Razer's musky perfume clinging to the inside of my nostrils, ten rum and cokes and liter of vodka in me, I'll tell her that I want that goddamn package." The man resumed wiping his window as I crossed Canal and proceeded up St. Charles soon approaching Lafayette Park as I had my first morning in New Orleans.

Men with facial scabs pushed past me hurriedly. They didn't signal for cigarettes or pay any attention at all to me. A woman began to shriek and point. Men and women arose from the grass, looked up and pointed. Others gathered their belongings and were dispersing in every direction, colliding with one another and falling.

I recognized the object of their attention, dangling from a large oak tree.

Emerging from Chief Petty Officer Deckley's torn flowery shirt were two long arms. I was not accustomed to seeing arms that long and did not understand why they would appear as they did. Deckley's arms were bound by ropes at his wrists then attached to the Oak's branch twenty feet above the ground. Two thin cords of flesh extended downward far beyond the end of the bone of his upper arm, to enter the sleeves of his shirt, presumably joining his body at the shoulder area. His torso twisted slowly a few feet above the ground. His legs hung below him, motionless, dark stains on both the front and back of his khaki pants, visible as his body slowly turned.

I knew what had happened. At the top of my lungs, I announced, "Strappadoed!"

I pointed at the turning corpse and bellowed, "Heesh been strappadoed!" The homeless turned toward me momentarily. Strappadoing had been one of Captain Morgan's favorite tortures; the action of hoisting his victim up by their arms served to dislocate them fully at the shoulder leaving them to hang by skin and strands of connecting tissue only.

I yelled, "The appearansh often fooled onlookersh ash it fooled ush. At firsht glansh appearsh as shum kind of optical illushun." In having so much to drink, I lisped in my explanation yet did not wince nor flinch. I lisped with abandon.

"Neither winsch not flinsch!" I yelled, viewing the scene in the park as if I were looking at a picture within a library book. I continued walking. "The other one was woolded!" I called over my shoulder. "Not thish one. Thish one wash strappadoed!" I turned and looked behind me. No one followed.

No one was paying attention.

I wasn't worried. I was in no danger.

I arrived at the intersection of St. Charles and Louisiana and turned right. I should have kept walking and turned right at Napoleon, but I turned up Louisiana instead. I did not know why I did, but I continued to walk up Louisiana until I passed a street sign tilted to one side: Freret.

I looked to my right and saw short brick boxes set in the middle of a dirt lot. The square buildings had little square windows and looked like photographs of Nazi concentration camp houses.

There was no concentration camp in New Orleans on Louisiana Avenue in 1982. Examining these little buildings made me uneasy, and I didn't understand what I was looking at, even with the rum, tequila, and vodka to mollify my vision.

These were structures, not houses.

People moved toward me between these structures, moving across the parched earth. I studied the small square windows of the concrete bunkers, these machine gun pillboxes. How hot it must be inside. An old black man, the same man whom I had seen my first morning in New Orleans, the haggard Zen Roshi, stood just beside a rusty stop sign, the only person in the street. I asked,

"Where am I?"

He turned and looked first at me then at the people walking across the dirt between the two pillboxes.

"Da Magnolia," he said. "And you need to start heading back that way." He nodded in the direction I had come. "Now."

I stood still.

Something was wrong. I shouldn't have seen machine gun pillboxes and people coming toward me. I didn't know what happened. I turned and walked; then ran. I ran all the way to St. Charles Avenue veering off the sidewalk every few feet in glancing over my shoulder. No one followed me.

Something was wrong.

28
SHITBIRD

Dan Shane had asked wouldn't you, wouldn't you, wouldn't you? And then pulled his hands apart, imitating the sound wires make just before they snap and cut a man in two: *Jjuh jjuh jjuh jjuh jjuh juh.*

I had agreed to do something but recalled only faded images, my memories stored on one-hundred-year-old decomposing cellulose. Drops of sweat expanded from pores on my legs and pooled in rills of exposed nylon mattress cover. I kicked the rest of the cotton sheets off my bed and lay still. This motion caused the room to tilt. I turned and saw Chief Petty Officer Deckley's business card on the night table. With this, the room tilted another ten degrees.

The nuances of nausea had become far more familiar than I had admitted to Eddie, the I.P.P. personnel manager. We had been given Monday off before the Training voyage. I was certain to remain ill through Tuesday morning when the Yul Brynner had been scheduled to get underway. The vomiting would continue for at least twelve hours followed by another six of dry heaving. Sliding my pocket notebook off the nightstand, I wrote with my head laying on the pillow:

My heart and soul retained the esophagus as its timepiece, adhering to its erratic contractions as a trainman synchronizes his pocket watch. My life will undoubtedly conclude in a torrent of vomit as I pass into the anesthetized state of awareness of all that falls within the rapidly diminishing angles of sight, smell, and hearing. Gastric odors, flatulent squeaks and smoky outlines of breasts will comprise my final reveries.

I closed my eyes and opened them; the room spun slowly. Moving off the bed onto all fours, notebook, and pen in hand, I crawled along the floor, out the door, and into the bathroom. I sat aside the toilet, created a subdivision heading, nausea, and wrote:

Bullfrog crawls from pilot's mouth; Japanese Zero careens toward battleship; frog hops against cockpit glass. White Rock nymphet alights on the rim of the bowl, cups hands, flutters wings, drinks. Mule appears, wearing a straw hat, rears back, kicks side of the bathtub; nymphet knocked into the toilet.

I placed my notebook down onto the rest room tile. Vomit pumped from my mouth as if from a well. Afterward, my arm stayed draped over the side of the bowl; my forehead leaned against the cool porcelain. I unraveled toilet paper, wiped my mouth and the back of my neck. I mopped vomit off the rim and dropped the paper into the water then flushed, watching it all spin around.

Dan Shane planned to hijack the I.P.P. training vessel.

I convulsed. The single strand of orange bile hung from my lower lip then dropped fell into the water.

Returning to my room, I lay on the bed for the next several hours and listened to the lodgers. Mrs. Gold came downstairs and made tut-tut-tutting sounds as she swept. I flinched each time her broom banged against my door. She paused outside my room, and I listened to her listening to me listening.

As soon as the son came back from his day of work, he argued with the father. The TV volume increased. In one instance, the father's voice rose and could be heard clearly above the din. "You follow the goddamn instructions. We get paid only if you follow instructions." With that, he left slamming the door behind him. With each passing hour, the son became increasingly agitated. I heard the slosh of a liquid rebound against the side of a bottle, followed by release of the vacuum seal. Clattering and bumping accompanied the sounds of chairs being tipped over as he moved about his living space. The television blared, channels were switched, finally settling on a wrestling event. I listened to the crowd cheer and the announcer scream. The son began talking to himself.

"I'm tired of goddamn waiting. We're just going to have to see about the goddamn instructions. I have a goddamn plan of my own. I'm going to kill that shitbird myself. Fuck the goddamn instructions."

I raised onto one elbow. The son entered the common area of the basement and bumped into objects. Doorknobs rattled, one after another.

The son's footfalls could be heard ascending the wooden staircase followed by the rattling of the living room doorknob. He descended. The bathroom door opened. A loud thud reverberated throughout the basement: the son had hit his head on the doorway. A long silence ensued followed by the rattle of shower curtain hooks sliding around the aluminum halo. Another silence was followed by metallic screeching then loud thumping. As the thumping persisted, the pipes vibrated below my floor. I rose to a sitting position. A slightly quieter grating of metal evolved into jarring echoes and loud clanking. Metal clashed against metal. Hearing free flowing water, I tried to stand but became dizzy and sat back down. A heavy object clattered against the bathtub. Water splattered against a wall. The water splattered more forcefully against the wall. I lay back tentatively, allowing myself to be lulled by the sound. No sooner had I closed my eyes violent tearing shook my bed. The son had heaved a heavy metallic object against the tub. I followed audible hallmarks of metal being deformed, twisted and bent. The sound of water cascading against the wall changed in its timbre. I guessed both shower taps had been turned wide open. The tub scooted. My eyes riveted on the thin panel of wood at the rear of my tiny closet, separating my sanctuary from the adjacent washroom. Water was being directed against this partition.

The door to the bathroom exploded outward and crashed against my door. The son murmured something to the effect of having fixed the plumbing.

He fumbled at my basement door lock.

I threw my legs over the side of the bed and stood, not knowing what to do. The son slid the towel at the base of my door to one side with his foot. Water continued to douse the paneling on the other side of my closet.

The tissue paper which I had placed in the keyhole was being pushed inward. I heard a slosh of liquid followed by vacuum release of the son's lips against a bottle. The tissue paper continued to inch inward.

Water pooled around the son's shoes and snaked into my room. Doubled over, I waddled into the closet as the paper plug dropped onto the floor. I leaned forward and with my left eye, monitored the tip of his ballpoint pen as it protruded through the keyhole, probing the air. The son had not known that the tissue had been dislodged and continued to probe. He cursed, the pen was abruptly withdrawn and his mouth now pressed against the outside of the lock.

"I know you're in there, shitbird, goddamn shitbird you!"

I was the shitbird!

The tip of the son's tongue extruded through the orifice of the lock like a pink amoeba. I withdrew farther into the closet, eyes twitching uncontrollably. Against my back, I felt the percussion of water showering the other side of the bathroom wall. Moving my head forward again, I observed saliva dribbling below the lock.

"I can see your light is on, you shitbird you."

The bulb inside my bedside lamp shattered. I sank to my knees. The son laughed. I heard him now moving around in his room. Creeping out of my closet, I examined the shards of the broken light bulb and noticed a gaping hole in the far wall.

In the center of this wound, a malignant eye observed me.

"Shitbird," the son's muffled voice spoke. The son pressed his mouth against the hideous hole just as he had against the keyhole.

"Goddamn, shitbird you! Are yew *dar dahring* in there, in your cage, on the papers in your cage?" The son laughed.

The son had fired a bullet through the keyhole. His gun, I suspected, had been equipped with a silencer.

Struck down by an abrupt and severe paralysis, I dragged myself back into the closet and listened to the son's laughter. Moaning like an animal caught in a trap, I pounded my legs with both fists. I reached back to palpate the region over my lower spinal column. I examined my palm for traces of blood. There was no evidence of a bullet wound.

I had been stricken with pure hysterical palsy!

I became angered at my helplessness and summoned the image of Don Canyon in full Ramses pose.

"I am not a shitbird!"

I spoke aloud with the same force of language the ancient senators addressed the ecclesia and rose slowly to my feet, placing my hands on hips. "I am goddamn Ramses, King of the goddamn Pharaohs!" I bellowed and swiveled my head from side to side.

"Shitbird," the son yelled. My legs collapsed. In my heart of hearts, I did not believe myself to be the embodiment of Ramses.

"Am I King of Siam or Sister of Baby Jane?" I asked aloud, pounding my uncooperative legs which felt to be made of wood.

Another lodger entered the basement area, and I listened with hope as he became engaged in conversation with the son. Their words were somewhat difficult to discern over the eruption of cascading water.

"What's going on?" he lodger asked.

The son whispered frantically to him. The lodger laughed in response to whatever the son had said. He replied, "You had better…" The lodger's comment became muddled. Footfalls thumped rapidly up the forbidden staircase once again. The son screamed at the top of his lungs,

"Mrs. Gold, they're trying to kill us down here!"

The son thumped to the bottom of the stairs and began banging and thrashing about the basement. He seemed to have momentarily forgotten about me although I noted that my door bowed inward precariously as he intermittently flung his body against it.

"They're killing me!" he yelled. "They're down here killing us all!" The son thumped back up the stairs, pounded on the door and spoke in a voice choked with pain.

"Open up, Mrs. Gold, they're killing us; they're killing us down here!"

The son thumped own the stairs, entered the bathroom and shrieked: "Oh my fucking God! Son of a bitch!" Pipes were flung followed by clanging of metal on porcelain. "They're killing us!"

The distinctive high-pitched voice of Mrs. Gold arose on the other side of her door at the top of the stairs. "What is it? Who's there?" she piped.

"Open up, Mrs. Gold, they're killing us all down here!" the son sobbed. He sobbed so convincingly that I wondered if, at that moment, whether a group of thugs in the communal space were indeed killing him.

"What's going on in my basement? Do you need help?" Mrs. Gold squealed.

"Yes, I need help goddammit Mrs. Gold. Open the fucking door. They're all around me down here killing us!"

There was a brief pause then I heard Mrs. Gold chirp, "I can't hear you! Hello? Hello? What is happening?"

Mrs. Gold would not open her basement door.

"What does it sound like is happening down here, Mrs. Gold? We're getting hacked to pieces down here. They're killing us!" The son was insistent with irritation in his voice.

Mrs. Gold's apparent inability to hear or comprehend what was happening was as irritating as the son's shrieks. I heard footfalls within the house above as Mrs. Gold moved around.

"Let me ask you something. Will you be my Supreme Court witness?" the son spoke with the lodger again. "She can take it to the town and city, but I'll take it to the Supreme Court. Just say you'll be my Supreme Court witness." The lodger mumbled something. I heard one of the outside doors slam.

Shortly, I heard the son's voice outside my basement door. "I've got a forty-four magnum, shitbird," he spoke through the keyhole. "Goddamn forty-four magnum." The son entered his room, passed into the communal space and ascended the stairwell and screamed, "He's got a gun, Mrs. Gold. It's a goddamn forty-four magnum it looks like! He's…"

I jumped at the sound of four gunshots. Faint high pitched chirping could be heard upstairs. Doors slammed. Shoes slapped through water as the son ran back into his room. His outside door slammed followed by another gunshot. The wood of my own outer door splintered. I heard sirens approaching from both directions on Napoleon Avenue. The son had taken matters into his own hands. His methodology was not rational.

I threw open the door to the communal area and studied the area. Within the bathroom, water sprayed up like a fountain from the base of the tub. Clothed only in tidy whities I tiptoed rapidly through the water-soaked basement and glanced up the stairway.

Mrs. Gold's door was ajar.

The son had blown the lock off! The door of the father and son's room also remained open. In seeing a shadow move along the far wall of their room, I pranced up the stairs, and entered Mrs. Gold's living room, where no lodger was allowed. On her front porch, Mrs. Gold cries sounded like a bird being attacked by a cat. I peered back down the stairs at the son leering up at me holding a freakishly large gun, its barrel poised vertically against his right shoulder. The gun was fitted with a silencer as I had suspected.

"Shitbird," the son said and spat.

Tucked in his belt was another gun which looked like Clint Eastwood's forty-four magnum. I heard more sirens approaching and walkie-talkie static outside the house.

"He's in my basement," Mrs. Gold's voice cracked. I turned to the antique table upon which Uncle Gambi's package lay. Someone spoke into a loudspeaker out front. I snatched up the box from Seville and as I did, heard banging on one of the downstairs basement doors.

"Come out with your hands on your head!"

The son cried out: "He's got a forty-four magnum in here. He's got a forty-four magnum."

The basement door was broken down; radio squelch and loud gunshots were heard. With Gambi's package under one arm, I darted down the stairs and collided with the son as he turned the corner, firing his forty-four magnum over one shoulder as if evading bandits on the Pony Express. The son pressed the barrel of the gun against my temple. My legs gave out beneath me and began lowing like a cow being lead through the slaughterhouse chute. I released several spurts of urine against the front pouch of my tidy whities.

"Hostage here!" the son called out. "I got my forty-four magnum flat against this shitbird's head." We descended to the base of the stairs, and all the New Orleans police officers gathered around, their guns drawn.

"Ten Forty-Four H," one of them said into his police radio. Static was followed by several more ten signals.

"You haven't hurt anybody, but you're in enough trouble as it is," one of the officers told the son. "Turn him loose."

I had been vomiting all day, was dehydrated, and the drunken son had taken me hostage after I had stolen the package from Mrs. Gold's off limits living room table. Mrs. Gold appeared from behind two police officers, moving through her basement making clucking sounds.

"These two I trusted," she said and threw her hands into the air. "Ruined, all ruined." She walked directly up to the son. I tucked the package behind my back. The son pushed the barrel of the gun against my temple. This hurt. I winced. She held her arm up and snapped her fingers in front of the son's face.

"You don't scare me. Give me the gun. He's a nice boy who works offshore. Give me your gun," she snapped her fingers again at the son's nose. I wished Mrs. Gold would stop snapping her fingers.

"You didn't open up the door Mrs. Gold when I was telling you I'm getting attacked down in your basement. They were attacking me, and you just stood up there behind your door." The son addressed the police in a louder voice. "I got my forty-four magnum, officers…I had to get my forty-four when they came back to kill us all. I captured this shitbird trying to get away."

The son now insisted that I was the perpetrator, the ringleader of the gang who had tried to kill them all, even though I was dressed for the massacre in nothing but urine soaked tidy whities.

"Give me," Mrs. Gold moved forward and jumped, trying to grab the gun out of the son's hand. The son pulled me to one side with Mrs. Gold following. The son pushed me between himself and the jumping Mrs. Gold. Mrs. Gold ran around behind me and chased the son. We turned several times in succession, and my head spun.

"Don't do that, goddammit, Mrs. Gold, you fucking bitch!" The police officers moved closer. I caught a whiff of my rancid armpits as we turned. I wished I had taken a shower earlier. At that moment, the father strode into the middle of the flooded basement and commanded, "Give me that fucking gun, you asshole!"

"Good," Mrs. Gold stated, throwing up her hands. "That's his father."

The father walked directly up to the son, knocked the gun upward, grabbed it out of his hand. "You blew it, Pancho."

The New Orleans Police pushed the son down onto the basement floor, pulled his arms behind his back, handcuffed him and jerked him upright as water sputtered from his mouth. I backed into my room and put Uncle Gambi's package directly into my duffle bag. Outside my door, I overheard Mrs. Gold say to the father, "I'm afraid you are going to have to leave immediately."

I decided that I would leave. A police officer interrupted my packing to record my name and contact information. Another officer asked several questions about the incident and my relation to the son. I did not tell them about the father and son's phony job or their animated meeting with my doppelganger at the Bonanza Steak House. I mentioned nothing about the strappadoed private investigator Deckley.

I needed to leave when possible and open Uncle Gambi's Uncle Gambi's postmarked package from Seville. I had to get all that information to my accountant as soon as possible.

29

BLOOD MONEY

Rid of my hangover through the invigorating participation in my near assassination attempt, I made my way to the YMCA on Lee Circle where I had previously noted a sign announcing Welcome in ten languages. After receiving my room key, I lingered in the lobby to observe the European students standing in front of the map rack. Each pointed in a different direction. I wanted to shout out:

For Godsakes be careful everybody!

Instead, I retreated beside the pay phone, cradled my pocket notebook in the crook of my arm, created the heading *YMCA* and wrote: *Hairy underarmed German and Dutch women wearing sandals, their boyfriends with blankets draped over shoulders, all unaware that criminals, like serpentine vapors, diffused through the lobby, waiting for any opportunity to pull the I'm-locked-out-of my-truck-trick or the look-over-there-what's-that-I-can't-hear-you-ploy.*

Closing my notebook using both hands produced a surprisingly loud report: Several of the Europeans flinched. I entered the elevator with a countenance flat as asphalt on a Texas panhandle highway. Once the door had closed, I made a chimp face and flared my nostrils several times.

On the building plan over the emergency stop button, a notation had been made beside the floor to which I had been assigned, the sixth: *American Males Only.* Unsure of the significance, I hummed as the lights blinked, one after the another: Two, three, four, five, six. The door opened with a bleak ping revealing a barren gray hallway, lit by a single flickering incandescent bulb. I missed the company of the backpack-toting Europeans, and would have gladly returned to the lobby and join one of their rap circles, but I had to accept that I was not only an American male but an American male notebook keeper. My journey remained solitary. On the wall opposite the elevator door, a sign hung:

No Guests Allowed in Rooms Past Ten PM.

The room, half the size of my quarters at Napoleon Avenue, appeared clean but smelled as if the walls, carpets, and bedding had been washed down in urine. I needed a shower after my day of protracted vomiting and opened my duffle right away, removing flip flops, a fresh pair of tidy whities and a towel. I wrapped the towel around my waist and cracked the door. The passage was empty. I followed signs to the shower room, passing a row of toilets separated by waist height partitions.

There were no doors associated with the stalls. The implication was obvious: Were I to have a bowel movement I would have to wipe like the wind careening across the Kansas plain, all the while guarding my genitals against the prying eyes of the other American males strolling past with their toothbrushes. And I could pen no graffiti aside the toilet roll rack, as much as I desperately wished to share with the world *the me of me*.

In entering the showering area, I came to an abrupt halt. An unclothed man stood under one of the nozzles, slowly and deliberately toweling himself.

The man looked military.

With a square jaw, bushy mustache and hair cut like a drill sergeant, he toweled and toweled. The floor surrounding the shower drain was dry, however, and I noted that the two shower heads present were separated by no form of partition.

The man was simply toweling himself, having concluded his showering, by the looks of it, some time before. The man's mouth contained an enormous wad of gum around which his jaws gyrated. He stared sullenly at me as he toweled. He then blew a bubble and held it in the inflated state for what seemed like an inordinately long time.

I couldn't take my eyes off the man's bubble.

The *pop* resounded throughout the shower room like a gunshot. I hopped into the air. Flinching because I had hopped, I winced because I had flinched.

"I noticed there were no doors on the toilet stalls," I stammered, took a deep breath, and casually flung my towel over the rail, revealing my penis and buttocks in the stark gray light. I assumed a modified Yul Brynner pose, that of an irritated Ramses, and manhandled the shower taps but jumped back, letting out a whoop as chilly water sprayed my belly button.

Applying my shampoo and scrubbing vigorously under my armpits, I held my eyes tightly and angrily shut. After a time, I peeked. The shower stall was empty.

I wondered where the military man went.

As my senses had been throttled by all manner of conspiracy, once back in the room, I dressed then straight away opened Uncle Gambi's package. Withdrawing twenty sheets of parchment, I sat down hard on the bed, confronted with a continuous and incomprehensible script, each letter joining the next without a break, all the way to the bottom of the page. Sums were present in a few margins and haphazard scribble which had been penned by the same hand as the original calligrapher, all reminiscent of Leonardo Da Vinci's mirror image shorthand. Heading each sheet were notations of another form, the initials A.G.I. then P de C, the word *legajo* followed by number and date.

Following a loud rap on the door, a woman walked straight into my room, strode directly past me to the window and opened it. In her arms, she carried a baby. Possessed of short-cropped gray hair, high cheek bones, and a nose pushed to one side like that of a prizefighter, she wore glasses and carried a hand-woven shoulder bag.

"Smells like you peed yourself." She said. "Did Danny jump ship?"

"Are you The Costa Rican?"

"Danny calls me that. The Costa Rican sounds like I work for the CIA. My name is Qucha. You met my brother Tommy."

"Tommy"

"At the library? He wore the eye patch; told you he had a peg leg and you believed him?"

"The Basque!" I exclaimed.

"Tommy pretends he's Basque. We were both born at Charity, but he changed his name legally to Erge Laztago as he came to strongly identified with Basque culture while he was in prison. Learning the language gave him something constructive for him to do. I'll give him credit for that. Danny and I have taken care of Tommy since he was paroled. It would probably come as no surprise to you that he organized the theater troupe and served as librarian at Angola."

I wondered what specifically about the Basque required *caring for?*

"This is my daughter, Maria Fortuna Shane."

The letters ETA had been tattooed between her thumb and forefinger on the hand which cradled Maria Shane's head. Her brother possessed this same tattoo. While at University, I recalled having come across a reference to these initials as associated, not only with that greatest author of automaton tomfoolery and ocular larceny of all time but with reference to a society that European nations linked to Basque terrorism. If this association only resided within her brother's imagination, I did not understand why Qucha would as well bear this mark.

"I'm here because I had been told that you got yourself into a fucking mess, and I understand it's about to become a bigger one. I love Danny to death, but Danny, and his roommate Kerry are not the ones you go to for help for this. Do you understand? So please listen. For the past two hundred years, the maps you hold have only been in a woman's possession. We never let a man go near them. There is a reason for that. My great Auntie Fortuna was Gambi's original *griffonne* lady. She was kidnapped by pirates straight off the streets of San Sebastian, put on a boat and sold into slavery. She woolded your Vincent Gambi in Galveston just like his relation was woolded under the expressway recently. Both got what they deserved."

I swallowed.

"Auntie Fortuna woolded Vincent Gambi then shot him with a musket. She put a hole in his belly the size of a bread loaf, took one of his pirogues and disappeared with every ounce of Lafitte gold that he had stolen. Her story was passed along from mother to daughter. I'll tell it to Maria one day. We don't know what she did for the few years after she killed him, but Auntie told me she might have lived with the Chitimachas on Grand Lake. We know there had been several small chests which she moved from place to place. She eventually showed up in New Orleans with her daughter Renee and set her up with one of the wealthy merchant's sons. The man gave Renee education. Before Fortuna died, she gave Renee the Gambi Bible, and inscribed educate your children inside its front cover."

"Even though her intention had been to build a school, if she had shown up with that amount of currency, they would have killed her. Not much has changed. Have you been over to Freret?"

Despite my state I remembered Sunday morning and the pillboxes set atop the arid dirt lot. I nodded.

"Renee, Fortuna's daughter, moved the treasure around and copied its locations onto maps you have which were passed from mother to daughter for six generations until your uncle stole them from Auntie. The week he took our money, she had contracts waiting to be signed to start construction of our school. She died six months after the theft. Mr. Gambi was hired at I.P.P. and used their equipment to locate the remaining underwater sites noted on Auntie's maps."

I felt sickened at her mention of these maps and how they had been appropriated.

"He tried to circulate some of the coins from one of the chests a few years later, so we found him. A contract was taken out by the others."

"The Lafittes?"

"Lafittes?" Qucha raised her eyebrows.

"Evelyn Razer is a hot blooded Lafitte." I had meant to say full blooded.

"Evelyn Razer is full of shit. That woman's grandfather was the last of the Sockserhausers. They were a German gang that used to go down to the Irish Channel and fight with meat cleavers. The only reason you're still alive is that she doesn't know where the treasure is buried."

Qucha used the exact words of Evelyn Razer's daughter. Surely this could not be the truth. Evelyn Razer and I were to be married. She was my trusted accountant.

"I should never have told Danny about the school. I don't know what he has planned but as usual, it's fucking out of control whatever it is. Men fuck it up. That's the way it's always been. I may have to kill you quickly, so Tommy doesn't do it slowly like he did your uncle and that dip shit of a private investigator."

Tommy was the New Orleans woolder, and Evelyn Razer was a meat cleaving Sockserhauser!

"No Gambi's were left on Cheniere Caminada after the hurricane," Qucha continued. "After Auntie died, I hired a detective to find the rest of your people. We needed to draw your uncle out again. Your father didn't want to have anything to do with blood money, so we left the bus ticket for you. I never thought you were stupid enough to come, but Tommy did. He told me all he had to do was chose the right book. He's good at sizing people up and knows his Dewey Decimal System."

Sartre's Introduction to Genet: I had been shanghaied by the power of suggestion. He had used precisely the right worm to bait his hook!

Qucha pointed at the documents spread out on the bed. "It's Spanish. The script is called *Processal,* used by the notary public. My mother's sister taught me to read this when I was ten. She didn't have any school, but she knew all of it. She taught me a lot and told me about my mother."

Qucha put on a pair of glasses and looked at me over the top of the rims. "There are rules for reading this." She turned the pages one by one. "Most of these notations are cargo manifests for slave ships." She pointed to the initials AGI stamped on each paper. "That's Archivo General de Indias. The largest repository of Spanish colonial records in the world are in Seville. Some of these are accounting papers from Cuba, some from Santo Domingo, *Seccion Venezolana del Archivo do la Gran Coloumbia,* this one's from Caracas."

"These are originals. He stole these from the archives and mailed it to himself. These were written in ink made from the gall of oak trees. High line content. They used very fine paper." She held up the paper to the light. "You have to understand certain complexities of the Spanish empire to understand how to use a manifest like this, what inferences to make. See," She pointed to a specific notation. "One hundred *pieze de Indias* were sold in Cartegena…that's one hundred units of slavery this particular ship had apparently been carrying."

"What?" I asked.

"One hundred units from the Guinea Coast? A single unit of slavery could be one healthy male or two women or three children. These units were a part of their economic system. People were also bought in Cartegena on this voyage and taken on board. See, *encadenada*, meaning enchained together." She pointed to another word, Bara. "These silver bars are double blood money. The Indians mined the silver in Bogota or Potosi that was used to pay for the Africans." She placed a finger above the marginal notation. "They have the shipper's mark and ingot numbers here. This ship also received gold bullion. This was a very rich ship after leaving the Gold Coast."

She turned to another page, examined that one then turned to another then another. "These are all similar records. There must be over twenty ships represented here." She looked at other pages. "These…are *Notas Diplomatica*, Spanish consulate in New Orleans…Spanish schooner was captured…blah blah other similar…." She turned to the next page and read, haltingly, ". . .the French, in number two hundred to two hundred fifty men, have fortified themselves completely in the Isle of Barataria where they have a mount of fourteen guns. They have taken possession of Cat Island and called it New France, and to that place and Barataria they take all their loot….That was Legajo one eight two eight, March eleventh, 1813."

Qucha removed her glasses. "He was trying to destroy all evidence for the fortune, to cover up the trail of blood money. These are valuable historical documents and they're being degraded the longer you keep them like that." She pointed to the bed and my duffle bag. "Tommy will go berserk if he finds out you have them. He had a reputation for stabbing inmates at Angola if his books were returned damaged."

Librarians were sobering and all too real individuals who paid heed to detail.

I bundled the documents and handed them to Qucha then reached into the duffle bag and retrieved Gambi's Bible. As it fell open on its front page was an inscription, long faded with two words discernible: "....mon fils..." I handed Qucha her book.

"Good. I have one for you. The one you returned. Didn't you bother to look inside?" She removed a book from her bag: Complex Analysis, the same book I had recovered from Uncle Gambi's shit strewn hovel and presented to him under the expressway. He had attested then that the book held no meaning. Trust nothing I've said were his final words.

Qucha said. "So, I'm a school teacher, right? Turn to page fifty-seven."

I turned to page fifty-seven and regarded the heading: Interpretation of a function of a complex variable as a mapping. I recognized Uncle Gambi's handwriting in the margin of the book's page. He had circled an equation and sloppily transcribed a set of coordinates: Angle = 0.34(pi), R= Y. A thin sheet of paper fell onto the floor. I could see this was the cut out portion of the French Quarter map Kerry Kelly and I had spent a great deal of time speculating over.

Qucha explained, "This transformation maps a horizontal line onto a circle. That piece of paper your uncle has provided allows you to plot his function. But there is one more piece of information you will need to plug in before you can dig: the unit of measure."

"You want me to go ahead and find the treasure?"

"That's the way it's done as it had been given to you through matelotage. Even Tommy was adamant about that. But if you don't figure it out soon, he'll torture you just the same. Or someone will."

I told her, "I don't know the unit of measure."

"He told you something or, you must have seen something. You may have been looking right at it and not realized, along those lines. He was not a stupid man and fully expected that you would find what he had intended for you to find."

She turned, holding her baby and walked out the door. In the hallway, she said, "If you do run into Danny on the beach, tell him that I will kill you all.

You think he was kidding about that?"

30
THE RIDE TO PASCAGOULA

On the morning of the training voyage, Grady Ranger had asked that I ride with him to the Pascagoula, Mississippi dock where the M/V Yul Brynner was tied up. I was grateful for the opportunity to thank him for what he did for me at Tyler's Beer Garden.

Grady Ranger may have just saved my life.

As soon as I sat down in the passenger seat, Grady Ranger reached across and gripped my hand. "First," he said, "I just want to apologize. It was none of my business what you were doing at Tyler's the night I showed up. You need to understand that. It would never be like that. But it was a good thing I was there after all, right?"

"Yes, it was a very good thing, Grady. Thank you."

"So we're good?"

"Of course."

Grady Ranger placed the company car in drive and arranged his hands upon the steering wheel in the ten and two o clock position. As we moved out of the city, I could not help recollect how Grady Ranger had removed his blond wig and pounded my doppelganger with unremitting and uncontrolled violence. This constituted a curious memory and the actions incongruous with the Grady Ranger I knew, a man who functioned admirably in his capacity as head navigation instructor within the Society of International Petroleum Positioning.

I glanced at Grady Ranger and noticed that his facial features had been altered in some subtle way. For several minutes, I could not put my finger on it. I glanced several more times and could not be certain that Grady Ranger was not wearing lipstick. It did not make sense that Grady Ranger would wear lipstick, however, while driving the company car to Pascagoula on official company business.

I doubted he was wearing lipstick and did not dwell upon this as several other more pressing concerns had been preoccupying me that morning. First and foremost of these was the prospect of riding an unstable training vessel without having performed a sufficient number of vestibular conditioning exercises. There was the more remote and disturbing possibility of Dan Shane forcibly commandeering the training boat to take it plumbing for treasure at fictitious ocean locations. And lastly, hanging over my head like the branches of a large Southern Willow, were the responsibilities and intricate enmeshments that my matelotage itself. My well-being depended on my ability to recover Uncle Gambi's final clue, the unit of measure, plug it into the equation from his text, *Complex Analysis*, then plot it on his fragment of the map.

I could not afford to be preoccupied with Grady Ranger's application of lipstick or his wearing of wigs.

Thankfully, Grady Ranger wished to speak of nothing in particular. He droned on and on about his calculus courses at the University of New Orleans and his weight loss regimen. He told me that several years ago he had weighed twice as much as he did presently and that he had been forced to "get his life back on track." My adviser at University had counseled me using those very words. I shifted in my seat.

"I have to do things in a certain way," he said, "If I don't, life gets the best of me. I don't think about the why anymore. Why am I here? Or, if loved ones die, how do I make sense of that? What are my reasons for continuing? Are there any legitimate ones? Who do I listen to? Which voices are correct? Do I follow society or my own inclinations? Where should my loyalties lie? All that. It frankly all makes me sad. I feel like crying, so I stop thinking completely."

Grady Ranger was sensitive and what he said made sense. If I understood him correctly, he at one time thought a great deal about life and death and the why of it all, but this made him so sad that he was forced to stop thinking. I studied Grady Ranger out of the corner of my eye.

Grady Ranger seemed to be wearing a tad of lipstick.

I understood that in not being accustomed to observe Grady Ranger wearing lipstick, my amygdala and fusinform gyrus, which hosted the facial processing areas of my cerebral cortex, resisted reception of unexpected input.

"I like to stay active, even if I am sitting at my desk," Grady Ranger was explaining. "I'll stand on one leg when I'm not doing anything. This conditions my core. But I forget to do it. I have all these opportunities throughout the day, but I forget. I'm imperfect." Grady Ranger was hard on himself. "When I'm driving, I'll flex my hips back and forth. We do too much driving. People don't realize that it's not healthy siting in a car or sitting at a desk all day long." Grady Ranger was trying to communicate healthy living practices as he drove. I appreciated this but was having a difficult time focusing, preoccupied with my other issues. I had no weight problem of my own. None of what Grady Ranger mentioned seemed to apply. In fact, as Grady Ranger upheld a positive outlook, I could not expect him to comprehend the significantly darker aspects of life that my previous weekend activities embraced, drawing me downward on their extended wings. Grady Ranger likely would understand none of this and moreover, the information might unnecessarily bother him. I had come to appreciate and respect his propensity to become markedly upset at deviations from protocol.

As morning light streamed through our car windows, Grady Ranger appeared stable and organized as he had been while on duty in the training facility. Only the relatively minor and uncertain issue of his lipstick application might suggest the contrary. His clothing had been pressed; his hair trimmed and neatly combed. He shared that he stood on one leg when he wasn't engaged in physical activity. As we drove on, he described the crew and instructors whom I was soon to meet once aboard the training vessel. This was immensely reassuring, and I relaxed considerably. Then Grady Ranger said,

"I've made a terrible mistake. But it's nothing you and I can't work out together. I think it will be really good. My mother thinks so too."

"Yes," I said. Grady Ranger sounded as if he wished to speak about the issue of our friendship. I was relieved that his agenda was that simple. We could be friends. He was likable and knew that it was best for me to embrace his wholesome health oriented outlook. I knew wholesomeness was the healthiest choice in the long run. And Grady Ranger was the embodiment of wholesomeness.

Grady Ranger said, "I guess you haven't heard. I assumed everybody knew."

"I. . .No, I'm not sure, but I don't think I have. . ." I hadn't heard; As this sounded ominous, I hoped Grady Ranger's health was ok.

"I was born Don Canyon's daughter."

I did not understand what Grady Ranger meant by daughter or what Don Canyon had to do with Grady Ranger.

"Now I am his son. I had gender reassignment surgery. Evelyn Razer is my mother. She was thirteen when she had me. Don Canyon and Evelyn Razer were never married."

Grady Ranger had shared a great deal of information in a short increment of time.

I nodded and examined Grady Ranger more carefully. He did not smile to suggest that he was joking. In studying Grady Ranger's face closely, I recognized the lipstick to be a pale pink shade with sparkling additives.

"I am on a daily Testosterone regimen. It's only 100 milligrams a week. That's not that much. I had my breasts removed. They were huge, like my mothers. I developed back problems."

I studied the door handle and then glanced over at the dashboard to verify the speed at which the car was traveling. In changing from woman to man and receiving testosterone injections, I wondered if Grady Ranger, were he to become upset, might be inclined to dismember me. I would not assume that the sex change personality was associated with cannibalism, bestiality or extremes of sadomasochism. Grady Ranger was the first person I had ever met who had a sex change operation. I examined Grady Ranger trying not to turn my head, using excursions of lateral gaze exclusively. In being at once Evelyn Razer's daughter and son, Grady Ranger served as Rhone's brother, previously her sister. I could now see the resemblance.

I understood why Grady Ranger might need a friend. I also understood that he had picked me to be that friend. I assumed this related to my background in Physics.

"I can't really talk to anybody about this in the company. I don't want to. People don't understand what I went through. You're the one person who looked at me as if I were human."

"You've met both my mother and father; you're educated and sensitive; I feel I can talk to you." Grady Ranger spoke with bitterness in his voice. "I'm just a masculinized woman." He pounded the steering wheel.

Grady Ranger was getting upset.

"That's ok. No, that's ok," I said, and regarded the road ahead of us. A truck was breaking fifty feet in front of us. Grady Ranger didn't appear to be paying attention to his driving as he was looking directly at me.

"As a kid, I couldn't see the goodness and beauty in myself. I couldn't make friends with girls. My mother was worthless. That's how I saw her, and I came to believe that if I was a boy I could please my father and I could protect my mother from male aggression. I resisted wearing girls' clothing. I'd play army with the boys."

I nodded toward the truck in front of us; Grady Ranger glanced at the road and thankfully slowed down. He then looked at me again as if he wasn't driving at all. I took the wheel and steered.

"No. Never take the wheel." Grady Ranger slapped my hand. "I was a temperamentally vulnerable child who easily developed high levels of anxiety. I see that now, but it took this to make me wake up. My mother used to have a great deal of difficulty with feelings. She was so young when she had me and she was depressed. You wouldn't know it, would you? I don't think my father respects women. He's so fucked up. Demeans my mother. And then there was me investing so much of myself to get his approval when the only thing he ever approved of was when I told him I was going to get the surgery he said good, and I thought at last, and my mother approved because she said it would make me tougher. 'The tougher, the better,' she says. That's her all over, but that's not me."

Grady Ranger whispered and not only whispered but whispered fast, taking his eyes off the road to stare at me. He whispered at an ever increasing rate.

"And then there was the company. I would take over but he wanted a son who could work with him in the company. I thought that was the solution but he already had a son only he won't speak to him because he's a transvestite; to his mind that's freakish; now he thinks I'm a freak too; little does he know we're a family of freaks but you have now become involved with my family of freaks. That may have been your mistake; maybe the biggest mistake of your life; just kidding but in some ways you're part of it and there's no turning back. She does try and bring my father and I together. He didn't even look at me after the surgery; they fashioned a penis; didn't even look at me; nothing is good enough for him and I can see now how it was all ONE BIG MISTAKE."

Grady Ranger pounded the steering wheel again; the car swerved. I gripped the dashboard.

"That's ok," I spoke loudly. "We're good, though. We're all good."

Grady Ranger slowed the car and again placed his hands in the ten and two o clock position. He said, "Thank you. Thank you for saying that because I was worried that we weren't. It means a lot you know. It carries me through."

"Ahh," I said.

Don Canyon had quite a few children by the sound of it. Grady Ranger had not mentioned Rhone. He had mentioned a transvestite brother but not Rhone. I did not wish to ask him anything which might upset him further. The family was rowdy in general with a certain theatricality which reminded me of my own. I wasn't surprised Rhone, his youngest sister, was such a hellion.

"I figured you would understand with your physics degree and all the reading you do. We make decisions thinking that our course of action is the greatest thing in the world then it turns out to be disastrous." Grady Ranger shrieked. He shrieked at the top of his lungs as he drove. I looked at the truck in front of us and held onto the dashboard again.

Grady Ranger was labile.

"I want it reversed," he shrieked. "I've changed my mind. I want to be who I am. Don't you see?" Grady Ranger calmed down suddenly and said, "And I wanted you to be the first to know. But I got so upset at Tyler's that I spilled the beans."

Grady Ranger chuckled. Relieved by his chuckle, I chuckled as well. So relieved was I that I found it difficult to stop chuckling.

"You did," I chuckled. "You spilled the beans."

I did not know Grady Ranger. Grady Ranger served as my instructor at the training school. Grady Ranger spoke as if he knew me a good deal better than I knew him.

Grady Ranger said, "I think you may have latent homosexual tendencies."

I turned and examined Grady Ranger. I did not wish to consider such matters. It was inappropriate, as chief navigation instructor, that Grady Ranger be speculating on a trainee's "subtexts."

"You have a hard time admitting it. My mother thinks so and so does my father, and Earl Short too. That kind of psychological profile would make us a perfect couple. I think about all that. I would be a quite the mannish woman for your latent homosexual man. I think you would like that. And I usually get what I want, Rodney Pepper. When I see something that I want, I am very persistent until I get it. I'm like the female version of Bam Bam from the Flintstones: *Bam Bam Bam!* You saw me *Bam Bam* the man at Tylers? I was protecting you, and right now I am looking straight at you, kiddo, and telling you that I'm having breast implants and big ones. I'm going to get my large chest back just for you. You obviously like breasts."

Grady Ranger reached across the seat and took my hand. I flinched. Grady Ranger became upset again and swerved the car back and forth across the median, in the same manner as Rhone. I wondered if Evelyn Razer swerved her car while upset.

"OK!" I yelled. "It's Ok." I didn't know what to say so I said, "No, I think you're the perfect mannish woman for me!"

Grady Ranger returned to the right-hand lane and spoke calmly. "You see. I was willing to kill us both if I couldn't have you. That's how deep I am into it. I can't tolerate any form of rejection right about now. It's unacceptable. So I won't. The time has come to put Grady Ranger first."

Grady Ranger laughed. He now seemed cheerful and asked, "Are you ready to make me super-happy, Rodney Pepper?"

I laughed and tried to recall how many times I had spoken to Grady Ranger in the course of my training.

"I have an apartment. I don't like you living downtown in those places. I've been worried sick about you." he said. "If you're with me, they won't hurt you. My mother won't let them, and I won't let them. Feel that muscle. Go ahead, feel it." Grady Ranger flexed his right bicep. At that moment our company car passed over the bridge from Pass Christian to Pascagoula on Old Highway 9. A large sign read *Engels shipyard*.

"There's the Yul Brynner, right over there." Grady pointed excitedly.

The Yul Brynner was a very big blue boat, quite a bit larger than I had expected.

"Please stop the car." I gagged. My vestibular nuclei reacted as a Geiger counter would in being exposed to a sample of radium. Grady pulled the car to one side of the bridge as I swung the door open and vomited over the rail into the Pascagoula River. I had become severely seasick subject to merely the visual stimulus of the training boat, tied up at its dock over two hundred feet away.

Grady Ranger got out of the company car, walked around to the railing and stood beside me. Despite our having had an extremely disturbing and provocative conversation, I did not wish for him to know that I had already become seasick in merely regarding the training boat.

I could let nobody in the company know.

"Bad eggs for breakfast," I said. A string of bile dangled from my chin. I pinched it off and flung it down into the water. I avoided looking at the training boat.

"Are you Ok?" Grady asked. "I worry about you." He placed his hand on my shoulder. We both leaned over the railing of the bridge. I gazed into the Pascagoula River then shut my eyes and wretched again creating another long strand of yellow bile which stretched from my lower lip all the way down to the water. The strand separated and plopped. At that moment another boat approached the bridge through the channel, quite a bit larger than the Yul Brynner.

"There goes a Pogey boat," Grady Ranger said.

Several black men were leaning on its railing, staring at us. I raised my hand to wave then lowered it. They did not wave. Every Pogey fishermen wore a cap and overalls. They did not wear shirts under the overalls.

"There's a plant up river at Moss Point." Grady Ranger added. As we looked on, a single puff of smoke erupted from a small smokestack. Two smaller boats were suspended on either side of the larger vessel. I was astonished to see a real wooden crow's nest, just like in the movies. Sections of large diameter hosing curled on the back deck. Grady followed my gaze. "That hose is for pumping fish into the hold. They can lift the net with those falls and that winch. The engine's in the after house; your fish holds in the middle. That one doesn't have refrigeration, so they have to come in every night." I nodded. The Pogey boat was transfixing. "And that's hard work what they do," was all Grady Ranger said. I nodded and climbed back in the car.

"See. That's all I want. Moments like these. Looking at the Pogey Boat with you. Nothing else. That's what counts, these little moments standing beside a friend. So many people don't understand that. They have missions. I think the world is insane and don't understand where the heads are with most people. They want too much or imagine something that doesn't exist. They delude themselves. It's tragic really. It's tragic when you miss what it is standing right in front of you."

I recalled Grady Ranger's sister Rhone saying something similar but was distracted. The big blue boat disappeared and reappeared behind trees and buildings as we drove toward the dock. We turned off the highway and passed through downtown Pascagoula then along smaller streets leading toward the river. In front of one of the wooden houses, a woman held a baby in one arm while speaking to a man leaning on the open door of a Pontiac convertible with headers and airfoil. A dog lay by the front tire of the car. The couple stopped their conversation and watched us pass. As we rounded a corner a small dock became visible alongside which the Yul Brynner was tied. I stifled further convulsions by focussing on the dashboard of the car.

"You may want to find your compartment below deck and take a short nap. I don't think the rest of the crew are here yet," Grady Ranger said. A nap sounded like just the thing. I waved to Grady Ranger as he got back in the car. I still liked Grady Ranger yet felt better that our car ride was over and hurried toward the hatch.

Grady Ranger called out, "Be sure to eat right and exercise while you're on the boat. I'll check in as soon as you get back, Rodney Pepper."

I waved goodbye. His pink lipstick sparkled in the bright sunlight. I felt badly that Grady Ranger had made the wrong decision and wondered what he had looked like with enormous breasts.

I went down below deck, found the bunk with my name on it and lay down to take a nap. As my nausea had not abated, I hoped I would acclimatize after getting a few hours of sleep.

31
THE MONKEY FIST

I swung my legs over the side of the bunk and dropped to the floor. Vomit sprayed out my mouth and nostrils onto the blanket folded on the lower bunk. Each time the boat descended, the muscles surrounding my stomach contracted and my mouth opened of its own accord.

"Six hours on six hours off. . ." Louis said.

Snit, snit, snit.

Through a break in my compartment curtain, I saw Kerry Kelly sitting on the edge of his bunk lighting a cigarette.

"Did somebody puke?" Louis asked.

As Earl Short had predicted, with little ballast the M/V Yul Brynner rolled over the ocean like a beach ball. My preoccupations with matelotage, pirate skullduggery, doppelganger subversion and Grady Ranger's obsessions subsided. The business of hands-on training and coping with my motion sickness became all encompassing. Despite the inordinate amount of time Kerry Kelly and I had spent on the beach discussing treasure hunting issues, once aboard the Brynner, the subject was not breached. The notations on Uncle Gambi's maps were all but forgotten as we settled into the routine of running imaginary seismic lines south of Dauphin Island.

Most shifts, I lay on the Nav Shack bench, incapacitated. The trainees and instructors accepted this and conducted their activities around me. One of the instructors, Sid, had grown up with my fellow trainee Mike. They had entered the Navy simultaneously, straight out of Gulfport High School. Most of their sentences began with the phrase in the Navy; both spent a great deal of time standing by the Nav Shack bench on which I lay, retelling Navy stories. I listened excitedly to every word.

"I loved Barcelona," Sid said. "There was this place there you'd go, and there was this dwarf woman there who'd go underneath the table and give you blowjobs while you drank your beer. She'd get underneath the table as soon as you sat down."

Louis pulled at his mustache and said, "Sometimes I wish I was back in the Navy, man."

"There was a guy on my ship who got himself discharged by whacking off," Mike said. "He whacked off in front of this ensign."

"No fucking way, man!" Louis said.

"He whacked off all over the ship. He would whack off nine, ten times a day, always in front of people. An ensign saw him doing it, so he got out," Mike said.

Louis said, "Rodney, they'd throw fags of the back of carriers, man. You'd hear about it. Somebody would get thrown off the back of the carrier, man, in the middle of the night and that would be it. By morning the guy could be a hundred miles away. If they didn't send a chopper out to pick him up right away, forget it."

Louis pulled at his mustache. The trainees fell silent, and I felt dizzy.

"It would take about two hours to turn one of those ships around, man and begin searching for the man overboard," Mike said.

Sid said, "That happened on our ship in the Indian Ocean, man. They found his body three hundred miles away two days later. If that happens at night, and even if they do turn around or send a chopper out you still might as well kiss your ass goodbye."

"Yeah, you can't find a man overboard in all that ocean at night. Even if it's calm," Mike said.

I lay on the bench imagining what that would be like to be alone not only in the middle of the ocean but in the middle of the night. I imagined what it would be like to feel completely alone.

Real-life Navy stories, the *snit snit snitting* of Kerry Kelly's lighter and the eddies of cigarette smoke intermingling with bacon grease formed the sensorial input aboard the Yul Brynner as one 6 hour shift passed into the next. I sipped Orange Crush from cans and continued to lay on the Nav Shack bench as if interned in an iron lung. I attended to my navigation exercises when called upon and vomited over the back deck at regular intervals, becoming accustomed to the sight of orange soda jetting from my nostrils, the sensation not altogether unpleasant.

After a week, I resumed my critical notebook review, bringing with me to the Nav shack bench one of my many paperback novels. I became thrilled for instance, when Mike, the ex-Navy diver, picked up Crime and Punishment and began studying it. He turned directly to the end, however, looked at the page number and closed it. "Five hundred and forty-five pages. No. I can't read a book like that. It's not real. Some people can read that; I can't. I'll read a true story now and then."

Later that shift Mike described a portion of his Navy diver's training program when the instructors would throw the probation diver, wearing his Kirby Morgan helmet, into a swimming pool filled with mud. The diver had to retrieve a seventy-five-pound weight from the bottom within a certain amount of time.

I wondered why I read books that weren't true.

Louis was the only other reader in the Nav Shack. He would sit pulling at his mustache while obviously enthralled by his paperback accounts of Navy Seals, the Special Forces in Viet Nam or Navy Fighter Pilots. The narratives appeared to sustain Louis' attention for long periods of time. He drank coffee and smoked cigarettes while turning his pages.

I observed Louis read the non-fiction accounts with a significant amount of curiosity.

"You have to read this one, man," Louis told me one day holding up *MIG Pilot* over the bench on which I lay; apparently the story of a Russian fighter pilot who defected with his top-secret airplane. Intrigued, I insisted on maintaining my ordered deportment in completing a study of Dostoevsky before allowing myself to consider *MIG Pilot*.

After several days, with a certain amount of skepticism, I began his book. Staying up my entire off-shift to finish it, I savored every last action packed morsel of *MIG Pilot*!

Never had I read anything so captivating or emotionally fulfilling as *MIG Pilot*. By its conclusion, despite my exhaustion, I violently craved more *MIG Pilot* and felt no small measure of bitterness in having spent so much time reading the classics. I felt an urge to bring my volume of F. Scott Fitzgerald short stories onto the back deck and hurl it as far out into the sea as I could. In imagining this foppish book floating like the abandoned sailor, alone in the vast ocean at night, I reconsidered. Instead, I created a book trading club to reconcile the classics with non-fiction on board the Yul Brynner. As a first step, I contributed my precious copies of *Crime and Punishment* and *Under the Volcano*, leaving them at on one end of the Nav Shack operating table. I simply lay and waited, becoming fully attentive whenever a trainee approached these volumes.

Louis finally picked up my Dostoevsky and brought it out with him onto the back deck. I experienced a thrill akin to Hemingway watching his pole bend after the giant Marlin had taken his bait! I arose and staggered over to the hatchway, unable to resist the opportunity to share Louis' joy as he read Fyodor's remarkable opening passage.

Louis was using the thick paperback to prop his head up while napping.

Another unpleasant literary surprise had been received at the conclusion of yet another shift while passing the open door of the instructor's quarters; I noticed a large cache of paperbacks on their night table, no less than thirty! Elated, even giddy to find that that our instructors had been rabid bibliophiles, I stumbled into the room as the crew were in the galley having dinner. I gathered several volumes up and began reading titles:

Big Stuff, Garter Snap, Length. . .

No designs were present on the book covers, and these titles were set in a standard Times New Roman type font. The author always sited underneath was Jicky, Evelyn Razer's nom de plume!

The instructors on the Yul Brynner had stockpiled in their quarters every single pornographic novel Evelyn Razer had ever written!

I sat on their bed and read *Garter Snap*. I became unaware of time and in hearing voices approach, I folded the book and slid it into my back pocket, ramming it tightly up against my notebook. With heart racing, I returned to the Nav Shack, brought my literary paperbacks directly down below and impatiently replaced them deep within my duffle bag. Having sampled both *Garter Snap* and *MIG Pilot*, I wanted nothing more than to spend all my shifts reading pornography and war stories to the exclusion of all else.

These plans had to be put on hold, however; that night our training routine suffered a significant interruption.

The sea had remained calm throughout the day, the sky cloudless. When not engaged in navigation exercise, it had been the trainees' practice to congregate on the back deck, lean against the rail and tell Navy stories, or in my case, to listen to Navy stories. On this occasion, Ricky joined us at the rail and pointed to a bright red light on the horizon.

"That's a seismic boat." The trainees gazed at the light in silence with only the sound of cigarettes inhalations. We were all radio navigation trainees. Soon each of us would begin working on just such a vessel. Far behind this red light was an even dimmer point of white light. "That's the radar reflector at the end of the cable," Ricky said.

"That cable's two miles long," someone said. We all looked at the red light then at the white light.

"They're probably using air guns," Ricky said. We were taught in the classroom that the air guns fired sound waves toward the bottom of the ocean which enabled the geologists to recognize oil deposits.

Earl Short had told us, "In the old days they used goddamn dynamite instead of fucking air guns to create these shock waves. Seismic boats would bloody well sink, and men died on the stern trying to set off the charges. Their arms and hands disappeared in big goddamn pink explosions."

I regarded the two lights at either end of the two-mile cable then turned my gaze to the stars, thick in the sky. I looked from one to the next, my seasickness abated. A slight breeze blew across the deck. The sea was calm. Ricky suddenly heard the intercom inside the Nav Shack and returned inside. He emerged several minutes later and announced,

"Captain Maury is on the radio with the Coast Guard."

"Something's going on, man," Louis said, pulling his mustache.

The trainees pushed themselves away from the rail, and turned their heads upward, eyes trained upon the Brynner's wheelhouse where a small red glow moved erratically just behind the window. Captain Maury was gesticulating while speaking over the radio. The trainees followed the trajectory of the Captain's cigarette.

In a moment, the Yul Brenner abruptly accelerated, making a wide turn. The trainees staggered across the back deck gripping the rail. Ricky came out of the Nav shack for the second time and informed us that Captain Maury had been instructed to proceed to a certain longitude and latitude to provide assistance to a sinking shrimp boat. He said that its Captain was drunk.

"We're the largest boat in the area. That's why the Coast Guard called us," Ricky explained.

I moved about the back deck as excitedly as a baboon who had smelled a ripe banana. The other trainees shared in my excitement. We had been called upon to execute a rescue at sea!

The trainees gathered at the stern to observe the wake behind the Yul Brynner. "We must be going at least twelve knots, man," Louis said. With nausea abated, my legs bowed of their own accord, feeling myself every inch the Liverpool sailor. A collection of lights appeared off our bow. As we drew closer, five shrimp boats were circling a sixth, bobbing in the darkness with outriggers extended. With the Yul Brynner's approach, the shrimp boats moved to a wider periphery, allowing us to move closer but appeared collectively to linger, as if eavesdropping on a conversation.

The shrimper in distress listed to one side, stern dipping under the water, its outriggers still extended, onboard lights extinguished. As the Yul Brynner approached, Maury trained a spot on the boat. A grinning man leaned against its high side railing, just outside the wheelhouse, arms crossed over his chest. Another man crouched over an open hatch in the middle of a back deck awash with seawater, frantically trying to operate a mechanical pump. Another could just be seen in shadowy silhouette within the wheelhouse itself, tilting a bottle upwards.

"Get that fucking light out of my eyes." The Shrimp Boat Captain slurred his speech and pointed toward the Brynner. Captain Maury manned a set of controls outside his wheelhouse and backed the Yul Brynner down.

As he turned his spotlight onto the struggling deck hand, my scream surpassed in frequency even an F6, the highest note associated with the Queen of the Night aria in its key of D minor, the key most often associated with tragedy: *Mein Doppelganger!*

Johnny Jupes squatted over an open hatch on the sinking shrimper's back deck, yanking wildly on the starter cord of a tiny motor. My eyebrows spuriously cocked, first right then left, then two lefts and a right. I peered hard at the silhouette of the man drinking from a bottle in the shadowy recess of the shrimp boat wheelhouse. I frantically sought Kerry Kelly with my eyes, feeling a dark foreboding at the vision of my nemesis aboard the very sinking shrimp boat our training vessel had been bidden to rescue.

As the pump motor would not start, my doppelganger paused, wiping his mouth with his sleeve. Hit by another wave, the shrimp boat lurched, and water cascaded over its fantail and into the open hatch. Johnny Jupes appeared no different than a frightened monkey, scooting backward on his buttocks, staring at the sea, wide-eyed. He remained seated for a moment then after the water had receded, crawled forward and began yanking on the cord of the pump. He shielded his eyes from the spotlight and peered toward the Yul Brynner, then convulsed and vomited into the hatch. Afterward, he again tried even more frantically to start the little motor. As he yanked and yanked, he glanced over his shoulder at the Shrimp Boat Captain, who continued to laugh and point derisively. My doppelganger clearly shared my tendency for seasickness and appeared to be the only crew member on board concerned with its sinking.

"Their stuffing box gave out," someone said. Captain Maury had apparently been on the radio with the other fishing boats. The sinking shrimp boat Captain had refused to call for Coast Guard assistance.

"Maury says their Captain is drunk as a fucking dog," Mike remarked.

"Their generator got wet and won't start," Ricky said, coming down from the bridge. The trainees gathered around him, smoking.

"It's the stuffing box," someone else repeated. The trainees from both shifts were now out on the deck.

"Their Captain is ripped to the tits."

"A Coast Guard helicopter is en route with an emergency pump."

"The stuffing box went out. Uh oh, the stuffing box went out," I spoke to the right then to the left, addressing the same trainee twice. I did not understand what a stuffing box was, but my initial impression was that it might bear some form of resemblance to a vanity case. I located Kerry Kelly and prompted him, "A stuffing box, isn't that…" I was hoping in doing so he would give me some indication whether or not our uncertain conspiracy which had been in the back of my mind, was in effect or not. He calmly explained to me that a stuffing box was the water tight interface allowing the drive shaft to pass through the hull and couple with the propeller. As he offered no hint of ensuing mutiny, I assumed that our drunken planning on that French Quarter Sunday morning at sea had been just that. Greatly heartened and unencumbered, I could now share in the state of general alertness pervasive amongst the trainees assembled on deck and participate in our dramatic rescue at sea.

Captain Maury came down the steps of the wheel house and shouted across at the shrimp boat captain, pointing at his outriggers. The shrimper didn't respond, staring at Maury, arms crossed over his chest defiantly. Maury stared at him, bellowed "shit," and then climbed back up to his wheelhouse. He addressed the stubborn shrimper over his PA system. He told him that if he raised his starboard outrigger, he would come alongside and throw a line over to support the vessel, allowing them to pump out the flooded engine room.

The drunken shrimp boat Captain shouted back. "I can't move the motherfucking outrigger. We got no power." He hawked up a large wad of phlegm and spat. I noted the splash of phlegm as it hit the water. Over the PA Maury then asked the shrimp boat Captain to cut down his outriggers. The Captain staggered away from the railing, pointed at Captain Maury and yelled, "I ain't cutting anything!"

He spat again then moved to the wheelhouse and took a drink from a bottle handed to him by the shadowy mate. I strained but could see no details of the second man. He returned to the deck and stood defiantly.

"We have to come alongside you to pass the pump," Captain Maury explained over his PA.

"We don't need no goddamn pump. He's pumping." The shrimper pointed to Johnny Jupes.

"The chopper's going to be here in five minutes," Maury said. I looked from Captain Maury to the Shrimper Captain then back to Captain Maury.

A wave washed over the back deck knocking Johnny Jupes over and drawing him toward the stern. He screamed and scrambled back toward the hatch as the drunk shrimper slurred instructions.

Johnny Jupes turned and stared at me across the void of the two vessels.

He appeared very angry. With a sneer, he turned his back and recommenced working over the hatch.

I was glad that Johnny Jupes had found himself in such a pickle. I hoped the next wave would sweep him off the deck and that he would sink to the bottom of the sea there to keep the company of a loathsome kraken, where he belonged. I was sick of stupid Johnny Jupes!

The heroic rescue at sea, perhaps the most exciting event of my entire life, was tainted only by the improbable presence of my confounding doppelganger aboard the vessel to be saved and a remote possibility of a nonsensical drunken mutiny. At the moment, however, my focus had to be maintained on heroic decision making taking place aboard the training vessel, embodied ideally by the likes of either a Yul Brynner or Charlton Heston, or someone, perchance, who could adequately duplicate their posturings.

The fact was that a Coast Guard Rescue Helicopter was rapidly approaching. The trainees were abuzz with excited banter. Louis stood beside me, pulled his mustache with vigor and said, "A seized rotor will start the helicopter turning around. If that happens, man, that's it. It drops like a rock."

Sid, the instructor from the other shift, who had worked on the deck of a carrier, explained, "That was my job in the Navy. I saw a Marine run underneath a Huey once as it was taking off. The rotor dipped, and the guy's head disappeared. His head disappeared just like that." He snapped his fingers. "Rotor knocked it half a mile out to sea like some motherfucking…you know, like one of those batting machines."

"Uh huh, uh huh," I said. There was no time for notebook entries. I internally reviewed the facts as I overheard them: The chopper had been dispatched from Mobile. We were expecting its arrival any minute with the emergency pump. Captain Maury had decided the pump would be more safely dropped onto our forecastle deck. With the chopper approaching, the other trainees, along with the Brynner's crew, were all staying within the enclosed superstructure at mid-deck where it was safe. The large mast, to which a cargo boom had been attached, rose twenty feet above the foredeck and possessed various wires and cables. Word got around that the Chief Engineer had remarked this mast "would make things difficult for the chopper with the Brynner rising and falling on the now ten-foot swells."

I wasn't concerned in the least. My inner voice was further invigorated by the sprinkling of Earl Short goddamnisms like gravy over mashed potatoes. The possibility of mutiny seemed completely unfounded given the proximity of the goddamn Coast Guard helicopter.

"The shrimp boat must actually BE sinking," I murmured. "Who knows what my goddamn doppelganger is doing there." I added a little more loudly, "And who fucking cares. That son of a goddamn bitch!"

I was letting off some long goddamn standing pent up steam.

I followed Sid to the bow. Sid had worked on a goddamn carrier deck, and I decided to assist him with the manhandling of the goddamn pump soon to be dropped by a goddamn chopper. Despite what I was told, there seemed to be no goddamn danger at all. I felt to be in absolutely no goddamn danger whatsofuckingever and would accompany Sid onto the goddamn bow and deal with the goddamn rescue chopper.

Soon a light appeared in the goddamn sky, and we heard the thumping of the goddamn rotors. I was right in the goddamn middle of everything.

"That's a Sikorsky H-52," Sid said. I nodded.

"A goddamn H-52," I said. Tears welled up in my eyes. The days of sleep deprivation and continual nausea had left me goddamn emotionally vulnerable. Here was a goddamn chopper, a real Coast Guard chopper flying in the night with blinking lights, the biggest and best goddamn toy I had ever seen.

"I would love to ride in a goddamn chopper," I said, my voice drowned out in the pervading din.

I had played with toy choppers when I was a goddamn child. I liked goddamn choppers, and one was flying goddamn straight toward us bringing us a pump for a goddamn sinking shrimp boat.

Sid pointed to the hatchway where the rest of the crew were standing and told me, "I would stand back if I were you. This is dangerous for everybody."

My inner voice was all-goddamned-out so I resumed internal dialogue without profanity although commenced a series of Egon Schiele hand signals directed at the pilot of the approaching rescue helicopter.

My ear drums bowed in and out with each displacement of air by the rotors above us. The noise drowned out my voice so I could speak my mind loudly and freely.

"Chopper one, can you copy!?" I yelled. "I want you to do exactly what my hands instruct you to do!" I moved in a crouch. "Even though my hands are assuming tense postures that the critical thinkers insist indicate masturbatory subtexts, Chopper One, I want you to understand the relatively straightforward concept of lowering a pump onto the deck of this vessel is our paramount concern at the moment. Ignore these subtexts, Coastie Pilot, and let's get this pump aboard!"

I could speak familiarly with the pilot yet with a degree of critical formality. Sid gazed steadily at the chopper without moving, I stood beside him and shouted into the deafening rotor noise, "We're like two Sargent Rocks crunching cigars!" I nudged him and laughed. His attention was on the chopper.

Someone had to be looking at it. That someone wasn't me.

The chopper circled the Yul Brynner slowly, shining a spotlight over the bow to assess the safest prospect for lowering the pump. The pilot leaned his head out the window.

I glimpsed his official orange Coast Guard pilot's helmet.

"Man oh man oh man oh man!" I laughed, glimpsing the striped helmet of the crewman peering down at us from an open door.

"I don't believe it." With their helmets visible, I projected my voice toward the chopper like a choked up John Wayne, shot in the thigh and lumbering up the Iwo Jima hill. "Boys, I need for you to drop down a few of them USCG helmets, the orange and striped ones that you're wearing. It's an emergency situation in addition to being a situation in general, and we all need to be wearing orange helmets, every last one of us, and won't be able to pull off this rescue without them strapped onto all of our heads."

I continued to laugh and cry simultaneously. The lowering of the pump constituted what amounted to one monumental and well-needed catharsis.

Oddly, within my happy reverie, I envisioned the tail rotor dipping and slicing off both of my hands. Despite the amputations, I imagined myself heroically thunk-thunk-thunking the newly placed striped orange helmet with my two bloody stumps then catching the pump in the crooks of my elbows, cradling it like a baby.

The hoist operator leaned out of the door and issued the pilot positioning instructions. The old kingpost bobbed within a few feet of the chopper's nose. The pump was lowered in a basket. As it landed on the deck, I leaped forward and did not know what to do. Sid pushed me to one side and deftly lifted the pump out of the basket.

That made sense.

The chopper pulled away, and I helped Sid carry the pump back to the stern.

Johnny Jupes and the Leaking Stuffing Box, I happily titled and didn't know what the hell was going on but wanted to involve myself even more intimately in whatever was going on. One of the trainees remarked, "If she sinks while we are tied up stern to stern…well, it could be bad."

I passed this observation on to another trainee as if it were my own. "You know if she sinks when we're tied stern to stern. I don't know," I shook my head grimly. I stood in the middle of the back deck assessing the situation with my hands on my hips.

I then noted Johnny Jupes holding a small coil of rope attached to a ball of some sort. Kerry Kelly remarked, "That's called a monkey fist. He's got a heaving line there." I nodded. I had never seen a monkey fist before.

I wanted to be involved in the catching of this monkey fist.

Johnny Jupes held the monkey fist in his right hand with the remainder of the quarter inch heaving line coiled around his left. Johnny began to swing the ball and the rope back and forth. I looked at Johnny and clapped my hands together signaling him I was ready to catch. Johnny stopped swinging the rope and stared. He cursed and spat then swung the rope back and forth again to prepare for throwing. The sterns of the two vessels were about ten meters apart. I raised my hands above my head and clapped them again.

"I got it," I called across. Several trainees studied me. Not one of them had offered to catch the monkey fist. I was taking the initiative.

Someone had to catch that monkey fist.

Johnny lowered his arms. He moved to toss the monkey fist. I moved in that direction. Johnny Jupes stopped and stared.

My doppelganger was clearly being difficult and didn't want me to have the honor of catching the monkey fist.

The mate clapped his hands behind me and signaled for Johnny Jupes to toss the rope. Johnny Jupes spat on the deck and heaved the monkey fist high over my head. I moved backward.

Having learned how to follow pop fly balls while playing center field in high school, I knew what to do. You don't back-pedal but move along a diagonal path.

"What are you doing, man!?" Louis shouted.

I jumped up into the air. The monkey fist knocked my hands away and cracked against my forehead. As I fell to the deck, the monkey fist made a very heavy THUMP just beside my head. The mate gathered the thin line then pulled in the thicker hawser. The Chief engineer came over and looked down at me then turned and waved up at the Captain.

"He's ok!"

I knew that the other trainees had gathered around me. Louis pulled his mustache and said, "You don't try and catch those things, man. They got lead in them. They'll knock you the fuck out. People have been killed by those things. You didn't know that?"

I could hear the shrimp boat Captain blurting out obscenities: Dipshit, moron, asshole! My head hurt; I became less aware of our rescue operation.

"The pump is going to have to be passed stern to stern," the Chief yelled up to the Captain. Captain Maury was again operating the outside controls. My vision blurred as I craned my neck. The Yul Brynner was backing down on the shrimp boat. Johnny Jupes stood in the middle of the deck. The shrimp boat captain still stood by his wheelhouse, still offering no assistance. The two vessels rose and fell upon the swells, each vessel slightly out of synchronization with the other.

I glanced through a gap in the railing at the shrimp boat. It rose and fell over the crests of the waves. A third person emerged onto the deck of the sinking shrimp boat. I looked up at Captain Maury. His attention was focused upon the stern of the Yul Brynner. Everybody's attention, in fact, remained on the passing of the pump.

"Coo coo coooo!"

Kerry Kelly was helping with the pump too and hadn't heard the signal. This third man on board the shrimper, with hair cut straight across the forehead, and an incomplete tattoo on one shoulder, waved at me. I was becoming exceedingly dizzy.

"Cooo coo coo!"

Both boats rose on a swell as the pump was heaved onto the back deck of the shrimper.

"Cooo coo coo!"

Kerry turned suddenly in a crouch and looked at me. I reached up and felt the lump on my head. It seemed to be getting bigger. I felt funny.

32
KARL

The galley was empty, the sky nearly dark when I climbed back onto the deck, assuming the instructors had allowed the trainees to sleep in following our heroic rescue. Moving my fingers over the large knot on my forehead; I tried to recall the events of the previous evening. With the Nav shack empty, I stepped out the hatch and stood at the stern. The ocean, uniformly gray and blanketed in mist, had become devoid of color. I heard gagging and turned. Johnny Jupes sat with his back against the bulkhead.

"I don't need no alcohol to feel right within myself. I'm one of the strong ones, praise God." Johhny Jupes arose with some difficulty, his face drawn and pale. Placing hands on both knees, he bent forward, retched then straightened. "I profiled yew." He tapped himself on the chest and staggered toward me.

"We're doppelgangers; that's why we're both seasick," I offered, feeling sorry for Johnny Jupes. He had undergone quite a stressful ordeal on the back deck of the sinking shrimp boat. I saw my doppelganger as a human being in his own right, fragile and mortal.

"We're not doppelgangers, dumb ass. I read your notebooks and made you believe that to be true. I made you believe that. My name isn't Johnny Jupes. My name is Karl. My granddaddy was a full blooded Sockserhauser. I took the name of your pretend baby hero because that was the easiest way into your head so I could dig out all the information I needed. Deckley heard me preach at the Mission on Magazine and hired me on the spot after seeing how much was in the collection plate. He saw that I was an evangelist. He had already found out through his government records that you were related to Gambi and promised me a share of the treasure if I profiled you. Deckley's dead, so I don't work for Deckley anymore. I'm getting that treasure all for myself. I need at least ten evangelism suits and six pairs of priest shoes. So you and I are going to trade places. I'm going up, and you're going down for that woolding you did under the expressway and for killing my boss in Lafayette Park in the nasty way that you did. I'm spreading it around that you did all that."

I did not like the sound of what Karl was telling me.

"I did not woolde my Uncle Gambi, nor did I strappado Chief Petty Officer Deckley. You have no proof."

I took one step back, glanced up at the wheelhouse but could glean no activity through the grimy window. Karl took another step forward.

"You'll be watching me preach in the pulpit on the penitentiary black and white day room TV."

My ex-doppelganger bent forward and wretched again. My head ached. I reached up to touch the knot on my forehead.

Karl had become privy to one of my private secrets, the name of my imaginary childhood hero, undoubtedly uncovering a reference in one of my notebook's nostalgic subdivisions.

I had been savagely duped: A doppelganger functioned as nothing more than a literary device. I looked down into the churning wake off the Yul Brynner's stern.

From the moment of my arrival in New Orleans, subject to the most profound of deceits and confidence games, my psychological profile had been extracted and assembled from private missives and employed to construct tailor-made misrepresentations.

"I may have been mightily susceptible to suggestion, but how could it be my fault?" I felt indignation. All this had not been fair in the least. "How could I have known that everyone I encountered would be telling me outlandish lies. Oh, I may have allowed a few scattered omissions of fact here and there but nothing more. I did not proclaim myself to be a psychoanalytic vestige of a disintegrating ego, or that I was a member of a long-standing secret pirate society. My fibs have been innocuous by comparison with yours. I want you to recognize that I am a human being in my own right. I need for you to acknowledge that I have a life aside from your own. I am Rodney Pepper. I have my own agenda and my own autonomy."

Karl stared at me. Having stated aloud what I needed to, I felt a whole lot better. I stood on the edge of the deck with hands on my hips. I assumed a full blown Ramses, King of the Pharaoh's pose when my ex-doppelganger Karl shoved me off the stern of the boat.

33
BUCKRA

Cold seawater forced itself up through my nostrils and expanded into the back of my throat. I clamped my mouth shut, and held my breath; turning over underwater, I heard the hum of the engine, a vast unknown stretching beneath. I kicked and thrashed just below the surface of the wake knowing the propeller spun like a circular saw a few body lengths away. I lifted my chin above the water and pumped my legs yet was no longer seeing the big blue boat.

Rising to the top of a swell, I glimpsed the Yul Brynner rolling from side to side at what seemed a considerable distance, farther than I would have expected. Despite my circumstance, I recalled Louis' story regarding the man thrown off the back of the carrier, how the current had carried him so far away in such a short while. The sky had darkened in the few moments since I had immersed. Dropping into another trough, the lights of the Brynner disappeared entirely. I swam in what I assumed to be the boat's direction, now and then glimpsing its red beacon at the top of the mast. Shortly, the light rendered only a dim reflection against the fog. Only gray murk surrounded me.

"God," I called. "Help me! I need help."

In desperate trouble, I needed a God who looked like me and felt the same things I did. The ocean forced itself into my mouth as I rolled over again. My sneakers became too heavy to kick, so I balled myself up and pulled them off one by one. I raised my head above the surface, took a deep breath, submerged, inhaled seawater and shot to the surface drawing in a breath.

Floating for an indeterminate time, born on one swell after another, the darkness surrounding me became complete. I tried to float on my back to conserve energy, kept my mouth closed and grew colder as the sea buffeted me. After a time, the water was slapped behind me. And I turned to face it.

Another break, this time, closer. I aroused myself and swiveled to face that sound, swallowed more water and coughed. My feet and hands could not function. My throat tightened as I choked with the idea of no hope. I was alone, completely, as I had tried to imagine. Only the evil son of a bitch Karl had observed me go overboard. He would not likely be sounding an alarm on the Brynner. In my back pocket, I palpated the metallic spiral of my notebook sandwiched against Evelyn Razer's pornographic paperback Garter Snap. I swallowed more water and kicked, attempting to float on my back. I grabbed or thought I grabbed my penis and scrotum, but could feel neither. I reached toward my face and similarly, felt nothing.

A sharp object struck my abdomen. The water was slapped behind my head then again toward my feet. Churning arose on either side of me. I heard voices singing and braced for the transition from ephemeral existence to eternal art. The slapping began, all around me. Struck in the mouth, I tasted salt. My ear stung, and I flinched; then my shoulder burned, I shouted, "Fuck shit" and swallowed more water. I withdrew first one ankle then my other knee. Nothing short of hell could have been emerging from the bottomless ocean depths. Enraged by the insult that I would die being eaten alive, like Danny Shane, I was ready to turn it at the drop of a hat and slapped the water, bellowing, "Goddamn God godammit!"

As soon as I shouted, I heard the singing clearly, originating from within, as my central nervous system in its dying state remained aware at an unconscious level only, approached by an amalgam of memory, not deities. I had not truly believed that my last minute prayers would be answered. Too weak to cry out, I marveled at the voices generated within, sounding like a gospel choir.

A fish leaped from the sea and hit me in the middle of my forehead! Another struck my ear, another my chin.

I was floating in the middle of a large school of fish!

A man's voice directly above me spoke: "La bas!"

"Ki!" another exclaimed. I tried to call out but choked on seawater.

"Shonuf buckra. Lok whut we kehtch." Shouts and murmuring arose within the fog. Black men in overalls and hats looked down at me over the side of a boat. Compressed by thousands of small fish and suspended in a net I watched the men attach hooks to a small hoist on the side of their boat.

"What you got?" A voice shouted through the fog.

"Buckra!"

"Bigun!"

Someone laughed. I was pulled roughly over on my side and gripped by my belt. No longer in the water, I lay on something hard. Farther into the fog another voice asked,

"Alive?"

"Yessir."

"On board?"

"Yessir."

"Then get that Tom over and bring in the line."

The men wore rubber overalls, some without shirts underneath. Some wore baseball caps, others wide brimmed hats. I had seen these men while vomiting over the Pass Christian Bridge into the Pascagoula River, the Pogey fishermen!

"I'm sorry about it all," I mumbled, recalling what Uncle Gambi said in the McDonald's, that my ancestors were slave traders, my treasure derived from the sale of humans dragged to the new world as cargo to be sold by the pound.

"What are you doing out here?" one man asked.

"Swimming," someone answered for me.

I spoke rapidly. "I was a white slave owner. I take full responsibility for it all. Full." I made it my first order of business to apologize on behalf of all slave trading descendants and to take full responsibility for their actions.

Someone coughed. The men stared at me. One spat overboard. I recalled how other races and cultures had adapted slavery, that it was a relative concept in some ways and was going to discuss those implications when I noticed a light on the horizon. We rose up onto a swell, and I could see another boat approaching. Men stood very still in this second boat peering steadily down at me. I heard quacking noises.

A loud voice penetrated the fog after the amplified click of a microphone key. "Stop yick yacking and purse the net, please. You pursed? If you pursed, then haul in that web." Men dispersed from the side of the second boat. There arose a mechanical whirring. I observed a portion of the net, in which it was now clear that I had been entangled, to be taken up by an on-board winch over a block suspended from a small davit. The fishermen stared. Someone placed a piece of canvas over my shoulders. Another reached out and pulled me toward him, grinning. He stared at me carefully then shoved me away. The men returned to the work of threading portions of the line through the top of the net.

"It was my people who enslaved you." I persisted, pointing at my chest. The men didn't look at me. I decided to begin at the beginning but was interrupted as a much larger vessel rolled out of the fog to come alongside the smaller, the same Pogey boat I had seen on the Pascagoula River.

"Get him the hell up here then strap that net up." I could see a man wearing khaki lean over the wheelhouse rail and point. The men in the smaller boat busied themselves. As we rose up on a swell, I found myself being silently passed upward onto the deck of the larger ship. Someone pushed me toward the wheelhouse outside of which a man dressed in khaki was yelling: "Strap that net and haul! Dry up and pump what we got right quick." I climbed a short set of steps and looked back down toward the deck. Two large davits swung over the side of the boat while a man turned on a winch. Hooks were lowered and attached to the net held between the two boats. I watched the fish boiling at the top of the net for a moment then entered the wheelhouse. The man in khaki sat at the wheel. A brown baseball cap with *Caterpillar* stamped on it just covered his white hair. He grinned.

"You off the Brynner?"

"Yes, sir."

"You on the Lisuhz now." He pointed to a brass plaque reading M/V Ulysses. "You're the one I heard about then, Pepper." The Captain looked me up and down and shook his head. One of the other fishermen entered the wheelhouse with a towel and pair of overalls. He was holding a mug of hot coffee. The Captain removed a miniature bottle of Bacardi Rum from a cabinet and emptied it into the cup.

"You tried to catch the monkey fist. Knocked you cold." I touched my swollen forehead. "Captain said you got loose on deck after that and walked off the stern. When they realized you were missing, the channel current had already taken you."

This account was not true. My evil faux doppelganger son of a bitch Karl had pushed me into the sea. I could not explain this to the Captain. I drank the coffee and regarded the miniature bottle of rum sitting on the Captain's chart table, recalling the miniatures just like it within Uncle Gambi's abhorrent cottage, the miniatures in the grass under the I-10 overpass by his body and the miniature on the roof of the automobile salvage garage. I choked on the coffee and began to cough. On the morning after Uncle Gambi had been killed, I had peed on the head of a large rat and just beyond him saw the same miniature. The little bottle was corked, and I had glimpsed something inside.

I knew exactly where I needed to go.

"So you're the young man who tried to catch the monkey fist." The captain repeated, looking out over the bow of his ship. "I'm Captain and net boss both on the Lisuhz hyeh. I'm in charge of everything and can hear everything that is said on my boats. A man can't whisper, or I'll hear it. So I was listening in on some of your bullshit." He paused and shook his head. "Pepper, you can't understand those colored men when they speak to you, right? Old man *Ribah*? You think a colored man speaks the way he does because he is uneducated? He says *hab* instead of have, *ribuh* instead of river. Do you know why, Pepper?"

"No, sir."

The Captain legs were firmly planted in front of his ship's wheel. He stared straight ahead as he spoke.

"There is no v sound in most African language, young man. Slaves spoke *Bantu* dialects. *Bena, Chuana, Kongo, Shambala, Zulu, Luganda, Swahili, Teke*...The Effik and Fante did not use an el sound. So the white man hears *sef* instead of self. The colored man spoke with the blade of his tongue higher in his mouth. The dropping of certain consonants sounds lax, doesn't it? Well, it isn't, and further, it is not lost to me that a great many of your Klu Klux Klansmen speak with Bantu inflections."

The Captain opened the wheelhouse door and spat into the ocean.

"I've got men on board from South Carolina that speak *Gullah*. Those men speaking like ducks? What you're hearing in Umbundu, they say *oona plat eye*. You evil spirit. You're an Albatross. You're a white boy swimming in the ocean. You're unlucky in their eyes, Pepper."

I was a little hurt by this. I had already apologized and taken full responsibility for the European slave trade.

"I was born in Kingsland, Georgia. Most of these men come from Georgia, South Carolina. Craven counties. See." He pointed out the wheelhouse window. "*Brevoortia tyrannus*. They call them fatback or yellow tail. You come up in the middle of a school of *Brevoortia Patronus*."

The Captain turned, walked to the window facing the back deck and placed his hands on the chart table. He observed the men on deck tie the smaller boat up alongside the larger ship. A large tube was lowered into the middle of the net itself. Fish were being sucked out and pumped into a hatch in the middle of the vessel.

"Too much work for the white man. He can't handle staying out under the sun. He can't handle the work. The Pogey too greasy, so he let the colored man handle it. So we handle it, and it's easy work for the colored man. Menhaden is a smelly fish." The Captain walked back over to his wheel and swung it slightly. He looked back out on the back deck at his men then again took his seat in the Captain's chair.

"When I knew you were in the net I called the Coast Guard to let them know you found. We'll bring you to Cameron. The Yul Brynner is tied back up in Pascagoula. They told me a friend of yours is going to be there to take you back to New Orleans."

The Captain closed his wheelhouse door and spoke more quietly. "I talked to your Captain Maury. He told me exactly what happened."

I could not be entirely sure what the Captain meant by exactly what happened. The Captain placed both hands on his chart table and gazed over the stern of the Ulysses. He continued.

"My wheelhouse is my home. I'm Captain, so I know everything there is to know about my boat and my crew. I need to know a little something about *buckra* and matelotage because now and then that becomes part of my job. It becomes part of my job because I have to protect my ship and my crew. I'm not interested in shortcuts or comshaw or pots of gold. There is no such thing. Someone tells me otherwise; then I know I've been drinking in the wrong bar." The Captain turned and looked at me. "And another thing. If a man hires on and gets the leans so bad he can't work, I'll fire him. I don't keep a binnacle list. That man is of no use to me. Usually, I'm doing both of us a favor."

The Captain stopped speaking, and we stood in silence. He pushed himself away from the chart table.

The Captain had finished what he had to say.

34
THE MOON WALK

Kerry Kelly, smoking a Winston, handed me a Pabst Blue Ribbon Tall Boy as soon as I stepped foot on the dock of the Cameron processing plant. We drank our beer as he steered the company car towards I-90.

"I wanted to let you know; I.P.P. is not my idea of shipping out, Cat. I'm dragging up. To tell you the truth, I miss my boy and can't let anything screw that up. So I'm fixing on heading down to the valley." Kerry threw his cigarette out the window. "I want him to come live with me. Maybe buy a little place; get that Bertram I'd been looking at, tie it up over on South Padre; live on it with him. He could go to school in Port Arthur."

Kerry Kelly had told me about his son before. He had given his boy up to his parents to raise years before; he had been partying too much back then. When Kerry Kelly had shown me the photograph of his son, his son appeared to be a miniature Kerry Kelly. I recalled how Kerry Kelly had stared at the photograph of his boy. He had stared at it for a long while. I had no boy and wondered what that feeling would be like to have lost his son like that.

"As soon as I get down to Harlingen, I'm going to the market and buying a bag of fresh vegetables. They eat tortillas down there, Cat. You can get fresh tortillas every day. Corn tortillas." Kerry Kelly pronounced the word tortilla carefully, with a Mexican inflection: tor-tee-yah.

Kerry Kelly lit Winston after Winston as we drank our Tall Boys. He described what life would be like once he got down to the Rio Grand Valley a place where they grew grapefruits. "Might just get my old job back with the railroad. Fresh tortillas, fresh vegetables, everything fresh down there..."

By the time we pulled up in front of the YMCA, each of us had finished three Tall Boys. Kerry Kelly was still telling me what he would do down in the valley. "The first thing I'm going to do is buy a fresh grape- fruit and tear it open with my hands." As we sat in the car, Kerry demonstrated the tearing open of a grapefruit with his hands and the motion of bringing the grapefruit up to his mouth. Kerry Kelly then remained quiet and stared out the front windshield. He removed two hundred dollars in twenties from his shirt pocket.

"I don't forget a favor, Cat."

Kerry Kelly had made good to his word and had one of the biggest hearts of anyone who ever shipped; just like Danny Shane was the fastest man to turn it that Kerry Kelly had ever met and that included the Gypsy Jokers.

"I only need a hundred," I told Kerry Kelly. He stared, shrugged, and returned half the money to his pocket.

"To be honest, even if you find the treasure, they may kill you anyway. I thought I'd just let you know that I was dragging up. I'll be leaving the car at the airport." Kerry Kelly threw his cigarette out the window. "Did you hear about Grady Ranger?"

I held my breath.

"When he found out you fell overboard, he walked out onto Jefferson Highway and was hit by a truck. He was lucky it only broke his leg, but I heard he got transferred up East." Kerry Kelly studied me." East is what they call the loony bin in Jackson, Cat. Sounds like he will be there for a while. Earl Short told me he was going through some kind of sex change."

"Jesus!" I was glad that Grady Ranger had only broken his leg. I felt sorry for Grady Ranger and also liked him. I wasn't sure if he was the right big boned woman for me but found the idea of massively large breasts intriguing. I hoped Grady Ranger would be happier one day, and wouldn't get so upset. I stood on the sidewalk with my duffle bag and watched Kerry Kelly drive the company car around Lee Circle on his way to the airport. I hoped Kerry Kelly's boy would come live with him and that he too would get what he wanted.

Checking back into the YMCA, I was assigned once again to the sixth floor, the domain of the American male. Once in my room, I inhaled the now reassuring odor of urine and removed from my duffle bag Uncle Gambi's book *Complex Analysis* along with the portion of ancient map he had placed inside it. I set off for Prytania Avenue.

The old rooming house had been boarded up; two by fours were nailed across the screen door behind which the landlady, her two teenage girls, the cat, and Karl had gathered the morning of my arrival. I peered through slats in the fence at the alley, strewn with debris, where children had shrieked, and adults had turned to stare. I questioned whether I had stayed in the house on Prytania at all; whether the actual house had been boarded up all along, and I had paid rent to a meta-physical gatekeeper existing only within myself; if everybody I had met dwelt within my psyche, that I was mad and should seek psychiatric counseling immediately. I had to trust this was not the case. Uncle Gambi's treasure existed. A goddamn treasure chest was buried in New Orleans.

Duplicating the route taken the day of my desk clerk interview, I turned up Erato and entered the vacant lot behind the automobile salvage garage. In walking along the fence to the rear, I examined the now excavated surface filled with concrete. I picked up a sharp rock and slammed it upon the base of a fence post, not at all certain this represented the same marker beside which I had stood showering the contented rat with urine. After a few minutes, the concrete split apart, and a small arm fell into view: GI Joe. I scraped more dirt away, and the soil collapsed downward. Within this space framed by a portion of old cinder block were wrappers, cans, and plastic bags. I broke off a small branch from a tree growing through the fence and used it to push downward into the hole past the mounds of rodent droppings and torn tissue paper.

Driving deeper into its recess, I pushed aside a Fig Newton wrapper and saw the miniature bottle of rum. With bare hands, I brushed more dirt away from the entrance to the den and hooked the bottle with my stick, pulling it toward me. Once in my hands, I uncorked it and teased out a tiny rolled up piece of paper: *Y equals thirty lengths of the scabbard.* I held in my hand Uncle Gambi's unit of measure.

Written while drunk and placed within the rum miniature then tossed onto the roof of the abandoned automobile salvage garage, this ordinant could now be plugged into the equation within my book. The result, in turn, would be plotted on my fragment of map, in doing so transforming theory into experiment and fulfilling my matelotage with its more-than-tangible reward of unbounded wealth. With Tall Boys in me, I felt that Kerry Kelly's warnings, while well intentioned and kind, had been unfounded. Nothing could hurt me now.

I gazed up at the cloudless sky and breathed, "We'll see who calls who a chump." I felt every inch the heroic Dick Van Dyke chimney sweep!

Giddy with the final clue now in my possession; I found it difficult to summon the discipline necessary to locate and dig treasure. I would much prefer to make my way down to the Quarter and see the sun come up on a bar-stool. At dawn, I would sit by the window at Mollys and slather a cheese-laden omelet into my mouth whether I could taste it or not, then emerge into disconcerting blue light framing rows of batten shutters converging to a vanishing point somewhere beyond Esplanade. Perhaps I would fire up Ole Cap Norris and drink water glasses full of the hiccough curing vodka once again.

"No!" I declared aloud and stamped my foot. I needed to solve my trigonometric word problem first. The center of the circle had been defined to be Andrew Jackson's monument. All I had to do was measure the length of the hero's scabbard.

At Woolworth's off Canal, I purchased a tape measure, a protractor, a draftsman's rule, a pocket flashlight and a small shovel. The cold ones had instilled within me the cavalier attitude of a freebooting law breaker. I proceeded directly to Jackson Square, climbed onto the statue and took my measurements. A tourist, ironically, took a photograph of me doing so.

"I am simply measuring his scabbard," I informed the man even though he and I were acutely aware the measurements taken represented not simply the dimensions of Andrew Jackson's sword but those of his metaphoric penis, in keeping with consensus of the psychoanalytic canon.

I sat on one of the benches and opened Uncle Gambi's mathematics text. The previously earmarked equation transformed, as Qucha had said it would, a line into a circle; the coordinates within the book clearly representing an angle and a radius. The angle would define the point along the circle's perimeter. As Gambi's solution became more evident and tangible, the notion of getting drunk summoned me with greater urgency. I had difficulty concentrating. I compromised and took a break. I made my way to the French Market, ordered a coffee with chicory, a baguette and smoothed my map on their table. After a few moments, having made several unit conversions, I double pursed my lips and said: "The solution is now self-evident."

The plotted point corresponded to an area of the levy on which, during my first hour of arrival, I had observed Uncle Gambi squatting and studying the Mississippi's turbulence.

Uncle Gambi sat himself directly on top of his own buried treasure.

Had Uncle Gambi been knowledgeable of the chest's whereabouts at the time, why had he allowed all this torment to unfold? The question was irrelevant: I would return after dark and dig in the dead of night. The echo of tugs dieseling around the Algiers bend would dampen the reverberations of my persistently thrusting spade.

I proceeded to the end of the moonwalk and examined my map. The calculations placed the treasure twenty feet behind the river's rocky embankment, a few feet past the last bench. I moved forward a few steps and studied the patch of yellowed grass corresponding to my plotted point:

A treasure chest lay buried below my feet.

Filled with no small measure of disbelief that my search had finally come to fruition, I hid my shovel, book and map behind a clump of bushes beside the railroad tracks and looked at the sun. Having time to kill until darkness, I decided to treat myself to one or two more cold ones at Mollys while perhaps munching on a little snack from their kitchen.

After my first cold one, I became filled with strong inclination to become drunk as a goddamn mangy dog. I ordered many double snakebites in succession followed by several shots of Barbados rum. With each shot, I assured the bartender,

"It's a little more expensive, but it's what I like."

I ate two cheeseburgers, a basket of onion rings and a bowl of chocolate ice cream. The more Schnapps and rum I drank, the more my head spun with the myriad of possibilities life offered. After coming into possession of my fortune, I might arrive at a thousand different crossroads, each with four times that many directions to travel. My stomach turned; there were too many choices. I turned to an older man sitting beside me and said, "I want to go in every direction at the same time, but I don't know which direction is the right one."

The man arose without a word and moved over to a window table. The bartender stood in front of me and said,

"That's the last one. You're bothering the customers."

I reeled out of Mollys and headed back to the Mississippi. A thick fog had moved in, and the moonwalk had become deserted. Being fully lit and now dimly regretting having had so much to drink, the search for my shovel extended for the greater part of an hour with an additional twenty minutes to relocate the discolored patch of grass.

I pressed the shovel downward with the heel of my foot and felt an immediate hollow resistance. Turning off my flashlight. I knelt and tossed clumps of sod aside like an excited badger digging for radishes. The top of an enormous and ancient wooden chest shortly revealed itself. At that precise moment, a voice directly behind me spoke:

"Thank you, bitch."

Evelyn Razer's breasts clamped themselves to either side of my neck like a pair of boxing gloves filled with molten lead. A cord slipped around my forehead and yanked taut. I gleaned the implication right away:

WOOLDED!

"People who write this sort of thing are freaks," she whispered, enunciating the eak of freak. I recoiled.

Evelyn Razer had called me a bitch then mockingly delivered my father's very words directly into one ear, derived from a kidnapped pocket notebook's *Familial Quotation* subdivision!

My life had been torn from me at the instant of gratification!

"I'm going to let your doppelganger woodle you." Evelyn Razer's deep laugh, while attenuated by fog, shook the ground on which I knelt. I also acknowledged at some level that Evelyn Razer pronounced woolde as woodle.

"Rhonie, shoot him if he starts to make noise," she said

As Rhone stepped in front of my field of view, I understood the caustic nature of the farce: *Rhone, the apple of my eye, was a man!* Rhone was Rhonie, Evelyn Razer's tranny son, the female impersonating brother to Grady Ranger, more than just a handful.

The woolding commenced as the cord tightened around my forehead. I smelled the disgusting stench of Karl's breath as he hissed into my ear, drenched in spittle: "I could have been the Six Hundred Club prime minister by now. They have two rooms full of gold and jewelry and just send people in. They put all their donations inside those two rooms, whatever the TV congregation sends in for Jesus and the preacher tells the people who work there to 'go on in and take anything you want.' That's what he tells them to do, 'to go on in.' I missed out on going in and taking anything I wanted because of yew. YEW! When I count to three Rhonie, you start pushing on that bar. I'll start pulling."

It sounded as if the son of a bitch Karl was giving Rhonie instructions as mundane as the starting of a lawn mower!

"One, two..." The tourniquet tightened. I mooed like a cow as vomit hosed from my mouth and splattering the grassy levy in front of me. The pressure increased across my forehead.

I never imagined bad things would actually happen.

"If he's going to make that much noise, then don't do that," Evelyn Razer said. "Just shoot him. Or give me the gun and I'll shoot him. We don't have time for this pirate bullshit."

The pressure eased momentarily while Evelyn Razer delivered her powerful admonitions and instructions.

"I want to see you woodle the motherfucker, Karl," Rhonie spoke excitedly. Rhonie was kissing up to Karl. Karl was the big man on campus. Karl was this, Karl was that.

Rhonie, just like her mother, had pronounced woolding as woodling. I began to beller like Faulkner's Benjy as he had run alongside the fence looking at the cows. I also evacuated the entire contents of my bowels directly into my tidy whities.

"Oh Jesus," Karl said. The pressure across my forehead momentarily lessened.

Karl smelled my shit.

"If he's getting too loud then do it over there." Evelyn Razer waved all of us farther down the levy. I caught sight of her tight turtleneck-shirted sidekick attempting to raise my treasure chest from the ground.

"I needed money for evangelism, so I took the job with Deckley to profile you," the more-than-evil-Karl went on. "And I was a little curious to see who this doppelganger of mine was."

"What?" I forgot for the moment that I was being woolded and listened closely.

"I'm not afraid to kill my own doppelganger," Karl continued. "But I don't feel anything right now. I should be feeling something around my own head if you're my doppelganger."

Karl apparently believed that he was still my doppelganger and in being my doppelganger expected he might be able to feel the physical pain in woolding me.

"You stupid nitwit, Karl,' I murmured. The cord tightened.

"I profiled all your self-esteem and all your abandonment issues in my report and used every last one of those against you. Deckley found out that you got tangled up in your oral stage and escaped reality with your pocket notebooks. That was all in my report."

What was this idiotic report Karl was raving on about? I titled: *Rodney Pepper and the Bleached White Bones of Death.*

My vision dimmed although I could just discern Evelyn Razer's turtle necked more-than-just-a-henchman hoisting the chest onto the grass. Although uncertain, it appeared as though Evelyn Razer was writhing on top of the now opened box, lasciviously and carelessly adorning herself with pirate jewelry. The pressure inside my skull mounted, and I fell to one side, uncertain whether my eyeballs hadn't already been forced from their sockets onto my cheeks. While Karl whispered, the tension on the cord around my forehead eased as he was concentrating more on the sound of his own voice than on the task of woolding, consistent with his evil son of a bitch personality.

"After I woodle you I am going to change my legal name to Johnny Jupes. I'll be known as Reverend Jupes in the pulpit."

Karl had also said woodle. I felt a measure of sorrow on behalf of the unparallelled dimwit Karl.

"I profiled you, so I know your mother and father are in entertainment. I am very interested in that. After I finish your woodling, and you're dead and gone, I'm going to take your notebooks up to New York where I'll be Reverend Johnny Jupes, your pastor and best friend on the face of the Earth. I'll be telling them how you fell in with the criminal element and became a criminal yourself and that you turned to Jesus, Praise God, in your dying breaths and whispered to me as blood was gurgling from your mouth that there were only three people in the world you loved, your mother, your father and the Reverend Johnny Jupes; and I'll be telling them that your dying wishes before God was that I get a Sunday morning television evangelism slot. I'll tell them a place in heaven for you was secured if I got that television evangelism slot even though I know you're going straight to hell. And if they don't believe me or agree to get my television evangelism slot then I'll woodle them both like I'm woodling you now, Praise Jesus, Praise God."

The evil preacher Karl was planning on extorting me from beyond the grave! The cord around my skull tightened.

The suggestion of a cloaked figure, a whisp or a cloud, passed in front of my eyes. I recruited each and every in-the-process-of-being-woolded-palsy-stricken- facial-muscle so as to cock one eyebrow and deliver my final simile, as Davey Crockett had swung his rifle upon the Mexican soldiers breaching the south gate of the mission:

"Like a shadowy sylph nimble and fleeting across the moor, at once static, with moss for feet, thorns for fingers, stunted firs for legs, my cocked eyebrows falls one last time, the final curtain, theater lights extinguished forever."

"What the hell?" Johnny Jupes exclaimed.

The phantom appearing in front of me was either summoned by my subconscious or represented the pruner himself. I heard a distinct grunt and watched as the turtlenecked muscle man fell to the ground on the other side of the excavated chest.

"Oh, Jesus." Evelyn Razer's voice raised impatiently.

The pressure on my skull resolved as the figure of Karl stepped in front of me and gazed back over my head. The same cloaked figure, which I could no longer consider a figment of my imagination, then landed between the two of us and drew a line across Karl's midsection. The apparition reached forward and pulled a scarf from Karl's pocket, turned and nailed it into the ground. My ex-doppelganger's body jerked forward:

This object was not a scarf, but Karl's intestines pulled directly from his abdominal cavity and staked to the earth atop the Governor Nichols levy!

"Fuck me." Evelyn Razer stepped forward and stood in front of Karl with her hands on her hips. She turned to regard some unseen agent beyond my visual theater.

"Sockserhauser whore!" The cloaked figure threw back her hood: Qucha, the Costa Rican!

"Basque terrorist bitch!" Evelyn Razer answered jauntily, hands still on her hips.

"Skank," Qucha replied.

"Did you know that your twat girlfriend works for the CIA, Rodney Pepper?" Evelyn Razer addressed me with unbridled venom. "Oh God, that smells."

I had shat in my pants and considered there to be a small measure of heroism in doing so.

The exchanges between the two women, one ambiguously evil, one ambiguously good, continued as I toppled forward, head coming to rest on a short mound of under-soil created by the digging process. The dirt felt cool against my cheek, providing a fleeting moment of respite. From this stationary field of view, I observed what transpired.

Karl, my ex-doppelganger, struggled to pull a gun from behind his back despite his disembowelment. While completing the forward motion, in attempting to raise the weapon's muzzle, the gun fell abruptly to the ground, perplexingly still affixed to his heavily tattooed hand and forearm. This arm holding the weapon landed with a jarring THUMP on the fresh earth directly in front of my right eye.

I frowned directly into the orifice of a gun barrel, its steel teasing my eyelash. No greater ocular threat could have been engineered by fate's author! Karl's fingers gripped the gun handle, his index finger remaining applied to the trigger, twitching in a limbo state of post amputation neuro-anxiety.

Karl spoke in a remarkably clear monotone, standing stock still, gazing at the amputated arm and his still unraveling intestines:

"Virtual castrations are evinced simultaneous to the denouement of the psychoanalytic subtext, followed by the actual and inevitable death of both…and final dissolution of the ego structure."

I was forced to admit Karl had concluded his synopsis admirably, as any University professor might and begrudged him a certain intellectual charisma. Instinctively I groped for my pocket notebook, forgetting my afflicted fingers would not budge, all the while my gaze riveted within the black pupil of the gun barrel; Karl's hideously disembodied index finger continued to twitch.

A second cloaked figure stepped into view and thrust an arm inward, unraveling the remainder of Karl's intestines, both large and small. Karl tried to run, more out of reflex than awareness. This action provoked further unraveling. He collapsed and writhed on the grass.

"Montbars, the Exterminator!" I shrieked, offering homage to the historical inventor of this specific atrocity.

I had become far more comfortable with the idiosyncrasies of my person, now curious as to what form my own execution would take. I hoped and trusted there would be a few moments available to inscribe one final entry into my pocket notebook then close it, as I always had made a habit of doing, like the castanet.

Johnny Jupes' right arm contracted, the gun jumped, and I flinched. At the precarious mercy of his trigger finger's neuromuscular junction, void of inhibition, the abhorrent idea of a bullet piercing my eye constituted a destiny not without irony as some portion of my brainstem must have appreciated in that I regained control of at least a portion of my synaptic junctions, finding myself able to flinch and blink uncontrollably. The rest of my facial musculature remained immobile as in the course of some agonizingly selective childhood nightmare.

A loud report occurred simultaneously to my forehead being struck by what felt to be a driving iron, rolling my body backward. Greatly surprised that death had proved so mundane, I blinked. Though dead, I could detect light. I blinked again and noted something solid occluded my vision. I could discern grass blades and the glow of Jackson Square off to one side. The solid object was slowly withdrawn upward by an unknown agent.

I found myself able to move my head. I was not dead, and my command of generalized motor function restored itself.

The object I now viewed was the bloody disemboweling cutlass deformed by the bullet strike at point blank range. The sword had transferred the resultant momentum directly into my forehead but pre- vented the projectile from penetrating either orbit, skull or brain. The saber had been thrust into the ground directly between the gun barrel and vulnerable eye at the last possible moment, just as might occur in the final scene of a cheaply concocted airport crime novel which one might read on the john while constipated.

Rhonie, in the meantime, ran up to Karl's body, knelt and sobbed, "Oh Johnny Johnny Johnny."

I felt unmoved, viewing the whole event clinically as if a were a 1950s research scientist wearing a floor length lab coat and holding a clipboard. I asked Rhonie, "Is his name Johnny Jupes or Karl?"

Rhonie turned his head and hissed. "You should be honored that he took your childhood hero's name Johnny Jupes both as his own and as his preacher name. He was to be known far and wide as Johnny Jupes the Evangelist!"

"Shut up you idiot," Qucha said.

"Don't talk to my son that way, terrorist," Evelyn Razer spat.

The women continued to bicker and hurl barbs as if part of a dysfunctional family seated at the dinner table. I came to an important conclusion, however: As Johnny Jupes and I had not perished simultaneously in a cataclysmic enmeshment of disintegrating psychic universes, customary in a doppelganger denouement. Johnny Jupes could not, technically, have been my doppelganger. I was not sure how I felt about that, neither sad nor glad although his carnage already lent a horrible stench to the moonwalk. Feces oozed from lacerated portions of large intestine. My own feces gave rise to an equally putrid insult.

Rhonie snarled, "He could have had you believing you were Abraham Lincoln if he had wanted. He read all those books in your bag and understood every last word, more than what you understood. There will never, ever be a television evangelist the likes of Johnny Jupes. And yes, I'm calling him a television evangelist because that's what he was. HE was the Reverend Johnny Jupes, not you!"

Rhonie still had a *thing* for the son of a bitch preacher even though he possessed obvious and significant defects of character, and of course, was now dead.

"We had plans to go to the pot bars in Amsterdam," Rhonie continued to weep. "I'm twenty-five, but Johnny told me I could pass for fifteen. Fifteen. He made me feel like I was fifteen. I'll have to go back to driving a cab because of you. I hate your fucking hippity hopping Rodney Pepper guts! I blame you and you alone for the way my life has turned out!"

This was painful for me to hear. I tried to offer myself a plausible explanation: Could Johnny Jupes have been an evil underminer acting independently of the ganger process, somehow defying psychoanalytic interpretation?

"No, me Croonie," a familiar voice spoke into my ear almost as if participating in my own inner dialogue. "We'll quietly take what's ours and let you continue to live out your life. Greed started it centuries ago, Macedonian."

Tommy, Qucha's brother, the Basque, Angola Librarian and *theatre troupe* director!

Despite my compromised posture and having shat my pants, I felt a surge of pride in being addressed as the Macedonian.

It had been Tommy who had put the disemboweling final touches on Johnny Jupes, modeled after Montbars the Exterminator.

"This is not an attitude with which to build a better world, me Saxon, me Anglo. Blood money must be transformed." He tapped the soiled saber. "This is the moral of the story and its only redeeming aspect."

A drop of blood fell upon my cheek.

Qucha said, "You didn't know it, but your only hope of staying alive had been to find your treasure and give it to me in public so there would be no misunderstanding. Now it's my problem. That's the law."

I was heartened by the promise of staying alive and prepared to purse my lips to offer a witty remark laced with satori-like awareness. Before I could, I received a whack at the top of my head, this one a lot harder than the previous.

35
THE DUTCHMAN

Awaking on the moonwalk bench to the dawn echo of a tug boat whistle, I rubbed the new tender lump on my head. Observing the river, I attempted to recall the events of the evening. I had ordered several double snakebites followed by several shots of Barbados Gold at Mollys then after having been refused service, proceeded to the moonwalk and may or may not have glimpsed Evelyn Razer adorning herself with golden trinkets or Karl's intestines unraveling from the center of his torso. The events were difficult to verify. I sat up and palpated my eyeballs with a single forefinger, gazed to the right then to the left confirming the adequacy of my extra ocular motion.

"Bilaterally," I remarked then paused: I had spoken with frog-like hoarseness.

I ran my hand across my forehead. The touch stung; I withdrew my hand.

I had been woolded and this woolding had left me with a nasty rope burn.

I tried speaking aloud again: "Not many people have been woolded and lived to tell the tale."

Sounding as if I had smoked three packs of cigarettes a day for forty years, I was elated. A man sitting two benches down stared as I spoke to myself. I gave him a thumb's up. He looked away with disgust.

I smelled something.

Standing up, I made my way to the far end of the moon walk. Several people arose as I passed, holding their noses and retching. I realized that I had shat myself and walked slowly to keep stable the collection within.

No stains of blood or spillage of bile or feces were visible on the grass although there were depressions and moist areas where the earth had been disturbed. I examined the ground for evidence of evisceration yet could draw no conclusions. My shovel and flashlight were nowhere in sight. Only my notebook and pen remained still wedged into my hip pocket. My copy of Evelyn Razer's Garter Snap, which had been present since my rescue by the Pogey boat, was also missing.

I removed my notebook and wrote: *From a state of being woolded to a state of not being woolded, I have awoken to a vacant stage, scenery removed, actors departed, a drama constructed then deconstructed. The only thing I have to show for it is a modicum of hoarseness and pants filled with shit.*

I closed my notebook. Despite this morose entry and a pervading sense of loss, I was pleased to have acquired hoarseness. I croaked a further truncated narration: "Once back at the Y, I would have to examine my face for evidence of hollowness. My underarms feel sticky in the morning heat. I smell my sweat, and its odor was infused with that of my own shit. The treasure has disappeared. Uncle Gambi is dead."

I had one final task to complete.

The familiar man with his white seafaring beard sat on the bench at the northeast corner Lee Circle facing the Y. He had been smoking his pipe as I approached and affixed his gaze on me as I crossed the street. He remained motionless; one leg crossed over the other.

"I'm looking for the Dutchman." I stood in front of him.

The man glanced at me and did not respond. A full minute of silence ensued. He took his pipe out of his mouth and sat with it on his knee. He gazed down St. Charles as if I had not been present.

"Do you know where I could find him?" I asked.

"He's usually around here," the man answered.

I nodded.

"Do you think the Dutchman can get me a ship?"

The man paused for almost another full minute, lit his pipe then billowed clouds of white smoke into the air, making kissing sounds with his lips. He removed the pipe from his mouth and pointed the stem at me.

"You don't get seasick do you?" Flexing his head forward slightly, his eyes became visible underneath his bushy eyebrows.

"I do," I said.

"Oh?" the man said and then looked down St. Charles Avenue. He turned back and asked, "You shit your pants?"

"Yes," I said.

He nodded and lit his pipe again. I stood in front of his bench for a few more moments. He said nothing more. I turned and walked slowly across the street through the doors of the Y.

The front desk clerk came out from behind his counter and waved at me. "Rodney Pepper?"

I nodded. He slid a piece of paper across the counter: Call Don Canyon.

My chest tightened. I had been fired for violating the I.P.P. tenet of no treasure hunting, and not only violating it but violating it with drunken abandon. Evelyn Razer had most likely already told on me.

I dialed the number, inhaled deeply and prepared to take my medicine. Don Canyon spoke hurriedly:

"You did well on the Brynner, Pepper, and survived admirably in the drink. I'm promoting you to overseas operator."

I had been seasick the entire training voyage, had been knocked out trying to catch the monkey fist then pushed off the stern by my mutineering doppelganger only to be rescued and mocked by Pogey Boat fishermen. No other trainee before me could have bumbled to such a degree. I could not possibly have done well.

"What I'm saying is that we don't need any lawsuits. I'm sending you to Brazil. You get your vaccinations and passport tomorrow then leave in three days. You'll be working on a pipe laying barge. They don't move."

I cleared my froggy throat, preparing to pledge my unwavering loyalty to I.P.P. when Mr. Canyon hung up.

"Brazil," I repeated. I knew nothing of Brazil. Brazil was a word, but that was all I needed, a word. I associated the word with people juggling grapefruits on their heads and tropical birds. The more I repeated the word Brazil to myself, the more excited I became. It would be as if nothing had happened, no woolding, no disembowelment, no treasure, no doppelganger, no nothing.

I could start afresh on a pipe laying barge off the coast of Brazil, once again the experimentalist and this time would not getting side tracked. *True Wisdom* undoubtedly awaited me there.

I came off the elevator and directly entered the partition less lavatory. A man seated on a toilet with his hands on his knees stared at me as I took down my pants and pulled down my soiled underwear to reveal my buttocks thickly encased in stool. I stepped out of my tidy whities gingerly and dropped them in the garbage receptacle.

"Oh dear fucking God," the man said, arose and waddled out the door without flushing or wiping. I hummed as I cleaned myself thoroughly using water from the nearby shower and paper towels, creating quite a pile in the trash receptacle.

"Nothing they haven't seen," I croaked.

I returned to my room still permeated by urine vapor and sat on the bed feeling as peaceful as I had in my entire life: I had survived my first woolding and hopefully, my last.

When I awoke the next morning, my pocket notebook lay as I left it on the night table, face up, open to the index page. Feeling refreshed, I made my way to the Hummingbird for breakfast and sat once again at the counter, drinking black coffee and eating two eggs over easy with buttered white toast. The man sitting next to me read the Times-Picayune. I regarded its front page not by enlisting lateral gaze muscles but by turning my head. I held my coffee cup just under my chin while I read.

Anonymous Philanthropist Donates Twenty Million Toward Construction of Freret Education Complex. At the bottom of the page, in a small box: Terrorist Bombings Overnight in Spain.

The man folded his paper, took up his coffee cup and stared over the rim. After mopping my eggs with the toast, I stared straight ahead at the Bun O Matic, wondering how many immunizations I would need to enter Brazil. Would the needles utilized be large or small, administered in the arms, buttocks, or both?

Romani and Basque Phrases with their Approximate English Translations

Romani:

lovina - beer, alcohol

bi-lacho - no good

kumpania - company, group

tachiben - truth

O lungo drom - the long road

love - money

Basque:

kaka zaharra - shit

pikutara joan - go to hell

popatik hartu - to be buggered

kabroi - bastard

atzelari - defender

Mutil hori tentelapikoa da - This kid is stupid.

lau garagardo - four beers

bietan jarrai - both continue

Basque cont'd

janzazu kaka - shit

larrua jo - fuck

zure ama emagaldua da - son of a bitch

ABOUT THE AUTHOR

A.F Knott has worked as a surveyor in the offshore oil industry, a lunch deliverer, a paper broker, a cyclotron engineer and a doctor. *The Trainee* is his first novel. He has two sons and lives in England. Visit him and his blogs at www.afknott.com.

Also by A.F. Knott
Ramonst

www.ingramcontent.com/pod-product-compliance
Lightning Source LLC
Chambersburg PA
CBHW070620260626
47161CB00007B/2506